AF182397

DANGEROUS HAVEN

by Luna Pierce

Arndell

Books by Luna Pierce

Brothers of Sin Series

Dangerous Haven

Twisted Enemy (coming 2027)

Praise for Dangerous Haven

"London and Archer's love story had me by the throat. Thrilling, decadent, and panty-melting hot, Dangerous Haven is dark billionaire romance at its best."

— Allie Oleander, author of Willing Prey"

Dirty, dangerous, and addictive as sin itself - *Dangerous Haven* is the billionaire fix I didn't know I needed. Must read!"

— Dana LeeAnn, Amazon Top 50 Bestselling Author

Dangerous Haven is a flawless blend of fresh and familiar, making you nostalgic for the 2010s swoony billionaires, while giving you a modern morally grey man for 2026.

— Tylor Paige, USA Today Bestselling author of Good For Her

DANGEROUS HAVEN

Brothers of Sin Series

LUNA PIERCE

Arndell

Arndell

DANGEROUS HAVEN

This edition published by Arndell, an imprint of Keeperton 2026.

Dharawal Country, 1 / 18 Manning Street, Kiama, NSW, Australia, 2533

Copyright © Luna Pierce 2026
EXCLUSIVE PAPERBACK CONTENT
Copyright © Luna Pierce 2026

ISBN: 9781923232556 Paperback

10 9 8 7 6 5 4 3 2 1

This novel is a work of fiction. Any reference to names, characters, businesses, places, events and incidents are products of the author's imagination or are used in a fictitious manner. Any resemblance to real persons, living or dead, is entirely coincidental.

All rights are reserved. No part of this book may be reproduced or transmitted in any form or by any means, graphic, electronic, or mechanical, including photocopying, recording, taping, or by any information storage retrieval system such as AI, without the express written permission of the Publisher.

Proofed by Claudette Cruz
Formatted by Books & Moods
Cover design by Emily Wittig

FSC
www.fsc.org
MIX
Paper | Supporting responsible forestry
FSC® C013604

Printed and bound by CPI Group (UK) Ltd, Croydon, CR0 4YY

Sydney | Washington D.C. | London

www.keeperton.com

To anyone who ever had to look in the mirror and fake a smile to get through the day...this one's for you.

Oh, and anyone who simps over tattooed, 6'5" grumpy billionaires in gray sweatpants...

Playlist

you should know where i'm coming from - banks

everything has changed (ft. ed sheeran) - taylor swift (tv)

touch it - ariana grande

don't blame me - taylor swift

run for the hills - tate mcrae

death wish love - benson boone

just pretend - bad omens

war of hearts - ruelle

constellations - jade lemac

pretty slowly - benson boone

the night we met - lord huron

i miss you, i'm sorry - gracie abrams

how did it end? - taylor swift

cardigan - taylor swift

hoax - taylor swift

i can do it with a broken heart - taylor swift

carry you home - alex warren

everywhere, everything (w/ gracie abrams) - noah kahan

trigger warnings

Dear Reader:

The contents of this book contain graphic material meant for mature audiences. Some situations and scenes are triggering, and I urge you to read through this list of triggers and make sure this book is suitable for you.

Parental abuse, human trafficking, suicidal ideation, catcalling, disrespect of boundaries, abused bodily image, alluded abused woman, mention of a dead parent, parental abuse, misogynistic men, death, alluded murder, foster system, broken bones from abuse, battered body, family feud, hemophobia and germophobia, armed robbery, murder and secrets, significant other death mentioned, drug use mentioned, mental trauma, PTSD, breaking and entering, assault, alcoholism, stalking, and explicit spicy scenes.

For a more comprehensive list of the triggers and where they are located (spoilers), please visit https://www.lunapierce.com/triggerwarnings

CHAPTER ONE

London

The first man who ever hurt me was my father.

Some of the scars he left behind have faded, some trigger people to gasp and ask what happened. Some are so fresh that only time will tell the permanent mark that will remain once the wounds close, and the skin shifts from a raised purple to soft pink. But some, some of them will haunt me long after he's been buried six feet under.

Ricardo Gardella was a vicious man, and he spared no one from his wrath. Not his so-called friends, not the mother of his child, not even his own flesh and blood.

He bought and sold people with no regard for their autonomy. He used money as a way to excuse his actions; his only motive was his endless greed. I was simply a part of the plan, a pawn in his twisted game that only he held the rule book for.

I used to think death would be my escape from his lifelong torment, but even after he's taken his last breath, he plagues me still.

I was lucky, really, that my father was hated so badly that no one wanted to do business with him.

That was, until he found someone as vile as he was to strike a deal for my hand in marriage.

Joe Vito.

A man more untouchable than my father supposedly was.

And so, I cling to my cast-covered arm and hobble off the final bus, putting over three thousand miles between me and the fate I never agreed to.

Rain pelts my face and I wince, squinting my eyes and desperately searching for cover. I shuffle my feet behind the people who exited before me and follow them over to seek refuge under an awning. Sniffling, I swallow harshly and glance around. A sign for Lincoln Square comes into my line of sight and relief washes over me. I'm close. I'm so fucking close.

It's been seven days, nine buses, and two pathetic truck-stop showers since I left that forsaken town in California. I'm blocks away from my final destination, and despite having no idea what lies ahead for me here, I cannot wait to find out.

My entire body aches, not just from the travels but from the injuries still healing. The doctor told me the casts on both my wrist and leg needed a minimum of four weeks until they could come off, but with my poor hygiene lately, the itching might drive me insane first. Everything else needs to heal on its own. The fractured skull, the bruised ribs and lungs.

My father made sure to make his last beating count, and boy was he close to making it stick for good.

As if the twenty-three years of abuse wasn't enough.

"Hey, baby," a raspy voice calls out, sending a spike of adrenaline coursing down my spine.

I ignore the sound, focusing ahead on the signs in the distance.

Yorkville.

Upper East Side.

Broadway and 62nd.

My gaze frantically searches for what I'm looking for, the crowd of people dissipating from around me when a break in the rain comes.

A hand grabs my shoulder, the fingers digging in. I shrink, recoiling away.

"Baby, where are you headed?" The question is followed by a cough, and then a loud belch and a laugh. "Excuse me." The apology is exaggerated and clearly sarcastic.

With too much force, I shift my weight onto my hurt leg and ignore the fierce rippling of pain as I advance from the creep. My good foot lands straight into a puddle, soaking my entire shin with disgusting street water. Tears glisten in my eyes, but I refuse to let them fall.

I'm this close, I remind myself, and put one foot in front of the other.

"Oh, baby, don't leave me—" But he trails off there.

Halfway across the street, I glance over my shoulder to see him slumped into the corner of the bus stop, his face pressed against the brown paper-bag-covered booze he's using as a pillow.

My shoulders release the slightest bit of tension, but it's nothing compared to what I'm going to experience when I finally get to where I'm trying to go.

It's then that I find the sign I was searching for, confirming that I'm only two blocks away.

Reaching into my pocket, I pull out the faded piece of paper with the name and address on it, my heart aching knowing the end is near. That safety is near. That a shower and a bed and maybe something to eat is near.

Ricardo may have made my life a living hell, but he was filthy rich, and by extension, so was I. But if living the way I have this week is what gets me free of men who think they can control me, so fucking be it—I'll gladly leave that all behind.

The streetlights illuminate the sidewalk through the hazy darkness of night.

I shake my leg, attempting to rid some of the water drenching it, and stare up at the building across the street. In my mind, I thought it would be grander, with a gated entrance and a doorman. But instead, it's a modest four-story building that blends in with the rest. The first floor houses a bakery with an elaborate Closed sign on the door and a laundromat with flickering lights. My attention falls to the door to the apartment complex, but once I latch onto it, I learn that it's locked.

My chest tightens as I take in the panel of buttons I hadn't noticed until now. Scanning each of them, I settle on the number 2202, the letters A. S. in faded markings next to it.

Just as I'm about to muster the courage to reach out and press the button, the door to the building opens, a man nearly barreling into me.

"Christ, I'm sorry, I didn't see you there." His features are soft, and it's immediately clear that his apology is genuine. He's conventionally attractive, with his dark hair, his dark eyes, and his tall stature. He holds the door open. "Here, let me get that for you."

I stare a bit too long, so long that I forget what I'm doing here and that I do, in fact, need to get inside this building.

"You were going in, weren't you?"

I blink, hoping it makes me look more human and less zombie-like. "Ye-yeah," I manage to blurt out. "I was. It's been a long day, forgive me." My voice cracks more than I'd prefer, and I regret opening my mouth at all.

It's then that his gaze loiters on my body, a quick pass that gives him enough time to realize how terrible of a condition I'm in. "Are you okay?" he asks.

It's a simple question, really, one that I don't know how to answer.

So, I force myself back to reality. "Yeah," I tell him, and step through the generous opening into the building, the air conditioning chilling my face the second I'm inside. "Thanks," I say as I continue forward, leaving him and that interaction behind me. Hobbling onward, I go straight toward the stairs, refusing to waste another second trying to locate the elevator.

I limp my way up the stairs, hating my decision more and more with each labored movement. I catch my breath at the top, my good hand gripping the railing until my knuckles turn white. I've come this far; I can't give up yet.

Stumbling, I glance at each door, wishing like hell the next will be 2202. It isn't until I reach the second-to-last door that I find my safe haven.

My hand twitches, my fingers flexing before they ball into a fist. With a final exhale, I knock on the door and await my fate.

Thirty seconds go by.

Then another thirty.

I knock again, this time a bit harder.

There's shuffling coming from inside, a clear indicator someone is in there.

Surely Silver told them when I'd be arriving. Shouldn't they be expecting me?

No answer.

My heart picks up its pace, so I pound on the door with the side of my fist.

A grunt is followed by the sound of locks clinking, and then the door opens.

What awaits me on the other side is nothing I could have ever imagined.

"Can I help you?" His voice is masked with irritation.

I look up at him as he presses one tattooed arm to the doorframe and holds the door barely ajar. And when I say look up at him, I mean look up at him. My neck tilts so aggressively that I'm not convinced I haven't reinjured myself. He must be six-foot-five at the very least.

His dark brown hair spills over onto his forehead, the color somehow matching his deeply intense stare. His jaw tenses. "I said, can I help you?"

His annoyance washes over me like a cold shower, my own frustration rising to the surface at the way he's treating me. Any level of attraction I held for him dissipates just as quickly as it came.

His icy glare flits behind me, his body inching closer as he peeks into the hallway, the scent of him, something like cedar and honey, concealing my own body odor.

"Aren't you going to let me in?" I finally blurt out, every level of sass I can muster lacing each word.

"Excuse me?" He almost chuckles but he masks it neatly.

Adjusting the backpack strap of my few belongings on my shoulder, I nod toward his apartment. "I was told I could stay here." I reach into my pocket and pull out the slip of paper with his name and address on it. "See. Here." I shove it into the space between us.

He hesitates before glancing down, his thumb grazing my hand as he takes it from me. I ignore the warmth of his skin on mine and imagine this entire thing being behind me soon enough.

"This doesn't mean anything," he says, shrugging and giving me the paper back. "Anyone could have written this down."

"I mean, that's your name, isn't it? Asher?" Why is he having such a hard time understanding what's going on? Silver told me I would be safe here, but instead, this guy is acting like he has no idea who I am or why I'm here.

The man exhales and shakes his head. "Archer, not Asher."

"I—I mean, that's a simple mistake." I study the smudged paper and Silver's poor handwriting. Is it possible I got the name *and* the address wrong? Maybe this isn't where I'm supposed to be. That seems like a reasonable explanation for the way he's treating me. I'd probably wonder why some random beat-up girl was knocking on my doorstep if I wasn't expecting her, either.

"But that's my address, yeah. Doesn't mean you belong here, though." The way he says it cuts through me like a hot knife on butter.

"Listen," I say, my temper rising. "I can't even begin to tell you the hell I've been through to get here. I haven't had a proper shower in days. My feet hurt, my body aches, and I am so fucking tired I could fall asleep right now, so unless you want me sleeping on your doorstep, you're going to let me inside. Silver told me to come here. He told me I'd be safe here, that you would help me, and that I could trust you. Was he wrong?"

He cracks the door open a bit more as he adjusts his stance.

"Wait, what did you just say?"

I narrow my gaze. "Which part did you not understand, big boy?"

"Did you say *Silver* sent you?" He does that thing with his jaw again and I can't help but wonder if he struggles with headaches, as fucking tense as he is.

Gently, I rock my head up and down. "Now we're getting somewhere."

"This is a mistake," he tells me, and grips the door.

My nostrils flare. "If you shut that door, so help me God."

I'm this fucking close to being free, I refuse to let anything stop me now.

CHAPTER TWO

Archer

Silver must have lost his fucking mind. First, he calls to ask me for a favor that could put me and my entire family in danger, and now he sends some random, borderline irritating, injured woman to my apartment.

I told him, I told *everyone*, that I was done. I was out. I don't want to be bothered. I don't want to be acknowledged or talked about or even thought of.

If I were a better man, I'd kill myself and get it over with, but someone has to manage the family's finances and be their tech person, and I don't trust any of them to do it. August, maybe, the eldest among us, only he's too busy running his own empire to learn the ins and outs of what I do. I don't want them to fail because I got a little down.

So, I made them a deal—I'd continue to run things, I'd continue to hack, as long as they left me alone.

It's been three years and still, no one can fucking grasp that I don't want to be bothered.

They know it, Silver knows it, every person in our industry from here to the West Coast knows to leave me the fuck alone.

But they want my help because they know I'm the one to get shit done. Silver asked for the favor because I am the only one who can hack into The Manor's security. And he must have sent this woman to my doorstep because he knows I'll be the one to *keep her safe*.

I cringe at those last few words, my heart icing over at the truth. I can't keep anyone safe, let alone some stranger I know nothing about.

I study her rain-soaked face, the bruises concealed under the red hair sticking to her cheeks.

"I can't help you," I tell her honestly.

Her hand presses firmly against the door. "I have nowhere else to go."

Chewing on the inside of my lip, I do something unexpected and step out of the way, giving her space to enter. I don't know why I do it, why I give in, but something about the look in her eye tells me it's my only option. "Let's talk about this inside."

Her face softens in the slightest, as if she's as surprised as I am that I gave in.

I shut the door behind her, closing us into my apartment, the area feeling strangely too small suddenly. This is wrong, I shouldn't have just invited a random beaten woman into my apartment. What if the cops come? I don't know who's working this shift and don't want to deal with bribing someone to put this all behind me.

It's then that I realize the screen on my computer is still lit up. I march over, leaving her at the door, and hit the button to turn on the screensaver. My task can wait until I don't have an audience.

"Were you watching porn?" she asks, the question and the cadence of her voice catching me off guard.

"No." I shake my head, way too seriously, and turn toward her. "I was working."

She glances around, almost skeptically taking things in. "What do you do?"

"I'm in tech," I respond with the generic answer I give most people who ask because it doesn't usually prompt any follow-ups.

"What does that even mean?" She focuses her attention on me, and I hate the way it feels like a giant spotlight just appeared out of nowhere in my dimly lit apartment.

Even from the distance between us, her eyes are bloodshot and droopy. She wasn't lying about being exhausted.

I slide my phone off my desk. "You said Silver sent you?"

The woman crosses her arms over her chest, one bigger than the other, telling me there's some type of bandage under the oversized sweatshirt she's wearing. Her outfit makes her seem even more frail than she already is, like she's a kid playing dress-up in their father's clothes. But that's the point, isn't it? To maintain some level of anonymity when you're on the run.

"Yes." She clears her throat. "Why do I get the feeling you had no idea about this?"

"Because I didn't."

She licks her lips and nods. "Ah. Okay. Well, that explains your response." She draws in a breath and tucks a strand of stiff hair behind her ear, displaying her discolored cheek even more.

Whoever hurt her wasn't messing around.

It's not your problem, I remind myself. *She isn't your problem.*

But isn't she? She *is* standing inside my apartment.

I dial Silver's number and press my phone to my ear. "I'll get to the bottom of this." The line rings, and rings, and rings some more before his voicemail picks up. "Give me a call when you get this," I say to his answering machine. "It's urgent." I don't bother telling him who it is, because if what she's saying is true, Silver more than likely was expecting my call, which tells me he purposely didn't answer.

That's probably why he didn't inform me of any of this to begin with, because he knew I would shut it down before it even happened. I would have insisted he find someone else, I would have gone somewhere and not been home, I would have done anything to avoid the awkwardness of whatever the fuck is happening right now.

"He didn't answer," she says, and I can't quite make out if it's a question or a statement.

I tap my phone against my chin and consider my options. I

want to tell her that I don't want her here. That I don't want anyone here. I want to insist that she leave and find someone else to help her. I want anything other than to deal with this.

Why can't people understand and respect that I want to be left alone? What's so hard with respecting boundaries?

When I left the life three years ago, I thought I made it clear, but apparently fucking not.

Couldn't Silver have asked quite literally anyone other than me? Why couldn't *he* have helped her? Clearly, her situation was dire enough that he sent her away, which begs the question, who is she running from? And why? But if I start asking those questions, I'll start to uncover a reality that I cannot escape from, and if I don't want to be involved in this, then I have to stay out of it.

Not. My. Problem.

"Are you just going to stare at me, or are you going to say something?" Her tone is snarky and makes me regret answering the door.

I fold my arms over my chest and lean against my desk. "I'm trying to figure out what to do."

"Well." She sighs and slides one arm out of the strap of her backpack. "Are you going to kill me?"

"What? No. Of course not." Not tonight, at least, but I don't mention that part. If she keeps getting on my nerves, I might.

But anyone who knows me knows that that's not true either, because even though I'm involved in illicit activities, I would never hurt her. Not after everything I've been through. I sigh as I realize that's exactly why Silver sent her to me.

"Okay then." She drops her backpack onto the floor near the door. "Then it's settled. I'm staying."

I kick off the desk and stand upright. "Wh-what? I didn't say that. You can't stay here. I could be an axe murderer, for all you know. Didn't anyone ever tell you it's dangerous to knock on random strangers' doors at night?"

She places her hand on her hip, jutting the thing out

dramatically, and that gesture alone is enough to show me her true personality, not the one masked by the desperate pleas for a place to hide out. "You're not a random stranger. You're Silver's friend, which by extension makes you my friend. And friends let friends crash when they're homeless and in need of help. So tell me, *Archer*, are you going to kick this friend out?"

The way she says my name grates at me in equal parts satisfaction and utter annoyance, and I hate that I can't quite figure out which is worse.

"We are not friends," I tell her, very matter-of-fact.

She shrugs and steps away from the borderline disgusting bag she left behind. She extends her hand. "Archer, London. There. Now we're on a first-name basis. That must be a step toward friends, right?"

I glare down at her, envisioning picking her up and carrying her back out of my apartment and outside. "How did you get into the building?" It suddenly dawns on me that she shouldn't have been able to.

She rolls her eyes. "I just did. Now shake my hand like a gentleman."

Reluctantly, I slide my hand into hers, noting just how fucking small she is in every way. A slight pang stabs me in the heart at the idea that someone could have abused her to the condition she's in now.

"Don't look at me like that," London says.

"Like what?"

"Like I might break."

Our hands, still locked together, linger between us, filling the awkward space. Finally, I release her and return my arms across my chest, the sensation of her skin on mine burning even in the absence of her touch.

"If you don't mind," she continues without letting me respond, not that I planned on it anyway, "I'd really love to take a shower." London tilts her head in both directions. "If you could just point me..."

"Right. Yeah." I march across the room, grab her bag from where she left it, and head toward the bathroom. "Restroom is through here. Uh, there're towels in that closet in there. Use whatever you need to. Do you, uh, do you have clothes to change into?"

Her face tenses, only just slightly, before she says, "No."

Whatever she was running from was so bad that she couldn't even properly prepare. I'm surprised Silver would send her off like this, but perhaps he didn't have a choice.

"I can get you something to wear," I find myself saying, unsure of why I'm entertaining any of this. "And while you're showering, I'll phone Silver again."

Her brows pinch together. "You'll *phone* him? What are you, elderly?"

"Whatever." I don't know why everything she says annoys me, but it does, and the sooner I figure out what to do with her, the better. I'm not meant to have other people around. It's better when I'm alone. I pause before I shut the door behind me and close her in, and nod at her arm. "Does that arm have a cast on it?"

London brings her arm toward her chest like she's weirdly protecting it. "Maybe. Why?"

"Because I don't think you're supposed to get them wet. Do you need to cover it or something?"

"No."

I gawk at her for a long minute before giving up. "Okay then." Dropping her bag into the bathroom, I leave her to find something of mine for her to wear. Given her visible injuries, I should probably stick to something baggy and comfortable. I quickly settle on a black T-shirt and a pair of gray sweatpants, snatching a pair of new boxer briefs just in case she needs something to wear under them.

Standing in the doorway, I watch her examine herself in the mirror. Her hazy gaze trails the finger she runs over her sunken cheek and peels the stuck hair off her face. Even battered, she's frustratingly beautiful and makes me wonder who could have treated her like this. Maybe it was an abusive partner or, knowing Silver was involved, it could have been a boss of some type. Regardless of who it was, it doesn't change the fact that she's here now, and the sooner she gets cleaned up, the sooner she'll be gone.

"Here are these," I tell her, and offer her the clothes. "The boxers are new, fresh from the wash. I didn't know what you needed."

London comes over, her gait slower and rockier than it was earlier. I hadn't realized she was struggling so badly with walking until now. "You're nice for a grump," she says, taking the clothes from me.

"I'm not a grump," I blurt out, even though she's not wrong. "And I'm not nice," I add.

"Whatever you say, grump." She's awful feisty for someone asking for help from a stranger. Clearly, she knows the people Silver hangs around with are criminals. I mean, Silver himself is a notorious fixer. Surely, she's not stupid enough to get too cocky with the wrong people. But maybe that's why she's in the condition she is—she mouthed off to the wrong guy.

I regret the thought immediately. I don't care what she said to *anyone*, man or woman, she didn't deserve what happened to her. I shouldn't, but a strong desire to figure out who hurt her washes over me, but I swallow it down and turn around, leaving the bathroom and trailing back into the openness of the living area.

Running my hand through my hair, I tug it back and off my face. "What are you doing, Archer?" I whisper.

CHAPTER THREE

London

With less caution than I should, I peel each layer of my clothes off, one by one, tossing them onto the marble floor. I chew at the corner of my lip and stare at my reflection, the person looking back at me unfamiliar and so very me all at the same time. There isn't an inch of my skin that isn't covered in either a bruise or dirt. My hair is ratty and matted together, the red dulled from the torturous week I've been through.

I force a smile, my eyes not quite getting the memo, and immediately relax my face and shake my head. I'll figure out a way to pretend, but right now I really just need a shower. Maybe that will give me the will to fight another day. I've made it this far, why give up now?

My feet stick to the cold floor as I make my way over to the shower, the entire thing bigger than I thought it was once I reach inside. On second thought, this entire bathroom is nicer than I expected, given the entrance of the building. Perhaps Archer remodeled it recently, installing what appears to be state-of-the-art everything, including a quad showerhead, water spurting from all directions when I turn the faucet on.

A slight chirping draws my attention to a panel in the shower with numbers on it, and I quickly realize it's temperature-controlled. I push the up arrow until it blinks red, indicating a warning for the water being too hot.

I step in anyway, not caring about the warning or the steam that ripples and fills the space. Tensing, I go through a few emotions one after another. Pain, pleasure, satisfaction.

Everything hurts, but it would have anyway, regardless of the heat.

Closing my eyes, I fully submerge myself, the molten water cascading over my face, my shoulders, and my entire body. I turn, tilt my head back, and let it wash some of the grime out of my hair. I struggle with the cast on my left arm, my fingers not quite moving the way I want them to when I run them through my long locks. I blink some of the droplets away and study the awkward thing stuck to my wrist. The itch has subsided, but only because the heat of the water is a bit more distracting.

I extend it toward the faucet shooting out of the wall and allow the water to rush through the opening, the water running murky for a moment before turning clear again. My stomach turns at the smell, and I wish like hell I could cut the thing off right here and now.

Luckily, one of the faucets detaches, so I use it to do the same to the cast on my leg, the part near my foot caked in debris from where I was walking on it.

Once I feel the slightest bit better, I study the various bottles on the shelves and come to the very sudden understanding that Archer must have a girlfriend. No single, straight man would have this brand of shampoo *and* conditioner, let alone a men's and women's bodywash.

Regardless, it doesn't matter; I'm not here to date Archer, I'm here to hide out until I can get a place of my own. But what if his girlfriend has a problem with that and I'm right back to square one, homeless and on the run?

I swallow the lump that forms in my throat and clear the thought. I can't think like that, not when I've finally found a sliver of peace. I'll worry about that tomorrow, when the severity of this situation kicks in.

To the best of my ability, I lather some of the shampoo in my hands and wash my hair, following it up with the conditioner. In the few moments of letting it sit in my hair, I pop the top on the men's bodywash, the scent of it an instant reminder of when Archer leaned toward me in the doorway. His golden-brown stare had bored into me, the color so strange and beautiful and intense, I was almost mesmerized by it. Only, I was more focused on getting inside of his apartment and taking a shower.

"Shit," I blurt out, seconds before I pop my head out of the opening and locate the closet he informed me the towels were in. Darting in and out, I leave a trail of water behind as I grab two towels and a washcloth, dropping the towels near the entrance and returning to the heavenly stream of water that leaves red marks on my already damaged skin.

I make quick work of washing my body, scrubbing each crevice and surface at least three times before calling it quits and standing under the stream for another few minutes.

Once I'm out and wrapped in the luxurious towels, I wipe at the mirror and take in my flushed complexion. My curiosity gets the better of me as I open every single drawer and cabinet, confirming my suspicions of Archer having a girlfriend when I spot the hair dryer and straightener, and well-stocked feminine-hygiene section.

I glance at the door, wondering what she must be like, and how Archer must act around her. If he's as grumpy with her as he is with me, there's no telling how *happy* the two of them must be together. Maybe that's why he acts like he has a stick up his ass—he's in an unhappy relationship. I shake my head to rid myself of the useless thoughts, my mind doing anything it can to distract me from the fact that I just spent a week escaping my arranged marriage and now I'm standing in some random man's bathroom, slipping my weakened body into his clothes and using his girlfriend's brush to attempt to untangle my hair.

With a curse, I slam the thing onto the counter and clench my jaw. "It's only hair, London, chill out."

A knock sounds on the door. "Is everything okay in there?"

"Yeah." I leave the brush behind and hobble my way over, plastering on my *everything is fine* face when I reach for the handle.

I open the door to find Archer leaning against the frame, his hand posted on the side, eyes fluttering from me to inside the bathroom then back to me again.

"What was that noise?" he asks like I set his apartment on fire or something.

"I was using your girlfriend's hairbrush."

Archer glares at me so intensely, it's almost as if he's trying to set *me* on fire. "I don't have a girlfriend."

"Oh." I shrug. "Fooled me."

He continues to watch me, and for a moment, I allow it, unsure of what he's trying to accomplish other than burn a hole through my forehead.

"Are you done yet?" I say once the moment has turned awkward.

Archer lowers his tattooed arm and steps out of the way. "I called Silver again, no answer."

I stalk out of the bathroom to find the couch made up with sheets, a blanket, and a pillow. Turning toward him, I offer what I can only hope is a polite smile. "Thank you," I tell him.

He runs his hand over his jaw. "That's not for you." He points to the door off in the distance. "You can have the bedroom; I'll sleep on the couch."

"What? No." I pat the corner of the pillow. "I'll take the couch, really. It's not a big deal." I should be grateful he's offering me his bedroom, but things are already weird enough that I just got naked and showered at his place. Do I really need to take things to the next level and sleep in his bed? Silver said I could trust him, but still, Archer is a stranger—even if he's a damn good-looking and grumpy one.

Archer's gaze flickers to the desk in the corner with the elaborate computer monitors adorning it.

I press my hand to my chest. "I promise I won't touch your computers, if that's what you're worried about."

He draws in a breath, his face almost unreadable. "I think you'd be more comfortable in the bedroom."

"I think *you'd* be more comfortable in *your* bedroom." I plop down onto the couch and stake my claim. "I mean, what are you, like thirty-seven feet tall?" I lower myself onto my side, stretching all the way out. "See, I actually fit, I doubt you do."

"I fit," he blurts out in a feeble attempt to defend his already weak argument.

"Okay, big boy." I drag my right hand under my head and adjust myself on the couch. "This is pretty comfortable, though." My eyes grow heavier by the minute, the exhaustion fully catching up and daring to drag me into the abyss.

"Are you hungry?"

"No," I lie, and beg my stomach not to betray me. I'm so fucking hungry, but I'm more tired than I am famished, and nothing sounds better than getting a solid hour of sleep without having to worry about some creep on a bus getting handsy.

"Are you lying?"

"No."

Archer contemplates my answer but decides to let it go. He points over at the open kitchen area. "Help yourself. There's stuff for sandwiches in the fridge, and there're snacks in the pantry."

"I'm a vegetarian," I tell him for no real reason.

"Oh, right. Yeah. Um, there's probably a vegetable somewhere in there."

I narrow my gaze up at him, his stature exaggerated from this angle. "Being a vegetarian doesn't mean I only eat vegetables."

Archer turns his hand over. "I don't know what vegetarians eat."

"Veggies, sure, but other stuff, like cheese, bagels, fruit, tofu, you know. Any of those things ring a bell?" I raise myself onto my elbows and wince at the pain. "Fuck," I mutter, accidentally breaking that cool streak I had going on.

"Are you hurt?" Archer's brows pinch together.

I let out a breath. "What do you think?" Swinging my legs around, I drape them over the couch, my feet dangling just before the ground, not quite reaching all the way. "I'm fine, though, really."

"You should see a doctor."

"Do you think I put these on myself?" I extend my cast-covered arm and wiggle my leg.

"Why are you so difficult?"

"Why are *you* so difficult?" I repeat, no doubt annoying the shit out of him. I don't mean to find such enjoyment out of bickering with him, but I do find it's sparked a light in this otherwise dim world I was living in. And since I don't have much else going for me at the moment, I'm going to keep this up as long as I can.

Archer tugs his bottom lip between his teeth and releases it a second later. "There's food over there. *Do not* touch my computer. If you need anything, I'll be in there." He motions to the bedroom he offered me and leaves me sitting there with a triumphant grin on my face.

Only, he doesn't go straight to the room, he goes to the bathroom first, a few curse words muttered from his lips when he enters.

My gaze skims his place but it's too dark to make much of anything out aside from the rough features of furniture and walls. The weight of my eyelids deepens, and I give in to the urge to return to a horizontal position, not even covering myself before I close my eyes and get drawn under into what I can only hope is a restful sleep.

Except it's nothing of the sort, because when I wake, my body is lined with sweat, my throat raw, and Archer is kneeling beside me, his sleepy face racked with panic, his hair tousled over his forehead.

CHAPTER FOUR

Archer

"London, you're fine, you're safe," I mutter to this complete fucking stranger.

Her bright green eyes flutter open, scanning frantically before settling on me. She sits up, her chest heaving as she catches her breath. "I was... I'm..."

I sit on my ass and lean against the table in my living room. "Are you okay?"

"Yeah, I..." London rubs at her neck, and her face, and then adjusts the shirt of mine that she's wearing.

"Do you want to talk about it?" I ask her, unsure of what I'm supposed to do in this situation. We don't know each other, but I can't exactly pretend like she wasn't just screaming like someone was trying to murder her.

"No," she says, stiff and a bit too sudden.

But I don't press it, because it's not my place. I am no one to her other than a person to crash at their place. Or more like come in like a tornado and destroy it.

After London insisted that she wanted to sleep on the couch, I thought I'd get ready for bed myself, but upon stepping foot in the bathroom, I had to first spend twenty minutes picking up after her. Once I gathered all her clothes, threw them in the wash, disinfected everything that they touched, and put everything back where it belonged, London was snoring on the couch. It was obvious she was exhausted from the journey getting here.

I tossed and turned for an hour, my mind unable to shut down enough to let me fall asleep, partly because I was waiting for the clothes to finish in the washer and partly because a random woman was sleeping on my couch. Stealing a quick peek at her, I switched the laundry over and returned to bed, only to stare at my ceiling for the next few hours. I managed to sneak out of my apartment without waking her and return half an hour later with her still fast asleep. Finally, my body shut down enough to pull me under, but it wasn't long until London's cries woke me from a dead sleep.

"I'm fine, really," she says, dragging me from my recollection of the night.

I scratch my chin and check the time on my watch. Nearly a quarter after six in the morning. "Do you want some coffee?" I rise from my spot next to her, everything about her becoming tinier once I'm standing fully.

She clears her throat, her voice hoarse. "Yeah, thanks." It's then that she seems to look at me, and I mean really look at me. Her gaze floats from my face to my bare chest, down my entire body. "Sorry, I didn't realize you weren't wearing a shirt." Her cheeks flush, but I can't tell if it's from the nightmare or not.

"Yeah, I run hot." I leave her behind to go straight to my room and grab the neatly folded T-shirt off my dresser and throw it over my head. I return a second later, calling out to her as I make my way to the kitchen. "How do you take your coffee?"

London yawns and stretches before rising to her feet. "What do you have?" Her face crinkles and she smacks her lips. "Do you have an extra toothbrush?"

I reach into the cabinet and pull a bag of coffee grounds out. "On the counter in the bathroom. Although I'm surprised you didn't find it when you were snooping."

"I was not," she lies.

I make the coffee, not daring to question her, because it's not like she'd tell me the truth anyway.

London joins me in the kitchen a moment later, opening the refrigerator like she's lived here her whole life. "Uh, that's weird."

She stares inside the fridge, and I grab two mugs from their home tucked away, ignoring her declaration.

"Archer." She glances over her shoulder at me. "Am I still asleep?"

"What?" I shoot her a quick look but grab the small container of sugar and a spoon.

"Cheese. Bagels. Fruit. Tofu."

I disregard her still.

"Archer," she says a bit louder. "Why do you have this stuff?"

Rolling my eyes, I sigh. "I went out and got them."

"When?" Her mouth gapes open.

"In the middle of the night?"

"Why?"

"Because I couldn't sleep."

"You couldn't sleep, so you went out and got the four things I mentioned I ate?"

"I got some yogurt, too; it's in the drawer. I didn't know what flavor you liked, so I got a variety pack."

"What if I don't like yogurt?"

I turn toward her. "You don't like yogurt?"

"Of course I like yogurt, who doesn't like yogurt?"

"Vegans?"

"There's vegan yogurt."

"Oh." I turn my attention back to the coffee, pouring both mugs full once it's stopped brewing. Without returning to the previous topic, I say, "There're a couple different milks in the fridge. Two coffee creamers, and there's sugar here."

London pauses, and I wish I could read her mind to figure out what snarky comment she's going to say before she says it, but instead, she opens the fridge and takes out the vanilla oat milk creamer. "What do you want?"

"That's fine," I tell her, mostly because I don't really have a preference.

I usually drink my coffee black, but since my morning is

drastically different than usual, why not mix up my coffee for the day, too?

She makes her way over to me, her cast dragging across the floor. "I thought you didn't want me here," she says with certainty.

"I don't," I agree.

"Then why did you get me food?"

I shrug, unsure of it myself, if I'm being completely honest. Maybe I was planning ahead, preparing for the conversation when Silver convinces me I should keep the stray woman who showed up on my doorstep. Usually, I'm more rigid with things, and my first instinct was to get as far away from her as possible, but maybe I could hear her out, hear him out, and try to do something good in my life for a change. She frustrates the hell out of me, but maybe last night was just a fluke and we got off on the wrong foot.

"Sounded like a good idea."

"Do you even like strawberries, Archer?"

"Who doesn't like strawberries?"

She walks over, yanks the container out of the fridge, and pops the top, pulling out a plump berry.

"You should really wash that—" But I'm too late. She puts the thing into her mouth before I can stop her.

London shoves the container back into the fridge and shuts the door with her hip, returning to my side, half-eaten strawberry in her hand.

Maybe getting her some food was a bad idea after all.

"Here." I shove a mug of coffee toward her. "But be careful, it's—"

She takes a drink, not bothering to heed my warning. London winces. "Shit, that's hot."

"If you'd have waited two seconds and let me finish my sentence, then you wouldn't have burned yourself."

London mumbles something under her breath and takes

the cup of coffee between her hands and strolls over to the stool at the island in my kitchen. I find myself holding my breath, the anticipation of whether she's going to make a mess unnerving me. How can one tiny human create such a disaster in her wake?

She settles into the chair, and I lean against the counter, my arms folded across my chest, waiting for whatever smart-ass thing she's about to say.

"This is a nice place."

I raise a brow at her. "Yeah?"

She nods. "Yeah. I mean, I couldn't really tell when it was dark."

I leave my post, stroll over to the window in the living room, and raise the blinds, light pooling into the room. I usually leave them closed.

"Have you lived here long?" London asks me once I return to my spot.

"Few years," I respond, my answer vague and hopefully satisfactory. Gripping my mug, I take a cautious sip of the coffee, careful not to burn myself the same way she did.

"Looks like you just moved in."

I don't respond.

"I mean, because it's so tidy."

"I like things tidy."

"I can tell."

I don't mention that the desire to have things in their place is almost overwhelming to the point that it unsettles me if they're not. I like order, I like control, I like knowing I can predict the outcome.

Nothing about the last eight hours has been predictable.

And I have a feeling the worst is yet to come.

"Do you need to leave for work?" She fiddles with the handle on the mug, almost like a weird nervous tic, and I'm curious if she knows what she's doing.

"No."

"Have the day off?"

"I work from home."

"Oh, that's nice."

I take another long swig of my coffee and set the cup on the counter. "Are you hungry?"

"I am," she tells me from her spot at the island.

"Cheese, bagel, fruit, tofu?" I ask her, naming the items in the order she had told them to me, and how I placed them in the fridge. Only, when I open the door and am greeted by the cold air pouring out, I notice that she shoved the still-open container of strawberries in with the takeout container from my Chinese a few nights ago.

"I can get it." London rises from her seat but there's nothing more that I'd prefer than for her to stay exactly where she is, unable to make any more messes or put anything else in the wrong place.

"I insist." I force the best polite tone I can muster. "What do you want?"

Hesitantly, she lowers herself back down. "I guess I'll have a bagel...half of one. And some strawberries. Do you have any cream cheese?"

I drop the container of cream cheese onto the counter across from her before she can even finish, her gaze darting from the food to me.

"Toasted?" I ask her as I reach for the bagels.

"Yes, please."

I pop the entire bagel into the toaster, deciding that I'll eat the other half so there isn't a random half in the bag, and turn toward the pantry, snatching the baking soda and vinegar off the shelf.

When I return to the counter, London is reaching for the carton of strawberries.

"You can't even wait for me to clean them?" I shake my head and take them from her.

"What was that saying about God made dirt..." London scowls like I stole candy from a baby.

"Dirt is gross, London. Aren't you afraid you'll bite into a worm or something?"

London's face tenses, and it's then that I remember she's a vegetarian. She gawks at the strawberry in her hand.

"I'm mostly joking," I lie, because it appears she's already been through enough lately, she doesn't need to worry about eating something that goes against her vegetarianism.

After a quick soak of the strawberries in the baking soda, vinegar, and water mixture, London grimaces watching all the debris go down the drain. "Wow, that actually is gross."

"I told you."

The bagel pops up in the toaster, but before I can get them, London hops out of her chair.

"Where are the plates?" she asks as she bites back some pain, which I don't think she notices me notice.

Why she's being so proud, I'll never know. I'm just a stranger, why does she think she has to act like she isn't suffering?

I nod in their direction instead of shutting her down, even though I really want to. If she gets the plates, there's a chance she'll knock something over, or worse, hurt herself in the process.

She surprises me by getting them and not doing either, not until she reaches into the toaster to get the bagel halves. "Shit." London flinches and shakes her hand.

"Did anyone ever tell you that you're accident-prone?" I walk over, get both halves out, and set them on the plate, ignoring the way her emerald eyes glare at me. "You need to be wrapped in Bubble Wrap."

"Yeah, well, did anyone ever tell you that you're grumpy?"

"Yeah, you. At least twice already." I continue back over to the sink, rinsing the strawberries and cutting the stems off before London can come over and do it herself, no doubt stabbing her jugular in the process.

I don't know why she's so hell-bent on calling me grumpy, though, because I'm not. I just prefer to be alone and not bothered. That doesn't make me *grumpy*.

"You really should be nicer to me," I say, glancing over my shoulder. "This is my apartment, remember?"

London brings both plates over and rummages through a few drawers before finding a knife. She slathers both bagel halves with more cream cheese than humanly consumable, and licks the thing clean. At least it was only a butter knife.

I cut a few strawberries and place them on her plate, and then some on mine. If I'm being honest, I've never really liked strawberries, but something about the way she was eating one made me want to reconsider...

"Do you have plans today?" London asks me.

"Yes."

"Oh." She picks up a slice of berry and pops it into her mouth.

"I have to finish the...project...I was working on last night."

"Oh," she says again, only this time her tone has shifted completely. "Right. Yeah. For sure."

"Why?"

"I was just wondering."

"Really?" I put the rest of the cut-up strawberries into a glass container, place them back into the fridge, and clean the sink of the stems, tossing them into the trash and wiping off the counter.

"Archer."

I look up at London, assuming that something is wrong. "What?"

Her face softens and it's the first time I'm really noticing the freckles that dust her nose and cheeks. She was in rough shape when she came in last night, but now, she's showered and sort of rested. "Sit down. Eat your food. Drink your coffee, it's getting cold."

I blink and see that she's brought my food next to where she was sitting, and she's returned to her seat. She pats the spot. "Come on, big boy."

"You talk to me like I'm a dog." And yet here I am, obeying as I walk over and slide onto the stool.

In a way, London reminds me of my sister—headstrong, tough as nails, and not afraid to call me out. I guess I'm not used to that from anyone other than her. My brothers and I have always been feared and respected, so for her to walk up in here and do nothing of the sort, I find it sort of admirable. Stupid, for sure, but a refreshing quality. Maybe that's why I haven't thrown her out yet. Maybe that's why I'm entertaining this entire shit show, because it's a strange change of pace.

"Good boy," London purrs, and takes a bite of her bagel, giving me a quick wink.

I'm easily a foot taller than her, a hundred pounds heavier, tattoos covering my body, and she's the one who seems to be calling the shots. If only she knew who I really was, and the things I'm involved with, perhaps she would act differently.

But for a little while, maybe it would be nice if we kept the dark part of ourselves hidden.

CHAPTER FIVE

London

I'm halfway through my bagel when Archer's phone rings. He slides it out of his pocket and immediately leaves his stool. He presses a firm finger in the air toward me and my heart stutters because I'm certain it's Silver that's calling him.

Archer confirms it a second later when he answers. "Silver."

"Can I talk to him?" I whisper-shout, and follow Archer as he tries to get away from me.

"Yeah, she's here."

I reach out toward Archer and attempt to tug at his arm but it's no use, he pulls away from me and turns around, extending his arm with his hand on my forehead to keep me at a distance.

"Chill," he mutters quietly to me.

I jut out my bottom lip and slump my shoulders.

Archer releases his hand slowly, and when I remain in place, he obliges me by putting Silver on speakerphone.

Silver's voice comes in ragged over the phone. "She's been through hell and back, Arch. Do me a favor and take care of her?"

Archer's intense stare meets mine, and he looks away. "A favor, huh? I thought we were already square after the last one, Silver?"

"We were, but hey, now I owe you one, okay? Anything. You name it. You know how this works."

"I'm out, Sil. You knew this. You knew it then and you know it now. You can't keep doing this to me."

"Listen, I wouldn't ask if it wasn't necessary. There wasn't anyone else I could trust to keep her safe."

"Keep her safe from what?"

"I can't say much over the phone, Arch."

"You're going to have to give me something, Silver. I need to know what I'm up against if you're expecting me to agree to this."

I swallow, my throat going dry at listening to these two go back and forth, talking about me like I'm not right here. I hate it, I hate the way it makes my stomach twist and my heart ache. I hate the fact that any of this is happening, that my father couldn't have just died and left me alone instead of haunting me with a man identical to him.

"Joe Vito," Silver says, those two words a complete statement.

Archer doesn't speak for a long moment, and I wonder what he must be thinking. If he's considering whether he should throw me out now, or later. But he surprises me when he chuckles, the sound so unfamiliar and strange. "Okay."

"You're good?" Muffled static follows Silver's voice.

"Yeah."

"I owe you one, Arch."

"Yeah, you do." Archer's gaze trails to mine as he hangs up on Silver and folds his tattooed arms over his chest. He draws in a breath and tenses his jaw. "Do I even want to know why Vito's after you?"

I shrug. "Probably not."

He rubs at his beard, and I wish like hell I could make it all stop. I don't want his pity, I don't want his help, I don't want anything from anyone other than to be left alone. But isn't that all Archer wanted, too? And now here I am, disrupting just that.

"It won't be for long," I add. "Just until I can get on my feet and find somewhere else to stay."

"He's untouchable."

"I know."

"If he's after you, this is a problem that will never go away."

"I just need a little time."

"He told me to keep you safe."

"All I need is a place to crash until I can find something else. Then I'll be out of your hair."

"How long?"

"I don't know, a month or two." The idea of living with a complete stranger isn't lost on me, but I don't exactly have any other options. I left everything behind when my father died, everything except the clothes I showed up here in and the injuries he left me as a parting gift.

"We'll need some ground rules," Archer says.

"Of course," I comply, because what other choice do I have in the matter?

"Do not touch my computers."

I roll my eyes. "Very protective of your porn stash, got it."

"I'm serious, London. Do not mess with them. Do you hear me?" He stands up straighter, as if he isn't already a foot taller than me, his voice stern with each word.

"I hear you, grumpy. What else?"

"No falling in love."

This time, it's my turn to laugh. But once I come down from the absurd remark, I realize Archer is stone-cold serious. "Oh, you weren't joking."

His intense stare doesn't look away. "I wasn't."

I walk toward him, my head tilting upward when I finally reach him. I pat his chest with my uninjured arm. "Don't worry, big guy. Plus, if anyone's falling in love, it's you." I leave him to return to the kitchen, his gaze hot on my back each step of the way.

Is Archer attractive? Absolutely. But could I see myself falling in love with him? Absolutely not. We're nothing alike. Archer is wound so tightly, he's set to explode at any given moment. He's grumpy, way too mysterious for his own good, and clearly a loner. The only thing we have in common is how familiar with the underworld we are. And that is not a good thing to build a relationship on.

"So then we're in agreement?" Archer joins me at the counter and goes to work clearing off where he was sitting.

"Yeah, Archer, no falling in love." I extend my hand toward him. "And I won't get on your computer."

He finishes rinsing his plate off and puts it in the dishwasher before giving me his full attention. Archer slides his large hand around mine, giving it a firm but gentle shake, like he's afraid I might break in half if he does it any harder. "Deal."

I release him after a long moment, ignoring the heat of his skin scorching my hand in its absence, and think about the rules we've set in place. I've come to terms with the "no falling in love" part, that one being the easiest of the two, but I can't quite figure out why he's so damn jumpy about his computers. It's clear he's into some kind of illegal activity, but what could be so bad that he's worried I'd see? Maybe he really does have some weird fetish and is embarrassed by it. I hate how intrigued it makes me, but I have to comply, otherwise I won't have a place to live for the next couple of months. I can't imagine it's going to be difficult to find somewhere else to live, but at least I have some time to figure it out.

First, I need to go shopping and get some clothes and necessities if I'm going to succeed at this whole starting-over thing. I can't do it in Archer's sweatpants and T-shirt, no matter how comfortable they might be.

"Are there any shops around here?" I ask him once I've drank the rest of the coffee he made me. "For clothes."

Archer pulls out his phone and clicks a few buttons before setting it down in front of me and zooming in. "See this." He points. "That's where we are." He zooms out. "Right here, there are a few shops, but they're high-end." He moves the map to a few blocks away. "Over here might be better."

I swat his hand out of the way and pick his phone up, exploring the map and what options are available. Without wanting Archer to blow a gasket, I quickly return his phone and offer a soft smile. "Thanks." I hop off the chair and pat the crumbs off my top. "Hey, by the way, where are my clothes?"

"I washed them." He motions toward his bedroom. "They're folded up on the dresser in there."

I narrow my gaze while trying to keep it sort of neutral and figure out his motives. Why would he wash my clothes? Why would he fold them? And why would he put them in his bedroom?

"Why?"

"Would you prefer them to be in a pile on the floor?"

"No, Archer, you know what I mean. Why are they in your bedroom?"

He comes closer, towering over me. "Because if you're going to be staying here, you're going to stay in the bedroom."

I should be intimidated by the way he's looking at me, standing so close I can feel the warmth of his body radiating from him. His tattoo-covered skin and his decadently intense stare should make me question what the hell I'm even doing here, but Archer has no idea where I came from, who raised me, and the depths of hell that man put me through.

My father may have been the first man to hurt me, and because of that, there isn't anything worse anyone else could do to me.

CHAPTER SIX

Archer

With only a few keystrokes, I locate Joe Vito, sleeping soundly in his bed in California, the camera on his computer giving me access to watch his breaths slow and steady through the screen.

I dig into his recent whereabouts, credit card transactions, and cell phone records. It isn't difficult to track a man like him when he's so fucking showy with everything he does. Twelve thousand at a strip club on Tuesday, another three thousand at dinner on Saturday, a payment to the yacht club he's been a member of since birth, passed down from his disgraceful father.

Joe Vito is fucking boring, but he's been around long enough to have respect from the *right* people, and because of the connections his father gave him, and the strings he pulls, he's untouchable.

He's like a cockroach that everyone *wants* to get rid of but ends up staying alive anyway.

Joe's private jet has been parked for over a month, the last known trip a week-long thing to the Cayman Islands, no doubt to assess the bank accounts he has there and make sure his affairs were in order. Pretty typical of a man like Joe.

I scan his driver's license information, his date of birth, March twenty-second, making him forty-three years old. Not an organ donor, go figure, not like anyone would want any piece of him when he's gone.

A few pushes of buttons later, three hundred thousand dollars have been transferred out, masked as a payment for his jet, but sent anonymously to a woman's domestic shelter in California. He'll never even know it's missing, let alone get to take credit for where the money went.

My cheek twitches, a smile forming and quickly fading the second London walks into the living room, her gait wobbly from that cast on her leg. "Hey, I'm going to run down to a few shops. I'll be back in a couple of hours."

I dim the screen and stand from my desk. "Give me a minute to shower and I'll go with you."

She waves her hand, dismissing me. "No, it's fine, really, I can go by myself."

"You're new to town, and you don't exactly get around easily, so let me take you." I leave out the part where I'm not even sure if she has any money to begin with. She wasn't exactly dripping in disposable income last night on my doorstep.

"I said I was fine," she snaps back, her tone rigid and defensive. "I don't need your help."

"Excuse me for trying to be a nice guy."

"You said it yourself, Archer, you're not a nice guy, remember?" She puts her hand on her hip, and it really makes me wonder if she realizes how pathetic she looks right now.

The salespeople aren't going to give her the time of day in this town, and it's not like she can manage to get to the more affordable stores on her own.

"Fine then, go." I motion to the door. "Be my fucking guest."

London blinks harshly like she's not understanding what I just said. Her mouth parts slightly. "I—I will." She marches to the door, not daring to glance back to see if I've changed my mind. She makes sure to slam it for dramatic effect, my chest tightening at how fucking frustrating that woman is.

I run my hand through my hair and head straight for the bathroom, taking the shower I said I needed and hoping it will allow me to cool off. I'm not used to dealing with people who aren't my immediate family anymore, now that I've isolated myself from everyone else.

I guess it doesn't help that London is one of the most infuriating humans on the planet, not quite setting me up for success with my new housemate.

What was I thinking in allowing her to stay? It goes against everything I've been trying to put in place. I'm disrespecting myself and my boundaries by going back on what I've told everyone—the second she stepped foot on my doorstep, everything started to crumble. Time has only proven that I'm not ready to be a part of society yet, nor should I be socializing with other people.

Washing my body, I notice that London has moved everything around in my shower. What's so hard about putting things back in their place? Why did she find it necessary to move the men's products? How does that even make sense? I close my eyes and let the water wash over my face, my hand rubbing the soap off my body, my fingers caressing the base of my shaft, noting just how hard I am for no fucking reason. I grip my traitorous cock as it thickens in my grasp and plant my other hand against the back of the shower, my entire body in the stream of water pouring down.

I stroke my cock, long and lazily at first, only to tighten and speed it up, almost ashamed of myself for being turned on right now. I don't mean to, but London's voice comes into my head, her snarky comments setting fire under my skin the same way her delicate hand did when she slid it into mine.

I finish abruptly, intensely, and am left there, my breath ragged and my chest heaving. "Fuck," I mutter.

But it isn't even a moment later that the realization hits me like a ton of bricks.

London is no longer in my apartment, meaning I am not watching over her, and my promise to Silver that I would keep her safe is nothing but a few meaningless words drifting away like my orgasm down the drain.

How could I let her get to me so badly that I'd do something as stupid as let her leave here with no money, no cell phone, no protection?

A minute later, I'm wrapping a towel around my soaked body and rushing out to my computer. In less time than it took me to get out of the shower, I've located London on a street camera outside of my apartment complex, only a few doors away.

I exhale, reposition my ass on the chair, and watch her through the screen. In preparation for her to move, I pull up two more angles and tap into the camera of the store she walks into, some overpriced boutique I've walked past a million times but never gone to.

The audio on the camera inside the store is muffled by the music playing in the background. I study London as she enters, her shoulders thrown back, fully confident she belongs there. The two women at the counter whisper something I can't quite make out and one nudges the other.

London skims a section of clothes, her fingers grazing each one.

The shorter of the two women steps around the counter and waltzes over to London. "May I help you?"

"I'm just looking, thanks," London replies in an even tone.

The woman clears her throat. "There's a clearance section over there that might better suit your needs."

London pauses, her body stiff and still, and I go tense with her, wondering how she's going to react given I've only known London less than a day and she's done almost nothing except argue with me about literally everything. Finally, without turning toward the woman, she says, "You should really stop trying to pass these last-season trousers off as this season." She grabs the hanger off the rack and shoves it toward the woman. "Are you so out of touch that you think anyone would pay full price for an off-the-rack, out-of-season knockoff?"

The woman gasps. "It's not a knockoff."

London points at something I can't quite make out. "See this stitching. Dead giveaway. This lockstitch is pathetic. Giovanni uses their signature herringbone here."

"But I..." The woman looks to her coworker for assistance, but by the time she turns toward London, London is already making her way out the door, her face pressed into a hard line, unbothered by the interaction.

Immediately, I click on another box, pulling the street angle of London up as she glances in both directions, deciding to go a bit farther away from my apartment. She isn't so far that I couldn't chase after her if something happened, but I don't love the distance she's putting between us, testing my ability to keep her safe.

She pops into another clothing store, this one less sterile inside than the last.

A round-faced woman greets her immediately. "Welcome to Charlotte's, can I help you find anything?" Her gaze meets London, and the second it does, she stops folding the clothes in her hands and focuses on London. "Oh my gosh, are you okay?" She rushes over, her fingers lingering in the air between the two of them like she wants to do something, but she's not sure what.

London inches back slightly. "Oh, I'm fine, yes. I do need some new clothes, though."

The woman nods her head. "Yes, of course, whatever it is you need, I can help you. I'm Charlotte, by the way."

"Charlotte Charlotte?" London motions around at the space inside the store.

"That's me." The woman smiles a sweet and innocent smile.

I lean into my chair, my bare back sticking to the seat. I ignore the awkward sensation and watch London look around the store.

"Are those the Rocco Couture from Italy?" London hobbles her best over to a table near the center of the place.

Charlotte follows her close behind. "Yes, they're lovely, aren't they? You're familiar?"

London nods and picks up one of the seemingly plain shirts,

turning it front to back. "I'll take one in every color, small."

Charlotte's mouth drops open as London walks away and continues to browse.

"These trousers, do you have them in a twenty-five?" She runs her hand along something else. "And these."

Charlotte quickly rushes over, snatching two pairs of bottoms off the table and adding them to the pile in her arms. "Why, yes, we do."

London turns toward her and presses her finger to her lips. "So that's five tops, two bottoms. I'm going to need a blazer, at least one pair of jeans, a cardigan, and..." Her gaze settles on the far side of the store. "That dress."

I can barely make out her last two words, she says them so quietly.

Charlotte follows her line of sight. "The Lorenzo. Only five of them were made. The silk gives it a timeless and elegant look, the dark green would go perfectly with your hair color and your complexion." She pauses and adds, "It's eight thousand."

My attention shifts to London, it not being lost on me how her shoulders seem to slump, even through the pixelated screen I'm watching her on. She nods her head slowly. "I'm going to have to hold off on that today." Without hesitating, she shifts back into action, scanning the store for something else. "Those black heels, do you have them in a seven?"

"Let me check." Charlotte rushes over, grabs the shoe off the stand, and drops the load of clothes onto the counter before disappearing into the back.

London glances at where she went then stops in front of the dress she was gawking at, her fingers barely touching the delicate fabric for the smallest second. She lets out a breath and leaves it behind as she rummages through the panties section, taking a handful of the dainty things into her good hand before placing them with the rest of her things.

Why she needs heels when she has a cast on her leg, I'm not exactly sure, but who am I to stop her? It's not like she'd listen to me anyway.

If I were her, I would have gone with something a bit more practical, like sneakers. It's safe to say London doesn't think the same way I do, though.

Charlotte comes out with a box in her hand, holding it out triumphantly. "Shall we try them on?"

London shakes her head. "Not necessary. I have a pair of them back home. Or, well, I did." Her voice trails off like she's lost in a memory. "I know they fit."

"Where is home?" Charlotte asks her. It's an innocent question, but considering the magnitude of the situation, I'm not sure if London should tell her the truth.

"Out West," she responds vaguely.

I loosen a breath at her smart answer. "Atta girl," I mutter.

"I've always wanted to go out West, I just haven't," Charlotte says instead of pressing London for any more information. "Maybe someday."

"Yeah, maybe."

"So, you're new in town, what brings you out here?"

London shrugs. "A fresh start, hopefully."

"I like that." Charlotte pats the pile of things that London has accumulated. "Okay, we've got a lot of your basics covered here. You mentioned a blazer and cardigan, what about..." Charlotte leads London to another side of the store, helps her pick out a few more things, and adds them to the stack. "These jeans here are a more relaxed fit and should accommodate that cast." Charlotte holds a pair of jeans out for London to take a look at.

"I'll take two of them, the dark wash and the light, please."

A woman walks in the front door and Charlotte greets her with a smile. "Let me know if there's anything I can help you find," she tells the woman as she starts to ring London's items up.

I squint to see the total but can't make it out. I punch in the information to the store's Wi-Fi, locate the point-of-sale system, pull up the order screen on my own, and watch the tally of items go up. It shouldn't be this easy to log into someone else's interface, and yet it is...

I guess Charlotte isn't protecting anything top secret, and an average person would never hack into her store. I'm not exactly an average person when it comes to hacking, anyway.

The total shoots from a couple hundred dollars to two thousand very quickly, and I wonder where London is going to get the funds to pay for this. Surely, she's not stupid enough to use a credit card that could be traced back to her, and I would hope she isn't carrying that much cash on her. She might be in a relatively safe area in Manhattan, but crime happens everywhere. On the off chance that she is stupid and has a card with her, I furiously type away to pull up the power to the store, ready to shut it off the second she whips a card out. My finger hovers over the button, watching in anticipation for which level of disappointment I'm going to have in her.

"Your total today is going to be two thousand two hundred twenty dollars and twenty-one cents." Charlotte starts to bag the items as she asks, "Will that be cash or card?"

London fidgets with the front pocket of her jeans, revealing a wad of cash a moment later.

I shake my head and rub at my jaw. How could she be so foolish? Didn't Silver tell her not to flaunt cash like that? Not to mention she's here to start over, shouldn't she have budgeted better and saved some of her money instead of spending it the first chance she got? But, considering she said she already had a pair of those overpriced heels, perhaps London is just showing her true, very materialistic, colors.

Once Charlotte has finished bagging everything up in four different, quite large bags, she counts the money that London handed her and makes change.

"Do you live around here?" London asks her, and reaches for a couple of the bags.

Charlotte scoffs. "Yeah right, *this* neighborhood? Too rich for my blood." She rips off the receipt and stuffs it into one of the remaining bags. "I'm in Hamilton Heights. It's not too far from here. You can take the A or D and be in Midtown in, like, twenty minutes."

"When you say too rich for your blood, what do you mean? How much are places around here?"

"I mean, you can't buy a studio around here for less than a million, and that's a fixer-upper. Something nice?" Charlotte laughs. "Who am I kidding, everything is nice in Manhattan. I'd say you're looking at over two million to buy something small. Five grand a month to rent something. I have one customer who pays eighteen thousand a month for a place a couple of blocks from here. Kind of depends on what you're looking for." She pauses and adds, "You looking for something?"

London shakes her head. "I'm staying with a friend for now." She takes the bags into her hands, struggling to hold them with her injured arm. She shifts them all onto the other. "Thanks for the help, Charlotte. This is a great place you have here."

"Of course, yeah, anytime. Don't be a stranger."

London lingers her gaze on the dress in the corner. "Hold on to that for me." She slips out the door before Charlotte can answer her.

I switch cameras, hating how the street views don't give audio, only visuals, and very shitty visuals at that. Still, I can keep my eyes on her while she, hopefully, makes her way back here.

It's uncomfortable, watching her struggle with the bags, but I can't exactly run down there and help her, considering she has no idea that I'm stalking her. I'm only doing it to keep her safe, though, not to be a creep. Silver asked for my help, I'm only following through on my word.

London slowly makes her way past the store where the girl was rude to her and catches sight of something across the way. She waits for the pedestrian sign to change and crosses the street, prompting me to change cameras again.

"Where are you going, little tornado?" I whisper as I hit the keystrokes on my computer and follow her.

London enters a coffee shop I've been to a few times; the bakery items are not so bad, and their coffee is what my oh-so-serious big brother would deem acceptable for his sophisticated palate.

It takes me far too long to gain access to their interior cameras, and when I do, I've already missed London speaking to someone. She smiles politely at another woman and says thank you as she leaves her bags behind with the stranger and heads toward the counter. Two men stand in front of her, the one directly in front glancing over his shoulder at her far too many times for it to not be blatantly obvious that he's checking her out.

"Hey, I'm Roger," he says, and turns himself toward her. "Can I buy you a drink?"

"Sure," London responds immediately.

I pinch my eyes shut for a brief moment. *Why, London, why?*

"I'll have a large cappuccino, dry, and whatever the lady is having."

"Vanilla latte, small." She keeps a bit of distance between her and the man, but it's not enough to not give him the wrong impression. Men are stupid and think everything a woman does is an invitation for them to harass them.

But maybe she likes him. Maybe she wants to get to know this guy and have a coffee with him. Who am I to step in the way of what might be true love?

The cashier takes his credit card, and it only takes me the time they're waiting for their drinks to pull up everything there is to know about this man.

He's married, a teacher, and with more debt than he could ever dig himself out of and a very expensive porn addiction. I'm surprised the nine dollars' worth of coffee didn't decline when the barista swiped his card.

"One large dry cappuccino and a vanilla latte for Roger," the bright-eyed, blue-haired barista calls out.

They each walk toward their drink, picking them up at the same time.

"Thanks," London tells him, and goes to walk away.

"Wait, that's it?" Roger calls after her.

She stops and turns on her heel, facing him. "Yeah, *Rog*, it is. You bought me a coffee, that's it. End of transaction. I said thank you, what would you prefer I do? Strip out of my clothes and bend over the counter? Not going to happen. Now, if you don't want me to raise my voice and tell this entire coffee shop that you just made a lewd comment about the no doubt underage barista back there, I suggest you move along."

"I said no such thing," Roger says, his third mistake.

His first was asking to buy London a drink, and the second was implying she owed him something in return.

London takes a step closer, her entire demeanor intimidating despite how freaking tiny she is. She's like a Chihuahua. "Who do you think they're going to believe, Rog? You, or me?" Her voice is so low, I can barely make it out, my hearing so fucking strained to listen in on this entire conversation anyway. Be great if she'd go to less crowded places. It would make my stalking easier.

Roger hesitates for a minute like he's considering whether London will follow through with her threat. "Crazy bitch," he mumbles before giving up and walking straight out of the coffee shop.

I let out a laugh, a strange sense of satisfaction rolling over me. Maybe London is more capable of taking care of herself than I was giving her credit for.

It has only been less than twenty-four hours since she stepped foot on my doorstep, I shouldn't assume I know anything about her. London might not even be her government name. Not that it's any of my business—Silver was right, the less I know, the better. I can't afford to care about her outside of my promise to Silver. I don't want to earn a favor with him, but Silver is a great ally, and someone I'd like to stay on their good side. As much as I want to be out of the life, it's impossible when I keep one foot in the door and my family is fully immersed in it. I was the stupid one for ever thinking I could escape it by staying alive. Maybe one day I'll come to terms with what happened, but the wounds are too fresh for that day to be today.

My attention returns to London when she moves from her spot near the counter and back to the woman she left her bags with.

"You good?" the stranger asks her.

"Yeah," London replies. "Nothing I can't handle."

"I wasn't worried about you in the slightest." The woman pulls a chair out for London. "Here, have a seat." She extends her hand. "I'm Grace, by the way."

Grace is well polished, not a lock of her blond hair out of place, her dress slacks perfectly pressed. Even from the view I have on my screen, I can tell Grace was born with money and privilege. She's conventionally pretty, but in a kind of way that screams politician's wife.

"I'm London." She settles into her seat and takes a cautious sip of her latte, more cautious than she was this morning when she burned herself. Perhaps she learned her lesson—has she never drank hot coffee before?

"You new in town? I haven't seen you around here before. Sorry, I don't mean to pry, I just feel like I know everyone who comes in here. Even Roger, the regular creep. He's mostly harmless, I'm sure."

London shrugs. "He paid for my coffee, that's all that matters."

"What did you say to him? He looked spooked when he left. I almost felt sorry for him." Grace drinks some of her coffee and pats the corner of her lips with a napkin.

"I may have threatened to tell the coffee shop he was a pedophile."

Grace's eyes widen and a giant smile spreads across her face. "You did not. That's hilarious. Wow. I think you might be my new best friend. Designer clothes *and* fearless. I love it."

"A girl's gotta do what a girl's gotta do..."

London tugs back the sleeves of her sweatshirt, revealing the cast on her arm, matching the one on her leg.

"Damn, you're worse for wear. Want to talk about it?" Grace spins the base of her cup, leaving a gap for London to fill in.

"Not really," London answers. "It's in the past."

Grace leans forward at the hip and lowers her voice. "Do we need to have anyone killed?"

I almost miss what she says because of the stupid fucking music.

I push a few buttons and shut it off, the barista near the register throwing up their arms as they say, "Wasn't me, I swear."

"Okay, that was nearly terrible timing," Grace adds.

London laughs. "Maybe your FBI guy heard you say that."

"Maybe *your* FBI guy heard me say that." Grace nudges London's shoulder playfully.

If only they knew it wasn't either of their FBI guys watching, but the random man whose doorstep London showed up on the night before.

CHAPTER SEVEN

London

Grace is great.

She's sweet, but not too sweet, not in an annoying way. She's classy, even though I can tell it's borderline from necessity. We sat there for a while, chatting about brands and places we had traveled. She was in Milan last spring; I was there the fall before. Our paths have almost crossed quite a few times, but not enough for us to have run into each other.

I vaguely told her I was new in town, and I love that she didn't ask too many prying questions. I could tell there was a part of her that wanted to, but she refrained. It's like she knew when to persist, and when not to. She's very sensitive to the delicacies of knowing when to ease off, and if I had to guess, she's had training on the matter.

She gave me her phone number, despite me telling her I didn't have a phone at the moment, but insisted I get ahold of her when I got mine up and running, and that we should get together again. Grace mentioned that she comes to that same coffee shop every other morning around the same time, and that if I'm ever free, I could join her.

It was nice talking to her, refreshing even, to say the least. Better than the conversation I've had with Archer so far. He's hilarious to mess with, but he's frustrating, and I can tell we have nothing of quality to chat about. Plus, it's different having a girl as a friend, as opposed to a guy.

Awkwardly, I do what I can to carry the bags the few blocks back to Archer's, keeping my chin held high while walking past the store with the bitchy clerk.

Every inch of my body aches and yet I carry on, because what other choice do I have? It was my idea to go shopping a split second after I arrived, so if anyone is to blame for my shitty recovery, it's me.

Well, and my asshole dead father who did this to me.

I smile at the thought of his death, knowing I'll never have to speak to, engage with, or even just exist around him ever again. The world became a better place the second that man met his maker. If only I had been the one to do it, but despite the lifelong torment he put me through, I have no regrets about not being the one to end him.

My thoughts flicker to Cora, the girl who was the catalyst in ending his life, and how she must be doing. I wish I could reach out to her, but Silver's warning overrides that idea every single time. She's better off without me, and if I want to keep her safe, I must leave her, and my entire life, in the past.

Maybe one day things won't be like this, but I can't hold out hope that I'll ever truly escape the fate my father sealed for me when he sold me to Joe Vito. A fucking business arrangement, one that never even came to fruition. It was all for nothing, and somehow I'm supposed to honor the end of the agreement even though I had no say in it.

"Fucking bastard," I mutter to no one but myself, and continue on my way to Archer's building.

It's strange to see it in daylight; the cityscape is much nicer when it's not dark. The street is relatively clean, and the buildings aren't as decrepit as I thought they were. It's sort of pretty, really, in a different way than things were in Los Angeles. There are more honking cars here, but the energy feels alive, nothing like it was back home. Plus, it was always so hot there. It's warm here, but comfortable, although I could do without the humidity.

I chew at the inside of my lip and trek the last few feet to Archer's place, loosening a breath and taking the entire thing in. It is much nicer than I thought it was, the details Charlotte gave me about rental prices coming back to me as I study it over.

Archer said he was in tech, but what does that mean? It's something illegal, which would explain how he can afford such a lavish place. Charlotte made it sound like a tiny studio was hard to come by, but Archer's is rather large for a one-bedroom. And everything appears to be new, like it was recently remodeled with the latest state-of-the-art everything. He claims he's been there a few years, but I beg to differ.

Hobbling, I make it up the steps and find the button I'm searching for. I press it and say, "Hey, it's me," into the receiver. It buzzes loudly a second later, Archer granting me access at record speed. Was he waiting for me? Or maybe one of his windows overlooks the sidewalk and he saw me coming.

In the time it takes me to finagle my bags through the front door, a large figure rushes down the steps and meets me.

Standing there, dark hair spilling over his forehead, his tattooed arms exposed in a tight-fitting white T-shirt, is Archer. He snags my bags out of my hands before allowing me to protest and turns around, making his way back toward the stairs.

"Uh, thanks?" I follow him and glance around. "Why aren't we taking the elevator?"

Archer barely tilts his head in my direction. "I don't trust elevators."

I narrow my gaze at his back and shake my head, not even wanting to dig into that one right now. Who doesn't trust elevators? How does that even make sense?

Archer practically leaves me in his dust as I all but crawl up the stairs. I'm slow, but eventually, I scale the last remaining ones. It's pathetic, I'm aware of that, but honestly, there's no point in rushing. It's not like Archer's apartment is going to disappear if I don't make it there in time.

But once I reach the top, I find Archer standing there, all my bags in one of his hands.

"Oh. I didn't know you were waiting for me." I have half a mind to add an apology, and yet I don't.

Archer opens the door with his free arm and holds it in place for me.

"Thanks," I tell him, and cross the threshold, a strange sense of safety returning to me that I wasn't aware I was lacking until this very moment.

Archer drops my bags in his bedroom and returns a second later, completely ignoring me and going to his computer. He pushes a few buttons and starts typing away like his inked fingers are on fire.

"Are you giving me the silent treatment?" I ask him from my spot near the door.

His keystrokes pause and his jaw tenses. "No."

"Oh wow, he speaks." I make my way toward him, and he grabs his mouse and clicks something away. "You've got to stop being so weird about your porn, big boy." I stop at the edge of the desk and cross my arms over my chest. "What is it? What's your weird kink you're too embarrassed I'll find out about?"

"I'm not watching porn," Archer says, his voice weirdly monotone. Finally, after what feels like a small eternity, his gaze meets mine. "Now if you'll excuse me, I have to get back to work."

I stare at him, unflinching. "Do you hate everyone, or just me?"

"Everyone."

"Cool, okay, so I'm not special."

"You're not."

I draw in a breath and exhale. "Another woman might take offense to that."

"Do you need something?" Archer ignores my remark and I'm not at all surprised.

I shrug. "What happened?"

"What do you mean, *what happened*?"

"This just doesn't feel like your normal level of grouch. It seems like something else."

"You've known me less than twenty-four hours, London. Why are you pretending you know what my normal is?"

"I suppose you could be right." I pause and then add, "But I'm not convinced I'm not right, either."

"Persistent, are you?"

I relax my arms and place one hand on my hip. "Does that surprise you?"

Archer maintains eye contact for a long moment and then breaks it, pinching his eyes shut temporarily before staring at his black screen. "I really do need to get some work done."

"Do you need any help?" I ask him, wondering if maybe this will get him to open up.

Archer's jaw tenses, his entire body following suit. Do I get under his skin that badly? I try to read him, to figure out what he's thinking, what he's going to say next, but he's impossible. Maybe I really should just leave him alone and stop poking at the theoretical bear.

"I don't want you leaving the apartment anymore," he says, his words catching me completely off guard, so much so that I can't even control my mouth from dropping open.

"Excuse me?"

"You're in no condition to be wandering around in an unfamiliar area. It's dangerous, careless, and unnecessary."

I laugh, like a full-on blunt chuckle. "You can't be serious."

Archer shoves his feet backward and rises from his computer chair, his stature towering over me.

I hate how fucking tall he is, it's rude.

"Are you trying to intimidate me, big boy?" I ask, tilting my head toward him. "Because it's not working." I point to my arm. "You see this?" And then my leg. "And this?" My nostrils flare.

"This is nothing compared to what I've been through, what I've fucking lived through. If you think for one second I'm going to let a man dictate any aspect of my life, you're sorely mistaken."

Archer shakes his head. "Don't put words in my mouth, I'm not trying to control you."

"Are you serious?" My eyes widen. "You just told me I couldn't leave your apartment. Fucking watch me." I march to the door, each step hurting worse than the last. The shopping trip took more out of me than I expected, both physically and financially.

"The fuck you are." Archer rushes past me with ease and puts his back to the door, crossing his arms over his broad chest.

I tug at him. "Get out of my way, let me out of here."

He remains firmly in place, my attempts to move him not even budging an inch. "You can try all night. I'm not going anywhere."

I give him one final shove and slump my shoulders, my breath ragged. I hate how my body betrays me in its weakened state. Suddenly, my vision blurs and my head spins. "I don't feel so..."

"I'm not buying it, London. That's not going to get me to..." But Archer doesn't finish his sentence, and the next thing I know, his arms are catching me as I sway uncontrollably.

Archer scoops me into his arms like I'm weightless, his dark gaze scanning my face.

"I'm fine," I mumble. "Put me down." But I don't wiggle out of his grasp, I don't move at all, I just succumb to his embrace and lean my head against him.

"I told you that you shouldn't go out." Archer carries me into his bedroom and manages to hold me with one arm as he drags back the blanket before laying me on his bed. "You need to rest, little tornado."

I blink up at him. "What did you just call me?"

Archer sighs, takes the shoe off my good leg, and covers me up.

"I feel fine," I lie, my eyes heavy, my head throbbing. I kind of want to throw up, but I'm too tired to care. I reach out lazily and graze his hand with my fingertips. "Don't go," I whisper, the two words coming out of my mouth without my consent.

Why would I ask him to stay? He's a stranger, and he hates me, and I can't deny that the feeling might be mutual. Still, I can't ignore that for the first time in what might be forever, a sense of safety washes over me when he's around. Maybe it's his apartment, or simply being thousands of miles away from home, or perhaps my father being dead—but whatever it is, Archer is attached to it whether I want him to be or not.

"I..." Archer's deep voice trails off like he's unsure of what to do.

"Please," I add. "Just until I fall asleep."

"You look like you're already asleep."

I let out a grunt and drop my hands, turning over onto my side. "Whatever."

A long silence fills the room, and I convince myself that Archer disappeared out of thin air. Once I've accepted this fate, he moves.

I expect him to leave me behind and return to his mysterious work, but Archer does the opposite and shuffles around the other side of the bed and climbs in next to me. I blindly reach for him, my hand landing on his solid torso.

He tenses but doesn't move me off him. He doesn't even complain that I'm touching him.

I reposition my face on the pillow, breathing in and basking in the scent of him that remains from when he was in here last.

Sleep calls to me, so close yet so far away.

This is really stupid, I think. The idea of lying with a stranger and finding comfort in it is beyond me. It must be the pain coursing through me that results in something so foolish.

Maybe a few hours of sleep will return me to my senses, and I can go back to pounding on his chest and bickering with him to let me out of his apartment.

Until then, I'm going to play pretend and act like we don't despise each other.

Because if I'm being honest, fighting with him is better than facing the reality that nothing will ever be the same again, and my life as I knew it is over.

CHAPTER EIGHT

Archer

I can't stop staring at London's tiny hand on my stomach, her fingers twitching as sleep finally drags her under.

Christ, she's infuriating for such a small human being, but when I look at her like this, I can't help but admire her beauty in a way I'm sure parents do when their screaming baby falls asleep.

And I know once London opens her eyes, she'll return to her normal self, poking and prodding at me until it drives me fully insane.

This was all such a stupid idea. Why I agreed to it, I'll never know. Part of me wishes I could turn back the clock and change the outcome of the situation, but I've lived too much of my life trying to alter the past and have had to come to terms with the fact that it's impossible.

Once we make our choices and the consequences fall into place, there's no going back.

I know I've tried, and no matter what I did, I can't fix what had been done, what had been taken from me. My heart aches at the countless things I tried, but it all resulted in the same outcome.

Flashbacks of blood staining her clothes, a lifeless body in my grasp, hushed pleas to save her.

It was all for nothing, and I refuse to allow my actions to result in another casualty.

Carefully, I pick London's hand off my torso and lay it on the bed, and with even more caution slip out of the room, leaving her behind to rest.

I slide my phone out of my pocket on the way out, taking a last glance at her to make sure I didn't disturb her. Silver's number is quickly located, and I press it a second later, hoping like hell the asshole answers.

"Yeah?" he says through the receiver.

"I can't do this," I tell him, making my way farther into my apartment so I don't wake London.

"Sure you can, Arch. I wouldn't have asked if I didn't think you could."

"You didn't ask, remember? You just dropped her on my doorstep." I shake my head. "I can't be responsible for her. This isn't going to end well."

"You're overthinking this, Arch. It's going to be fine. All you have to do is keep her safe for a little while."

"A little while? It's Joe Vito. This problem isn't going to go away on its own."

"Trust me, she's not exactly on his priority list right now. Don't worry, this thing is going to blow over soon enough." Silver's voice becomes muffled as he tells someone else something and returns to me. "Arch, I've got to jet. I'll be out of town for a while. Promise me you'll figure this out. My girl will kill me if you let something happen to London."

"You're doing this because of some girl?"

"Hey," Silver snaps at me. "She's not just *some girl*, she's *my* girl."

"Same thing."

"Can you handle this or not? I need to know I can count on you."

"Yeah, you can count on me." I hang up a second later, not caring to hear any more excuses or guilt trips from Silver. What's done is done and I can't change that; the only thing I can do is figure out how to handle the cards that I've been dealt and navigate this London situation as best I can.

Even if it drives me insane.

I slide into my computer chair, stealing a peek at my bedroom to ensure London is still in there. My fingers dare me to dig up every piece of information I have on her, but I refrain, not wanting to involve myself any more than I already am. The curiosity is overwhelming, yet I know if I succumb to it, I'll never be able to truly escape this situation.

My phone screen lights up with Ivy's name across it.

"Shit," I mutter, and swipe the call to accept. "Hey, what's up?"

"What's up?" she quips back. "What's up is I've been waiting at the restaurant for twenty minutes for you. Did you die? Are you being held captive somewhere?"

"I...I'm sorry, Ivy. I got held up with something. I can't really talk about it."

"Can't talk about it? Are you serious? Hold on." Muffled sounds fill the end of the line. "I'll take another pinot. Yeah. Thanks." She returns to me a second later. "Arch, listen, I love you, but you know you have to leave that apartment sooner or later, right? It's been three years. It's time you moved on. I'm sorry, really, you know I've always been there for you, and I always will be, but I'm going to have to put my foot down. You have to leave. I'm going to stage an intervention. Yeah, that's what I'm going to do."

"Ivy," I say to get a word in. "I'm sorry, seriously. I had every intention of meeting you, but..." My gaze lingers on my bedroom. "Something came up. I promise I'll explain, I just can't right now."

Ivy laughs dryly. "I don't buy it, Archer, and quite frankly, I'm insulted you think I'm going to fall for this yet again. We can't keep doing this. *You* can't keep doing this. Do you enjoy staying cooped up in your apartment all the time? You're getting pale, too pale. You're probably deficient in vitamin D. I'm concerned about your health, Arch, really. This isn't good for you."

"My health is fine," I reassure her. "I take a handful of supplements daily, Ivy. I even started eating fruit."

"Huh. Really? Or is this another lie?"

I walk to my kitchen, snap a quick picture of the cut-up strawberries, and send it to her. "There, check your messages."

"Why do you have a package of tofu?"

"I, uh, I was at the market and the lady told me it was a good source of protein." I hate myself for not just telling her the truth, but I don't have a grip on the situation enough to involve her yet.

"I mean, she's not wrong, it's just weird." Ivy smacks her lips. "This pinot is not pinot-ing." She raises her voice. "Excuse me, waiter. Is this pinot or gamay?"

A brief exchange follows, and I wait patiently for it to end.

"I knew it," she tells me. "They tried to pass a gamay for a pinot. Anyway, yeah, what were we talking about? You standing me up, that was it."

"I'm sorry, Ivy. How many times do you want me to say it?"

"I'm starting to think you don't love me, Arch. It hurts."

I roll my eyes at her dramatics. How could I not love her? There isn't much I wouldn't do for Ivy. I would die for her; I would kill for her. But I guess I draw the line at being able to show up on time or leave my apartment when she demands that I do.

"You know I do. I promise I'll make it up to you. Give me some time," I tell her.

"Fine. But you better be glad I love the bread here, because the carbs are making up for my missing date."

"I'll send you an edible arrangement of bread, how's that?"

"Don't make promises you can't keep, Arch." Ivy clears her throat. "I'll see you on Sunday." And then she hangs up.

I exhale, the guilt adding to the festering feelings nagging at me from every direction. I did have every intention of meeting her today, I just lost track of time when London came fumbling into my life.

Returning to my computer, I type away until I find what I'm looking for, ordering Ivy the biggest bread basket I can find to be delivered to her office. I add an "I'm sorry" note and punch in my credit card information. It's just bread, but I refuse to not follow through with another promise and disappoint her any more than I already have.

I run my hand through my hair and lean back in my chair, remembering the last words that Ivy just spoke to me. *I'll see you on Sunday.*

Here's to hoping I don't disappoint her again.

CHAPTER NINE

London

I wake up in Archer's bed, a bit confused but feeling better. My stomach growls as I catch the scent of something coming from what I can only assume is the kitchen.

Slowly, I uncover myself and slide out of his bed, careful not to get dizzy by getting up too quickly. My recollection is hazy, the argument Archer and I had by the door coming back to me as I make my way out of the room. My cheeks redden when I see him, the memory of asking him to stay returning to me, too.

Ignoring the thought, I lick my lips and continue toward him. "What are you doing?" I ask upon my approach.

"Just in time." Archer pulls a skillet off the stovetop and dumps some of the contents onto two plates near him. "You must be hungry."

I shrug. "I could eat." I step closer, trying to look over his shoulder at what he made. "What is it?"

"Go sit down, I'll bring it to you."

"That didn't answer my question."

Archer glares at me. "Do you want to eat or not?"

I throw my hands up in defeat. "Fine." And go to where we had breakfast this morning. It suddenly dawns on me that I have no idea what time it is, and because Archer has closed every single window blind, I can't tell if it's still daylight.

He slides a plate in front of me, and another in the spot a couple of seats down. "You okay with water?"

"Yeah, that's fine."

"Ice or no ice."

"Ice."

I poke at the food while he gets our drinks. "Are you going to tell me what I'm about to eat, or is this some weird game to add to your mysteriousness?"

Archer sets my water in front of me. "It's teriyaki tofu, brown rice, and sautéed Broccolini."

"You can cook?"

"It's as simple as following instructions. Anyone can cook." Archer sits on his stool, grabs his fork, and pauses. "Do you have a problem with what I made?"

My brows rise and I shake my head. "No. Not at all. I'm just surprised, is all." I stab a piece of the tofu and pop it into my mouth, almost moaning at the taste. "This is good." I eat another bite. "Really good."

Archer and I eat in silence for the remainder of the meal, not that I care much, considering how hungry I was. He finishes before me, helping himself to another plate of food and topping off our waters.

I rub my stomach once I'm done and wipe my mouth with a napkin. "Thanks for dinner."

"You're welcome," Archer says, almost like it was painful for him to get out. He takes both plates without giving me a chance to help, rinsing them in the sink and putting them in the dishwasher.

It's then that I notice other than the skillet, the rest of the dishes are already done from his preparation of dinner. He makes quick work of scrubbing, rinsing, drying it off, and putting it away.

He places his hands on the counter and stares directly at me. "Can I ask you a question without you biting my head off?"

"I wouldn't bite your head off," I scoff.

Archer tilts his head as if to question me silently.

"Fine. What's your question?"

"How did you pay for the things you bought earlier?"

I blink at him, unsure of what exactly he's asking me. "What?"

"You came back with bags. Clearly, you purchased the items, right? How did you pay for them? Cash or card?"

"Oh. Cash. Why?"

"How much was it?"

"I don't know," I lie.

"You know damn well how much it was, London."

I scoot myself off the chair. "Don't patronize me, *Archer*." I leave him behind and head toward his bedroom, desperate to get away from him. I thought maybe we might finally start getting along, but here he is, asking questions he shouldn't be and putting his nose where it doesn't belong.

"I'm not patronizing you." Archer takes off after me, following me into his room.

"Sure sounds like it, big boy."

Archer reaches for me, stopping me in place and turning me toward him. "Stop calling me that."

I look up at him. "If it looks like a duck, and quacks like a duck..."

"You are so childish." He releases me but remains firmly in place. "And stupid."

My mouth drops open. "How dare you call me stupid!"

Archer rushes over to where the bags sit in the corner of his bedroom. "I know this stuff wasn't cheap, London. You can't carry about that much cash with you. It's dangerous. You have this false sense of safety and it's going to get you—" He stops abruptly and lowers his voice as his gaze floats across my body. "Hurt."

"Wait." I place my hand in the air between us. "You're mad because I used cash? Not because of how much I spent?"

"What would you do if someone saw you carrying that much cash and decided they were going to take it from you? You can't trust so easily, London. This isn't a safe neighborhood. If you insist on using wads of cash to pay for things, all I ask is that you let me come with you."

"I don't need a bodyguard."

"I didn't say you did, but for fuck's sake, have a little common sense." Archer runs his hand through his hair, messing it up. "I don't know your past, and I don't want to know, okay? But the way you lived your life before has to stop. You're living in *my* apartment and Silver asked *me* to keep you safe. I can't do that when you bolt out of here, looking like that and carrying that much cash on you."

"What's wrong with how I look?"

Archer pinches his eyes shut and rubs his temple. "Woman, do you fail to recognize the cast on both your arm and leg, how frail you are, how you can barely walk three feet without struggling? I'm pretty sure a second-grader could overpower you."

"I refuse to be confined to this apartment *and* you."

"Well, I'm sorry, but you're going to have to get used to it. I won't let you leave if you can't follow a few, very simple, rules."

"I don't like rules."

"Do you like staying alive?" Archer's brown eyes stare at me so intensely, it sends a chill down my spine.

"I only have cash," I tell him, because it's the truth. I couldn't use a credit card if I wanted to. I left all of them behind, and the package from Silver only had five thousand dollars in it because he was under the impression I was bringing my own stash, only that plan was foiled when my house was set on fire, everything I owned going up in smoke. It was a small price to pay for my freedom, even though my new circumstances feel nothing of the sort.

Archer leaves the room without a word, disappearing into the openness of the rest of his apartment. "Here," he says on his way back in, something in his hand that's outstretched to me.

"What is it?" I settle my sight on his offering, that familiar black card I knew and loved all too well. "I can't take that."

Archer grabs my hand and shoves it into my grasp. "Don't use that cash anymore. Use this. I'll get you a purse to put it in. Something with a crossbody strap to make it harder for someone to take from you."

"What? No. I can't take this, Archer. Are you out of your mind?"

He meets my gaze again, and this time, something unfamiliar settles between us. "Probably."

CHAPTER TEN

Archer

Three days go by, and I can't tell if it's felt like an eternity or the blink of an eye.

We've fallen into somewhat of a groove. I sleep on the couch, and she takes the bedroom. Not like I've done much sleeping anyway. Most of the nights have been spent catching up on the work I haven't felt comfortable doing during the day and lying there staring at the ceiling wondering what I did for such a fucked-up life.

The days consist of us not speaking to each other much. After I gave London my black American Express card, it seemed to shut her up. She hasn't left the apartment and hasn't even attempted to. Not that I would have stopped her. I told her if she took the card, it would be acceptable, and considering I was going to track her every move if she did leave, I wasn't too concerned about her leaving. Maybe my warning about the neighborhood being unsafe scared her into staying put, but considering how much she's been sleeping on and off these past few days, it might just be because she needed the rest.

We haven't bickered, not really, we've just sort of coexisted, eating our meals in silence, going about our days together but separately.

Considering how the first twenty-four hours went, I didn't think London could keep her mouth shut, and yet here I am, continuously surprised by every aspect of her showing up in my life.

I left for about forty-five minutes before she woke up this morning, running down to the market and grabbing some more groceries. I'm not sure London even knew I was missing, since she was still asleep when I got back.

I've tracked Joe Vito's whereabouts these past few days and nothing indicates he's looking into anything on the East Coast, let alone poking around in Manhattan. Perhaps Silver is keeping him busy from going after London, or he did a good enough job of hiding her that Joe doesn't know where to look. It was smart sending her here because London and I have no connections and nothing to trace her to me.

London closes the cover on my iPad and lays her head on the side of the couch, her attention turned toward me, her stare burning a hole into the side of my head.

"Can I help you with something?" I ask her without taking my eyes off my computer.

"I'm tired."

"Take a nap."

"I don't want to take a nap."

"I can't help you, then."

"I want a coffee."

"You know where the kitchen is."

"That coffee is boring."

I peel my gaze from the account I was hacking into and focus on her. "It's *boring*?"

"Yeah." London drags her bottom lip into her mouth. "I want a fancy coffee."

"What is a fancy coffee?"

"You know, like a latte or something."

I put my head in my hand and rub my temples. "Just say it, London."

"Please..."

I start shutting my computer down without hearing the rest. "Please, what?"

"Will you please go get me a latte?"

"Anything else, Your Majesty?" I rise from my seat and snatch my wallet and keys off the desk.

"Do you have any other book recommendations? I just finished the last one."

I walk over, pluck the iPad from her, and poke a few buttons. "Here. You can choose from any of them, they're all included in the membership."

Her eyes light up like I just handed her the world, only it was a sort of endless supply of books.

"Oh, there's a romance section. Now I don't have to read your stuff."

"I like romance novels," I tell her, even though I can't recall a time I ever read one. She doesn't need to know that, though.

"You are such a liar, Archer..." She trails off like she forgot something. "Wait, why do I not know your last name?"

"Probably for the same reason I don't know your last name."

"Smith," she responds, very matter-of-fact.

"My last name used to be Smith," I confess, the words surprising even me.

"Used to be? What do you mean?"

"Um." I walk away, straightening the trinkets on the table in an attempt to come up with a response. I settle on the truth. "I grew up in the foster system. I was assigned a name. Joseph Smith."

"And you didn't want to keep it?" London watches as I fidget.

"Never felt like me. When we all aged out, we changed our names."

"We who?"

"My brothers and sister." My stomach coils at admitting this information. I don't deny that they're my siblings, but I haven't spoken of our origin story in so long that it's uncomfortable to talk about. "Anyway, I'll be back in a few minutes. Don't leave." I slip out the door before London can question me any more and my mouth can continue to betray me by answering her.

I shake the unease off me as I jog down the steps and out the front door. It doesn't take me long to get to the coffee shop London had met Grace at and place an order. I spot the cameras I had watched her on and glance around at the patrons while waiting for the coffee.

"Hey," the woman beside me says. She smiles and tucks her dark hair behind her ear.

"Hello," I reply.

"How's your day going?" she asks me.

"Uh, fine. You?" I inch a bit away from her and cross my arms.

"It's going well, thanks." She clears her throat. "Listen, I don't do this often, and I'm sort of putting myself out there, but you're an attractive guy, and I was wondering if maybe you wanted to, I don't know, get coffee sometime."

I point to the counter where the baristas place the finished drinks. "I'm getting coffee now."

"Yeah, but like, together. You know? Like a date."

"Oh."

"I mean, unless you have a girlfriend, or boyfriend, whatever your preference, that's fine, too."

I shake my head. "I'm flattered, really, but I'm not looking to date."

She steps closer and lowers her voice. "We don't have to date if you don't want to." The woman bats her eyelashes in what I can only assume is her best attempt to seduce me, only it's not working.

She's attractive, sure, but I'm not in the time or place in my life to even entertain such an offer. How would I even begin to explain the random stranger who started living with me earlier this week? Let alone the crime my family is forever entangled with. People like me don't date just anyone—they find people already in the life and either hook up or get married, there's really no in-between. I'm not interested in either of those options.

"Order for Archer," the blue-haired barista calls out, and sets the drinks on the counter.

I rush over, grab them, and mutter a quick "Sorry" before leaving the woman who propositioned me behind.

Once I'm outside, I let out a sigh of relief, my chest tightening at the entire interaction. I fucking hate leaving my apartment. I can't stand having to deal with other people.

I return to the refuge of my apartment building and decide to check the mail, relieved when I find the things I had ordered inside. Shoving the boxes up under my arms, I carry them and the coffees up the stairs.

"Hey, Archer," Camille, the neighbor right next to me, calls out. "Damn, got your arms full. Do you need some help?"

"I'm good, thanks, Camille." I continue forward, not letting the challenge stop me.

"So, I'm not sure if you saw the bulletin board..."

"No, what's up?" I adjust the packages under my arms and give her my attention.

Camille has always been kind without prying anything out of me that I haven't been willing to give her. I appreciate her respecting my boundaries, and, in turn, I've always been cordial with her.

"I'm going to be going out of town for a while, a year, actually, maybe two, and I'm going to be subletting my apartment. I wasn't sure if you had anyone in mind. You know, since they're going to be your new neighbor, I thought I'd give you a heads-up."

"Oh," is all I can manage to get out, the information somehow catching me off guard.

"Listen, no major rush. I'm not leaving for another six weeks. But I'm going to be interviewing applicants, so if you have anyone in mind, just let me know. I'd appreciate it."

I nod without saying anything and she seems to accept that.

"Anyway, I'll let you go. You seem..." She points to my full hands and arms and chuckles. "Later, Archer." Camille starts down the steps. "Oh, hey, tell Ivy I said hey!"

Except it isn't Ivy that's in my apartment, it's London.

CHAPTER ELEVEN

London

I swing the door open the second Archer gets closer and hold it for him to enter.

"Uh, thanks?" he says.

"Who was that?" I ask him without hesitating.

"Who was what?" Archer continues inside and sets the two coffees on the counter before taking the packages from under his arms.

"The girl you were just talking to."

He turns toward me, his gaze narrowing. "Were you stalking me, little tornado?"

I roll my eyes and march over, pointing at the coffees. "Which one is mine?"

"Either one."

I take one and suspiciously sip it. "Is this a vanilla latte?"

"Yeah, why? Is that not what you wanted?"

"I didn't tell you what I wanted."

"Oh. I, um, I just guessed." Archer opens one of the boxes he brought in with a knife and pulls out a shoe box I could never mistake. "Here. These are for you."

"You bought me Christian Louboutins?"

"It's not what you think." He flips the lid to reveal a pair of stark white tennis shoes with red bottoms.

"You got me sneakers?"

"Well, the ones you came here in were worse for wear, and you only bought yourself heels when you went out the other day. I figured you could use something more practical."

"What's in the other box? Did you get yourself a matching pair?"

"No." He gives the box his attention, carefully opening it and pulling out two satchels. "I didn't know if you'd want brown or black, so I got both." Archer reveals two Saint Laurent crossbody leather bags with gold chains.

"I'm confused." I stare at the items and then at him. "Why would you do this?"

"Why would I do what?"

"Buy me, like, seven grand worth of stuff. You've known me four days and I've done nothing but annoy the hell out of you."

Archer shrugs, his plain black T-shirt bunching over his tattooed biceps. "It's just money, it's not a big deal. You needed a purse, I said I'd get you one, and now I did. And the shoes, I mean, you needed shoes, and I know you like brand-name things, so I thought these would work."

"Are you saying I'm materialistic?"

Archer runs his hand over his jaw. "You love to put words in my mouth, don't you?"

"That wasn't a disagreement."

"I did not say you were materialistic, London. I am simply giving you something you need. That is all. Don't make it into something it's not. Just say thank you. Actually, no, don't even do that, I didn't do it for a thank-you." Archer huffs and storms away, dragging his computer chair out and sitting on it with a bit too much force.

I stand there for a long moment, grab his coffee, and walk it over to his desk. "Thank you, Archer. For the coffee, the shoes, and the purses. It was very thoughtful of you."

He snatches his coffee and takes a swig before setting it down on the coaster he keeps near his mouse pad. "You're welcome."

A smile creeps across my face. "Did we just defuse our first argument?"

"That wasn't an argument."

"Look at you arguing about whether it was an argument."

"London, I need to get some work done."

"Okay, fine, but first, you're not going to get out of telling me who that was in the hallway."

Archer exhales dramatically and faces me. "That was Camille, our neighbor. Satisfied?"

"I'll be satisfied when you give her my name for a potential sublet of her apartment."

"You're joking."

I throw my arm up. "Why would I be joking? It's perfect. We both get some privacy, and you can still keep an eye on me. What's not to love?"

"We are not going to be neighbors." Archer returns his attention to his computer, typing away at who knows fucking what.

Since I've been here, Archer has gotten these screen covers that prevent anyone who isn't directly looking at the screen from being able to see anything he's doing.

"We can't be neighbors, but we can be roommates? How does that make any sense?"

"I said *no*, end of discussion." Archer doesn't even glance my way, his lips pressed in a line, his eyes trailing whatever he's doing.

"You wouldn't have to worry about me finding out what's on your computer if I got the place next door," I tell him as I leave him and return to the kitchen where my new shoes and bags are.

He doesn't say anything, not that I expect him to. Archer isn't exactly one of those people who feels the need to get the last word in. His silence usually speaks volumes by itself.

I want to ask him about Camille, her apartment, and the lingering questions that remained when he left earlier in a hurry to get our coffees. Like what his actual last name is, and why he seems so strangely protective of talking about his siblings. Or maybe I'd ask how he knew my coffee order when I hadn't told him what it was. But I don't, because now isn't the time and I don't want to push my luck. If I'm going to continue living with him, I have to find the balance between annoying him and completely pushing him over the edge.

***

THE NEXT DAY

"Hey, how much do phones cost?" I ask Archer from my spot on the couch.

He shifts his focus from his computer to me. "What?"

"A cell phone. How much do they cost? I want one."

"Monthly, or the cost of the phone itself?"

I guess I hadn't thought there was a different cost for both. I've never had to think about money in the past, I just went out and got things, and my father paid for them. One of the perks of being under his constant torture.

"Both," I tell him, and plop his iPad onto the cushion next to me. "And where do they sell them?"

"What kind of phone do you want?" He types on his computer, and I can't tell if he's paying attention to me or not.

"I don't know. What do you have?"

He doesn't say anything for a long moment, and I contemplate throwing a couch pillow at him but I don't think I know him well enough to gauge how he would react. I decide to clear my throat a bit too loudly. "Hello?"

"I ordered you the latest edition; it will be here the day after tomorrow. The plan is included. Will that be all?"

"I don't even get to choose the color?"

Archer licks his lips. "I got you a gold one."

"Oh, well, I guess it'll match the bags."

"That's why I chose that color."

"You really think of everything, don't you?"

"I try to."

I almost laugh at his response, knowing damn well that Archer is a massive control freak, that's why he thinks of everything. It's hard not to wonder why he is the way he is, but I'd be an idiot to think I could ask him and he'd tell me the truth.

"Do you want some privacy?" I hop up from the couch and Archer glances in my direction.

"You're leaving?"

"I'm going to take a shower. Is that okay, big guy?"

Archer immediately returns his attention to the computer. "Yeah."

I roll my eyes and make my way toward the bathroom, my cast scraping against the floor. Counting on my fingers, I attempt to do the math on when I can get these things removed.

"What's today?" I mutter, unsure of how long I've been here. The days sort of melt into each other, and considering I spent the last few resting, I can't be certain how long it has been. Either way, I should only have a couple more weeks until I'm free of the obnoxious coverings. Maybe I should find a doctor, that way I can get them removed immediately instead of having to wait around on one.

The bathroom door latches shut behind me and I strip my clothes off as I head to the shower. I turn the water on and crank the heat up, the room filling with steam within seconds.

I sigh, stepping under the scorching water and tilting my head up, realizing that I need to wash my hair. I had been avoiding it since that first day, considering how difficult it was to navigate with my arm in a cast. Sure, I have access to my fingers, but they're not as strong as my other hand, and the cast sort of disallows me from having full control over them.

I wash my body instead, holding off on washing my hair for now. The bruises have shifted their colors, faded reds, purples, and greens covering most of my body, my torso with the brunt of the damage. Luckily for me, I can conceal it under my clothing and minimize some of the sad stares.

Everything still hurts, though, from my head down to my toes. I thought the pain would have subsided, but I have to remind myself that my father nearly killed me two weeks ago, that doesn't go away overnight.

Even taking deep breaths is difficult, my injured lungs still healing, too. The headaches have died down, a steady throb that intensifies randomly.

He's abused me countless times, but the fractured skull was a new addition to his résumé of damage he's inflicted on me.

I put my arm in front of the faucet and rinse the inside of my cast out, the water nowhere near as disgusting as the first time I showered at Archer's place. I cringe at the memory of how dirty I was when I showed up on his doorstep. I can't believe he let me inside. Not that I look much better now, but still, I was disgusting, to say the very least.

The water courses over me another few minutes and I decide it's time. I need to wash my hair, I can't keep putting it off. I didn't exactly do a good job the last time I washed it, some of the shampoo no doubt remaining in my hair after I got out of the shower.

I squeeze some of the shampoo into my hand, still wondering why Archer has women's products in here. I go to lather it with my other hand and the entire lump of shampoo slides out and plops onto the shower floor.

"Fuck," I blurt out, and go in for another pump of the product. I manage to hold on to it this time, and raise my arms to work it into my hair, my ribs aching at the new position my body is in. "Fuck," I say, this time a bit louder. "Fuck, fuck, fuck." Tears well in my eyes and I lower my arms to my sides. Maybe I can find a salon nearby and pay to have my hair washed. But considering how much money

I spent on clothes, I don't really foresee having the luxury of paying someone to wash my hair in my future. I have nearly half the money I came here with and no idea how I'm going to get any more.

The door to the bathroom bursts open, and Archer rushes in a second later. "Is everything okay?"

I cover what I can of my private parts. "What the fuck, Archer?"

"You sounded distressed," he says, his voice still clipped, like he's not convinced someone isn't in here trying to murder me right this second.

"Have you ever tried to wash your hair with a cast on? I *am* distressed."

A long pause fills the steamy room.

"Hello? Some privacy?" I say, hoping he'll get the hint and get the hell out.

But instead, Archer reaches into the shower area and pokes at the panel on the wall. "You really shouldn't use that hot of water. You're going to hurt yourself."

I chuckle. "More than I already am? I'm pretty sure the water is the least of my worries, big boy."

Archer steals a glance at my body as he pulls away, his arm lingering, water droplets forming on his tattooed skin. "Christ..."

"Take a picture, Archer, it lasts longer."

He shakes his head. "No. Your...I didn't realize you..."

"Spit it out and get out." I continue to attempt to conceal myself, the cast covering most of my bare, soaked chest.

"Your entire body, London. You're bruised all over."

"Tell me something I didn't know."

Archer blinks a few times and I wish he would just spit out whatever it is he's thinking and go away, leaving me to stew in my embarrassment and the hot water. "Get out of the shower," he says, the words confusing me.

"Excuse me?"

"Sorry, I mean, when you're done, obviously. Get out of the shower and I'll wash your hair. We can do it in the sink in the kitchen."

"I'm not going to have you wash my hair," I protest for no real reason.

"Why?"

"I..." I struggle to find anything to say for the first time in my life.

"I'm not taking no for an answer." Archer reaches inside and takes the shampoo and conditioner off the shelf. "There, now you can't do it yourself."

"Dude, I'm naked here." I move to shield myself as he comes closer.

"Chill, I'm not trying to look at you like that."

"Wow," I scoff. "Thanks."

"Well, do you want me to? Make up your mind, little tornado." Archer walks away, going over to the counter and wiping the water off the sides of the bottles in his grasp. "I'll be in the kitchen when you're ready."

He leaves a moment later, not giving me a chance to protest or say anything.

I stand there, a bit dumbfounded, and crank the heat back up to where I had it, mumbling under my breath at Archer and his audacity.

It takes me two whole minutes under the blazing water to come to my senses.

The situation isn't ideal, but Archer is offering to wash my hair, something I can't manage on my own. Sure, it's weird and awkward, having some man I met a few days ago washing my hair, but I don't really have any other options unless I suffer my way through it myself.

I pat my body dry and wrap a large white towel around myself before making my way out of the bathroom and into the kitchen, my wet feet leaving a trail that will no doubt infuriate Archer. It's just water; it will evaporate eventually.

When I arrive in the kitchen, I find Archer rolling a towel up and setting it near the sink. His gaze flickers up at me, returns to his task, but then quickly falls on me again.

"Hey, so I, uh, I was thinking it would be easiest for you to lie on the counter and put your head in there." He points to the long island where the sink is located.

"Okay." I stroll over and stop next to the counter, realizing I can't boost myself up with my injured arm.

"Right, yeah." Archer seems to understand the problem immediately, and comes to my side as I face him.

I look up and put my arms out to give him space.

"I'm going to touch you, okay?"

I swallow and nod.

Archer puts his strong hands under my armpits and lifts me onto the counter with ease. His eyes meet mine, his grip still tight and gentle all at the same time.

"Thanks," I whisper, our faces just a breath apart.

"Yeah." Archer releases me and steps back. He walks around the side of the counter. "Lie back," he says, his hand hovering behind my head. "I've got you."

With his help, I comply, resting my neck on the towel he had bunched up and leaning the rest of my head into the sink area.

He turns the faucet on, adjusting the temperature too many times until he gets it right. Archer covers my forehead with his left hand and pulls the nozzle down to spray my hair. The water is lukewarm at best.

"You can make it hotter," I tell him.

"I'm sure you'd like that."

"I would, you're going to freeze me to death."

Even with his palm covering my eyes, I can make out him shaking his head.

"Were you personally victimized by hot water?" I ask him.

He stops, moves his hand, and says, "What?"

"It was a joke, Archer. Have you ever heard of those?"

Archer doesn't answer me, yet continues his task, returning the nozzle a second later to put some shampoo in his hands. He lathers it up before running his tattooed fingers through my hair, and I'm not entirely sure I haven't died and gone to heaven when he massages my scalp.

"Fuck," I mutter, but nothing like the fucks I was letting out in the shower.

"Am I hurting you?"

"No, not at all. That was a good fuck." I close my eyes and savor his touch.

Archer scrubs all around my head, even getting the base of my skull and around my ears. It's fucking pure bliss, and I don't want it to stop.

"Other than your arm and leg, what's wrong with you? So I know." His question completely pulls me out of the blissful moment. Leave it to him to ruin something so damn good.

"What?" I peek through one lid at him.

"Your injuries. Clearly, you're worse off than I thought you were."

"Oh. It's not that bad."

"Not that bad. London, your entire body is one giant bruise."

"If I tell you, will you let it go?"

Archer rinses my hair, covering my forehead again to save me from the splatter. "Maybe."

I exhale and think through my list of injuries. "Fractured right leg, left wrist, skull. Bruised and collapsed lung, I mean, it's not anymore. Um, what else? Broken ribs, some cuts and scrapes, nothing too crazy." I lick at the inside of my lip, where it's still a little swollen. "I think the stitches on my lip have already dissolved."

Archer stops everything, his mouth hanging open when I glance up at him. "London..."

I roll my eyes and point to my head. "If you keep looking at me like that, I'm going to do the same to you. Now, finish my hair or I'm going to do it myself."

"Do I even want to know where that scar on your stomach came from?"

I sit up, wincing from the abrupt pain. "I'm done."

Archer carefully puts his hand on my shoulder, his tattooed touch burning through me. "Okay, I'm sorry, let me finish."

Reluctantly, I go along, because what other choice do I have? It's not like I can do my hair myself, at least not well.

He applies conditioner from mid-length to my ends, combing his fingers through and cautiously tugging the tangles out.

With the conditioner sitting in my hair, I reposition my neck toward him. "I think it's only fair you show me a scar or two. I mean, you just saw me naked. We need to make this even."

Archer raises a brow and plants his hands on the edge of the counter. "You want me to get naked?"

"You wish I'd want to see you naked."

"You don't want to?" The muscles in his arms flex and it's everything I can do not to shift my attention from his face to study his chiseled body.

"Archer, are you flirting with me?" I wink at him. "I didn't think you had it in you. Is that why you stormed into the shower to get a peek?"

"I did not storm in there."

"What else would you call that?"

"Okay, well, it wasn't to look at you. I thought something was wrong."

"You always think something's wrong. What's with that?"

"I think it's time to rinse..." Archer reaches for the faucet and rinses my hair, spending way more time than I expect him to on it. He grabs all my hair into his fist and squeezes any excess water out before grabbing the towel he had sitting off to the side and ruffling it around my head.

I sit up, carefully, and reach for the towel, our hands grazing in the process. "Come on. I think I earned at least one scar. Or hey, maybe tell me about one of your tattoos."

Archer sighs and runs his hand through his own hair, the dark locks falling back onto his forehead. He lifts his shirt, only slightly, and points to a puckered, ink-stained spot on his stomach. "Here."

Not caring at all that I'm a towel away from being naked on this stranger's counter who just washed my hair, I extend my hand and press my finger along the raised spot. "Gunshot?" I ask him, even though I can't imagine it would be much else.

"Yep."

I glide my hand along his stomach until I reach his back, feeling for one on the other side. "And there's the exit wound." I turn my face toward him. "At least it was clean and straight through."

"Why do you know about gunshot wounds?" he asks me, his stare intense. Archer reaches back and grabs my hand, bringing it around to his front. He hovers it over his stomach, across his abs, and onto another scar, then another. The next one surprises me; the length and texture are drastically different. This scar is longer and jagged.

"Knife?" I ask him, unsure of whether I'm right.

"Yeah." He lets go of my hand and puts a step between us. Archer folds his arms over his chest like he's hoping it will prevent me from finding anything else out about him.

"Guess we both have our secrets," I say, scooting myself off the counter before he can help me get down. I nearly lose the towel wrapped around my body, but I catch it as it tries to fall off.

"Guess so." Archer doesn't take his eyes off me, and it leaves me wondering what he's thinking, a thought I'm almost always assaulted with. Sure, I know how to make him mad, but aside from Archer being a grumpy control freak, he's sort of a mystery. One I find myself unable to not want to figure out.

But I'm no stranger to secrets, and sometimes they're better left buried.

CHAPTER TWELVE

Archer

Two days have passed since I washed London's hair, and I can't get the entire experience out of my head. It's fucking frustrating. The image of her bruised body is burned into my memory, and despite only knowing her for a week, I feel strangely protective of her.

I mean, that's a given, considering Silver's main objective was to find someone to keep her safe.

Where was his plan when someone beat the shit out of her? Why couldn't he have watched out for her then? Why did things have to get as bad as they did for Silver to finally step in and say enough was enough?

I try to rid myself of the nagging thoughts and questions, but they bubble up and disrupt everything—my sleep, my work, my every waking thought.

The buzzer to my apartment goes off, abruptly bringing me back to reality. My gaze flits to the bedroom, where London is with the door shut, and then to the front. I rush over and press the button.

"Who is it?" I ask.

"Uh, delivery for Archer S—"

I cut him off before he can continue. "Come on up."

It takes the guy far longer than it should to reach my door, and once he does, I see why. His nose is practically buried in his phone. He shoots me an apologetic glance when he approaches. "Sorry, my girl's mad at me. I'm sure you understand." He holds the small box out to me. "I need a signature."

I ignore him, scribble on the pad, and take the box from him, shutting the door on him a second later.

Once inside, I go straight to my desk and open the box,

revealing the phone I ordered for London. With the bedroom door still closed, I quickly adhere one of the smallest trackers I have in my stash to the back of her phone, holding it up and wondering if she's going to notice it doesn't belong.

She's a smart woman, but I don't think she's quite that observant.

I swipe at the screen, turning it on and going through the automated prompts, plugging in a brand-new email when it's asked for, and shutting off the unnecessary location services.

London comes out of the room and goes to the kitchen, pouring herself half a glass of water and chugging it down. She leaves the glass there, on the counter, and I can't help but wonder if she does it on purpose to drive me insane.

Spoiler alert, it does.

She approaches, and it's then that I take her in—a pair of dark jeans and a fitted white top, the heels she bought herself on the one foot that doesn't have a cast on it.

"You're not seriously wearing that, are you?" I ask her.

London snatches the black bag I had bought her off the table and does her best to walk without limping. "What's wrong with what I'm wearing?"

"You're wearing heels...and a cast."

"And?" She pauses and points at the phone in my hand. "Is that my phone?" London snatches it out of my grasp without letting me answer. She looks it over and swipes her finger across the screen. "Cool, thanks, what's my number?"

I join her next to the couch, towering over her shoulder. "Click settings, then phone. That'll show your number. But you need to be careful who you give it to, you can't just—"

London pivots her body and places her hand on my shoulder. "Simmer down, big boy."

I glare at her. "Wait, where are you going?"

"Out." She opens her purse and plops the phone inside.

"What do you mean, *out*?"

"It's Sunday, Archer. I've been out of your apartment once this entire week. I'm going out."

"It's Sunday?" The recollection of my conversation with Ivy hits me like a ton of bricks.

"Are you okay? You look like you're having an aneurysm." London squints her eyes at me and pokes at my cheek.

I gently swat her away. "I'm fine. That's fine. Have fun."

"That's it? No protesting? No lecture? You're going to let me go?"

"Mm-hmm," I mumble, and take a peek at my watch, flinching at it being half past noon. I'm already thirty minutes late and I haven't even gotten ready yet. Ivy made it clear that she was sick of my shit, and here I am letting her down once again.

"Okay," London says, a hint of surprise in her voice that isn't lost on me. I don't have the time to do any of the things she mentioned. She's made it this far in life, I must assume that she'll heed my warnings and not be a complete idiot when she leaves my place.

"Don't leave town, please," I instruct her, the words slipping out too hurriedly. "Stay within a four-block radius."

"Are you going to tell me not to talk to strangers, too? Maybe not to get into strange white vans?"

My rushed nature halts and my entire body goes tense. "London," I say through gritted teeth.

"It was a joke, big boy." London pats my shoulder again, but it does nothing to ease the worry. Only, the wrath of Ivy comes creeping back in.

"I put my number in your phone," I say. "Call me if you need me." I open the front door and shut it a split second later. "Oh, wait, hang on." I rush over to grab the spare key I had made for her off the stand. “Here’s this.” I hold it out to her, a sort of electric energy pulsing between us I don’t have time to decipher. Perhaps it’s my anxiety getting the best of me and nothing is there at all.

“You’re being weirder than usual.” London takes the key from me and slides it into her purse. “Are you on drugs?”

“I’m not on drugs.”

“Maybe you should be.”

I ignore her remark. “The access code is 2220.”

“So original.”

“I didn’t make it,” I tell her.

“I would hope not.” London nervously motions to her body. “How do I look?”

I let my gaze wander, regretting it the second my heart skips a beat. “You look fine,” I respond, my tone even.

“You sure have a way with words.” London reaches for the door handle, and I reach for her, pausing her from going any farther.

“Be careful, please?”

“I will,” she tells me, a sense of honesty lingering. “I’ll be back in a few hours.”

“Okay. Make sure you use that card. Get whatever you want.”

“Whatever I want? Okay, maybe you do have a way with words.” She slips out the front door, a piece of me going with her. I fucking hate how she’s crawled under my skin in the week that she’s been here.

Once she’s gone, I rush to the bathroom, turning the temperature to a reasonable degree, and take the quickest shower I ever have, drying off so quickly that I almost forget to hang my towel up. I’m throwing my arms through the sleeves of my shirt and trying to button my jeans when a voice calls out from my front room.

My chest tightens. Why would London be back already? Maybe she forgot something. Maybe she changed her mind. Either way, if I can't get rid of her soon, I'm going to have to explain...

"Arch, honey, we need to talk," Ivy murmurs from her spot standing at my bedroom door.

I rush toward her, grabbing her shoulders and guiding her out of the room that has London's stuff all over it. "Hey, let's chat out here."

Ivy throws her arms up. "You might be older than me, taller than me, but you know I'm prepared to kick your ass, right?" She shrugs me off and places her handbag on the counter, opening it to pull out a compact. She powders her nose and snaps it shut, dropping it into the bag. "How many times are you going to stand me up before I do something about it? This is getting old. I'm done making excuses for you." She tilts her wrist toward her. "Noon. Once a month. That's all I hold you to. Everything else, sure, make excuses for...but for Christ's sake. I'm not asking for too much. One Sunday. Your brothers get it, why can't you?"

I shove one of London's shirts under a couch cushion and attempt to tidy up while Ivy isn't paying attention.

Ivy is pretty small, probably shorter than London, but she grew up around four of the most ruthless men in this town and is trained to kill in various forms. I do have the advantage of being taller and stronger than her, and I'd never lay a finger on Ivy, but I'm not sure if I could hold her off. She's like a ticking time bomb. Soft and sweet on the outside, dying to murder someone on the inside. She gets it honestly, though; her twin brother, Seven is a homicidal maniac.

I've killed people, but for necessity. Seven does it for fun.

"Are you even listening to me?" Ivy turns around, her heels clicking against the floor in my kitchen. "Archer. What are you doing?"

I stop dead in my tracks, my heart pounding out of my chest. I hate lying to Ivy. I hate making her upset. And yet here it is, the only thing I can manage to do.

"I'm just straightening up," I tell her.

Her dark brow arches and she takes a full scan of the room. "What's going on here?"

"What do you mean?" I swallow harshly.

"Your place. It's a wreck. And..." She sniffs, then sniffs again. "Have you been using that bodywash I left here?"

"I, uh, I can explain." But no words follow, and I wish like hell I could come up with some reasonable explanation for why it looks like a tornado came through my apartment.

Luckily, the front door flies open and saves me from having to say anything.

"There's my least-favorite brother," Leo says as he marches in, his arms extended as he pulls me in for an aggressive hug. He slaps my back hard. "Can't believe you stood us up, Arch. What the hell?"

I hug him back, my apartment feeling smaller and smaller as Seven and August come in, too.

August thumbs something on his phone and shoves the thing into his pocket. "Sorry, dealing with a crisis."

"Oh, what's new?" Ivy says, rolling her eyes.

August shoots daggers at her before turning his attention to me. "Brother. Are you well?"

"Why do you talk like you're fifty-five?" I ask him, the comment suddenly sounding like something London would have said.

London, shit, I need to check on her.

I rush over to my computer, type a few things, and sync her tracker to my phone, the loading screen taking far too fucking long.

"What are you doing, Arch?" Ivy starts toward me but stops when Seven dramatically drops a couple of brown bags onto the counter. "Geez, Sev, what crawled up your ass?"

Seven goes to my fridge and opens it wide. "What's to drink?" He scans the contents and slams the doors shut, the whole fridge rattling. He shifts his focus to the cabinet off to the left, taking a full bottle of tequila out and popping the top off it. After taking a giant swig, he wipes at his mouth and holds out the bottle. "Oh, did you want some?"

"I'm good," I tell him, and make my way toward the kitchen, hoping everyone else will, too, instead of noticing how my apartment is nothing like how I usually keep it.

"I only have an hour," August announces.

"Guys." Ivy raises her voice. "Everyone. Sit down, now." She takes the bags and drops them onto the table in my dining room. "I said now."

Seven mumbles something but lowers himself onto a chair, leaning and throwing his tattooed arm over the back of it. "Pull that stick out of your ass, baby sis."

Ivy slams her fist onto the table. "You are two minutes, *two* fucking minutes, older than me." She takes a deep breath and lets it out slowly. "I don't care who you are, what you've done, who you've killed. I am going to stab each and every one of you if you don't sit down, right now."

I walk over and grab a stack of plates, returning to the table a second later and setting them next to the brown bags. Without saying a word, I sit on one of the chairs and wait for the lecture I'm about to get to begin.

Leo and August follow, August unbuttoning his suit jacket and folding it over his chair first.

"Great, glad we could all get on the same page about something for once." Ivy pulls out several Chinese takeout boxes and slides each one of us a plate. She sits on a chair and waves her arms. "Eat."

Each of us grabs a box, pops it open, and shuffles them around the table to who likes what. I pass her the carton of noodles and say, "I'm sorry, Ivy. I'm an asshole."

She looks at me, her eyes glistening. "You *are* an asshole."

"Glad we agree on something." Leo smacks me on the back

again and digs into an egg roll.

Ivy gasps. "Seven. Is that blood on your arm?"

"Oh, shit." Seven laughs. "My bad." He flicks at it like it's going to make the dried mess disappear.

I point to the bathroom. "Go wash up. You know better than that."

"It's not my fault he was a gusher." Seven huffs but stands, goes to the bathroom, and washes the rest of his crime down the drain.

"Who did you kill?" Ivy asks him when he returns.

"Uh, I don't know."

"What do you mean, you don't know? How can you kill someone and not know who it is?"

Seven shrugs. "No, really, I don't remember his name. Gary something, maybe."

August clears his throat. "Greg Walters."

"That's right." Seven snaps his fingers and points to August. "That's who it was."

"You're a sociopath, you know that, right?" Ivy shoves a forkful of noodles into her mouth.

"Probably." Seven eats some of his spicy chicken and I'm just glad the focus is on someone else for a change, and not me.

"What's a sociopath?" Leo asks as he gets up from the table and makes his way to the kitchen.

Ivy clears her throat like she was ready for this question, this moment. "A sociopath is someone who shows no regard for right or wrong *and* ignores the feelings of others."

"Uh, Ivy, babe, if that's the case, I'm pretty sure we're all sociopaths." Leo returns a moment later with a soda in his grasp.

Ivy waves her finger in the air. "No, sociopaths cannot feel empathy and remorse. You might blur the lines of right and wrong, but you have feelings. Seven doesn't."

Seven clutches his chest dramatically. "I'm right here, baby sis."

He laughs sharply and continues, "Ah, who am I kidding, I don't give a fuck."

"Case in point," Ivy says. "I mean, he's a psychopath too. True Gemini nature. This is where you charm people, manipulate and use them to your advantage."

August and I sit there, quietly eating our food, and exchange a glance.

I reach for my phone, doing a quick look at the tracker and noting London's whereabouts. She's at the coffee shop she met Grace in, and has been for quite some time. If I were alone, I'd pull up the surveillance feed and see exactly what she's doing, but my nosey family would want to know what I'm doing and who I'm watching.

"And what am I?" Leo asks Ivy. "I'm sure you've psychoanalyzed all of us."

"I have." Ivy grins like the Cheshire cat. She wipes at her mouth before answering him. "So, I'd say you have textbook narcissistic tendencies."

"What makes you so sure?"

"Where do I start? Hm, well, you are super competitive, materialistic, arrogant, jealous, hypersensitive to criticism, you avoid responsibility like the plague, you're insecure—"

Leo puts his hand in the air. "I think we get the point, Ivy." He shakes his head and mumbles under his breath. "I'm not any of that stuff."

Seven scratches his chin. "I think I have that too."

"Is that a new tattoo?" I ask him, a design consisting of a bunch of dark angled lines that don't really make any one specific thing covering his throat.

He tilts his head, exposing the flaky area. "Yeah, itches like hell."

"You're snowing all over the dining room table, Seven. Go put some lotion on that thing," I tell him.

"Carmen was asking about you," Seven says. "Said it's been a while since she's seen you."

"I ran out of ideas." For a while, I did nothing but get tattooed, scheduling an appointment every few days, covering section after section of my body, hoping the pain would do something to ease the empty pit in my chest, but it never worked. And once I finished my arms and the front and back of my torso, I decided to take a break.

"Let's talk about what's wrong with August," Leo blurts out.

Ivy shifts her gaze to August, something concealed I can't quite make out being spoken between them. "Same as Archer. Control issues. Although Archer is a germaphobe and August is a workaholic with an unhealthy dose of perfectionism."

"You get one degree in psychology and think you're—" August blurts out, his tone no doubt surprising all of us.

I slide my phone back out, ignoring the argument between August and Ivy, rest it on my thigh, and watch the tracker dot of London stay in the same spot. My chest tightens at the thought of her having found the tracker and removing it. I frantically push a few buttons and locate the Find My iPhone feature, breathing a sigh of relief at seeing it in the same spot, too. Maybe she has no idea I put it on there. Maybe she really is just hanging out in the coffee shop. That makes the most sense.

"Don't talk to me like I'm a child," Ivy says, pulling me from my own little world.

"Guys, seriously," I speak up. "Can we have one meal without fighting? We're all we have. Can we pretend like we like each other?"

Ivy clenches her fists and shakes them loose. "Fine." She pats her dress pants and returns to her seat.

August immediately shifts the conversation like he wasn't just being a giant asshole. "How's business, Arch? Anything I should be aware of?"

Ivy rolls her eyes so aggressively, I'm concerned they're going to pop out of her head. "Always business with you," she mutters.

August turns toward her. "Do you have something you'd like the rest of us to hear?"

Seven reaches for the bottle of tequila he brought to the table, takes a long swig of it, and watches things unfold. "I missed this."

"No, August," Ivy says, her tone laced with venom. "By all means, let's talk business."

"Investments are up," I tell him. "Finances are solid. We aren't taking a hit quite as bad as the West Coast sector, but considering the fallout, things could be worse for them."

"And security?" August adds.

"Do you doubt my abilities?" I ask.

"Not at all, but I understand you've been under some stress."

"Some stress? Are you serious?" This time it's my turn for my cheeks to get hot with anger at August.

"I didn't mean any offense." August leans back in his chair. "It's perfectly within my nature to question the integrity of things."

The integrity of things, is he fucking serious? I've done nothing but keep our family affairs in order, how dare he question anything I do? He's lucky I'm still involved, let alone contributing in the manner I do. A thankless fucking job, that's what this is.

Seven slams the tequila bottle on the table, drawing all our attention toward him. "How come no one asks me about business?" He belches and follows it up with a hiccup.

"Because all you do is kill people," Ivy chimes in. "Tell me, what have you done this week *other* than kill people?"

"I, uh..." Seven trails off and gets lost in his recollection. "Wait, I broke that guy's kneecaps on Tuesday. That counts, right?"

"Sure." Ivy gives Seven a soft, yet condescending smile.

I'm taking in the curve of her cheeks, noticing how it doesn't quite meet the eyes, when my entire life flashes before my eyes as the door to my apartment opens.

Seven reaches for his waistband gun, Leo doing the same, as Ivy slides the small dagger she keeps in her ankle holster out.

I hear her voice before I see her, and do nothing but fucking panic. "Put your weapons down," I whisper-shout to my family.

They comply partially, holding them behind their backs as London steps into the apartment, her friend Grace, who I haven't officially met yet, on her heels.

Fuck, fuck, fuck.

London starts. "Oh, shit, I didn't know you had company."

"Company?" Ivy calls out to me over her shoulder. "Who the fuck is this?"

I rush around the table and make a face that hopefully says *Please put the fucking weapons away* to my family. "Uh, this is..." *Come on, Archer, think of something, anything. Perhaps something clever or elaborate to explain why two random women are standing at the entrance of your apartment.*

"I'm London," London says, marching straight up to the table and leaving Grace behind. She extends her hand, and for a long moment, I forget that she has a cast on her leg. How she's managing to walk so well in one heel, I'll never understand.

Ivy stares at London, at her hand, and with such poise, flips the dagger into her left arm and conceals it while shaking London's hand with her right. "I'm Ivy. Pleasure."

The two of them size each other up and I'm not certain my heart has ever beat harder than it has at this very moment.

I step forward, my mouth opening. "London is staying with me for a little while."

Ivy whips her head toward me. "I'm sorry, what?"

Seven glides the tequila bottle across the table, his sight locking on Grace, who remains quiet. "And what do we have here..." He saunters over to her, licking his lips and looking at her from head to toe. "Damn, baby girl. Are you an angel, because..."

Grace holds her finger out toward him. "Immediately no."

Ivy chuckles, Grace's comment breaking the thick tension between her and London. Although I'm not sure London gets the memo.

Grace keeps her head high as she bypasses Seven's borderline offensive remark and makes her way over to the rest of us. "I'm Grace."

"Right, yeah." I shift to the group. "London, Grace, this is August, Leo, Ivy, and...that's Seven." I reach out to Grace. "Archer."

Grace shakes my hand, firm and quick, to the point.

"Nice to meet you," Leo tells her.

"Pleasure is all mine," August adds.

Ivy scowls at August like he's done something wrong, but I'm not sure what. "So how do you two know each other?" Ivy flits to me and London.

"Oh," London begins. "We're friends of friends. I'm new in town, an extended visit, if you will. Archer was kind enough to let me crash here until I got a place of my own." She walks over, gripping my shoulder between her arms. "Archer's such a nice guy, you know?"

Ivy laughs. "Yeah, sure is." She plants her hand on her hip and I wonder how much sass my apartment can take before it implodes. I've been dealing with a heavy dose of it all week with London, and with Ivy added into the mix, it's a recipe for disaster. "Why didn't you tell us about this, Arch?"

London speaks up without giving me a chance to. "It's my fault, honestly. I've kept him rather preoccupied." She pats my chest. "Haven't I, *Arch*?"

I chuckle nervously and consider how quickly Ivy is going to murder London, especially considering London's current condition. Still, she doesn't seem to be backing down despite having a disadvantage. Maybe she's crazier than I gave her credit for.

"As truly entertaining as this all is..." August peels his jacket off the chair and shoves his arms into each sleeve. "I must be going."

"I cleared your schedule today, what could you possibly have going on?" Ivy barks at him.

"Things, dear, things." August straightens his collar. "Brother, it was great seeing you. Let me know if you'd like to continue that conversation." He shoots me a quick look and nods stiffly at Leo. "Brother."

"What about me?" Seven protests, throwing his arms out to the sides, the tequila bottle still in his grasp.

"And you, Brother, are an alcoholic." August grasps Seven's shoulder on the way to the door, slipping out without another word.

Leo slips his gun into the back of his pants and tucks his shirt over it slyly. "I should probably get going, too."

"You guys are the worst." Ivy pouts. "Once a month, that's all I ask."

"What's once a month?" London asks her.

Seven leans against the back of my couch, his obvious stare glued to Grace.

Most women fold to Seven's passes, even if they're degrading and a bit repulsive. They're usually drawn to his dark hair, endless tattoos, and mismatched eyes, one green, one blue. He's got a sort of *moth to a flame* kind of vibe, only people don't realize it until he's chewed them up and spit them out. Seven really is the most psychotic of us all, making each one of us question our loyalty from time to time. He's unhinged, and if it weren't for Ivy keeping him in line, keeping us all in line, our entire empire would crumble.

Grace acts like he's some drunk at a bar, not bothered by him enough to give him a second glance. It's kind of comical, watching him shoot his pathetic shot and getting turned down.

"Dinner," Ivy tells London. "Once a month, all I ask of my brothers is for a family meal."

London stiffens next to me. "Brothers?"

"Yeah, Archer didn't tell you?" Ivy meets my gaze. "You ashamed of us, Brother?"

CHAPTER THIRTEEN

London

My entire body relaxes at hearing the words out of Ivy's mouth, and a second later, I'm realizing how fucking foolish I must look, hanging on Archer in some sad attempt to mark my territory for no real reason.

He's a grown-ass man. Even if Ivy wasn't his sister, what on earth gives me the right to act the way I am? I've known this man for a week, and we've both made it clear we aren't interested in each other like that. Perhaps it was the two mimosas I had at the coffee shop going to my head. That must explain it.

Or maybe it was the possibility that a girlfriend would be a reason for me to lose my safe haven and have nowhere else to go.

The shampoo and conditioner, it wasn't a girlfriend's, it was his sister's, which also justifies the feminine products in his bathroom.

"I have a brother," Grace adds out of nowhere, probably in an attempt to defuse the weirdness of the situation. "He's older by a few years. What about you guys? What's the age difference?"

Ivy turns her focus to Grace like she's grateful for a question she can answer without giving too much away. "Seven and I are twenty-six."

"Oh, nice, me too. When's your birthday?" Grace says.

"June ninth." Seven approaches from the living room. "Will you be my birthday present?" He tucks a strand of bright blond hair behind Grace's ear, and she doesn't even flinch.

"In your dreams, lover boy." She takes one solid step away from him and looks at Ivy. "You were saying."

Seven hisses like he touched a hot stove and drinks down more of his tequila.

"Dude, really?" Archer goes for the bottle, but Seven's reflexes are catlike, moving it and himself from Archer's reach.

"We're twins, Seven and I," Ivy continues. "The youngest of us all. And then there's Archer, thirty. Leo's, um, Leo's thirty-two, and August is thirty-six. London, how old are you?"

"Aren't you not supposed to ask a woman her age?" Archer says.

"That usually only applies to men asking." I smile politely. "I'm twenty-three."

Ivy licks her lips and I know without a doubt that she's about to stir the pot even more. "Are you two hooking up?"

"Oh, yeah, good question, baby sis. I want to know if they're fucking, too." Seven leans against the wall, the bottle of tequila held firmly in his tattooed hands.

"No," I say before Archer can. "We aren't fucking. We're just... friends."

"Are we?" He raises a brow at me.

"Yes, Archer, we are friends. Is that okay with you?"

As if the wheels are turning in his head, Archer struggles to find an answer. Sure, we've only known each other a week, but we're friend adjacent at this point, right?

Leo clears his throat by the front door. "This has been fun. I'm leaving now. Bye." He waves and slips out the front door, leaving the rest of us behind.

"Oh, I'm starving, is that lo mein?" Grace points to the table where a bunch of Chinese takeout containers are.

"Yeah, help yourself," Ivy tells her. "August and Leo are gone, so those chairs are open. "Oh, but—" She rushes over to another seat. "Don't touch these ones."

"What's wrong with those?" Grace asks her.

"They're Seven's and, well...he's kind of gross."

"Am not," Seven protests, stalking over and returning to his seat. "I washed my hands." He tips back the tequila and drinks some of it, my mouth watering at the idea of more booze flowing through my system.

"Can I have a drink of that?" I surprise myself by asking him.

Seven hesitates before grinning, exposing his canine teeth which appear to be filed down into a dramatic point. "Be my guest."

"London..." Archer warns, but I ignore him, putting my mouth on the opening of the bottle and drinking some down.

It's hot, warms my throat and stomach, and sends a tingling sensation throughout my body. "That's good," I tell Seven, and return the bottle to him.

He's strange—outwardly attractive with that tall, muscular, tattooed thing going on, but there's something about the look in his eye that tells me he's more trouble than he's worth.

And I don't exactly enjoy the way he looks at Grace like she's a piece of meat he's ready to tear into.

I settle into the seat next to Archer, Grace taking the one next to Ivy, as far as she can get away from Seven. It doesn't stop him from gawking at her the entire time.

"Are you single?" Seven asks her with no regard for the rest of us.

"Are you?"

Seven props his tattooed elbows onto the table and rests his head on the bottle. "I can be anything you want me to be, baby girl."

"One, don't call me baby girl. Two, what makes you think I want anything to do with you?" Grace takes the box of lo mein that Ivy slides to her. "Oh, thanks." She digs right in and I almost laugh at how she shuts Seven down.

I don't know much about Archer, but it's clear he's involved in some shady shit. And considering my background, I wouldn't put it past this bunch to be a family of criminals in one way or another. Grace is nothing of the sort. She comes from money, and I haven't fully uncovered her backstory, but I think it has something to do with politics. She is the exact opposite of us, and here she is, not intimidated in the slightest. Maybe if she knew the truth, she'd act differently.

Who am I kidding—I'm well aware of part of the truth and I still act like I'm not afraid of them.

They can't hurt me any more than my father already has.

"You're feisty," Seven says. "I like that."

"No," Archer speaks up finally. "You like that she's not interested in you, you sick fuck. Leave her alone."

My cheek turns up into a grin, but I don't let it fully come to the surface. Instead, I eye the selection of food and wonder if there's anything that doesn't have meat in it that isn't already spoken for.

Archer shoves a sack toward me. "These are vegetable egg rolls."

"Oh." I hesitate. "Are you sure?"

"Yep."

I take one, carefully biting off the end and confirming that he's telling me the truth. The buzz of alcohol flows through me, settling my nerves.

"Are you vegetarian?" Ivy asks me from across the table.

"I am."

"I almost went vegetarian once, but it's hard...I like burgers too much."

"When you witness your dad gut a...pig...right in front of you, it kind of makes you change your mind." Only, I edit part of the story to include the truth I'm willing to tell. My father didn't gut a pig, he gutted a man, and then dismembered him and fed him to pigs. Who knew watching that at seven years old would make you turn vegetarian? I don't tell them any of this, though.

"Damn, that's brutal." Ivy shuffles her lo mein back and forth. "I don't think this has meat in it, does it?"

She turns to Grace, who shakes her head. "It can, but these don't, no."

"Hm, maybe I'll reconsider…"

"There's tofu in the fridge," Seven says out of nowhere.

Archer blinks at him. "And?"

Seven shrugs and shovels a forkful of food into his mouth.

He reminds me of one big intrusive thought, never holding back and just saying the first thing that pops into his head. Maybe he doesn't have a filter and that's why he's so…out there.

"So, how long will you be staying here with Arch?" Ivy puts her arm over the back of her chair and folds one leg over the other, getting comfortable and no doubt arming her arsenal of questions she's preparing to grill me with.

"A few weeks, until I find another place. I already have a lead if Archer will put in a good word for me."

Archer clears his throat. "Camille says hi, by the way."

"Is she moving? I love Camille, she's great. Tell her hello for me." Ivy runs her tongue across her teeth, probably in search of any food she may have missed. "Her place is great. Same size as Archer's, except it's a two-bedroom, since she didn't randomly demolish a wall and decide to renovate."

"I'm sorry, what?" I say.

Ivy motions plainly around the area. "Arch took a sledgehammer to the place. Tore down the wall between the rooms and made it one big room and an even bigger bathroom. I think the kitchen is different, too, isn't it, Arch?"

"The kitchen is the same, V. It was one, tiny wall. It's not a big deal."

"I'm telling you, I think there was another wall…"

"Okay, fine, there was one other wall, that's it." Archer acts like he's a child being scolded by a parent, and I find it so strange to watch him interact with someone else, especially this way.

"Wait, you took a sledgehammer to the wall? Why?" I ask him, and take another bite of the egg roll.

"Because I can," he says dryly.

"He was having sort of a...psychotic break," Ivy adds.

Seven leans forward, closer in the direction of Grace. "Do you wanna hook up in the bathroom?"

Grace tugs her bottom lip into her mouth like she's considering it. "You know what. Head on in there, I'll meet you in a minute."

Seven's eyes go wide, showing off their different colors. I hadn't noticed that until now. "Wh-what? Really?"

Grace shrugs. "Sure, why not? You seem persistent enough not to let this go."

Seven hops up, taking his tequila bottle with him, and rips his shirt off, throwing it onto the floor on his way to the bathroom.

My gaze meets Grace's, who remains firmly rooted in her seat. "You're not going, are you?"

She bunches her brows and shakes her head. "Are you kidding me? No way."

Archer chuckles. "He's going to be pissed."

"What's new?" Ivy says. "He's always mad about something."

"Ivy. What do you do for work?" I fidget with the wrapper of the egg rolls and try to guess what bullshit answer she's going to give me. Will it be as generic as Archer saying he's in tech?

"I'm in PR," she tells me.

"Oh, nice," Grace speaks up. "Who do you work with?"

"I have a few clients, some more labor-intensive than others. Right now, my focus is on August and his companies."

"What does August do?" I pry.

"A plethora of things, really. Essentially, he's a venture capitalist, but it is a bit too broad to narrow down to one specific thing. What about you? What do you do?"

It's not hard to notice Ivy is quickly deflecting the topic of conversation, something her work in public relations has primed her well for.

"Nothing at the moment, since I just relocated." I hate not having some fantastic job to brag about, but it's not a lie that things are a bit up in the air for me right now, so I do the same thing as her and turn the focus on someone else. "What about you, Grace? We talked briefly about work but nothing too in-depth."

"I'm in event planning for the city, mostly charity events."

"What the fuck?" Seven calls out from the bathroom entrance. He snatches his shirt off the ground, throwing it over his shoulder. "Come on, Ivy, let's fucking go."

Ivy rolls her eyes. "Very well, Brother." She looks to Archer. "Walk me to the door?"

"Yeah," he says without hesitation. "Of course." Archer hops up and follows her over while Seven approaches the table.

Archer pauses, watching Seven intensely.

"Give me your number," Seven says to Grace. "We can go out sometime."

Slowly, she turns toward him, tilting her head up at his exposed chest. If it weren't for his personality, Seven would be attractive. He has everything working in his favor. The tattoos, the height, those weirdly mismatched eyes, and the dark hair. Even his filed-down teeth add a strange sort of sex appeal. But the second he opens his mouth, every ounce of attraction falls to the wayside.

"I think she said no," I say from my spot at the table.

"I didn't ask you," he quips back, a bite to his tone.

I stand, ignoring the pain shooting up my cast-covered leg. "I don't care that you didn't ask me. Leave her alone."

Seven looks at me, his stare so penetrating, it sends a chill down my spine. "What did you just say to me?"

"You heard me."

Grace immediately stands, putting herself between Seven and me, even though the table is there anyway. "Give me your phone."

Seven's jaw tenses, that little bulge on the side flexing as his nostrils flare slightly. He shifts down, now at Grace's level, his height drastically different from hers. Is that what Archer and I look like standing next to each other? "Why, so you can give me a fake number?"

Grace pulls her phone out of her back pocket, unlocks the screen, and hands it to him. "There, put your number in."

He hesitates like he's not sure if she's telling the truth, but then decides to take her phone. He pushes a sequence of buttons and a second later, his phone rings and stops. "There." Seven gives me one last death stare before returning her cell. "Don't make me come over there and wipe that look off your pretty face," Seven says through gritted teeth, each word a bit blended into the next.

Out of nowhere, Archer appears, gripping Seven's shoulder and shoving him. "What the fuck is wrong with you? You don't talk to her like—"

But Seven doesn't let him finish, no, he reels back his arm and slams his fist against Archer's face, blood splattering Archer's rug and dining room floor.

I gasp, my feet moving without my brain even catching up.

Archer, red pooling from his nose, doesn't falter when he punches Seven back, a crack that could only be Seven's nose echoing in the space.

"You fucking bastard," Seven yells. "I'll fucking kill you." He hits Archer again in the face, and harder in the gut.

Archer doesn't let up. He smashes his fist into Seven's jaw like he's been waiting far too long for this to happen, like this isn't just about what happened here today, but something else, something bigger.

"Stop it," Ivy screams into the chaos. "Both of you, fucking *stop.*"

But neither of them does. They keep hitting each other, over and over, blood staining their faces, fists, and everything in a two-foot radius.

Archer swipes his leg so fast, I almost miss it, knocking Seven's legs out from under him, and climbs on top of him, hitting him repeatedly in the face, a sort of anger in him being unleashed that I didn't know he was capable of.

You've only known him a week, I remind myself, and realize I'm living with a stranger. *You know nothing about him, London, you stupid, stupid girl.*

And even though I know I should be more afraid, there's something in me that's ignorant to the fear, having lived with my father all my life. I'm no stranger to violence.

"You." Archer hits him. "Fucking. Bastard." Every word is another blow.

"Cut it out, Archer, you're going to fucking kill him." Ivy reaches for his shoulder, but he shrugs her off, rage blinding him.

"Archer," I say, my voice quiet. I clear my throat. "Archer."

His attention flickers to me, only for the briefest moment, but it's enough for Seven to buck his hips in just the right way to knock Archer off him and pin him under his body. Archer wriggles, but it's no use. Seven seized the moment and is now in control of the situation.

Seven wraps his hands around Archer's throat, squeezing tighter and tighter, my heart constricting with his grip. "I'll fucking *kill* you."

Archer gasps and pries at Seven's fingers but it's futile.

"Stop," Ivy yells into the chaos again. "Seven, stop!"

"Step back," Grace tells Ivy and me, her hands out to signal to us.

I clutch my chest, unsure of what's going to happen, what she's going to do.

She looks around, latching onto the chair she was once sitting in, and picks it up. For a second, she struggles, but then this strange calm washes over her. Grace draws back, chair in her grip, and drives it sideways and forward, crashing it over Seven's back. Wood splinters, chair legs go flying, and Seven goes still and then falls to the ground as Archer gasps.

I'm on my knees in a flash, my hands finding Archer's cheeks. "Are you okay?"

He blinks up at me and coughs, blood sputtering out. "I'm good," he croaks. Archer lies there for a long moment and looks from Grace, who holds the remains of the chair in her hands, to Seven, who's unconscious next to him. "Good job."

Archer takes Ivy's arm and she helps hoist him to his feet. He runs his palm over his face, flinching and flexing his jaw.

"You okay?" she asks him, her face pinched with concern.

"I'm fine." Archer sucks in a breath. "This place, though, is a fucking disaster." He kicks Seven, nudging him onto his back. "Is he dead?"

Grace stoops and studies Seven seriously. "No, he's still breathing."

Archer reaches for Seven's hands, moving them and hooking his arms up under Seven's armpits. "Grab his feet," he tells Ivy. "Help me move him."

Ivy complies without question, taking Seven's ankles into her hands and wiggling forward to get a more solid handle on him. "Why is he so heavy?" she mumbles.

The two of them scoot their way closer to the door but Ivy loses her hold twice.

"Never mind," Archer huffs. "I'll just..." He hoists Seven's large but semi-lifeless body onto his shoulder with a grunt. "Get the door for me."

Ivy rushes over, opens the door, and disappears through it with her two brothers.

"What the fuck," I mutter into the eerily quiet space.

"Where's the dustpan?" Grace says out of nowhere.

"What?"

"We need to clean this up." She points to the mess. "We can't leave it like this." She goes straight into the kitchen, dropping the remains of the chair into the trash, and looks through cabinets until she finds what she's looking for, then goes to work doing exactly what she said.

"Grace," I say. "Are you okay?"

She turns to me. "Are you crazy?"

"Are you?" I pause and then add, "Why did you give him your number?"

"You have no idea who they are, do you?"

CHAPTER FOURTEEN

Archer

"Are you sure you're okay?" Ivy asks me, her face scrunching up as she examines mine.

"Yeah. I'm sure." Nothing a cold shower and a few days of licking my wounds won't fix. I've been worse off and recovered, we both know that.

She seems to buy my answer, not pressing on my injuries or what just happened any more. "What's the deal with you two?" Ivy says to me from the entrance of my apartment building.

"Nothing." I cross my arms and do everything I can not to go back down to his car and stab my brother for being a dick to London and her friend. Why London decided to test him, I'll never know.

"You're lying."

"I am not."

"Why is she staying in your apartment, Archer?"

I take a breath in. How much should I tell her? What information does she need to know? If I give her something, maybe it will shut her up and get her to let it go.

"What's his deal lately, anyway?" I try to divert things back to Seven because then maybe she'll forget her train of thought.

"He seriously needs to get it together," Ivy tells me. "It's embarrassing." She barely pauses before ripping right back into me. "But don't try to change the subject. I need to know what's going on, right now."

"Keep it down." I step toward her. "Nothing is going on. A friend asked me to keep an eye on her and keep her safe for a little while. It's temporary, Ivy, nothing to worry about."

"I'm not worried, I'm just confused. You hate people. You

barely speak to us. It's insulting you're letting some stranger crash when you can't even show up to family dinner."

"I know, I'm sorry."

"I'm so fucking sick of hearing you say sorry. I need actions, not some weak-ass apologies." Ivy's face softens. "I get it, Arch, you've been through a lot. But we all have. We've all lost someone close to us. We can't lose you, too."

"You're not going to lose me."

She tilts her head. "Then why does it feel like I already have?"

"She means nothing to me, Ivy. This is all a means to an end. I'm doing Silver a favor, okay? I'm simply paying a debt." I don't add that the last part is a lie. I fulfilled my debt to Silver when I hacked into The Manor's impenetrable security. My hands were clean of him and honestly, he's lucky I even allowed him to ask me something so fucking foolish. But a debt is a debt, and I owed him a favor. Now, he owes me one, one that I never asked for, one that has done nothing but wreak havoc on my life from the second she stepped foot on my doorstep. "Soon enough I'll get rid of her, and we'll put this all behind us. But until then, she's going to be here, okay?"

"You promise?" Ivy looks up at me, her saddened eyes tearing at my heart. She's desperate to fix the cracks in our broken family, but I don't know how much more we can take before things fall completely apart.

"And wait, Silver? Seriously? I thought you were *done,* Arch?"

"I'm trying to be. It's not my fault no one will respect my wishes."

"I know it's hard with how things are. We're trying to legitimize all of August's affairs...but it's hard. There are too many threads tying everything together. The entire empire was founded with..." She trails off, not finishing her sentence, but both of us know what she's referring to.

August saved us, but in order to do so, he had to hustle in any way he could, doing the unspeakable to gain enough to get us out.

"It's especially hard when Seven is the way he is," she continues. "God, it's like every time I put out one fire, he's set a dozen more things ablaze." She shakes her head. "I love him, but I hate him so much."

"Don't worry about the August stuff for me." I put my hand on her shoulder, realizing how bloody it is. "I don't mind managing the finances. I get it. That shit doesn't bother me. It's having to deal with the face-to-face, talking to people, being reminded of..."

"I know," Ivy says. "I wish I could make that happen. I'm trying."

"I should get up there before the blood sets into the rug." And before London decides to get on my computer and poke around it with Grace. I've never left her alone in there for this long, at least not while she was awake. Usually, I slip out when she's sleeping and has no idea I'm not there.

"Sorry about your apartment. I wouldn't have brought him here if I knew he'd act like that."

"It's Seven. We should always expect the unexpected with him."

"Are you ever going to forgive him?"

"Do you think I should?" I ask her, an honest question.

"Probably not." Ivy leans in for a hug. "That girl has a crush on you."

"No, she doesn't, you're just being an overprotective sister."

Ivy releases me but keeps her hands on my shoulders. "Archer. You are a dumb boy. I'm telling you, she has a crush on you. I know these things. And you must have one back because you just beat the shit out of your brother for her."

"I would have beat the shit out of Seven for anyone."

"Touché."

"I don't have a crush on her," I confirm. "I can't stand London.

And I can't wait until she moves out. She's a disaster. She never stops yapping and she can't even pick up after herself. I know toddlers with better habits than her. She's a spoiled brat."

"Okay, okay." Ivy throws her arms up. "Whatever you say."

"She's like a tornado," I mutter so quietly, I'm not sure Ivy can make it out. "Anyway. Be safe. You sure you don't want me to call a driver?"

Ivy dangles the keys to Seven's Rolls-Royce between us, a smirk on her face. "And miss the chance to drive his baby?"

"He's going to kill you."

"Nah…I'm the only person Seven would never hurt." Ivy jogs down the stairs and disappears from sight as I punch the access code into my building and dart inside, the ache in my face settling in now that the adrenaline of the situation has started to wear off.

I make my way through the front door, stopping in my tracks when I find most of the mess that Seven and I caused missing. Grace and London kneel at the rug, scrubbing at it furiously. I chew at the inside of my lip, knowing damn well they're probably ensuring the stain is setting in.

But when I approach, I'm even more surprised by most of it being gone.

Grace meets my gaze. "Vinegar and water. Always works like a charm."

"Where'd you learn that trick?" I ask her.

"I'm a woman, we're accustomed to blood getting on things." But there's something concealed in her reasoning that feels like it isn't the whole truth. "Whoa. Check out your face."

London glances over at me, her expression unreadable, unfazed, as if she's bored by my face. She averts her attention to the stain, scrubbing it with a dash more elbow grease. She doesn't say anything, and despite only knowing her a week, it seems very uncharacteristic of her.

"That bad?" I say, raising my fingers to graze over the sensitive flesh. "It probably looks worse than it is." I point to the mess they've managed well, something I didn't think London was capable of doing. "Thanks for that, by the way."

"No problem." Grace finishes her spot and stands. "I totally broke your chair, though, my apologies."

I rub my neck and let out a nervous laugh. "I should probably be thanking you. Seven may have made true to his promise if you hadn't."

London huffs, shoves off the ground to stand, and marches off, tossing the rag she was holding onto the kitchen counter on her way out of the room. She goes into the bedroom and slams the door.

"That ought to be fun dealing with." I cross my arms, catching sight of the blood all over me. "Listen, I should get a shower."

"Oh, yeah, for sure." Grace awkwardly gives me the rag she was cleaning with. "Here's this. Sorry again about the chair."

I walk her to the door. "I'm sorry for my brother, he's kind of an asshole."

Grace chuckles. "Think so?"

"I think you're the first woman to not immediately fall for his charms."

"You call what he did charming?"

"You'd be surprised what kind of shit Seven can get away with and then still get the girl."

"Well, don't worry, I'm immune to Seven's *charms*."

"Never say never," I tell her, but secretly hope that she's right. Seven could use someone like Grace to balance him out, but he'd corrupt her before she even got a chance, and she seems like a pretty nice woman who deserves better than him.

"Thanks for the Chinese, though." Grace gives me a sweet smile and slips out the door.

I lean against the door, my back to it, my head resting on it.

"What a shit show." I scan the room, searching for anything out of place that needs to be put back. The food remains on the table, a breeding ground for bacteria at this point. I'll need to go over the rug again to make sure the girls did a good job removing the blood, and go over the floor, too, both with stain remover and disinfectants.

My cheek throbs, the entirety of my face no doubt swelling up with each passing second. I should ice it to control the swelling and minimize any long-term damage, along with popping a few anti-inflammatories just in case.

When did I get that table? Will I be able to order another chair? Or will I have to live with an uneven number? I guess I could throw the whole thing out and order a brand-new set. The idea of Seven's blood somehow getting overlooked and existing on something I eat on grosses me out more than I care to admit.

I should tidy up and then shower, that way I can properly clean any of his remains off me prior to tending to my own wounds.

And then there's the matter of whatever the fuck London is upset about. Maybe she gets uneasy around violence, especially considering what happened to her recently. I must remind myself that not everyone grew up the way we did, so a fight like that isn't normal and is cause for alarm.

Do I comfort her? Do I leave her alone?

"One thing at a time, Archer," I whisper to myself, and get to work.

It doesn't take me long to go over the mess we made, considering Grace and London made a lot of progress while I was tossing Seven's body into the back seat of his Rolls-Royce. He can worry about the stains in his seats himself, that isn't my problem.

I toss all the food in the trash, take the bag out, and throw it into the garbage chute. I go over the table three times—once to do a general sweep, another to clean it, and one to disinfect it.

My shower water is murky as the remnants of my fight with

Seven get washed down the drain. I scrub at my hand, massaging the soreness of my knuckles, and recall the blows against his head. I was so fucking angry. I still am. Seven had no right acting like that. He's an arrogant asshole who has no limits. I'm his family, and somehow that doesn't matter. Although I wasn't exactly holding back either.

Taking a look in the mirror at my battered face, I tuck the towel around my waist. I scan my features, not alarmed by the swelling, having seen my face like this a million times before.

It's then that I realize I didn't bring any clothes with me, and London has shut herself in the bedroom. I guess I can't put off confronting her forever.

With a sigh, I exit the bathroom and make my way over, knocking lightly on the door.

"Go away," London calls out.

"I need some clothes," I tell her, the truth.

She grunts, and a long second later, opens the door, stepping back to let me in.

I go over to my dresser and pull out a pair of boxers. "I'm going to put these on now," I warn her, and drop my towel.

"Fuck, Archer." She shields her eyes and turns her back.

"Do you want to talk about what happened?" I ask her, and look for a pair of gray sweatpants.

"Not really. Do you?"

"Not really," I confess. My brother and I got into a fight, it's not a big deal, but that doesn't mean it isn't to her. "I'm sorry you had to see that," I add.

London drops her hands and glares at me. "That's what you think I'm mad about? The fight? I don't give a shit about you and your brother arguing. I mean, he almost killed you, and that was pretty fucked up, but I'm not mad about that."

I stop what I'm doing and face her. "Wait, this is you *mad*? I don't understand."

"Of course you don't, you're a dumb boy."

I stare at her, trying to understand what the fuck she's getting at.

"You're such an asshole, you know that?"

I run my sore hand through my hair. "I'm confused. How am I an asshole? I got into a fight with my brother because of you."

London crosses her arms over her chest. "I'm sure you would have fought him for anyone, seemed like you were just looking for a reason."

"What the fuck are you talking about? Did you not provoke him? Or am I totally losing it?"

"Your brother is an asshole, too."

"I mean, there's no denying that."

"You really don't get it, do you?" she asks me, her tone serious.

"I don't. Can you spell it out for me?"

"I don't know, Archer. Can I? Or am I dumber than a toddler, too?"

I blink at her a few times, piecing together what it is that she is and isn't saying.

"Or maybe I'm just a means to an end, a favor you never wanted, a disaster even? Or better yet..." London takes a step forward, the space between us shrinking and expanding all at the same time, the tension growing thicker by the second. "Maybe I'm just a spoiled brat."

Everything clicks into place—London isn't mad about the fight, she somehow overheard the conversation I had with Ivy out on the front steps.

"You eavesdropped? How?" I ask her, not sure why my brain is choosing to focus on that tiny detail.

"That's the angle you're going with, big boy? You're mad that I heard you say some shit you wouldn't say to my face? Just admit it, Archer, you can't wait until I move out. Say it to my face." She inches toward me, her face tightened with anger.

I move closer to her. "You *are* a spoiled brat! Is that what you want to hear? It's not a lie, London."

"You are such an asshole!" London pokes her tiny finger into my chest. "I can't stand you."

"Great," I tell her. "I can't stand you either."

But in the time we've been bickering, we've somehow come closer and closer, until our bodies are almost touching, a hairsbreadth between us.

She tilts her head up at me, anger lining every word she speaks. "I hate you so much, you know that?"

"Good, I hate you, too."

"Good," she snaps back at me. "Then we agree."

"Finally, we agree on something."

I tower over her, our bodies swaying like magnets avoiding each other, the push and pull threatening to tear us apart. But instead, without even fucking thinking it through, my hand cups the small of her neck, my thumb next to her ear, my mouth pressed onto hers.

London doesn't hesitate, she kisses me back, her lips frantic and eager. Our tongues meet, dancing together like they're the only things keeping each other alive. Her hands wrap around my bare torso, her skin fire against mine.

My cock throbs, my heart sputters, and I want nothing more than to throw her onto the bed and rip her clothes off, savoring every inch of her and making her climax so hard, she regrets ever talking back to me.

She presses against me, and I drag my fingers along the base of her head, grabbing a fistful of her hair and tugging firmly. London moans into my mouth and I nearly come undone. But the second my arm grazes against the cast on hers, I come to my senses, releasing her immediately.

London stands there, panting, her arms outreached, still

lingering on my body. "Fuck," she whispers.

"That..." I swallow harshly, the burning remains of her mouth on mine replaying over and over in my head. "That was a mistake. I shouldn't have..."

London drops her arms, recoiling into herself as she takes a step back. "Yeah, you're right." She pats down her hair and wipes at her lips. "That was stupid." Her gaze trails my body, no doubt noticing the bulge in my boxers. "That can never happen again."

"Never," I repeat, my head knowing damn well that she's right, my cock not so much in agreement.

London and I would never work. We're like fire and air, the two of us resulting in nothing but an explosion that would ruin us both. Not to mention it would make our living arrangement hell. Everything she does drives me insane, and I'm certain she feels the same way.

"Your boner is telling me otherwise," London says, that familiar sarcastic tone of hers returning.

I adjust my dick and turn my back, going to my dresser and locating the sweatpants I was searching for to begin with. "I just kissed a hot girl, what do you expect?"

"You think I'm hot?"

"Don't get any ideas," I tell her, and slide into the sweatpants, adjusting the waistband. "This would never work."

"Because of your face." London leans against the wall, her gaze glued to me.

"What's wrong with my face?"

"Have you looked in a mirror? You look like shit."

"You looked like shit a week ago." I eye the entrance of my bedroom and wish I could slip through it to be alone with my thoughts.

"Wow, rude much?" She pauses, then adds, "I'm still mad at you, by the way."

"What's new?" I hold my breath and walk by her, not releasing it until I'm on the other side.

I wasn't lying when I said kissing her was a mistake and that it can never happen again, but it's going to take a minute for the rest of me to catch up to that unfortunate reality.

CHAPTER FIFTEEN

London

"What do you mean, you two kissed?" Grace says louder than I'd prefer her to. "Give me every juicy detail."

"A girl doesn't kiss and tell." I play coy and sip my latte, returning it to the table in the coffee shop and pretending like I'm not going to tell her everything.

It's been two days since that wild evening with Archer's family, and my lips have never felt lonelier. It would be cliché to say it was the best kiss of my entire life, but I'd be lying if I said it wasn't.

I can't stand Archer, but something about it makes me want him more. How can something so wrong feel so right?

"You just told me you kissed!" Grace shoves me playfully. "Now, spill."

"I confronted him about the conversation between him and Ivy."

Grace gasps. "You didn't?"

I nod. "Yep. Well, kind of. I mean, I made it clear I knew. Brought up all the highlights."

"Shit, London, I'm sorry." She winces and fidgets with her coffee. "Then what happened?"

"We were standing there in his bedroom; he had just gotten out of the shower. He still had little water droplets all over him, and he came strutting in with only a towel *barely* wrapped around his waist." I get lost in the mental image for an embarrassing second. "Anyway, we started arguing, each one of us somehow getting closer to the other with every single jab, and the next thing I know, Archer's got his tongue down my throat and we're making out."

Grace's hazel eyes go wide. "Oh. My. God. That's so hot. He was practically naked."

"I mean, he was for a minute."

She shakes her head and holds her hand out. "Excuse me, what?"

"Right, yeah, I forgot that part. He went to his dresser to get clothes and dropped his towel right in front of me."

"Did you see it?"

"No. But he has a nice ass." I take another drink of my coffee and hide my smile from watching Grace lose her mind. "He changed into boxers, then we fought. Yeah, that's the order. But get this, afterward he put on gray sweatpants."

"No," is all Grace says.

"Yep. Like, come on, man, you're already a six-foot-something tattooed, chiseled god, you don't need the sweatpants too."

Grace chuckles and leans back. "Wow. And I mean, wow." But then she bends at the hip and moves closer. "What does this mean? Are you two going to become something? Hook up? Date? Get married and live happily ever after?"

"Immediately no," I say the same words that she said to Seven when he tried hitting on her. "Archer and I couldn't be further from alike. I'm not kidding when I say I can't stand him. He's hot, there's no denying that, but he's an asshole. Plus, I'm still not over him saying all that shit about me. He didn't even apologize." And now that I think about it, he confirmed the comments when we were fighting.

Grace smiles politely at an older man who walks by and returns her attention to me. "Yeah, that was kind of fucked up. Maybe he was heated from his fight with Seven." She shrugs. "Maybe give him the benefit of the doubt."

"No, absolutely no way. Plus, we both agreed it was a mistake. That can't happen ever again. I don't want to complicate things anyway."

"I guess that makes sense."

"What about you, though? Are you going to entertain Seven?"

Grace laughs abruptly. "Immediately no." She reaches into her purse and pulls out her phone, poking a few buttons and showing me the screen. "Look at this."

It's a text thread with Seven, except he's the only one talking.

SEVEN

Did you hit me with a chair?

SEVEN

That was fucked up.

SEVEN

It really hurt.

SEVEN

You could kiss it better.

SEVEN

Do you want to fuck about it?

SEVEN

I'll let you hit me with a chair again...

SEVEN

If that's what you're into.

I scroll to the bottom. "Wow, he's down bad."

"He's going to have to get over it." Grace drops her phone into her bag. "He's vile."

"He's kind of hot, though," I admit. "In a psychotic way."

"He's not terrible-looking, but you think you and Archer are opposites?" Grace motions to her body. "Miss Prim and Proper, a senator's daughter who spends her time planning charity events, and him, doing God only knows. He's the textbook definition of trouble."

“Could be fun,” I say over the top of my mug. “You could use a little danger in your life.”

“No. I refuse to deal with another shitty man.”

“I respect that,” I tell her, and recall the events of that night. Seven was a drunken idiot making passes at Grace every chance he got. Archer was tense and withdrawn, typical. Ivy was guarded but curious, her every response toying with the truth she was willing to give. August was polished and put together and it felt like he didn’t want to be there, something that seemed to bother Ivy even though she tried to not show it. But Leo...

“Leo was kind of cute,” Grace says at the same time I’m thinking about him.

“He was, wasn’t he?” It just wasn’t as glaringly obvious as the rest of the guys. Leo was calmer, more even-tempered, and a bit unbothered by everything going on. He was wearing designer clothes from head to toe, his appearance well-thought-out and put together, but not like August was. August had a dapper vibe about him, and Leo was giving a more casual, sophisticated look.

“I didn’t notice it until now.” Grace taps her finger to her mouth. “Maybe Leo is the brother we should be after.”

I put my hands up. “Not it.” I’m familiar with the inner workings of a dysfunctional family, but I’d prefer not to get involved with another one. “You know Seven will murder him, right?”

“Could you ask Archer for his number for me? Actually...” Grace gets her phone again, furiously typing away and leaving me hanging. She smiles triumphantly and pokes one final button before signaling to me to be quiet and putting the phone to her ear. “Hey,” she says into the receiver. “It’s Grace, we met Sunday night at Archer’s place. I’d love to get together for coffee. When are you available?”

She stops talking, and I watch her assertiveness take hold.

“Great, yeah, that time tomorrow works for me. I can meet you there." Grace hangs up and sets her phone down. "And that's how it's done."

My eyes widen. "Did you really find and ask out Leo that quickly?"

"Like it was hard." Grace shrugs and grins, her bubbly personality almost contagious if not for everything that's happened to me.

I used to be like her, despite everything that I've lived through, but I find it particularly hard to pretend lately. The worst should be behind me, and somehow it feels like my father still has his claws stuck in me.

"No, but really, how did you find his number?" I ask her, wanting to learn her sleuthing ways.

"Leo owns Sin Casino. It only took a little digging to cross-reference documents and find his personal number. Easy-peasy."

"Casino owner...huh. I don't know what I expected, but it wasn't that."

"Right?" Grace downs the last of her coffee and checks her watch. "Listen, I should get going. Unless there are any other juicy details you left out."

"Not that I can think of." I stand and drink the rest of my latte, too. "But you need to update me on this Leo situation."

"Excuse me," a voice interrupts.

I scan until I lock eyes with a man, his face familiar, but I can't quite place him. My chest tightens. No one should be familiar. Not here. Not yet. Does he know who I am? Did I get so complacent that I forgot I'm supposed to be hiding out and starting over?

"Sorry," he says. "We never really officially met. The other night, in front of the apartment complex. I'm Drew." He extends his hand.

"Drew, hey." I shake his hand and it's not until I fully lock my eyes on him that I place him as the guy who let me into Archer's building over a week ago when I showed up that night. "Yeah, I remember you." My body takes a long moment to relax. The threat I thought was staring me in the face is actually a nice guy.

Grace reaches out to him. "Grace McCallister."

He shakes her hand too. "Drew Kingsley, pleasure is all mine." Drew focuses on me again. "I'm sorry, I don't think I caught your name."

"London," I offer, almost following it up with Gardella. But London Gardella died in California when her father was set on killing her for helping her friend. "London Smith."

"Beautiful name," he says, a polite smile on his handsome face. "I know this is probably too forward, but would you want to go out sometime? Get dinner with me? My treat, obviously."

My first reaction is to tell him no, to turn him down and walk out of here with my head held high. That's what the old London would have done. The old London was picky, and never dated—her dad wouldn't allow it.

We have to keep you pure, London girl.

No one will pay me top dollar for a whore.

You're worthless if not for what you can give with your body.

I'll kill any man that even looks at you.

And he held his word to that promise, my heart aching at the bloody memory I can't escape no matter how hard I try to push it aside.

"Yes," I find myself saying. "Are you available Thursday?"

Drew nods, a hair too enthusiastically. "Of course, yes. I'll let the firm know not to schedule any late meetings. Have you been to Rao's?"

"I haven't," I tell him.

Grace chimes in. "You have a table at Rao's?"

"What's so special about Rao's?" I ask them.

"Only people with VIP access can get in. It's passed down from generation to generation. Getting a table is impossible unless you know someone with one. Plus, I mean, it's on the river."

"What do you say?" Drew ignores Grace and doesn't take his eyes off me. "Dinner at Rao's Thursday?"

"Sure, sounds great."

"Don't sound so enthused, London," Grace teases.

"Oh." I perk right up. "Sorry, I was thinking about what I'm going to wear." The dress at Charlotte's comes to mind, but there's no way I can afford it on such short notice, and since Archer called me a spoiled brat, I don't think I'll be using his black card to pay for it.

"I'm sure I have something you can borrow," Grace suggests.

"What? No," Drew chimes in. "Let's go shopping." He tilts his expensive watch face toward him. "I have about forty-five minutes to spare. I think there are a few shops around here. What do you say?"

I look at him, unsure of what angle he's playing here. He doesn't know me, we met briefly, and I mean so briefly, I'm surprised he recognized me in the daylight.

"My treat," he adds. "Really. I mean, I'm asking *you* out, the least I could do is make sure everything is taken care of."

"Damn," Grace mutters with a grin. "You two have fun. I've got to go."

"It was so great to meet you," Drew says to her.

Grace makes her way to the door, motioning with her hand and mouthing for me to call her later.

"What do you say?" Drew asks once we're alone in this coffee shop full of people.

"What the hell"—I snatch my bag off the table—"why not?"

Drew smiles, and it's so strangely wholesome. He guides me out, his hand on my lower back even as he opens the door. Once we're outside, he sticks his elbow out for me to hold on to. He's so fucking formal and chivalrous, and I should be swooning, but I don't feel anything at all.

"How's your day going?" he says to me while we walk down the sidewalk together.

"Oh, um, pretty well, thank you. What about you?"

"Better now." Drew winks at me and points ahead. "What about in there?"

The shop where the girls were bitches to me. A perfect place to walk into with a hot guy on my arm and his credit card prepped to get me whatever I want.

"Yeah, that works."

My chest flutters at the idea of showing him off, but then I remember the comment Archer made about me being a spoiled brat.

So what, maybe I am. At least I'm not a grumpy asshole.

"After you," Drew tells me, holding the door open. He follows me in, the store clerks flocking toward us without giving us time to even look around.

"Can I help you find anything today?" the blonde says to him, her eyelashes fluttering more than a normal rate. She doesn't take her eyes off him long enough to realize I'm the same girl from before. But I sure do recognize her.

"We need something for dinner," he tells her, and glances down at me. "A dress, perhaps? Or whatever you're more comfortable in."

"A dress, yes," I confirm. "Long, though." I make a quick gesture to my casted leg.

"Formal? Casual?" The woman finally meets my gaze, her breath catching. She coughs. "Excuse me, I'm so sorry. Had something stuck in my throat." Her eyes water and her cheeks redden, and I can't contain the happiness that floats through me. It's pure fucking joy to witness her stumble over her words.

"We're going to Rao's," he tells her. "So maybe something with a sleek elegance to it, but not too formal."

"I have just the thing." She points toward the back of the shop. "If you'll just follow me."

We do, his hand on my back as I focus on not stumbling over my own feet. This cast is not easy to walk in, especially with the lopsided height difference with my shoes.

"What happened, by the way?" Drew whispers on our way over. "I mean, you don't have to tell me if you don't want to."

"I'm clumsy," I lie. "Silly little accident."

"Are you okay?" he asks, genuine concern lining his question.

"Oh, I'm fine. Nothing to worry about. I should have these off in a couple of weeks." I hold out my arm and remember I still need to find a doctor around here who will see me and not drill me about information. How much do doctor visits cost?

"When dinner goes well, we'll have to plan something for when they're off. Maybe we can go dancing."

I tilt my head toward him. "Counting on it going well, are we?"

"A guy can hope, right?"

"What about this?" The clerk interrupts us to show off a pale-yellow long dress.

At first glance, it's pretty, but she and I both know damn well that redheads don't look good in pale colors. This bitch is trying to sabotage my outfit and still get a commission.

"Beautiful," Drew says, nothing wrong with his remark.

"How about something with a richer color?" I suggest, my tone neutral even though I'm considering strangling her with the straps of the yellow dress.

"We have this pink one over here." She strolls over to another soft palette dress, and I imagine fashioning the hanger into a point and stabbing her in the eye with it.

"Do you know anything about fashion?" I ask her.

"Excuse me?" she snaps back.

I want to explain to her that the colors she's picking out will do nothing but wash me out in the most unflattering way, to educate her on deeper colors, like dark green or browns. Hell, even a bubblegum pink would be better than the one she's trying to convince me of.

"How about this one?" I break off from Drew and trace my fingers along the delicate fabric of a dark purple dress, so dark it almost looks black. In the right light, it's a stunning shade of aubergine.

"Try it on," Drew encourages.

"Let me get that for you." The clerk cuts in front of me, snatching the hanger off the rack and turning toward the fitting rooms. "If you'll follow me."

Drew settles into a cozy chair in the back and waits patiently as I slip into one of the fitting rooms and start taking my clothes off. I suppress a curse when my top gets stuck on my cast and try not to get frustrated when it happens to my jeans too.

The dress manages to cover my leg well, concealing it so you can't even tell I'm hiding anything underneath. My wrist is another thing, but unless I opt for a long-sleeved thing, I'm screwed. I'll have to make do with what I can.

The tag catches my eye and I reach for it, suppressing a gasp at the twelve-hundred-dollar price. I can't expect this stranger to spend that much money, can I? I mean, Archer bought me two designer bags, a pair of shoes, and a cell phone, and we'd only known each other a week. Surely I could be okay with a dress.

I step out of the room and walk toward Drew, his eyes lighting up and sparkling bright.

"Wow," is all he says.

I do a spin, careful not to fall and hurt myself any more. "It might be a bit much," I tell him, not quite mentioning the hefty price tag.

"It's perfect...you're perfect." Drew stands, getting the attention of the clerk who's gossiping with another coworker. "We'll take this one, please." He slides her a silver credit card.

"You don't have to," I protest, despite very much wanting this dress. It's gorgeous, and I haven't felt this pretty since *before*.

"I insist." He swivels his finger in the air. "Do you want shoes? Accessories? Anything else?"

"No, I have shoes that would go great with this." The ones I picked up from Charlotte's.

Drew doesn't bat an eye when the clerk brings him the card reader and finalizes the transaction. He taps the card on the receiver and returns it to his money clip.

I slip back into the dressing room, letting the dress slide off my shoulders and onto the floor. I hang it up, catching a glimpse of myself in the mirror. The poor lighting casts the worst shadows on my already not-so-great appearance, deepening the shades of faded purple and green covering me. I place my hand gently on my ribs, wincing at the soreness that's still present. My gaze trails over the jagged scar on my stomach and the memory comes flooding back in.

It was a hot afternoon, and my father had been toying with his favorite pet. That*'s what he called the girls that came to and from our house, and one of them was supposed to bear him a child—a son. Having a daughter was pointless, he said. He needed an heir. Someone to carry on the family name. Someone who wouldn't disgrace him.*

Of course, he couldn't get a wife of his own, so he bribed and bargained for women who might be fertile enough to provide him with a baby. It was disgusting and repulsive, but there wasn't anything I could do about it. I spoke up a few times, questioning why he did what he did, but my words were met with his abuse, so I learned if I wanted to stay alive, I had to accept, or at the very least turn a blind eye, to his antics.

I always hated him; I don't ever remember a time when I didn't. And somehow, that hatred grew with each passing day. I fantasized about killing him, torturing him, even. I considered all the ways I could end his life—his threats making damn sure I never did.

He hurt me, sometimes when I didn't do anything to provoke it. He was like that, unpredictable and volatile, and after a while, I realized I had to just stay out of his way.

I felt bad for the girls that came into our house, some of them barely legal. In the beginning, I tried to help them, to come up with elaborate plans to spike his drinks when I knew he'd be having them over in an attempt to subdue his abuse. His wrath was inevitable, but I figured if I could help take the edge off, maybe it wouldn't be so bad.

He was no fool, though, and he quickly figured out what I was up to, beating me until I was unconscious time after time.

I stopped helping them for a while, staring straight ahead when his pets came into the house. It killed me in a way he could never manage.

It wasn't until one of them directly came to me that I snapped back to reality.

Madison was her name. She was beautiful, as were all of them, her eyes dimming each day that passed in his presence. Over a few weeks, we spoke in hushed whispers throughout the house, coming up with a code to exchange ideas and come up with a plan. If I couldn't save myself, maybe I could save her. I had to hope things weren't completely hopeless.

My father was a sick man, dragging out the torment in a slow and cruel kind of way. He was tracking her cycle, too, waiting for the time to finally plant his wretched seed.

The goal was to put extra sleeping medication in his brandy and pray that he passed out before his plan would see its way through. We'd buy ourselves a few hours to make it look like things happened, and we'd figure out how to move forward.

But I didn't find out until much later that my paranoid father had bugged nearly everything I owned, giving him access to every private detail about my life.

So, when I casually tried to slip the medicine into his drink, he barged in, calling me out with his hand wrapped around my throat.

Madison begged him that she had nothing to do with it, throwing me completely under the bus.

My father grabbed the nearest sharp object, a corkscrew wine bottle opener, and drove it into my stomach.

I remember gasping for breath, my eyes wide, my mouth gaping. I couldn't believe it. He had hit me, punched me, kicked me, thrown me into things, but my father had never done something so...damaging.

I slid down the wall, my hands cupped around the thing sticking out of my stomach, blood pooling all around me, and watched him turn to Madison. At first, I thought he was going to fuck her right there, make me witness him defiling her, and in retrospect, that wouldn't have been the worst thing that could have happened.

Instead of that, my father fisted her hair and forcefully rammed her head against the wall.

She screamed, the sound burning into my memory so vividly, I could still hear her cries haunting me now, as I lay there, unmoving, unable to do anything other than suffer.

He ripped her shirt, exposing her breasts, and shoved her hard onto the floor of his study.

With great force, he kicked her in the gut, tossing her frail body more. Lazily, he waltzed over to the table next to his chair he smoked cigars and drank dark liquor on, and pulled out a revolver.

"Please, please, I'm so..." Madison cried out. "I'm sorry." She had found her hands, palming the floor and scooting back, unable to do much else other than inch away from him.

He flipped open the thing that held the bullets, my heart pounding harder with each passing second until he slammed it shut and pointed it at her.

"You are nothing more than a fucking common whore, you're a dime a dozen." His voice was thick and phlegmy, like he had something caught in his throat.

"I'm sorry," she spat out again, her gaze meeting mine this time.

I still wonder to this day if that last apology was meant for me, or if it was her attempt to forgive herself for her sins. I'll never know.

Because the next thing I knew the gun went off, the reverberation settling over me, my ears ringing. Her body thudded hard on the floor, red covering the space around her. Madison gurgled for a solid minute as my father watched, but he gave up halfway through, my sight never leaving her, not until he turned his fury on me.

He stepped around the blood coating the floor like it was spilled milk, careful not to get his loafers dirty. My father didn't even look at me bleeding out, slumped against the cabinet on his way over.

I sucked in a breath, everything numb and lit on fire at the same time, my hands still around the wine opener jammed in my stomach.

He rifled through his liquor cabinet, knocking things about in his search for something I'd soon discover. A knife, meant for cutting the lime wedges he sometimes used in cocktails.

My father knelt down, something that took him great effort, and ran his gaze over me. "You have disobeyed me for the last time, London girl." He clicked his tongue before latching on to the wine opener and yanking it out. "Now, I'm going to fucking gut you. Maybe then you'll realize the error of your ways."

He didn't even give me a chance to process his words before driving the knife in, my lungs letting out a blood-curdling scream. Everything turned white, my vision betraying me. Maybe I shouldn't see this anyway.

He dragged the blade along my flesh like a child coloring outside the lines, tearing me open wider, and I screamed, wanting it to stop, wanting it all to stop.

I'd never wanted death more than I had in that moment.

But for the life of me, I couldn't give up, not yet. I don't know why I did it, I don't know why I didn't let him finish me for good right there, because living another day under his thumb would be reliving this day over and over.

Still, I was weak, and I couldn't take any more of the pain, I couldn't fathom the idea that this was the way I would die. I had barely lived, why did he get to take that away from me?

That was the day I learned to think like him—saying the only thing I could think of to save my life. "Sell me," I sputtered. "Sell me to someone," I begged. "I have to be worth more alive than dead."

This made him pause, my idea somehow intriguing him enough to think about it.

He thought long and hard, so long I started to black out from the pain, but I clung to that silence, hoping like hell it might mean something other than my demise.

And so, he removed his hand from the knife, brought himself to his feet, and towered over me. "If you live, I'll consider it."

He spat on the floor and left me there, somehow with a sense of thankfulness that he chose the floor instead of me.

I wasn't sure if I'd have the strength to overcome what he did to me that day, but I wore that scar as a constant reminder that nothing could ever hurt me as much as he did.

I trace my fingers along the jagged edge and shiver the memory away, one I hate reliving but find myself facing every time I look at my naked body. Once I'm dressed, I return to the clerk with the dress in my hand.

"I'll get that bagged up for you," she says.

I ignore the condescending tone in her voice and nod stiffly. "Sure."

"Everything okay?" Drew asks me, his hand resting on my back.

"Mm-hmm," I mumble, and shift away from him. He hasn't done anything wrong, but I find no comfort in his touch, and right now, all I desire is to be tucked away in Archer's room.

CHAPTER SIXTEEN

Archer

I cannot fucking believe London agreed to go on a date with that…that…scumbag.

Pacing in front of my computer, I keep glancing at the street cameras showing me London while she walks back to my apartment complex with Drew fucking Kingsley, Camille's older brother.

I can't stand him and his stupid pretty boy face.

Do I know much about him to justify this visceral response? Not really, but my gut feeling should count for something, and I don't like the dude.

She shouldn't be going out with him, and she shouldn't be allowing him to walk her home.

They pause at the entrance of the apartment building, and by the time I realize I don't have audio, they finish whatever they were saying, Drew taking London's hand in his to kiss the top of it.

"Fucking show-off," I mutter, and wait for her to come inside before I close out the footage and pull something else up. Only, I don't have it in me to play pretend, so I shut the screen off and make my way over to the door, opening it when London approaches.

She steps inside, not saying a word, the garment bag in her grasp.

"Did you use the credit card I gave you?" I ask her, knowing damn well she didn't.

"No."

"You used cash?"

"No." London kicks off her shoe and leaves it scattered on the floor, completely out of place.

"How did you pay for it, then?" I lock the door and wait for her to answer, my arms crossing over my chest.

"I'm not really in the mood, Archer. Can we fight about this some other time?"

"You just don't want to tell me," I press. "Why?"

She turns toward me, her eyes meeting mine, something hidden in her expression I can't quite place. "Because it's none of your fucking business, that's why."

"What the hell got into you?" I step closer. "Did something happen? Did he do something?"

London narrows her gaze. "Did *who* do *what*?"

"Drew," I blurt out.

"How did you know I was with Drew? Did you stalk me? How do you even know his name?"

"He's Camille's brother. I saw you out front. Don't be so full of yourself, I wouldn't stalk you. Now, I answered your questions, you answer mine."

"Drew bought it, okay? Are you happy?" London rolls her eyes so intensely that I swear they must have touched the back of her head.

"Why?" The word almost comes out of my mouth like a growl. I can barely recognize the strange sensation running through me.

"Why are you being such an asshole, Archer?" London lets out a breath. "I'm not in the mood."

"You kiss me and then let him buy you a dress?"

"Excuse me? *You* kissed me!"

"It was a mistake."

"I'm well fucking aware, Archer. And it won't happen again. Ever. Plus, you're a bad kisser anyway." London turns on her heel and storms away, slipping into my bedroom and slamming the door shut. A second later, she yanks the door open and pokes her head out. "I have a date with Drew on Thursday. You have two days to get over it and yourself." She closes herself back in, and when I glance down, both of my hands are balled into fists.

I fucking hate that she has this effect on me, and despite my better judgment, there doesn't seem to be anything I can do about it.

***

Two antagonizing days later, London spends far too much time getting ready in the bathroom.

We barely spoke the last forty-eight hours, each passing second adding to the wall building between us. It's strange being in this close proximity to someone but feeling so far away. I can't stand it, but it's partially my doing.

I should have never agreed to allow London to stay here in the first place, that mistake compiling on top of all the others.

I absolutely never should have kissed her—that was reckless of me, stupid, even. I couldn't help it, she was frustrating the hell out of me and the only rational thing my brain could come up with was to shut her up.

London steps out of the bathroom, my attention glued to the computer screen in front of me. I refuse to look at her, to witness whatever she spent hours on in the bathroom.

She clears her throat and makes her way to the table her purse is sitting on, her heel clicking against the floor.

When I don't acknowledge her, she continues to the door. "I'll be back later, don't wait up for me." London doesn't bother waiting for my response, not that I was going to give her one anyway, and leaves a second later.

I hurriedly start typing on my computer, pulling up the camera feed from outside my apartment complex where Drew is already waiting, a Jaguar parked out front that must belong to him.

I watch him watch her, his face lighting up the second she approaches. She gives him a soft smile, but even through the pixelated feed, I can tell it's not genuine.

They exchange a few words before he escorts her to the car, opening the back door for her and shutting it. He moves around to the other side, climbing in and no doubt telling his driver they can go. The car takes off and it dawns on me that I don't have access to their journey to the restaurant. As long as they stick to the plan, I've already gained access to Rao's and am fully prepared there, but until then, I'm in the dark.

Unless.

Fingers moving swiftly, I pull up London's cell phone information and see about hacking into the camera, turning the camera on to give me audio inside of the car. But my search is halted when I realize London has shut her phone off, my pulse picking up at having hit a dead end.

I'm going to have to accept that for a little while I won't know what's going on, even if it kills me a little inside.

I google Drew until I find his phone number and attempt to hack into his device, but the service is too unsteady to let me fully connect.

"Fuck." I slam my fist against the desk, my fingers still swollen from my fight with Seven.

I haven't spoken to him either, but that's how our family usually operates. We fight, we don't talk, and then we pretend like nothing happened. It's not the healthiest, but neither is our entire family dynamic.

The next forty minutes are agonizing as I dart from street cam to street cam and watch them crawl through traffic toward the restaurant.

I hate that I wasn't more prepared, but I didn't think this through, something that isn't like me at all. I'm always calculated and precise, always on top of the things that could go wrong and every variable that might pop up. But when it comes to London, my head gets jumbled and I make mistakes. I cannot afford to mess up, not again, not with her.

Switching the feed to the camera outside of Rao's, I hold my breath as Drew steps out of the car and comes around to open London's door. He holds out his hand, her dainty palm sliding into his. He guides her onto the sidewalk and toward the entrance of the restaurant.

London's dress fits her curves well, the delicate fabric hugging every inch of her in the right places, and somehow concealing the cast on her leg. She walks with ease, not alerting anyone that her leg is even injured.

My phone rings, stealing my attention, Leo's name across the screen. I click the green button and put it on speakerphone, my gaze returning to the computer.

"What do you need?" I ask him.

"Why do you assume I need something?"

"Because you never call me just to talk."

He clears his throat, hopefully signaling he's getting to the point of the call. "That deal with August and the Branford brothers."

"What about it?"

"Did it go through?"

"Why?"

"Inquiring minds want to know." He pauses. "Come on, Arch, you can tell me. I won't tell anyone."

"Why didn't you call August and ask him?"

"I did. He has his calls going through Ivy and she wouldn't say shit."

"Maybe that's for a reason."

"What did I do?"

"It's not what you did," I confess. "It's what you might do. You're hotheaded. You act on impulse. It's a sensitive deal, and August can't afford any chances."

"So it didn't go through, then...because you'd tell me if it did." Leo continues, "What don't I know? What's the holdup? What's got August's panties in such a bunch?"

"I have to get going, Leo, I'm in the middle of something."

"You making a move on London, is that it?" He chuckles. "Ivy doesn't trust her, you know?"

"Ivy doesn't trust anyone," I tell him, because it's the truth. I'm surprised she trusts us, and we've been there for each other through shit that no one should ever have to go through.

London walks through the restaurant, Drew's hand on her lower back, his body entirely too close to hers. I wait until she's seated and contemplate my next move. It's not that I don't want her to have a good time, I just don't want it to happen with *him*.

"Come on, Brother. I promise I won't act on it. Tell me what's going on, I won't take no for an answer."

I consider my options—I could easily hang up on Leo, but his persistent ass would keep calling, and then no doubt show up to my apartment and ruin any chance I have of keeping an eye on London. But if I tell him, I'd be going against my family's wishes and potentially ruin the deal they're working on. Something is getting ruined either way. There's a chance he keeps his word and his mouth shut, though, and that's a gamble I'm going to have to take.

"The Manor brothers," I confess. Our rivals, our biggest enemies, the bane to our fucking existence. They hate us, we hate them, it's a vicious cycle of who can fuck over who worst and, in this case, they're trying to get in the way of the deal we're trying to make with the Branford brothers.

It should have been simple, completely easy-breezy. We offered them a handsome rate for their side of town, and in exchange, our territory would expand, giving us a stronger foothold in the East Coast sector. They've lost their asses the last few years while Johnny Jones has expanded into their area, but with our backing, we could push out what he's trying to infringe on.

"You're telling me the Manor brothers are trying to sweep in and take the Branfords?" Leo's voice thickens with anger and I start to regret my decision to tell him the truth.

"Are you surprised? They've been trying to regain what we took from them years ago."

London says something to the waiter but I can't make it out because of having to mute her screen.

"I have to do something about this. *We* have to. Come on, Arch, you're not going to let them get away with this, are you?"

"When are you going to realize that I'm not the knocking-heads type anymore, Leo? I'm done. This is as involved as I'm going to be, and if I'm honest, it's too much."

"You're going to let them walk all over our family name like that? Where's the Archer I used to know? The one that would fight for his family. The old Archer would have threatened their family, at the very least, if not put a bullet in one of their foreheads to prove a point."

"I would not have killed a Manor brother, Leo. You're out of your mind. That would be like them killing one of us. Have you forgotten the treaty?"

The treaty was put into place many, many years ago after a long-running feud between our family and the Manors. The eldest brothers got together, August and Reid, and came to an understanding, a written one, one signed in blood, with the main point being that there would be no murder attempts on either family, by either family. A fistfight here or there was blurring the rules a little bit, but for the most part, we stuck to it, mutual respect forced by wanting to protect our families.

There were a few other stipulations, like properties would not be attacked, and any children born by any of us were also off-limits. But things like meddling with each other's business affairs were not off the table, and right now, they were fully trying to undercut and steal this deal out from under us.

"Who gives a shit about the treaty?" Leo blurts out.

I snatch my phone off the desk, bringing it closer to my mouth when I say, "This is why August doesn't trust you, Leo. You're arrogant, and that arrogance is going to get one of us killed. Don't you fucking remember why we started this? You may have been out partying with Seven, too fucking drunk to recall when our family was falling apart, but I was there, I remember, and it was August and I who had to dig us out of the hole you led us into."

"Geez, Arch, way to kick a man when he's down." Leo feigns hurt when I know damn well it's his ego taking the brunt of the damage. "You act like I don't care."

"Do you?" I ask him, a genuinely serious question. "Because I can't tell half the time, Leo. It seems like the only thing you care about is how many girls you can sleep with and how much money you can launder through that casino. Not to mention all the other shit you're doing through there. I heard about those diamonds that went missing. Wonder where I'd find them, Brother?"

"Where else do you expect me to launder money? You shut me out of the other places. You're being unreasonable, Archer. I'm doing this for the family, to build our empire, and what are you doing, sitting in your apartment all alone because you got your heart broken?"

"How fucking dare you." I hang up the phone, not wanting to hear another word of what he has to say. Does he not realize that I control most of our finances and if I wanted to shut him out, it would be as simple as pushing a single fucking button?

I release a sobering breath and return my attention to the screen, watching as Drew excuses himself from the table. With a few keystrokes, I pull up more camera footage and follow him to a deeper part of the restaurant where he pulls out his phone.

"Hey, baby," he says into the receiver. "Yeah, I miss you, too. I can't stop thinking about you." He goes quiet and I assume the other person fills in the silence. Drew glances in the direction he came from and continues. "We'll see each other soon enough, okay? I hate being away from you. I love you, don't forget that." He hangs up a second later and shakes the hand of a man who walks near him. "Sir, how's it going?"

"Ah, business is booming, my boy," the older man responds. "I appreciate your help with that...situation."

"Yes, of course. Happy to be of assistance. You let me know if there's anything else I can do for you."

"Well, since you're asking..." The man glances in both directions and leans in closer. "I've got this broad my nephew knocked up. She's threatening to tell his wife if he doesn't make things right."

"And what would you like me to do?" Drew asks him.

"Get rid of her."

"I see."

"Do we have an understanding?"

"Get me her information and I'll take care of it."

The way he says *it*, so nonchalantly like he isn't referring to a human being, a pregnant one, makes my jaw tense.

I dial London's number a second later, the dial tone skipping straight to voicemail.

"Fuck," I mutter, and run my hand through my hair. That's when my sight lands on the person sitting a couple of tables away from London, an old acquaintance of mine from my old life. I skim through my phone and locate his number, hitting Call as soon as I find it.

It rings, and rings, and I keep my eyes glued to the screen and hope I didn't get this wrong.

He picks up a second later. "Long time no see, pal."

"Do you see that redhead to your left about twenty feet?"

"What? No hello, how are you? I thought we were close, buddy."

"Unless you want me to expose every single escort you've hired to the local tabloids, I suggest you do exactly as I say."

"Shit, man, hang on, don't get so hasty." He turns around, scanning and locking his sight on London. "The hot one sitting by herself?"

"Choose your words carefully, Jack, otherwise they'll be your last."

"Fine, fine. What do you want me to do?"

"Go give her your phone."

"What?"

"Did I stutter?"

Jack gets up and approaches London, her head doing a double take as he gets right next to her. "You've got a call."

"Excuse me?" London says with great hesitation.

"Tell her who it is," I speak loud enough so he can hear me.

"Archer," London calls out, and snatches the phone from Jack. "What the fuck do you want?" Her voice is hushed.

"You need to get out of there, London. You don't know who you're on a date with."

"I don't know who I'm living with either, and that doesn't seem to stop me. Pretty sure my date is harmless, big boy." She smiles politely, if a bit falsely, at Jack.

"I'm warning you, London. I wouldn't joke about this. You need to go."

"I shut my phone off for a reason, Archer. Because I wanted to have a good evening. I think I deserve that, don't I? Why do you have to ruin this for me? What's wrong with you? And to bring some random stranger into this." She covers the speaker and says "No offense" to Jack.

He shrugs and takes a piece of bread from the basket on London's table and bites off a chunk.

"You need to listen to me," I try to make her understand. "He's not who you think he is."

"Yeah, well, neither are you, and neither am I. I'm a grown-ass woman. I can do what I want, Archer. Now, if you'll excuse me, I have a date to finish." She disconnects the line and gives Jack his phone back. "Sorry about that," she tells him.

"No worries, I understand how frustrating Archer can be." He nods stiffly at her. "Have a nice evening, miss."

"Thanks. You, too." London dusts off the wrinkles in her dress before returning to her seat, taking a quick glance around to no doubt see the damage caused by our conversation.

But luckily everyone seems so focused on themselves that they don't pay her much attention.

"God damn it, London," I gripe.

I skim the layout of the restaurant, do a search to pull up the schematics, and go to work doing what I do best—hacking.

It takes me two entire minutes to shut the electricity off, the entire place going dark except for the occasional cell phone someone is staring at. A dozen patrons let out a collective gasp, and I can barely hide the triumphant smile on my face. But why stop there? I disconnect the phone lines, throw a signal blocker in place, and focus my attention on the street outside. If I can just...

With a final click of the Enter key, I send the traffic lights flashing, cars blaring their horns and locking up their brakes. "That ought to stall them." I move what I can over to my cell phone, putting the tracker of London's phone in one corner, and two video feeds split across the rest of the screen.

I rush to the front door, grabbing my keys off the table on the way out. Instead of going out the main entrance, I make my way to the parking garage below our building, rush straight toward my motorcycle, and shove the key into the ignition. The voice of my sister floats through my head and I reluctantly slide my head into my helmet before shifting into gear and launching myself out of the parking spot.

I dart through traffic, not stopping at a single red light or Stop sign. I go onto sidewalks, drive on the wrong side of the road, and cross one-ways in the wrong direction to get there as fast as my bike will take me. I accidentally clip a car's mirror, my arm taking the brunt of the hit, pain rippling through me. My back wheel comes off the ground as I skid to a stop to avoid hitting a woman pushing a stroller, and then once it returns to the pavement, the front wheel goes up as I speed away.

I push myself and the bike harder, faster, until my forearms ache from the force of the ride.

Except when I lock up my brakes in front of Rao's, I realize London's location has changed and she's now a block away from me. Revving the motor, I go back into action, zipping away from the chaos erupting outside of Rao's and following her trail.

I spot his stupid car up ahead and I blaze through the traffic between us to catch up to them. Making a fist, I bang on the back window and ride alongside the vehicle. I hit it harder and yell, "Open the fucking window."

The thing goes down a moment later, Drew sitting closest to me. "Can I help you?" he calls out to me.

"Pull over," I tell him.

He doesn't comply, he doesn't even entertain me—instead, he reaches for the button to roll the window up.

But I prepared for that, so I put my hand between the window and the frame as it starts to roll up, my hand getting smashed in the window but not before I start yanking it aggressively and buckling the entire window from its pane.

With one final tug, the window shatters, a shard of glass still in my fist. "I will ram this through your throat if you don't stop this car."

"Don't stop," London calls out. "Driver, keep going."

I accelerate and shoot ahead of the car, slamming on my brakes and stopping myself in front of the vehicle. If they want to keep going, they're going to have to kill me first.

Drew's car screeches to a halt and a moment later, both back doors open as horns blare from all around us.

London rushes over. "Are you out of your fucking mind?"

I hop off my bike and yank my helmet over my head with my free hand, the other still holding on to the glass, the sharpness slicing through my palm. "Put this on and get on the bike, London." I shove my helmet toward her, but she crosses her arms.

"What's the problem here?" Drew says as he approaches, his sight finally landing on me and realizing who I am. His expression shifts immediately. "I'm sorry, I didn't know it was you, Archer."

I step toward him, sirens blaring in the distance, and nudge the piece of glass into his torso. "If you ever so much as look at her again, I will fucking end you. Do you understand?"

He nods briskly and sweat glistens on his upper lip. "I do."

"You're just going to let him intimidate you?" London mouths off to Drew. "You fucking coward."

I drop the glass, no longer having any use for it, and move closer to London. Without her consent, I slide the helmet over her head, not giving her a chance to protest, and buckle the chin strap tightly.

"What the fuck, Archer? I'm not getting on that thing with you." She motions to her dress.

"You get on the bike willingly or I'll put you on the bike myself." I ignore the commotion around us, not giving a fuck about anyone or what they might think.

"I'm not getting on there. You can't make me." London keeps her arms crossed, her head bobbling with the oversized helmet.

"Fair enough." I scoop her into my arms with ease, turning to walk toward my bike.

"Archer!" she gasps, and pounds at my chest.

A second later, I hoist the two of us onto the seat. "Put your arms around my neck, little tornado." I position her small body in my lap, using my left hand to secure her legs over my leg. Her cast is awkward and bulky, but I make it work because I have to.

"This is fucking insane," London yells through the helmet.

"Shh," I tell her, and start the engine. Leaning forward, my torso presses against hers as I shift into gear and take off from this random street corner.

London remains quiet for the entirety of the ride back to our apartment complex, her grip around my neck tight and lasting. I make sure to stop at every red light and Stop sign and obey the speed limit. I don't care about breaking the law, but the way she's riding with me leaves too many opportunities for something to go wrong.

It isn't until I pull us into the parking garage and shut off the engine that London seems to come back to life.

"Get me off this death trap," she whines.

I lift her into my arms, hop off the bike, and carefully set her on the pavement, turning my attention to the bike and pulling the key out of the ignition.

"What the fuck, Archer, I can't get this stupid thing off." London fumbles with the strap at her neck and I can barely hide the smirk on my face watching her struggle. "What's so funny?"

"Stop." I flick her fingers out of the way, unhook the strap, and hoist the helmet over her head, leaving her red hair a complete mess. "There."

London shoves her hand into my shoulder, but I don't budge. "I can't even push you, you're like a fucking statue."

I return my helmet to the bike, lock it into place, and disregard her comment.

"This way," I tell her as I walk away, leaving her behind in the garage. I glance over my shoulder once to confirm she's coming, her face scrunched and her cheeks flushed.

"Are we not going to talk about what just happened?" London marches after me.

"Can we not do this right now?"

"Then when, Archer? I mean, what the fuck, you had to ruin my date, didn't you? But why? I want to know why."

I reach the stairs leading us into the building and turn around to face her. "Because your date wasn't worthy of you."

London stops abruptly, craning her neck to look up at me. "What is that supposed to mean?"

"Just trust me." I run my hand through my hair and wish like hell this entire situation would be over.

"No." She shakes her head and puts her hand on her hip. "I won't just *trust* you. I don't know you."

I let out a sigh and return on my journey into the stairway, London grabbing my arm once we're inside.

"Damn it, Archer. You're going to have to talk to me. Tell me what the fuck is going on. You can't be an asshole and get away with it. I deserve an explanation."

I pinch my brows, my back still to her. "Do you ever shut up?"

"Make me."

"What are you, a child?"

"No, I'm a grown-ass woman who's pissed off her birthday was ruined."

I tilt my head toward her, my resolve softening. "What?"

"Yeah. And all I wanted for my birthday was to have a nice dinner, and maybe get laid. Is that so much to ask for? Living with you is unbearable, sorry I wanted a release."

I snap around, caging her against the wall in one solid motion, my hands on both sides of her head. "You wanted to fuck him?"

London swallows and keeps her gaze on mine. "Does that matter?"

"You want a release? Is that what this is about?" My breath mingles with hers and my mind runs wild at the thoughts consuming it, my cock already aching in my pants. I shouldn't feel this way, I shouldn't think these thoughts, but I can't stop myself and I don't know if I'm even trying.

"Yes," she whispers.

I look into her eyes, mine darting back and forth between them. "And you don't care who it comes from?"

She shakes her head, her breath ragged.

Without allowing my brain to catch up with my dick, I crouch in front of her, my hands hovering along her legs. "Do I have your consent?"

London bites her lip. "What are you going to do?"

"Exactly what you want." I stare at her through my lashes, not daring to take this a single inch further until she gives me permission. I might find her to be the most frustrating person on the planet, but I would never touch her without her consent. "Do you want me to do that, little tornado?"

She nods, but that isn't enough for me.

"I want you to say it," I tell her.

"Yes, Archer," she pants. "Please."

I wish I were a better man, one that would be able to walk away from this, keep his composure and not get so fucking worked up during every interaction with her. But I am not a good man, and right now, all I can think about is what she must taste like.

Gripping the fabric of her dress, I rip the slit in the side and run my nose up her thigh and give my hands a chance to explore her soft skin.

London gasps and follows it with a moan, the sound going straight to my throbbing cock.

I reach her lace panties, run my thumbs under the dainty material, and growl when I feel how fucking wet she is already. I stop what I'm doing and tilt my head toward her. "That better be for me, not him."

"I...I promise," she whimpers, and runs her hands through my hair, tugging me toward her center. London steps apart, opening herself wider for me, an invitation I hate that I want in the first place.

I bring my face closer, breathing in her scent—so fucking sweet—and blowing hot air over her pussy. I kiss her through her panties and savor the taste of her seeping through the sheer fabric. Reaching up, I take both sides into my hands and slowly tug them down and over her legs. With the panties still in my hand, I skim the fabric over her thigh and across her center, teasing her before running the fabric over her entrance.

She moans and tilts her head back. "Please, Archer."

I shove a finger inside of her, the panties wrapped around it, and fuck her with it.

London whimpers and tightens around me, so I send another finger into her.

"You like that?" I ask her, knowing damn well she does but wanting to hear it from her lips.

"Y-yes," she moans, the sound echoing in the confines of this parking garage staircase.

I lift her leg over my shoulder and fuck her deeper, my lips grazing her clit. I apply pressure, kissing her and swirling my tongue around her as I rock my panty-covered fingers into her tight, soaking pussy. I angle my fingers, caressing her G-spot and making her shiver under my control. I shove more of the lace inside and release my hand, both of them going to her center to spread her apart. I lick and suck on her, drawing my name with my tongue so her pussy knows who's bringing it pleasure, and who it belongs to.

London digs her nails into my scalp, practically begging with her hold on me.

In one swift motion, I position her other leg over my shoulder and rise to my feet, holding London's sweet pussy in front of me while she holds on. She doesn't protest, she doesn't ask to be let down, and I don't think I would even if she did. I'm a man on a mission, and I won't stop until she's finished and dripping on my face.

London bucks her hips gently, fucking my face and moaning with every motion, her fists holding on to my hair.

I swirl my mouth all over her, careful to only graze her clit, not quite giving in to what she wants just yet. She deserves a little punishment for what she's put me through, and a little sexual frustration is a small price to pay.

But with each labored breath, her sweet juices coating me as her body aches with want, I find myself unable to withstand giving in. I maintain a hold on her with my left shoulder and arm, and free my right hand to return it to her aching pussy. I penetrate her, using the friction of the drenched underwear to fuck her hole and suck on her swollen clit.

Her entire body tenses and rattles, her orgasm hitting her hard and fast, the most beautiful moan leaving her and filling this parking garage staircase. I finger-fuck her all the way through it, not letting up when her clit pulsates against my tongue. I smile and savor her taste, knowing damn well this fleeting moment is soon to end.

"Oh. My. Fucking. God," London says.

Carefully, I release her, leaving her panties inside of her and lowering her onto the ground. I hold on to her as she gains her footing. "God had nothing to do with that, little tornado."

She braces herself on my arm and wobbles. "I don't think I can walk," she admits.

I scoop her back into my arms and carry her the rest of the way up the stairs and into our apartment complex, going straight to our place and not stopping until I've laid her on the bed in my room.

"I think that was a bit overkill," she admits. "You didn't have to carry me all the way in here." London scoots back onto her elbows, her legs parting slightly, reminding me of the fabric tucked into her.

"Do you want me to get that?" I ask her, chewing at my lip and dying for another taste.

What the fuck is wrong with me? I can't stand her and yet I can't get enough.

London, her gaze lined with lust from only moments prior, spreads her legs. "Be my guest."

I shouldn't want this. I know I should stop. I've already gone further than I should have, but that doesn't seem to stop me from climbing between her legs, hooking my arms up under them and dragging her onto her back. I bury my face, my mouth sparing no regard for her aching core. I don't care that she just came; she's going to come again if I have any say in it.

I pinch her clit between my lips and she bucks against me, her body wanting the release almost as badly as I do.

"Kiss me," she says through labored breath. "Archer..." London drags my head up to hers and I let her, giving her a taste of herself as my tongue enters her mouth, our teeth practically banging into each other's as we try to deepen the kiss.

I press my body into her, my cock hard in my pants and dying to penetrate her tight hole. But I won't allow it. Not yet. Not like this. Sex is something we can't come back from, even though I can't be certain what's happening right now won't already complicate things.

London spreads her legs wider and moans as she grinds against me.

I crush myself into her, her wetness soaking through my pants, my cock so painfully hard, I'm not convinced it isn't going to snap in fucking half in its confines. I run my hand over her chest, tugging the strap of her dress down and exposing her breast. Breaking away from our heated kiss, I skim my tongue over her skin and pop her nipple into my mouth, sucking on it as it pebbles. Desperate to feel her lips on mine again, I cup her breast, circling and massaging her nipple as our mouths meet, a frenzied hunger consuming us. I continue to rock my hips against her, noting all the ways her body moves and bends under me, wanting to memorize the way it breaks, too.

"Fuck me, Archer," she cries against my mouth.

But I won't do it. I can't. Because once we do, there's no coming back.

I ignore her request and slide my hand down between our traitorous bodies and rub her clit, applying just the right amount of pressure for her to climax even harder than she did before, her moans suppressed by our kisses. I swallow every single one of them down like it's the only thing giving me life and bask in her quivers until I'm certain she can no longer take any more. I release my hand, give her one final kiss, and collapse on the bed beside her.

London lies there, her head back, her gaze on the ceiling, her breath labored and clipped. She licks her lips and swallows, and I watch her so intensely, I locate a new constellation of freckles I hadn't noticed before on her cheek.

She turns her head toward me. "You still didn't get them out."

"Oh, my apologies." I move between her legs, both resting over my shoulders, and breathe her in for what should definitely be the last time. Pinching her panties between my lips, I tug, her pussy tight as I slowly pull them out of her and wish I could go back in time and do this all again.

London stares at me. "That was a first."

"What was?" I ask her, and drop the panties into my hand.

"Being finger-fucked with my own panties," she admits.

"How was it?" I ask her, curious for a performance report even though I'm sure the two powerful orgasms say enough.

"Terrible." She smirks. "You're a bad kisser, remember?"

I glare at her, wondering why she's going to ruin the moment, but realize that's what got us in this situation from the start. Not wanting to participate in the bickering match she's no doubt prepared to launch into, I slide off the bed, her cum-soaked panties still in my grasp. "I'm taking these, by the way."

"What? Why?" she asks, her eyebrows raised.

I'm at the door when I turn back and tell her, "I'm going to go jerk off in the shower."

It's up to her to determine whether I'm being serious.

CHAPTER SEVENTEEN

London

I wake up with my mouth dry and my body still throbbing from last night. For a split second, I convince myself that it wasn't real, that it didn't happen, but when I glance down at the ripped dress I'm still wearing, it all comes flooding back to me.

Archer's hands dancing over my skin, his lips on mine, his mouth and tongue doing all the right things and sending me over the edge not only once, but twice.

My pussy pulses at the thought, but then I take the entire thing full circle and recall him riding like a maniac down the street, banging on the window until he ripped it out, and then bolting in front of us and making us stop in traffic.

I jump out of bed, not bothering to take a look in the mirror or brush my teeth, and rush straight into the living room where I know with certainty I'll find Archer.

He sees me coming, frantically getting in a few keystrokes before shutting off his screen.

"How did you know where I was?" I ask him, not even trying to hide my frustration.

"What?" Archer leans back in his chair and faces me. His gaze skims my body, probably wondering why I haven't changed out of this dress yet.

"Last night. Don't act stupid, Archer. You found me in Drew's car."

He shrugs, so nonchalant, I wish I could slap the look right off his face. "I saw you leave the complex yesterday."

"That doesn't answer how you knew where we were." I glare

at him. “You were behind the power going out, too, weren’t you?”

Archer shifts in his seat. It’s not much, but it’s enough to signal that he’s about to lie. “I have no idea what you’re talking about.”

I step closer. “Don’t you fucking lie to me. You cut the power. You followed us. You were the one who ruined my date.”

Archer rises to his feet, and it’s moments like this where I’m reminded of how fucking tall he is. His tattooed frame towers over me and does nothing but make me angrier. “I cut the traffic light, too, little tornado. What are you going to do about it?”

My nostrils flare. Did he just admit to everything I accused him of? That wasn’t what I expected. Nor did I think he’d add to his list of grievances.

“You are just so…” My chest heaves. “God damn it, I hate you.”

A sly grin forms on his face. “You didn’t hate me when you came on my mouth last night.”

“It only makes me hate you more.” I narrow my gaze. “And it’ll never *ever* happen again.”

“We’ll see.” Archer takes my chin in between his thumb and finger. “Perhaps I’ll remember that when you’re begging me for more.”

“You fucking wish. If you wouldn’t have ruined my date, I would have been fucking him instead. I would have been better off. I only hooked up with you because it was available.”

“You don’t mean that.”

“Oh? Watch me. I’ll find someone else to fuck by the end of the week.”

“It’s Friday,” he reminds me.

“Good. It won’t be long until I get you out of my system. Maybe I’ll bring them back here and fuck them on your bed.”

Archer’s jaw tenses and his expression hardens. “You will do no such thing.”

“Is that a dare?”

"I'll promise you one thing, London. If you fuck another man, it will be his blood on your hands, not mine." Archer's steady gaze doesn't break away, and it's then that his identity comes back to me.

Archer Sin is one of the notorious Sin brothers—a family of criminals who lie, steal, cheat, and kill their way through this town, not a single person willing to go up against them. They run a tightly concealed illegal empire where I'm not sure anything is off-limits. I heard whispers of them back in California, but I had never come across any of them, since my father insisted I stay out of the family business. Logically, I know I should fear Archer, but something in me thinks that if he was going to hurt me, he would have done so by now.

"Do you understand me?" Archer says.

"How did you do it?" I ask him, ignoring his question.

"Do what?" He raises a brow and seems to consider me for a long moment.

My gaze flits to the computer behind him, then back to him. "It was on there, wasn't it?" I step around him and point at the monitors. "What do you do on here, Archer? You spend all day just typing away." I make a dramatic display of me pretending to type on a keyboard.

Archer's chest rises. "You swore you wouldn't touch my computer."

"Yeah? I also swore I wouldn't fall in love," I snap at him. "Don't worry, neither of those will be happening." I cross my arms, my stupid cast scuffing my other wrist. "Tell me, big boy. You claim you don't have some porn obsession. Then what is it? What are you hiding on there?" I pause, and when he doesn't answer, I continue, "Just admit it, you're a hacker."

Archer's fingers twitch like he wants to ball his hand into a fist, but he doesn't. "No, I'm not."

"I don't get why you're so secretive about it. Everyone knows who you are. Who your family is. Stop pretending like you aren't what you are."

"That's not who I am. I gave that life up a long time ago."

I motion from the computer to him. "Doesn't really look like it, big boy."

Archer swallows harshly and his gaze meets mine again, this time something else hidden in his eyes. "Wait, you knew who I was and still chose to come here?"

"I didn't know that first day," I admit. When Silver sent me here, the only information I had was Archer's first name, last initial, and address. Silver told me he was a friend and that he would keep me safe. I figured he was connected to the life somehow, but it wasn't until Grace told me that I started piecing things together. Still, it doesn't change the fact that I'm here, and that I'm not going anywhere.

Archer stands there, waiting for me to fill the silence.

"I'm not afraid of you," I tell him.

His intense stare threatens to undo me as he says, "You should be."

CHAPTER EIGHTEEN

Archer

London and I haven't spoken in forty-eight hours and I don't know what's worse, her silent treatment or her incessant nagging. Part of me wishes she'd go back to yelling at me about nothing and everything instead of closing me out.

But closing me out is what is best for us. Every time we talk, we argue for no real reason, and it ends in the same heated passion between us that neither one of us can seem to ignore.

This is better. London is here temporarily, and once she's gone, I'll return to my life of solitude. My life of numbing the pain and ignoring everything else as much as I possibly can.

"Will you wash my hair?" she asks me, the sound of her voice startling me from my daze.

I blink a few times and turn toward her, unsure of whether I imagined her to begin with.

"Uh, hello?" She snaps her fingers in front of my face. "Earth to Archer."

I clear my throat and stand from my desk. "Yeah." I make my way over to the bathroom but notice she's already got the supplies sitting in the kitchen on the counter. How unaware was I that she managed to do that without me noticing? I change my course of action and go to the counter, my mind begging to be anywhere but here.

London stands at the end of the island, her hands to her sides, her eyes trained on me.

"Right." I approach her, grab under her arms, and hoist her onto the counter.

"Are you okay?" she asks me while lying on her back. "You're being weirder than usual."

"I'm my normal weird," I tell her, and turn on the water, adjusting the faucet until I get the right temperature.

"Are you going to keep giving me the silent treatment?" London looks up at me from her position on the counter, her eyes squinted when I bring the nozzle over.

"I thought you were giving *me* the silent treatment," I tell her, and rinse her hair, making sure to cover her forehead and not splatter her too much. I lather some shampoo into my hands before massaging it into her hair, paying special attention to her scalp and not pushing too hard. The last time we did this, she mentioned a skull fracture, and I don't exactly want to make that worse.

"Truce?" London says, and I can't tell if she's being genuine or not. "I mean, I'm still mad at you for ruining my birthday, but you kind of made up for it."

"How about I let you ruin my birthday? Then we can call it even?" I rinse the shampoo from her hair and squeeze as much water out as possible before putting some conditioner through her ends.

"Deal." London closes her eyes, and for a minute, it's like she's enjoying this. "Hey, we should probably go to the grocery store."

"Yeah, we're getting low on supplies. I was going to go tomorrow morning, but if you want to go..."

"I've never been."

I stop moving and look at her. "What?"

London shrugs. "We had a housekeeper, and I'm pretty sure she went."

"Okay, yeah, we're definitely popping your grocery store cherry, then."

"Ew, that makes it sound gross."

"We can go when we're done with your hair, if you want." I finish getting the conditioner out, smoothing some of the tangles, and wrap her hair in a towel. "I can blow-dry it for you."

London sits up, holding the mass of her towel-covered hair, and looks at me, a hint of suspicion lining her brow. "Why are you being nice to me?"

"I'm not. I'm just trying to avoid hearing you complain for an hour." I wipe off the counter and grab the supplies, taking them back to the bathroom where they belong. "Come on," I call out to her.

Once I've put everything away, I plug the blow-dryer in and point to the counter for her to sit on.

London scoots on top and turns to face the mirror.

I brush through her hair carefully, not tugging too much on the tangles that appear, and not scraping her with the bristles when I get near her face. Each motion is slow and steady, my attention too focused on such a mundane task. It takes me at least ten minutes to fully blow-dry London's hair, our gazes meeting in the mirror from time to time. I go over it one last time and shut the thing off, twisting the cord around it and setting it under the sink.

"I was thinking about braiding it," she says, her fingers reaching for her red locks.

"I saw you trying to braid it a few days ago," I admit. "Can I try?"

"Sure." London lowers her arms and steadies a breath as she watches me in the mirror.

A strange pressure falls on my shoulders, a sort of performance anxiety I've never experienced in the past. I push the sensation aside and focus on my task, divvying her hair into three sections at the top and desperately trying to remember the instructions from the countless YouTube videos I scoured. After smoothing out the rest of the hair, I cross the sections, bringing hair into each one on the other side. I repeat the movement, adding hair and crossing it over, only getting hung up twice and having to backtrack. Once I'm at the bottom of her head, I finish the braid without adding any more hair and hold it steady while I reach into the drawer for a hair tie.

Examining my creation, I doubt myself and come to terms with the fact that doing hair is not in my level of expertise. It's sort of bumpy, and some of the sections are bigger than the others, not to mention it's crooked.

"Let me start over," I say, but London moves from my grasp, her hand gently skimming the hump of the braid.

"Holy shit, big boy. I didn't think you had it in you." She turns her head and checks it out in the mirror, pivoting and moving all about to get all the angles. "You braid better than me without a cast on."

I chuckle and rub at my neck. "You don't have to lie."

"I'm not lying," London tells me, and hops off the counter. She approaches, right in front of me, and stands on her tiptoes, pressing her lips on my cheek. "Thank you."

I remain there a long moment after she's gone, unsure of what just happened.

We went from arguing, to hooking up, to the silent treatment, to her thanking me for doing her hair.

Just when I think I've gotten things figured out, she goes and throws me completely off.

***

London doesn't take much longer to get ready, which only continues to confuse me. In the little over a week I've known her, nothing she does is quick, and some things I'm not mad about...

I dismiss the thought of my lips on her pussy and watch her as she makes her way to the front door, the brown purse I bought her in her grasp. "Are you coming or not, big boy?"

"Right behind you." I follow her over, grabbing my keys off the table near the door. "Want to take the bike?"

She glares at me and it sends a strange satisfaction coursing through me. I'm not one for purposely antagonizing someone, but she dishes it enough to take it from time to time.

I make certain the lock is secure, checking it twice before continuing. My feet stop in their tracks when my sight lands on Camille coming up the stairs. "Shit," I whisper, knowing damn well London has already spotted her.

"Arch, hey!" Camille says once she spots me. I wasn't sure how mad she'd be at me for what I did to Drew, but so far, she doesn't seem bothered. Maybe he was too much of a coward to mention it.

"Hey, Cami." I awkwardly wave and catch London's questioning stare.

She darts right around me, extending her hand toward Camille. "Hi, Camille, I'm London."

Camille shoots me a glance and shakes London's hand. "Nice to meet you."

"Same to you," London continues. "Listen, I don't mean to be too forward, but I heard you're going to be subleasing your apartment. I'd love to be considered."

"Oh, you're in the market for a place?" Camille studies London from head to toe, probably trying to determine whether she can afford to live in this neighborhood.

"I am. I'm new to town. I'd love to stay around here." London clears her throat. "I'm sure Archer would vouch for me, right?" She turns toward me, her expression looking like a mix of "please help me" and "if you don't, I'm going to kill you."

"Uh, yeah. Definitely," I lie. Even if London didn't drive me insane, she's a mess. I'd never willingly let her rent from me, especially if I wasn't there to pick up after her. London will destroy Camille's place in a week, two max. But right now, I'd rather keep that a secret because there's no way Camille is going to choose London over any of the other applicants who have no doubt a better renter's history than her.

"Okay. Sure. I'll think about it. Maybe we could chat over coffee sometime. Are you free next Tuesday morning?" Camille says to London, no doubt just being polite because we're neighbors.

"Absolutely," London tells her enthusiastically. "Works for me."

"Great, just give me your number..." Camille opens her phone screen and hands it to London, who has to pull her own phone out and locate the digits.

"Sorry, new phone. I haven't memorized it yet."

Camille laughs. "I get that. Anyway, it was good meeting you. I'll text you Monday with a more specific time and place, my work schedule changes from day to day."

"Sounds good, see you later," London says.

I offer her a wave and she disappears behind the door of her apartment.

"I wouldn't hold your breath," I tell London, and make my way toward the stairs. "I'm sure she's had dozens of applicants."

London stops in her tracks. "You act like Mister Big and Bad and have no sway over who she chooses? I would think you'd be thrilled about this. The sooner I find a place, the sooner I'm out of your hair. Not to mention it's the closest I can be without being inside your apartment, allowing you to keep your word to Silver until I get things figured out. Why don't you want this?" Her eyes widen. "You like me living with you, don't you?"

"No. I don't. What did you call it...*unbearable*? Yeah, it's that." I leave her and head down the stairs, not wanting to continue this conversation.

"That's the only explanation there is. Either you want me to live with you, or it's something else, and until you tell me what it is, I'm going with the former." London follows me, her pace slower than mine, reminding me she's still injured, even if she pretends like she's fine.

"I don't want you to live with me, London. You're a disaster." I lead her to the front entrance of the complex and open the door for her, my gaze already scanning outside at what's going on.

"Ouch." London steps through, her head held high in her attempt not to feign hurt from my remark. But she and I both know it's true. "You're not fun to live with either, big boy."

"Yeah? How so?" I position myself between London and the street and walk beside her on our way to the corner store.

"The clean-freak thing is a bit much. And heaven forbid anyone even blink in the direction of your *precious* computers." London talks with her hands, and I fight the urge to shut her up the same way I have in the past.

"Please," I huff. "You're being dramatic."

"I am? Are you serious? Everything has to be in its specific place. It has to be tiring constantly arranging and rearranging things."

"I wouldn't have to if you put things back where they belong."

"It's not just that. Have you counted how many times you check the windows daily? You'd think there was a sniper out there you were watching out for."

"They're bulletproof," I let slip out.

"What?"

I sigh. "The windows, they're bulletproof."

London throws her hands up. "Of course they are. Is there anything you aren't prepared for?"

We reach the corner store, and I pause with my hand on the door handle. "I wasn't prepared for you." I open it a second later, and the store clerk greets me once we're inside.

"Archie!" the old woman says, and rushes around the counter to wrap her arms around me. "My favorite customer. And who is this?" Her big, round eyes get even bigger as she gawks at London. "A girl. He's never brought a girl in here."

"Ruth, this is London. London, this is Ruth," I say to them.

"London." Ruth smiles a borderline toothless smile and shakes London's hand. "Oh, sweet angel, what happened to your arm?"

"I'm accident-prone," London tells her.

Ruth laughs and nods. "Me too, my girl, me too."

"I'm going to grab a basket," I tell them, disappearing for the nine seconds it takes me to walk to where Ruth keeps them. When I return, Ruth and London stop talking, both of their lips pinched together like they were already sharing secrets.

Another customer walks in, the doorbell ringing to signal to us. I eye him suspiciously and split my attention between him and them.

"What happened to your face?" Ruth asks me, her question coming as a surprise.

"What's wrong with my face?"

She motions to hers. "It's all bruised. Have you been fighting again? What have I told you, Archie...?"

"It was Seven," I cut her off without letting her continue her lecture. "No big deal. Brotherly thing, you know how it goes."

Ruth nods. "All too well." She turns to London. "I've got this sister I want to strangle at least once a week. When I tell you we—"

The man who walked in a minute ago approaches the counter and Ruth stops her speech.

"Let me help him and I'll let you get your shopping done." She slips behind the counter and pushes a button on her register. "Is this all for you, honey?" she says to the man.

But there's something strange about his posture, the sweat forming on his brow, the anxious tapping of his foot.

Without another thought, I shove London into an aisle at the same time the man pulls out a gun and points it at Ruth. "Give me all your money and no one has to get hurt." He turns, shooting the gun into the air and waving it around.

"What the fuck was that?" London asks me, her face strained as we crouch down low together.

I press my finger to my lips. "Shh," I whisper.

She nods, and I wonder if she truly understands the gravity of the situation.

Taking a deep breath through my nose, I silently exhale and think through every possible scenario I can come up with, my one and only goal being to get London out of here safely. But each path leads me to the same outcome, and if I don't act quickly, there's no telling what additional variables could be added that I haven't considered.

"Stay here," I tell her. "Do not move. Do not come out until I come for you. Do you hear me?"

London blinks up at me through her lashes and stiffly nods again.

With another sobering breath, my heart beating evenly in my chest, a part of me I haven't acknowledged in far too long comes alive. Like a switch flipping inside of me, I rise to my feet and turn toward the man threatening to ruin everything. I march out from behind the aisle, not even flinching when he catches sight of me and thrusts the gun in my direction.

I walk straight toward him, right into the line of fire, and before he can fully process how fucking insane I am, I grab his wrist, twist it, and disarm him. His mouth drops open, his eyes wide with disbelief as I turn his weapon on him, shoving it into his chest.

"Who the fuck sent you?" I say to him, my voice barely raised. My gaze flickers to Ruth just long enough to confirm she's unharmed, and then I focus on this ignorant asshole.

"Wh-what?" he blubbers.

I stare into his eyes, noting how his lip quivers and his hands shake at his sides.

"Get on your fucking knees," I tell him, the rage inside of me building with each passing second. I hate the familiarity of the feeling, and how much I welcome it despite hating it more than anything. I loathe how calm I am with a gun pressed in my palm and the barrel trained on another man.

"Puh-please," he begs as he drops down onto the ground. "I didn't mean to, I'm sorry."

I narrow my eyes at him. "You didn't mean to, yet you brought a weapon in here? In my fucking neighborhood? Do you not know who the fuck I am?"

He studies me carefully, and the moment he realizes, he tears up. "I didn't know, I wouldn't have agreed."

"Agreed to what? To whom?" I push the gun into his chest.

"I—I can't. They'll kill me."

"Who will kill you?"

He pinches his lips together like he's afraid the secret will spill out.

I drag the gun up his neck and across his face and rest it on his forehead. "The only one you should be worried about right now is me."

A siren sounds in the distance, but I pay it no attention other than registering it in my awareness. This man might be afraid of the police, but I'm not.

"I'm going to give you to the count of three," I tell him. "One..."

"Please, please, no."

"Two."

"I'm begging you, I don't know anything, I'd talk if I could."

"Three," I mutter as I pull the trigger, the sound deafening and the reverberation rippling up my forearm.

His body thuds against the floor of Ruth's shop, his blood splattered around and pooling on the linoleum.

"Sorry about the floor," I say to Ruth, who stands there on the other side of the counter.

"That's okay, Archie." She offers me an apologetic smile and steps around the side to take in the dead body bleeding out.

With the gun still in my hand, I return to the aisle I left London in, shock settling through me when she's still there. "Holy shit, you listened," I tell her as I round the corner.

She stands, her emerald gaze locked onto mine. "Did you just kill someone?" London marches right past me, stopping in her tracks when she locates the body.

"Uh," is all I respond, the realization that I murdered someone in front of her hitting me like a ton of bricks.

"What are we going to do about that?" London glances back at me, her face scanning mine for answers.

"It was self-defense," Ruth blurts out. "He was robbing the shop, Archie stepped in and took things into his own hands. He's a hero. That's my story and I'm sticking to it."

London's brows bunch and she brings her hand to her chest. "I wasn't blaming Archer." She meets my gaze again. "I wouldn't do that. You know that, right?"

Truth be told, I practically blacked out when the threat appeared, the old version of me stepping into my shoes and doing what needed to be done, but now that I've returned, I don't know what to expect from London. Sure, she's familiar with crime and danger, but maybe I just took things entirely too far. Just because I'm used to this life doesn't mean she is, too.

"Archer," London murmurs.

I slide my phone out of my pocket and flick the screen to life, dialing a number I haven't dialed in a while. It rings twice before it connects, a thick voice on the other side.

"Officer Robinson."

"I need you to send a small team to Ruth's place on the corner. The usual guys, no one else."

A slight pause is followed by, "How many?"

"One," I tell him.

"I'll personally see to it."

"Thanks," I say before hanging up and looking over the gun in my hand, noting the serial number that was filed down on the side. I let out a breath and focus on Ruth. "Someone should be here soon to clean this up. Are you okay?"

"Of course, Archie, I'm fine. Are you okay?" Ruth reaches out toward London. "You okay, honey?"

"Yeah, I'm fine," London says, her voice strangely calm.

Maybe she's in shock. Maybe she's waiting for the opportunity to bolt out of here and never come back.

But instead, she opens her mouth again. "What about the groceries?"

"What?" I ask her, not quite following.

"We came here for stuff for the apartment."

"Right." I tuck the gun into my waistband.

"Take whatever you need," Ruth insists while grabbing another basket and shoving it toward me. "Did you make that tofu like I told you to?"

"Was that your recipe?" London asks her as her gaze shifts from me to Ruth.

Ruth smiles politely. "I take it you're the reason he's buying tofu?"

"Guilty," London admits, her cheeks reddening but only slightly. "It was great, by the way." London takes the basket, ignores the dead man on the floor, and chats to Ruth about tofu.

"Keep an eye on the door," Ruth tells me, and turns her attention to London. "I have these new black bean burgers you might like. Here, let me show you." She guides London down an aisle, the distance between us tugging at me, itching me to move closer, to be there, just in case something happens again. I shouldn't feel this way, but having London around gives me a sense of purpose, and I don't want to fuck up the one task I've been given.

Taking my phone from my pocket, I dial August's number and walk toward the door, eyeing everyone on the sidewalk as they pass.

"Arch, what's going on?" August says through the receiver.

"They sent someone to Ruth's shop."

"What are you talking about?"

"The bodega on the corner, the one in my fucking neighborhood. They sent someone to make it look like a robbery."

"Did you ever consider it was a robbery?"

"All things considered, I'm appalled you're being so dismissive."

August sighs. "Has the situation been handled?"

"Yes."

"Did you question the person?"

"He wasn't giving anything up." I recall the shock on the man's face as I pressed the gun into his temple. I ignore the part of me that missed having that control.

"I see." August clears his throat. "And you think it was the Manor brothers?"

"When I asked him who sent him, he said they'd kill him. Who else would it be if it wasn't us? I can't imagine Leo or Seven would send someone to shoot up my grocery store."

"I mean, I wouldn't put it past Seven..."

"We're brothers; we fight, we make up, that's what we do. This time was no different."

"What's the deal with the girl?"

"I didn't call you to talk about her."

"What do you want from me, Archer?"

"Nothing, August," I bite back. "I'm trying to make you aware, is all. Take it or leave it, but if we don't get a grip on this situation, who's to say they don't take over our territory? I should have known when I took a step back everything would fall to shit."

"Excuse me?" August cuts me off. "Nothing is falling to shit.

Don't you dare disrespect what I'm doing here. *You* are the one who resigned from your position. *You're* the one who wants nothing to do with things. I won't tolerate this from you."

A familiar man in uniform struts down the sidewalk, a few men close behind him. "I've got to go," I tell him. "The cops are here."

"Good, handle the situation," August says before I hang up the phone and return it to my pocket. I open the door, the bell chiming, and hold it for the men to enter.

"Archer." Officer Robinson shakes my hand. "This is Officer Peterson, McKenna, and Charles. You want to walk us through things?"

I glance at each guy and tip my head toward the dead man. "Came in, tried to rob the place." I pull the gun out, holding it with my shirt and wiping my prints off it before handing it to Officer Robinson. "This is what he used. Serial number is wiped," I tell him when he turns it over and looks for one.

"You heard 'em." Robinson tucks the gun up under his biceps. "Let's get this cleaned up."

Officer Peterson locks the front door and stands guard while the rest of them go to work. I leave them to find London and Ruth, who are near the produce section.

I take the basket from London, the weight of it no doubt too much for her to carry in her condition. "Did you find what you needed?" I ask her.

"And some," she confirms. "Is everything okay?"

"Yep."

"Thank you, Archie." Ruth pats my arm. "You take good care of me."

"Speaking of which, can I talk to you?" I pull her aside and disregard the strange look from London. Lowering my voice, I say, "I'll give you ten grand to close up for an hour every Sunday so we can come in without any other customers."

Ruth shakes her head. "That's absurd, Archie, I won't let you do that."

"I'm insisting." I stare at her, wanting her to understand just how serious I am. If I have to bring London in here one more time, it sure as hell better be when no one else is in here. Why take the risk if it's not necessary?

"What time were you thinking?"

"Whatever time works for you," I tell her in my attempt to make this easier on her.

Ruth rubs her chin. "We do have a slow period between nine and ten in the morning."

"Works for us. I'll bring cash." My thoughts wander to the man I made a mess of. "I'll send some extra for cleanup."

"That's absurd and not needed. You really do take great care of me, Archie. It's the least I could do to repay you. This store wouldn't be here, I wouldn't be here, if it weren't for you."

"Don't mention it," I say, actually wishing she wouldn't.

"Take whatever you need. And if I can offer a little advice..." Ruth leans in close. "You should marry that one."

"What? No. We'd kill each other." London and I are nothing alike, and the only thing we manage to be consistent at is fighting with each other. Taking things further than we already have would result in nothing good for either of us.

Our relationship is fleeting, simply a means to an end, a favor where I'm trying to hold up my end of the bargain.

"Whatever you say." Ruth grins and winks at me, leaving me a moment later to attend to the cops who are bagging up the body in the front of her shop.

"You need anything else?" I ask London, who is aimlessly scanning the tray of tomatoes like she's trying to busy herself.

She points her finger in the air like an idea has hit her and marches away. "Bagels, we definitely need bagels." London latches onto a pack and tosses them into the basket. "Can we get supplies to bake cookies?"

"You know how to bake cookies?" I follow her into the wrong aisle, putting my hand on her lower back and guiding her in the right direction. A few minutes ago I thought she was going to bolt out of here, and now she's considering baking. I guess it just goes to show how little we know about each other.

"No. But I can follow directions." She holds out her hand. "Give me your phone."

"What? Why?" I stop in front of the baking section.

"To find a recipe, duh."

I narrow my gaze. "Where's your phone?"

"I left it at home."

Something about the way she says *home* cuts right through me. I swallow it down and snatch a bag of chocolate chips off the shelf, turning it over and giving it to her. "There's a recipe right there."

"Oh." London plucks the bag out of my hand and gathers the ingredients, one after another, filling the basket more and more.

We finish finding all the items and head to the front of the store, where I insist Ruth checks us out, and I pay for everything. With two stuffed brown bags, London and I leave the store, and the crime scene, and head back to our apartment.

I gravitate toward her, ready to throw myself over her in case anything happens, but remind myself I'm being irrational. The attempted robbery had nothing to do with London, and more so to do with me. If anything, London is in danger because of my presence in her life. If I were smart, I'd put distance between us to keep her safe, but at the end of the day, making her someone else's problem doesn't seem like the best option.

"What made you want to bake?" I ask her, the words slipping out of my mouth surprising me.

London draws in a breath and releases it, her head facing forward on our walk back. "I had this maid once. She was my favorite. She baked a lot. And anytime anything bad happened, she'd make me something. We never talked about it, she never pried, but she'd leave a plate of cookies or muffins or a pie, you know, whatever she came up with, and would leave it in my room. I always knew that if something happened, I'd at least have that to look forward to... until I didn't."

"What happened to her?" I ask, knowing damn well I'm going to regret the question.

"My dad killed her," London says so nonchalantly like it's nothing out of the ordinary, like it's as plain as telling someone the time. She doesn't flinch, she doesn't show emotion, she simply keeps moving forward, one foot after the other, her head held high.

I find her confession both startling and comforting—the London I'm peeling the layers off of is nothing like the London I thought showed up on my doorstep two weeks ago.

CHAPTER NINETEEN

London

Archer shot and killed a man three days ago and all I can think about is how fucking itchy the casts on my arm and leg are. I shove a wooden spoon between the fabric and my skin and attempt to dig at the spot on my arm, but it's no use. I need them off and I need it now.

I pull out my phone and google how to cut a cast off, quickly realizing I'm going to need something called blunt-tipped shears. They're sort of inexpensive, but I don't want to use Archer's credit card to order them, and I'm not sure if there's a store nearby that sells them. I locate a hardware store a few blocks away and wonder if Archer would throw a fit if I left, the answer no doubt being yes.

He gets pissy over everything. You'd think he cared about me by the way he grows so protective, but I'm well aware it's because of his obsessive-compulsive disorder and has nothing to do with me. He'd act this way toward anyone living in his house—I'm no exception.

"I'm going to meet Grace," I lie as I gather my bag and walk past him at the computer.

He stops typing immediately. "You never meet her at this time."

I shrug. "So?"

He swivels in his chair toward me. "You're acting suspicious."

"You are."

Archer crosses his tattooed arms and looks up at me. "What aren't you telling me?"

"What aren't *you* telling me?" I blurt out, the only thing I can think of in the moment.

"You're not leaving unless you tell me what you're doing." He glares. "The truth."

"I'm...uh, I'm going to look for a job."

Archer stares for a long moment and then laughs abruptly, the sound short and clipped and so fucking patronizing. "Right."

"What? You think I can't get a job?"

"With what skills?"

"I have skills."

"Do tell, the floor is all yours." He motions for me to continue.

"Asshole."

"That is my skill, not yours."

"Whatever," I huff. "I don't care if you don't believe in me, I do. I can get a job, watch." It's then that I realize I had no intention of going out and getting a job, but now that I've walked into the lie, I can't exactly deviate from my plan. And as much as it frustrates me to admit, Archer has a point—I don't have any useful skills. I refuse to tell him that, though.

"Okay," he says, his tone even and calculated. "Have fun with that."

"At least I don't sit around all day typing away on my computer. What kind of job is that?"

Archer's jaw tenses like I struck a nerve. He rises to his feet, his hand planted on his desk as he leans toward me. "An important one."

"Hardly," I respond with a bite to my tone. I don't know why he has me so fucking defensive about this, but I couldn't stop if I tried. The only thing I can think to do is prove him wrong. "I'm leaving."

Archer remains firmly in place when I walk away and storm to the door, only shooting him a final glance before I leave his apartment.

I release a breath on the other side and pull myself together. This is not the energy I need if I'm going to get a job. I'm only a few steps away from Archer's front door as someone jogs up the stairs.

"Hey," Camille says, her smile reaching all the way to her eyes.

There's something so wholesome and genuine about her that sort of sets me on edge, and the more I take in her features, the more I see her brother, who Archer threatened on the street during our date.

"Hey," I reply. "I was just—"

"Oh my God, I never texted you." Camille covers her mouth but drops it immediately. "I am so sorry. You have no idea how busy my schedule has been. I don't know each day from the next. I can't believe I forgot, actually, yeah, I can, but seriously, I'm so sorry. Will you forgive me?"

"Of course," I tell her, the vague recollection of our agreed-upon coffee date resurfacing—her memory not much better than mine. "Don't sweat it."

"How can I make it up to you?" She peeks around me. "Are you busy now? Do you have a minute? We could go now, but I understand if you already have plans. No Archer today?" She barely takes a breath between each word.

"No, his grumpy ass is in there working."

Camille laughs. "Sounds about right. He never leaves that place."

"I'm free, though, if you want to grab a coffee now." Why not add one more thing to the to-do list that's piling up? Getting a job will make Archer mad, I might as well add securing an apartment too.

"Yeah, let's go. You good with the place down the street?"

Camille and I make our way downstairs, having the most basic small talk the entire journey to the coffee shop. We cover the weather, a new restaurant in the neighborhood, and we even touch on sports. I mumble and nod along, my mind struggling to stay with her as it focuses on the other things I'm supposed to be doing.

"Tell me about you, London," Camille says while holding the door to the coffee shop open.

I force a smile. "Not much to tell. California transplant, just trying to get my footing here and start over."

"What about hobbies? What do you like to do for fun?"

I think about her question, and I hate how it *feels* so simple, that an answer should immediately pop into my head, but nothing comes to mind. "I like to read," I confess. "And bake." I'm not that good at the latter, and yet there's still something so comforting about it that I enjoy.

"Oh, that's cool. I never was very good at baking, or cooking. I don't follow directions well." Camille shuffles in to line behind an older man with silver hair. He orders a small black coffee, pays with cash, and is gone in less than a minute.

We place our orders and settle into a small table, my back to the patrons and unease creeping up my spine.

I shake it off and move to the spot closer to Camille. "Better spot to people watch," I partially lie.

"No doubt." Camille taps her chin. "This is what I like to do for fun. Make up stories about other people and try to imagine what their lives are like." She points to a man in line with a briefcase. "This guy. Public defender, twice divorced, only sees his kids every other weekend, struggles to get it up in bed."

I suppress a laugh and nod along. "Spot-on." I scan the crowd, settling on a young duo at a table in the corner. "Those two, first date. She's trying to come up with an excuse to leave."

"One hundred percent."

A barista brings our drinks to our table and I fidget with the handle of the mug, not quite wanting to burn my mouth just yet but wanting to have a sip. "What do you do for work?"

"What don't I do?" Camille sighs. "I'm a personal assistant, which means I do grunt work twenty-four-seven. It's not all bad, but it's unpredictable and a bit overwhelming at times. I love it, I do, but sometimes I forget what it's like to have a life."

"That sounds terrible, why do you do it?"

"It pays well."

I nod like I understand even though I've never worked a day in my life. I won't tell her that, though, because then she probably wouldn't lease me her apartment.

"I'm confused. You're a personal assistant but you're leaving town, that's why you're subleasing your place?"

"Right, yeah, that. The guy I work for has this acting gig, it's sort of a big deal. The project is contracted for a year, but it could be longer. Anyway, instead of hiring someone there, he offered to relocate me."

"Damn, he must like you." I test the temperature of my latte.

Camille shrugs. "Or doesn't want to have to train anyone else. Or doesn't think anyone will put up with his shit."

"That bad?"

"He is the most high-maintenance man I have ever met." Camille tucks her hair behind her ears. "I leave the first week of June, and if I'm being honest, I haven't liked a single person I've interviewed."

"Oh?" I try not to come across as desperate, but I'd be lying if I said hearing that didn't make my entire body perk up. "How come?"

"I'm a vibe person, if that makes sense. And they were off."

"No, I get that," I tell her, and motion to myself. "How are my vibes?"

"Not bad, actually." She laughs. "Doesn't hurt that I trust Archer's judgment, too. He's a good guy."

I want to pry, to ask more questions about him, but that would insinuate that I don't know him very well, and her understanding is that we're closer than strangers who got forced together a couple of weeks ago.

"He is, isn't he?" Archer isn't a terrible guy, that's for sure. Not considering the kind of men I'm typically accustomed to being around. And compared to my father, Archer is a fucking saint. A saint who happened to shoot a man in the head earlier this week, a man who is clearly hiding some big, terrible secret that weighs him down to the point he's hiding out in his apartment and pushing away anyone who attempts to get close to him.

Who am I to judge him for what I have no idea about? Archer might be grumpy and get on my fucking nerves, but we both have a past that haunts us, and I find it strangely comforting that I feel like we have that in common despite everything else about us being so opposite.

"I met Archer a few years ago when he moved into the building. I was trying to drag a couch up the stairs. I can't tell you how many people walked around me without offering to help. It was like I was inconveniencing them, you know? Anyway, Archer, all big, bad, and scary he is, turned this couch sideways and carried it up himself. I was in fucking awe, I had no idea how he did it, but he did, and sure, maybe he did it so I would get out of his way and he could get to his place, but he didn't make me feel like a burden the way everyone else did. I could tell there was something sad about him, and I was no stranger to that either. Throughout the years, he's just always been there when I needed him. Even if it was something stupid, like borrowing a screwdriver, or opening up a jar. He's reliable, and he offers help without ever expecting anything in return."

Camille pauses and I study her getting lost in her train of thought. I have half a mind to ask if she has a thing for Archer, but I don't imagine that will help my chances of securing her apartment. Instead, I let her simmer in her daydream and wait for her to return.

She blinks and her eyes meet mine. "You two would make a cute couple."

Her statement catches me so off guard, I nearly choke on my coffee. I wipe my mouth and nervously chuckle.

"He seems to like you," Camille says.

"I'd say *like* is a massive overstatement. Archer tolerates me."

"How long have you two been hooking up?"

I almost lose it again but maintain my composure. Camille is nothing if not direct, and I sort of love that about her. There's no beating around the bush, no leaving any thought unsaid. "We aren't hooking up," I confess, although it's not entirely the truth.

Archer and I have fooled around, but it was in a heated moment of frustration. It didn't mean anything. Not to him. Not to me. If anything, it was a careless mistake that shouldn't happen again. It would only complicate an already complicated situation.

Camille's eyebrows rise ever so slightly. "Could have fooled me. The tension between you two is palpable."

I nervously sip my coffee and beg my mind to settle on anything other than the feeling of Archer's hands on my body, his mouth on mine, his tattooed fingers buried inside of me, hitting me in all the right spots like he has a secret blueprint of my body.

"Sorry, I'm being nosy." Camille puts her hands up. "That's your business. We're here to talk about the apartment. So, it's a two-bedroom, eighteen-hundred-square-foot space. You'd get access to the on-site gym and an assigned parking space downstairs. I'm fairly certain I'll be gone for two years but guaranteed for a year. It's four thousand a month, which is a steal because the other units rent for closer to ten grand. My dad pulled some strings, that's why I want to sublease it to keep the contract in place. Otherwise, it would bump up to the full price. Hmm, what else?"

I take in all the information, skipping over the parking garage where Archer explored my body, and get caught on the four thousand dollars a month. The old me wouldn't have even blinked an eye, but considering I'm down to a little over a thousand and I don't have any money coming in, the realization that I might be too broke to live on my own hits me. When have I ever given up that easily, though?

"It all sounds so amazing," I tell her.

She reaches across the table and places her hand on mine, giving it a gentle but firm squeeze. "I think we should do this, what do you say?"

My eyes light up, unable to conceal my excitement. "Are you serious?"

"One hundred percent." Her phone buzzes on the table and she glances down at it, her arm gliding across the table to swipe the screen open. "Go figure, I have to run. Duty calls." She stands without taking her eyes off her phone, rapidly typing something and practically slamming the Send button. "We'll be in touch, okay?" She focuses on me, reaching out to give me a brisk hug.

"Of course. Thank you, Camille. I appreciate this more than you know. I promise you made the right decision."

"I feel good about it." Camille touches my shoulder before turning on her heel and bolting out of the coffee shop, leaving me and our coffees behind.

I settle back into the seat, the gravity of things pulling me down. On the one hand, this is great news—in a few short weeks I'll have a place of my own—but on the other, I have no idea how I'm going to pay for it.

Four thousand dollars a month is forty-eight thousand a year. I'll have to find something that brings that in at the very least, otherwise, I'll have no money to pay for anything else.

Resentment builds at having left everything behind because of my father. If I had access to any of my accounts, or hell, any of his, none of this would be a problem. I'd have the funds to cover rent for years and years to come.

The fact that I had to endure a lifetime of his wrath and ended up with nothing other than the scars is enough to make me want to bring him back from the dead just to inflict a little pain on him for a change.

But I wouldn't risk it, even if it were possible, because that man would claw his way into the living and make damn sure I was punished for his demise.

I study the customers that come and go, sipping the coffee Camille bought me. Workers move gracefully behind the counter, taking orders, fulfilling them, and communicating well despite the unpredictable rush that comes and goes. A bit farther away, a giant window gives us access to the kitchen area, where a woman with tightly curled hair darts from one end to the other, a bowl in one hand and a measuring cup in the other. She stops in front of the counter, dumps the cup into the bowl, and frantically looks around, latching onto a wooden spoon near her, her expression softening but only subtly.

Leaving both mugs of coffee on the table, I move closer to the register, waiting in line patiently but keeping my sight on the glass. Once I'm at the front, the cashier smiles politely at me.

"Another vanilla latte?" she asks.

I point in the direction of the kitchen. "Does she need help?"

The cashier stares at me blankly. "What?"

"The woman in the kitchen. Does she need help?"

"Oh." She glances over her shoulder at the lady darting around the kitchen. "Actually, yeah, probably. Do you have baking experience?"

"Yes," I blurt out without giving it any thought. I've baked before, that counts as experience, right?

"Sasha, take over for a second," the cashier tells another worker. "Come here," she says to me.

I follow her over and she taps on the door before opening it. "Andrea, do you have a minute?"

The woman stops in her tracks, flour on her face and her hair bouncing on her brow. She blows it out of the way. "Not really. What's up?"

"London was inquiring about a job."

Andrea gives me that same blank look that the cashier had just moments prior. "Seriously?"

"I'm sorry," I speak up. "I saw you through the window. You looked like you needed help."

"Can you follow directions?" Andrea asks me from her spot still standing there.

"As long as a man isn't the one giving them."

Andrea cracks a smile. "Men don't do directions."

"Then I don't see the problem."

She slides her gaze to the casts on my body.

"Don't worry, I can keep up," I reassure.

"How much longer until they're off?"

"Hopefully only a few more days." The whole point of today was to leave and find something sharp enough to cut them off, and here I am, committed to an apartment and trying to get a job.

"When can you start?"

"Immediately," I tell her.

"The pay is twenty-two an hour. The hours are shit. Wash your hands and come on."

The cashier gently taps my back and says, "Good luck," before returning to her post near the register.

I stifle the smile that creeps across my face and comply, going over to the sink to wash my hands.

Getting a job and an apartment in one fell swoop is pretty awesome, but it will be nothing compared to the satisfaction of proving Archer wrong.

CHAPTER TWENTY

Archer

Even though it's been a few days, I still can't believe that London was only gone less than an hour and she managed to land a job.

How?

I fought the urge to prevent it from happening and decided to go along with it. The whole point is for London to get back on her feet so she can move out, and yet I can't help but feel resistance.

The job isn't far, and their security is lax enough that I can easily gain access to various feeds throughout their building. If she was going to get a gig anywhere, this would be the most ideal. She doesn't have to take a bus, taxi, or train, and if something happens, I could be there in two minutes flat.

I finish my daily scan of what Joe Vito is up to, and conclude that he doesn't seem that interested in locating her. Maybe Silver overestimated the threat or did a good enough job of making her disappear that he doesn't even know where to look. Either way, it's made my task of keeping her safe that much easier.

Perhaps I should accept the independence she's gaining because it's putting her one step closer to getting out of my hair.

I thought London having a job was going to be painful, but so far, nothing bad has happened. That doesn't mean I haven't been watching her intensely every moment she's been gone. It's distracting. My work is suffering. And if I don't get my head out of my ass soon, I might make a costly mistake I cannot risk. I'm getting things done, but mainly when she's fast asleep in my bedroom, and I can guarantee she's safe and sound.

My investigation of the man who tried to rob Ruth's place was unsuccessful—one dead end after another. I'm not convinced it didn't have something to do with the Manor brothers, but I haven't found anything to give me irrefutable proof yet. And without that, none of my own brothers will take me seriously. They call me paranoid and tell me I'm overreacting, and honestly, I'm kind of starting to believe them.

I didn't use to be like this. I was always pretty thorough and collected, but this Archer second-guesses and triple-checks everything. There are things I miss about the old me despite it being better that he stay buried in the past.

London slams the front door shut, jarring my attention from the computer I'm mindlessly typing code on. I've been trying to hack into security footage at a high-end gentleman's club on the West Coast for the past hour to no avail. I'm getting sloppy and it shows.

She doesn't bother looking in my direction, which is a dead giveaway that something is up. London continues into my bedroom, her purse clutched to her chest. She doesn't visibly seem injured, but her body language tells me this isn't her normal behavior.

This is what I get for not watching her every second she's gone. I thought having her feed in the background and paying attention every so often would be enough. Yet here I am, clueless about what's going on because I was focused on anything other than her for a change.

London slips out of my room and darts straight into the bathroom, shutting the door behind her.

I make my way over there in a rush, tapping on the door. "Are you okay?"

"Yeah," she calls back without hesitation.

"Why are you being weird?"

"Why are you?" she responds. "Maybe I have to poop, leave me alone."

“Are you sick?” I ask her.

“I’m fine, Archer. Leave me alone.” Her tone is clipped and pointed but it does nothing to settle my unease.

I remain there, one arm on the doorframe, and wait for something, anything.

“I know you’re still out there,” she says through the door. “Go away.”

Breathing through my nose, I attempt to calm my nerves and not break this door down right now. “I’m not going anywhere until you tell me what’s going on, London.”

She grunts. “You are so annoying, you know that, right?” Muffled sounds come through. “Just give me a few minutes and I’ll be out.”

I keep my arm on the doorframe and consider how hard I’ll have to kick to open the door. Only, if I’m not careful, London could be in the crossfire, and that would make things worse than they already are. I don’t want to hurt her, I just want to know what the fuck she’s hiding from me.

An entire minute passes and my nerves have done nothing but grow wilder. “London, I’m giving you to the count of three and I’m busting the door down.” I hate myself for being this way. “One...” I pause and give her a chance. “Two...”

“Jesus, Archer,” London huffs. “Hold on.” She unlocks the door and turns the handle, opening it slightly.

I peer at her, inside the bathroom, and back at her. “What are you doing?”

“Why does it matter?”

“It matters,” I all but growl. “Let me in.”

“You’re being a psycho.” London keeps the door barely ajar, hiding herself behind it.

“And you’re being secretive. Did something happen? Did someone hurt you? Tell me and I’ll make it right.”

London narrows her gaze. "Are you listening to yourself right now?"

"Step away from the door." As forcefully as I can without shoving her out of the way, I push the door and step into the confined space, my sight scanning the room and searching for answers.

"You can't just barge in here and..."

That's when I locate the bag on the counter from a local hardware store and the thing sitting on top of it. I snatch it off the counter, turning it over in my hand and trying to make sense of what I'm looking at.

London hugs her arm to her chest and it finally clicks what's going on here.

"Let me see it." I hold out my hand and she reluctantly puts her casted arm into my palm, the edge of the cast snipped from the blunt-edged scissors she attempted to smuggle in here. A million thoughts run through my mind, like how could she be so stupid? Why wouldn't she go to a doctor? Why not ask me for help, or at the very least, someone else? She's going to hurt herself if she's not careful.

"I don't want a lecture, Archer," London says. "So if you're going to give me one, you can get the hell out."

"I'm not going to lecture you," I tell her, even though I really fucking want to. Chewing at the corner of my lip, I realize the only path forward is to play nice. "Let me help you."

"I don't need your help," she snaps at me, and pulls her arm away. "I was doing fine without you."

I ignore the strange sensation cutting through me at her jab and continue. "It's not an option. I either help you or you can get out." So much for playing nice.

"You wouldn't." London glares at me and I match her intensity, stepping toward her.

"I would." I put my hands on London's waist and hoist her

onto the counter without giving her a chance to protest. "Now sit here and shut up."

Surprisingly, London doesn't disagree, and even puts her arm on her lap instead of hugging it to her chest.

"Good girl," I tell her, and line the scissors along the edge of the cast. It doesn't take me long to carefully cut through the cast, pausing once I reach the end. "Are you in any pain?"

London swallows harshly. "No."

"I'm going to pry it apart," I tell her, and hope like hell enough time has passed for her arm to be healed. If it were up to me, London would be in a doctor's office having this done, but I'd be a fool if I thought she would wait to let that happen. Once London makes her mind up about something, she stubbornly won't let it go.

"Okay." London keeps her eyes on her arm as I grip her cast gently, but firmly, and pull at the sides.

The cast cracks and gives way, revealing her frail arm underneath.

London loosens a sigh and brings her other hand over to caress the no-doubt tender skin.

"Are you sure you're okay?" I ask her.

She nods rapidly. "I'm great." London extends her fingers and contracts them, turning her wrist over and bringing it toward her. "I feel like I just lost twenty pounds."

"You should probably take it easy with that thing for a while. Maybe get it checked out."

"Can you not ruin this moment for me?" London pushes my chest to move me away before hopping off the counter and unbuttoning her pants.

"What are you doing?" I blurt out.

"Uh, taking my pants off so you can cut the other one off."

"Right. Yeah." My chest constricts as London slides her jeans over her ass, revealing a pair of dainty lace panties, similar to the ones I fucked her with and ended up stealing.

"Put your tongue back into your mouth, big boy." London smirks and steps out of her pants completely, leaving her in just her fitted top and panties.

Maybe it's a good thing she didn't go to some random doctor to have this done.

I do my best not to eye her too much and focus on the cast attached to her leg. I'm not always a gentleman, but for her I'll try.

London inches toward the counter, pressing her hands to the sides to lift herself. I get there first, my palms gripping her waist and putting her back up there before she can hurt herself.

"You shouldn't apply pressure to that arm this soon," I tell her like I'm trying to come up with an excuse for why I'm touching her.

"Whatever," she responds, and repositions herself.

Kneeling in front of her, I start at her foot, holding her leg steady with one hand and using the other to run the scissors up her cast. The material is easier to cut through than I expected, and it takes no time to make my way to the other side.

"Are you ready?" I ask her once I've cut the length of the cast.

She nods stiffly.

Repeating the same movement as her arm, I pry the sides of the cast open until it pops and reveals her leg.

"Gross," London says immediately. "It's so hairy."

"I think that's normal," I tell her.

"Normal and gross. I'm so ugly now."

My jaw tenses. "Don't say that about yourself."

London rolls her eyes. "Don't be so dramatic, I'm joking." She wiggles her toes and rolls her ankle to get a feel for her newfound freedom.

"Are you in any pain?"

"Not at all."

I hate that I can't tell whether she's lying or not. London could be actively bleeding to death and I'm not sure anyone would notice. She might be annoying as hell at times, but she refuses to let on that anything ever bothers her. It's a quality I respect and know all too well.

Rising to my feet, I help guide London off the counter and onto the floor, gently setting her down to get her footing. "You sure you're okay?" I study her so intensely that I accidentally spot a freckle I've never seen on her cheek.

"Stop looking at me like that," she says, her green eyes meeting mine.

"Like what?"

"Like I'm about to fall apart. We've been over this before, Archer."

"How do you want me to look at you?"

I stare into her unwavering gaze and hate the desire that overwhelms me. I shouldn't want her the way I do, and yet nothing could compare to how badly I want to grab her face and kiss her. She infuriates me—why can't that be all that it is?

A smirk forms on her face like she can hear my fucking thoughts, making me break eye contact first. I release a breath and busy myself with picking up the discarded pieces of her cast, piling them in my arms and doing what I can to put anything between us.

"We should have a drink," London suggests. "To celebrate."

"Okay," I say while leaving the room so she can put her pants on or do whatever it is she needs to do. But once I'm at the trash can, I find myself unable to throw the casts away. They serve no purpose, they have no use, why can't I just toss them?

"You have no idea how much better I feel," London says while coming into the kitchen.

I drop the pile behind the trash and shut the pantry door. "I bet," I tell her, and avoid eye contact as I make my way over to the cabinet where I keep my liquor. "What kind of drink did you want?"

I open the door and scan the options. Tequila, vodka, whiskey, and rum are at the front, concealing pretty much everything else needed to make just about any mixed drink. Even a few bottles of wine I had picked up here and there and tucked in along the side. I glance over my shoulder. "Or did you want to go out for a drink?"

"Staying in is fine." London settles on a stool at the island. "Let's start with tequila."

I grab the bottle, put a few ice cubes into two small glasses, and make my way over to her.

She takes them from me, pouring some of the liquid into both, more in one than the other. She pushes the fuller one toward me.

"Trying to get me drunk?" I ask her, and take it anyway.

"Maybe." London raises her glass. "To starting over."

"I can cheers to that." I clink my glass against hers and we down the tequila, the warmth of it flowing down my chest.

"We should play a drinking game," London says.

I lick the remains of the tequila off my lips. "That sounds dangerous."

"Are you afraid?" London refills our drinks, making sure to fill mine a bit higher.

"No. Are you?"

"I'm the one who suggested it." London crosses her legs and teeters a bit like she isn't quite used to not having that bulky cast off yet.

"What are the rules?"

"Truth or drink," she says. "A question is asked. You can either answer it or drink."

"What happened to dare?"

"That usually follows." She winks at me and it's everything I can do not to react. "So what do you say, will you play with me?"

I down the tequila in my cup and wipe my mouth. "Why not?"

London smiles, and I hate the way it warms my chest more than the tequila. How is it possible to both not be able to stand someone and want them at the same time?

"But," I interject. "We need sustenance. What do you want to eat?"

"What do you think I want to eat?"

I stare at her for a long moment. "Do you think I can read your mind?"

"Can you?"

"You want lo mein and veggie egg rolls."

Her smile widens. "See, you can!"

I shake my head, pull out my phone, and place an order for entirely too much food, but when drinking is involved, it's better safe than sorry. Once I'm finished, I get us both large glasses of water and slide onto a chair at the island, one between us.

"You are so boring," London says while taking a sip of her water.

"You'll thank me tomorrow when your head isn't violently pounding."

"Who said my head isn't always violently pounding?" London turns toward me. "Okay, I'll go first. Hmm. Oh, I've got it. Why are you so grumpy?"

I scowl. "I'm not grumpy."

"Do you want me to get a mirror out for you, big boy? I mean, the wrinkles between your brows. You're going to need Botox if you keep that up."

I do what I can to relax my face.

"Were you always this uptight?" London persists.

"That was two questions," I inform her. "Were you always this nosey?"

London shrugs. "Yeah, probably." She pauses and adds, "See

how easy that was?"

"What?"

"To answer a question."

"Oh." I twirl the glass of tequila before putting it to my lips and downing it in one swallow. "There. Now it's my turn." But the moment the opportunity presents itself, I realize I have no idea what I want to ask her. Sure, there are a million burning questions, but none of them are appropriate. Like who she really is, and what actually brought her here? How did she get involved with Joe Vito, and what is her connection to Silver?

"I'm waiting, big boy." London leans against the counter and keeps her eyes glued to me.

"I...I pass."

London sighs. "You're so boring."

"Thanks."

"It wasn't a compliment."

"I have a question," I admit. "Why are you always trying to pick a fight?"

London blinks a few times like she's taken aback. "I do not."

"You're lying and you know it."

"Fine," London huffs. "I mean, it's not necessarily on purpose, but you're fun to mess with. You get flustered easily." She fidgets with her glass. "You're going to have to ask me harder questions, otherwise I'm never going to drink."

"Maybe I'm not trying to get you drunk."

She shifts right into her next train of thought. "What was your longest relationship?"

I have half a mind to drink the tequila she pours into my glass, almost as if she's expecting me not to answer, but realize I have nothing to lose by giving her this information. "Six years."

"Damn. I don't know what's more surprising, the fact that you answered or that you were in a relationship for six years."

I force a laugh. "Yeah."

"What happened? Did she break up with you?"

My gaze lowers and the memory of what happened comes rushing in. I open my mouth, unsure why I'm admitting the truth right now when I've done everything I can to bury it for the past few years. "She died."

London's lips part, her expression softening and her hand reaching forward to rest on mine. "I'm so sorry, I never would have asked if I knew."

I pull my hand away, the reaction so quick and aggressive. "It's fine. You didn't know. It's in the past, anyway."

"Still, Archer, I'm sorry." My name on her tongue and the tequila coursing through me almost numb the loss.

"What about you?" I ask her, both to deflect the pitiful look on her face and to derail this from being all about me. "What was your longest relationship?"

"Six months."

"What happened?" I ask, unsure if follow-up questions are part of the rules.

London stays quiet for a long moment before drinking the tequila in her glass. Her face pinches slightly and she licks her lips. "Good job, you made me drink."

"That bad, huh?"

"Yep," she says while pouring herself more tequila. "Let's talk families. Tell me about your parents."

"Never knew them," I admit easier than I expected.

"Wait, what's the age gap between the twins and August? How did you not know them?"

"That's a lot of questions, little tornado."

"Help me make it make sense," London pleads.

"We're not blood-related," I confess. "Well, Ivy and Seven are. They are twins. But the rest of us, there's no blood relation."

"But you call each other brother and sister."

I run my hand through my hair, unsure of how much of this I want to share with her. Any other time, I'd clam up and not say a word, but the back-to-back shots have my inhibitions and my lips feeling a bit loose. "We grew up in foster care together. We bounced from house to house but would always end up back together in the group home. We were the only constants in each other's lives, and after a while, we started looking out for one another. I guess a sort of unspoken bond formed, and it turned into something stronger than a blood connection. We made a pact to be there for each other, and the rest is history."

"Interesting," is all London responds, and I hate that I can't read her mind to fully grasp what she's thinking about my admission.

I grow uncomfortable in my skin at having told her all that information and shift in my seat. "What about you? Tell me about your parents."

"They're both dead."

It's not that I expected that to be her answer, but I don't find myself at all surprised. I guess neither one of us is a stranger to losing someone.

"What happened?" I ask, even though I know damn well it isn't my place to. It must be the alcohol talking at this point.

"My father killed my mother when I was three years old."

My mouth goes dry and I'm not sure what to do with my hands other than reach out and place them around London's, cupping them in a way that begs for her to understand that I'm here.

She stares blankly, her eyes shifting back and forth, lost in a memory. "Most people, when something traumatic happens to them, their mind blocks it out, files it away as it tries to protect itself. Me? I remember everything bad that's ever happened. Starting with that day."

"You don't have to—"

"There was blood everywhere," she whispers. "I walked right in it. It was warm and sticky and I remember being so confused, and so worried, because my dad hated messes. I was three and knew that. Knew that he would be so furious when he found it. I grabbed a rag, followed the trail of red, and thought if I could find the source, maybe I could stop it from getting worse.

"It wasn't until I stumbled over her lifeless leg that I realized she was where it came from." London blinks stiffly. "Her eyes were open, her mouth parted. She wasn't moving and I couldn't understand why. I put my arms around her, hugged her, and lay there for I don't know how long, thinking maybe if I stayed with her, it would fix things. Shortly after, that's when the maid found me, covered in my mother's blood from head to toe. She had to pry me from my dead mother."

The buzzer to the apartment dings, loud and intrusive.

London seems to snap out of her trance and hops from the stool. "Food's here."

CHAPTER TWENTY-ONE

London

I rush over to the door, my legs somehow easier and harder to walk on now without the cast. It's strange that I only wore it for a short period, but it seems like I lost some permanent piece of me.

Archer walks past me, putting himself between me and the door. He hits the buzzer and gives the takeout guy access to the building. "Go sit down, I've got it," he tells me with that *do it or else* look on his face.

I roll my eyes and return to the kitchen, topping off our tequila and taking a long swig of the water so Archer doesn't give me shit about it. My entire body is warm with the alcohol, and for the first time in a long while, my head and shoulders feel lighter.

A minute passes before Archer comes over with a large brown sack in his hands. He sets it on the counter and carefully rips open the bag, taking one thing after the other out and setting it on the counter.

"How much stuff did you order?"

"Does that count as a question?" Archer glances up at me through his thick lashes and goes back to work pulling everything out. He strolls over, grabbing two plates, setting one in front of me, and shoving a stack of napkins between us.

"Thanks for the food," I tell him, digging into the box of lo mein.

"No problem." Archer dumps some noodles onto his plate and pops a giant piece of broccoli in his mouth.

"And for the place to stay," I add.

He shoots me a glance. "You're welcome?"

"What?" I shove his shoulder playfully.

"You're being nice," Archer says. "Must be the tequila."

"Oh, whatever."

We eat our food in silence for a little while, the only sound other than our chewing is the faint music that Archer put on playing in the background.

I bite the end of an egg roll and pivot the stool toward Archer. "What's your favorite color?"

Archer finishes swallowing the food in his mouth and pats his mouth with his napkin. "I didn't realize we were going to get so personal with our questions."

"Oh, come on."

His gaze meets mine, something so intense in the way he's looking at me. "Green." Without taking his eyes off me, he reaches for his glass of tequila. "This is because I'm thirsty."

I smirk at him. "You sure do loosen up when you've been drinking."

"The more I drink, the less there is for you." Archer sets the cup down. "I think it's my turn."

"Ask away, big boy."

He leans a little closer, his tattooed arm resting on the counter. "Did you mean it when you said I was a bad kisser?"

My cheeks redden and there's nothing I can do to conceal the heat flushing my entire body. I consider my options, opting to take my glass of tequila and down it.

Archer doesn't even try to hide the grin on his face. "Thought so."

"You're the worst," I tell him, despite us both knowing I'm lying.

"Okay."

I go right into the next question. "What's your favorite tattoo?"

Archer lifts his shirt, exposing his ink-stained skin, and points to a lock that's just over his heart.

"Where's the key?" I ask him, the limit to my questions seemingly endless tonight. I'm not sure where this game begins or ends anymore, and the insatiable hunger to learn more about this mysterious man only continues to grow.

Archer drinks, not wanting to give me the answer to my question. Or maybe because there is no key to his heart; it was lost somewhere along the way when the woman he was in love with died.

"We've covered relationships, parents, siblings...what else is there?"

"Politics and religion?" I suggest sarcastically.

Archer chuckles. "I'd rather drink."

I grab my glass and raise it in the air between us. "You and me both." I tip it back, swallowing the liquid for no reason other than wanting to keep this buzz going. This is the first time in a while I haven't felt so heavy, and I want nothing more than for it to last, even if it means the uncertainty of whether I'll have a hangover tomorrow or not.

"It's kind of terrifying, really," Archer says.

"What?"

"How you can talk about something so traumatic and then immediately pretend like everything is fine."

"Who said I was pretending?" I eat more of the egg roll and hope Archer doesn't see right through me.

"We might not know each other well, London, but I know you better than you think."

I swallow the bite in my mouth. "What do you want me to do? Break down and cry because something bad happened to me? If I did that every time, I'd never stop crying. You think I'm annoying now, imagine me crying twenty-four-seven."

"You're allowed to process your emotions."

"Says the grumpy guy who hides away in here by himself."

"I'm not by myself."

"You were until I got here. And I guarantee you still would be if I hadn't. Admit it, as much as you hate this, it isn't all bad."

"I didn't say I hated it," Archer deflects.

"You didn't need to. Pretty sure you telling your sister how terrible I am was enough."

"She thought we were hooking up. I had to make her understand it wasn't like that."

"Uh-huh."

"What do you want from me, London? An apology?" Archer pauses. "I'm sorry, okay? I'm sorry I said that shit to Ivy."

"I think you're just sorry I heard it."

Archer rubs his temple and glides his hand through his hair, some of it spilling onto his forehead. "You're going to be the death of me, you know that?"

"I know," I say with a smile, and continue eating my egg roll. "Can you add me as a beneficiary before you die? I missed out on any inheritance."

Archer laughs, and for once it's genuine.

"You think I'm funny."

"Yeah, sure. That's it."

"How much will I get?" I ask him. "Couple hundred grand?" I scratch my chin. "What's Archer worth?"

"A few bil, probably."

I almost choke on my saliva. "I'm sorry, what? Did you say million?"

"Billion, with a B, baby." Archer winks at me and shoves a forkful of noodles into his mouth, the alcohol no doubt lowering his filter enough to admit he's filthy rich.

My phone buzzes and I flip it over to see a text from Grace.

GRACE

Hey. Next Friday. You busy?

I thumb back a quick response.

ME

Not sure, what's up?

GRACE

Clear your schedule. Double date.

ME

Wait, what? With who??

I ignore the way Archer watches me on my phone, his stare unsettling me more than telling him about my father murdering my mother.

GRACE

Me and Leo. You and one of his friends.

"What's wrong?" Archer asks me.

"Oh, nothing. Grace wants to get together next week." I leave out the part that it's a date, because if I have learned anything about Archer, it's that he is too much of a control freak to let it go. He's made it clear he isn't interested in me in that way, so what's the harm of going out with someone who might be?

"She seems nice, I like her," Archer admits.

"Well, if you want to date her, you better get in line behind two of your other brothers," I tease him.

"I don't want to date Grace. I'm allowed to like someone without *liking* them."

"Are you mansplaining male and female friendships?"

Archer takes in a deep breath and I almost smile at how easy it is to frustrate him. "London."

"Archer," I mock. "Wait, let's go back to you being a billionaire. That was a joke, right?" I sip some of my tequila, noting how it goes down smoother than before, the telltale sign that I'm drunker than I realize.

"Do you want to see my bank accounts?" Archer drinks his tequila, and for the first time all night, it's him that refills his glass. He keeps the bottle near him like he's hoarding it all for himself. He and Seven might not be blood-related, but they sure are selfish with their liquor.

"I believe you," I say, despite being dangerously curious about Archer's financials. "How is that possible, though? What do you do?"

Archer shrugs. "This and that."

"Drink." I point to his glass. "If you're not going to tell me, you have to drink. That's the rules, remember." I laugh for no real reason, my face all hot and warm and smiley.

"God damn, you're pretty when you smile," Archer says, his glassy eyes meeting mine.

"So I'm ugly when I'm not?"

Archer frowns. "You know what I mean." He hops up from his chair and holds his hand out to me. "Let's dance."

"Wow, you really are drunk, aren't you?"

He sucks down more tequila and almost drops his glass getting it back on the counter. "I'm buzzed. Let me live."

I take in the mess he left behind on the counter, knowing damn well he's going to hate himself for that tomorrow. But that Archer can deal with it, because right now, this Archer wants to dance with me.

Sliding my hand into his, he surprises me by twirling me to his chest, my body hitting his with a thud.

"Sorry, was that too aggressive?" Archer's words blend together slightly, the alcohol numbing his otherwise sharp, calculated tone.

"Not at all," I reassure him.

He moves me to the soft beat of the music playing in the background, a piano with a delicate melody. Our bodies fall into rhythm with ease, him leading me around his living room.

Archer twirls me around, dips me backward, and holds me close, our heartbeats in sync, our breaths mingling. I sort of wish there was a way to freeze this moment in time because, as beautiful as it is, it won't last.

"Where did you learn how to dance?" I ask him, regretting it the second it's out of my mouth.

I feel the shift in his energy a millisecond before I see it slip across his face.

Archer slows down, his hands loosening their grip.

I try to hold him to me but I feel him slipping away. I want him to stay. I want to keep him close. I don't want to lose this momentary bliss where everything and nothing is right all at once.

"I shouldn't have asked," I say, hoping it will fix my mistake. My head swims with booze and desire and the things I want to tell him. That I understand. That I'm sorry. That he's not alone in his sadness.

"It's my fault," he declares. "It's my fault she died."

"What? No. I'm sure it wasn't. Don't blame yourself."

Archer releases me completely, his hands in the space between us. "I can't keep you safe. I can't keep anyone safe."

"That's not true." I reach out and place my hand on his shoulder. "You didn't do anything wrong."

"She didn't want anything to do with the life. I should have listened to her. If I would have listened to her, she'd still be alive." Archer's breath hitches.

"Here, sit down." I guide him to the couch, grateful that he complies and sits down. As much as I give him shit and tease him, there's no way I could force him to do anything he didn't want to. Archer is tall, and strong—he could crush me without breaking a sweat.

Archer leans back and runs both of his hands through his hair. "I hate this. I hate feeling this way. I hate saying any of this out loud. Fuck. I shouldn't have drunk. I'm sorry."

I face him and pull my legs up onto the couch. "Hey, don't apologize. Sounds like you needed this. Maybe you need to get it out. Vent a little."

Archer shakes his head. "I'm good now. I've reeled it back in."

"You don't have to, Archer. Talk to me. Tell me about her."

"Can't I just drink instead?" He turns his head toward me.

"We're not playing a game anymore," I tell him while placing my hand on his shoulder. "This is real."

"I hate thinking about it," he says. "It hurts."

"Sometimes the things we love most in life hurt us. That doesn't make it any less special, any less worth it. As painful as it is, not everything lasts. It's a fucked-up reality, but it's true."

"I can't do it again."

I pinch my brows. "What do you mean?"

"This. Us. I can't risk losing you. That's why I panic every time I don't know what's going on. It's like it's happening all over again." Archer shakes his head. "Why Silver would do this to me, I don't understand."

"Hey, you're not going to lose me. The situation is handled. It's fine. Joe has no idea where I am. He thinks I'm dead. You have nothing to worry about. Unless someone found out I was alive and explicitly told him, he's never going to find out. And the only other person who would want me dead is already dead. The threat is nonexistent. You have nothing to worry about." I'm not even lying. Silver did a good job cutting the loose ties and making sure my escape was clean. Other than my father, there wasn't anyone else who was aware of the business deal, and if I were Joe, I wouldn't be publicizing that he made such a deal with a dead man. All my father's assets were seized by the Feds, so there isn't even anything Joe can do to get his money back.

If Joe wanted to find me, he would already be causing chaos.

Unless he's licking his wounds until the opportune time. The thought sends a chill up my spine, but I ignore it because calming Archer down is more important than anything else at the moment.

Archer sits up and riffles through some of the books on the coffee table in front of us, flicking the pages until he finds what he's looking for. He slides out a photograph, holding it in his hand while cupping his chin with his other one.

I lean closer, taking in the picture, my eyes settling on Archer, a different version of him, a happier one. He seems lighter, and freer. And then next to him, a face that haunts me to this day.

I blink a few times, trying to make sense of what I'm staring at, but the image doesn't clear.

Same eyes. Same hair. Same nose. Same everything.

My chest tightens, and I go from being buzzed to completely sober in a split second.

Flashes of a fight come into my mind. Screaming. Begging. Pleading. Gunshots. My father. His wrath. His bloody loafers and his vile breath.

I wanted to save her, to save myself, but I couldn't.

I did everything I could, but it wasn't enough. Not for her. Not for the girl in the photo.

The same girl I almost died trying to save, the reason I have a jagged scar across my stomach. The same girl that died at the hands of my father.

Archer isn't the reason why Madison is dead, I am.

CHAPTER TWENTY-TWO

Archer

My head aches, but it's nothing compared to the regret I have of saying things I should have kept to myself. London and I shared trauma I'm not convinced either of us has shared with others, and I don't know whether it's a good or bad thing.

I feel closer to her, but I hate showing weakness. I hate how vulnerable it makes me.

But then there are moments from last night I don't hate—like slow dancing in the living room and laughing at each other while we were eating. I didn't mind opening up to her, it's just everything else that comes along with it.

*Feelings...*gross.

London steps out of the bathroom, a towel wrapped around both her body and her hair. It's sort of a gut punch seeing she no longer needs, or even wants, me to wash her hair. I had gotten used to it, looked forward to it even, and I regret not enjoying it a bit more when it was happening.

Life's strange like that—you don't realize in the moment that it's the last time, and once it hits, there's nothing you can do to turn back the clock.

She doesn't look in my direction as she makes her way into the bedroom and shuts the door behind her, a coldness to her today that wasn't there yesterday.

Did I share too much? Did I overstep? Did a wedge get put between us that can't be removed?

I shake my head and remind myself that it's better this way.

She's doing me a favor by icing me out. Because that's what we both should be doing. It's clear that we aren't compatible—it must stay that way.

Still, that doesn't mean we don't have insanely palpable chemistry that is off the fucking charts. Just the memory of how sweet she tastes is enough to make my cock ache for her.

I continue my task, typing away at my computer, slyly removing funds from one account and moving them to another. I might be a bad man, but there are worse men out there, and I fucking love stealing from them and donating to charities they'd never be caught supporting.

I do this seven more times, stealing over three million dollars to spread across various charities, my actions completely untraceable. I'm double-checking my family's investments when London comes out of the bedroom, her towel-dried hair hanging over her shoulders.

"Do you want help with that?" I ask her.

"I'm good," she says, and goes into the bathroom.

I chew at my lip and try to force away the rampant thoughts of not fully understanding where her head is at. Maybe she's hungover, too. Maybe she regained some freedom from getting the casts off and just wanted to wash her hair herself. I can't imagine asking for help in the first place was easy for her, so not needing it now, it makes sense for her to go back to her old ways. Still, I wish she knew I wasn't bothered by helping her. I enjoyed it.

It's nice to feel needed.

After a quick recap of the whereabouts of Joe Vito, I mark him off my to-do list for the day. The guy is boring, predictable, and honestly, a total fucking waste of oxygen. He spends most of his time at the same few clubs, spending entirely too much on bottle service to buy friendships, and has his hand in countless illegal activities that I would never approve of. Don't get me wrong, I've done my fair share of shady shit, but I draw the line at women and children. I don't respect men because they don't deserve it, but women are doing their best to survive, so there's no way I'm adding to the shit they have to worry about.

Call me a feminist, or maybe just a decent fucking human being.

The sound of the muffled blow-dryer comes through the bathroom door, and I picture myself in there, drying and brushing through London's red hair. I got pretty okay with it toward the end, picking up a few new braiding techniques and learning how to use a round brush to style her hair while drying it. I had no idea so much went into doing hair until I wanted to make sure she was happy with hers.

My phone rings, and a picture of Ivy lights up the screen.

Reluctantly, I answer. "Hey, sis," I say into the receiver.

"Arch. How are you? What's going on?"

"Not much," I tell her while keeping my eyes on the bathroom door. It's not like she can leave without me seeing it happen; I don't know why I'm so fucking drawn to where she is. I wouldn't put it past London to accidentally drop the blow-dryer in the sink with the water running, though. She's accident-prone like that, and a bit ditzy. "What's up with you?"

"Busy with work, as always. You know, August keeping me busy."

"How is he?"

Ivy sighs. "He told me you called the other day."

"Oh, great. What did he say?"

"Something about you're paranoid the Manor brothers had something to do with a robbery in your neighborhood."

"I don't think I'm being paranoid," I tell her.

"That's what a paranoid person would say."

"Explain it to me, Vee. He came in with a dirty gun, said he'd get killed if he told me who sent him. Who else could it have been?"

"You know they're not the only family that doesn't like us, right? We have enemies coming from every direction."

"Which is all the more concerning. Who's to say they're not allying to take us out? We're going to have to make a power move if we want to maintain control."

"And what do you suggest?"

"You're the PR specialist, isn't this your thing?"

Ivy laughs. "A suggestion or nudge in the right direction wouldn't be the worst."

"I think we need to reach out to Johnny Jones. He and his wife have a huge sector. If we could ally with them, we'd have more territory. A stronger footing." I pause and then add, "They have connections out West, too. And if I'm not mistaken, I might know a guy."

"Are you listening to yourself? You might know a guy? Really?"

I shrug even though she can't see me. "What's the worst that could happen, they decline? We need to do something, or they're going to overpower and push us out."

"I'll have to discuss details with August. He has the final say in these things."

"I think you're underestimating how much control over him you have. August would do anything you said."

"Anything other than listen to me."

"It's worth a shot. I'd hate to see us lose everything we've all sacrificed so much to build."

"It's not going anywhere."

I lean back in my chair, my sight still on the bathroom door.

"What's going on with you and that girl? Is she still there? Will you be at the family dinner?"

"Nothing is going on between us. Yes, she's still here, for another few weeks. You'll have to remind me about dinner."

"Sunday at noon. Promise me you won't fight with Seven."

"I can't make that promise," I tell her, especially with London on the line. He overstepped by getting aggressive with her, and that's something I refuse to allow to happen again. "How about this? I promise not to kill him. Everything else is on the table."

Even through the phone, I can tell that Ivy rolls her eyes and switches ears. "You're the worst, Arch...but who am I kidding, I want to punch Seven in the face from time to time too."

"I don't know how you don't. I would have consumed him in the womb if I were you."

Ivy grins so much, I can hear it in her voice. "You have no idea how many times I've considered it. That man, well, that fucking child, he drives me insane. I'm sick of cleaning up his messes. It's getting out of hand, and I'm at the point I don't know how to help him. He needs professional help but he refuses to talk to anyone. He just wants to push me away, and all I'm trying to do is be there for him."

"Maybe he needs you to be there for him in a different way." But once the words are out of my mouth, I come to terms with the fact that Seven really is unwell in the head. He lacks remorse and empathy and any consideration for his own, or anyone else's, safety. If he weren't family, I'd have nothing to do with him. He's too much of a loose cannon.

"I don't know what else to do, Arch. I've tried everything. I'm at a loss."

I sense the shift in her tone, the seriousness of everything she's said and hasn't said. I just wish there was something I could do to help her, to help him, but at this point, I think Seven might be a lost cause. The trauma he's experienced molded him into who he is, there's no denying that, but I think things go deeper than trauma and more into who he is as a person fundamentally.

"Anyway," she says before letting me get a word in. "What's going on with you? Tell me more about this girl. How long did you say she's crashing at your place?"

"She has a name, you know."

Ivy sighs. "That doesn't answer my question."

My mind floats back to last night, the game London and I had played. If only I were able to take a shot instead of having this conversation with my sister. "I think she's getting an apartment in a few weeks. So not much longer."

I loathe the tightening that forms in my chest. How can I look after her when she's not living inside my apartment? Next door isn't *that* far, but it's farther than I'd prefer.

"I have a bad feeling about her, Arch."

"You have a bad feeling about everything, Vee. You have trust issues."

"I trust you."

"Well, that's a given. I'm a pretty trustworthy guy."

"I don't know about all that." Ivy pauses. "Dinner, the Sunday after next. Can you handle that?"

"Where?" I ask her.

"If I say your place, will you promise not to go out of town or change the locks?"

"Chinese?"

"Keeps everyone happy. But maybe hide the booze from Seven this time."

Seven's drink of choice is tequila, although I don't think there's an alcohol he would pass up given the opportunity. And considering the dent London and I made in it last night, as long as I don't replenish it, he shouldn't get too fucked up with what's left. Maybe I'll go ahead and put a lock on the cabinet door just in case.

London comes out of the bathroom, her hair dried and in soft waves dancing around her shoulders. Even from this far away, I can see a light layer of mascara and a shade of lipstick I've never noticed her wear before. She avoids my gaze, going back into the bedroom and coming out with her purse a second later.

"I've got to go," I tell Ivy, and hang up the phone, sliding it into my pocket as I hop up from my desk. "What's up?" I meet London halfway to the door.

"Just going to work." She barely looks up at me, and unease settles over me like the cold of night.

"Oh." I take a breath in and exhale. "Want me to walk you?"

London adjusts the bag over her shoulder, still not quite focusing on me. "No. I'm good. I'll be fine." She moves to the door and I reach out and catch her arm.

"Is everything okay? Between us?" I want to punch myself in the dick for asking such a question. It sounds so desperate and pathetic, and if I had a time machine, I'd erase it from existence.

"Yeah." She nods. "Of course it is. Sorry, a lot on my mind is all."

There's no denying that London is going through a plethora of shit, but still, I'm not convinced she's telling me the truth. And it isn't exactly my place to pry. Just because we have these moments of closeness doesn't mean we are anything other than strangers forced to live under the same roof. The sooner I come to terms with that, and I mean fully fucking grasp it, the better.

I guess I thought something in our dynamic shifted last night. I shared things I don't talk to anyone about, and maybe I'm an idiot for thinking it brought us closer together.

"I'm here," I tell her. "If you need to vent, get it off your mind."

"Thanks." London gives me a fake smile before slipping out the front door and leaving me behind to wonder where things went wrong.

***

Almost a week of awkwardness ensues as London does everything she can to avoid me. She's civil, but the most concerning thing is the lack of arguing with me every chance she gets. That's how I know with one hundred percent certainty something happened that she's not telling me. London loves arguing, getting on my nerves, and doing whatever she can to drive me insane.

But aside from only talking to me when directly asked or necessary, London hasn't made a single quip at me all week. She's even been picking up after herself and not leaving messes everywhere she goes.

I thought I would prefer it this way. The Archer who opened up the door to her bloodied and beaten was frustrated with her entire existence, but now all I want is for it to come back. I've tried poking to see if I could get something out of her, but she's put every wall possible between us, and I'm at a loss for how to move forward.

I suppose the only thing I can do is leave what I thought we had in the past and focus on the task at hand—keeping her safe and getting her on her feet. I don't want her to go, but I can't make her stay, not when she clearly doesn't want to be here.

London has been in my bedroom for over an hour, getting ready for her date with Grace. Part of me is glad she's getting out and going and doing something with her friend; maybe that will make her feel better. And the other part of me wants to shake her and ask what happened, what went wrong, why she shut me out completely.

Although there's a larger part of me that wants to kick myself for caring and wondering why any of this matters to me. I'm getting exactly what I wanted. This was always a means to an end. London's stay was never permanent. And yet why does it ache this fucking badly?

The door to my bedroom opens and London steps through, wearing an olive-green dress, making her hair and eyes pop that much more. I steady my breathing and pretend to type something on my keyboard, hitting buttons that don't do anything other than piss off my computer.

London clears her throat, my attention returning to her faster than it should. "I'm leaving," she says. "I'll be back in a few hours."

I stand, not sure what else I'm supposed to do, and fight the urge to rush across the room and kiss her.

God damn it, Archer, pull yourself together.

"Okay" is all I can get out.

London hesitates like there's something else she wants to say. She drags her bottom lip into her mouth, tugging on it before meeting my gaze. "Can you do me a favor?"

Instinctually, my foot moves, then the other, my body gravitating toward her. "Anything."

She tilts her head up at me as I approach. "Can you please give me some privacy tonight? I know you like to keep a close eye on me, but for a change, can you just accept that I'm safe, and I'll let *you* know if something happens?"

My stomach drops. I hate the idea of not following her out of this apartment. It goes against everything in me. I'm supposed to keep her safe, how can I do that if I'm not watching her closely? What if this is the one time something bad happens because I was respecting her wishes?

"London, I..."

"Please, Archer." London stares up at me and it's everything I can do to keep my cool with the way her eyes meet mine.

I fucking hate that I feel this way, that I feel like I'm losing my cool.

I swallow the lump in my throat, along with my pride. "You swear to me you'll be careful?" I ask her.

She nods. "And if I need anything, you'll be the first person I call." London pulls out her phone, pushes my contact, and lets it ring once before hanging up. "See, now you're all the way at the top."

Agreeing with her terms goes against everything in me, but I don't exactly have any other options unless I forbid her from going.

And London has made it clear she's not a fan of being told what to do. Things are already sort of weird between us, I don't want to make it worse by disrespecting her wishes.

"Okay," I finally say.

Her face lights up and she stands on her tiptoes to press a soft kiss on my cheek. "Thanks, Archer." London leaves without another word, my heart going out the door with her.

I smack myself and mutter, "Get it together, you idiot. You barely know her. This isn't real."

London has been in my life for just shy of four weeks, and we've been stuck in forced proximity together—that has to be the reason I'm so fazed by this. I've spent the last few years alone, only going out when necessary, and doing everything I can to avoid any and everyone. I got quite used to living life that way. Then came London like a fucking tornado, wrecking everything in her path, my life and peace included. Sure, we have this strange chemistry unlike anything I've ever experienced, but it's because we're both so different, which means we'd never actually be compatible. I have to get it through my head that this is fleeting and the only reason I'm interested is because it can't happen—it would never work, not in a million years.

Not to mention London has put distance between us since our drunken night together. I was under the impression it brought us closer, but her coldness the past week tells me otherwise, and if I'm not mistaken, I'm pretty sure she can't wait to get out of here. If I really care about her, I can't stand in the way of that.

Sliding into my computer chair with a sigh, I come to terms with the fact that I'd rather make London happy than keep her to myself, despite the tugging at my chest to do the opposite.

I can't be selfish, not with her.

So I go to work, typing away until I've infiltrated Camille's Wi-Fi next door, and scan the data to find her banking information.

Twenty minutes later, I deposit money into her account and send her a text message.

ME

Hey, Camille, it's Archer. London mentioned subleasing your apartment, so I went ahead and sent you the first and last months' rent and the first year. Let me know if you need more. You know where to find me.

If I can't have London here, at the very least I could have her next door. I just hope it's enough freedom to not push her any further away than I already have.

I sit back, my eyes glued to my computer monitor, my fingers practically begging to locate London. I cross my arms, uncross them, sit forward, run my hand through my hair, and rise to my feet. Maybe if I move away from my computer, I won't be compelled to break my promise of not stalking her.

Pacing around the living room, I fight with myself and the desire that's building like a volcano ready to erupt. I could just take a quick peek and make sure she's fine, and perhaps that would settle the urge.

"No," I tell myself, and march to the kitchen, dragging out the remains of the bottle of tequila we shared together. I flick the cap onto the counter and tip the bottle back, taking three heaping gulps. It warms my chest, burning and temporarily distracting me, but not long enough.

With zero self-control, I return to my computer, not even sitting down before my hands find the keyboard, my fingers having a mind of their own as they type away. It takes me an embarrassingly short time to find her, and when I do, I pause, my finger resting above the button that will bring up the camera feed.

I shouldn't do it. I can't do it. I won't do it.

But my finger keeps inching closer, and closer, until I do the very thing I shouldn't.

It takes my eyes a second to adjust as they scan the room, searching and doing everything they can to locate her red hair.

My heart stops upon locating her, Grace sitting across the table. But it's then that I realize they aren't alone...Leo is there, too, and so is another man. I clench my fist, not even fully meaning to, and lean down to take a better look.

A round of cocktails is delivered to the table and London smiles politely at the waitress. The man next to London puts his hand on her shoulder and says something, but I can't hear him over the thudding in my head, my heart beating so fucking hard that it's in my ears.

I stand up and turn around, dragging both of my hands through my hair. "Calm down, Archer. She's allowed to be on a..." But I can't even say the word *date* out loud. It's like the word is forbidden from my vocabulary when it comes to her and someone else.

Is this why she asked for privacy? Because she had a feeling that I would watch and find out she was on a date with someone else? Why wouldn't she have just told me instead of lying by omission?

You ruined her last date, I remind myself, the memory of blasting through intersection after intersection on my motorcycle coming back in a flash. I ripped the window out of that guy's car and stopped traffic to insist she get out of the car and come home with me. And that followed me cutting the power to the restaurant she was in, but it was for good reason. That guy was being shady as fuck. I was doing her a favor and getting her out of harm's way.

Who's to say this guy is like the other? Maybe he has good intentions. But who am I kidding, he's probably friends with Leo, which means he's not far from being scum of the earth. Leo is a playboy, rotating women left and right, only keeping them around just until the new starts to wear off and discarding them for another the second he gets bored. He's never committed to anyone longer than a month or two, and it won't be long until he does the same thing to Grace. I'd be concerned for her if I wasn't sure she's only dating him to piss Seven off, which is another thing entirely.

Do I love that Grace is icing Seven out and going behind his back to date his brother? Absolutely. Do I worry for her life because of how deranged my brother can be? One hundred percent.

Either way, she isn't my problem, and right now, the only concern on my mind is what London thinks she's doing with this guy.

I lower the volume coming out of my speakers; maybe that will suffice to give London the freedom she asked for. I'm just watching, not listening, that must count for something.

But when he puts his hand on her shoulder again and she smiles at him, I restrain myself from shoving my fist through the fucking screen.

I breathe deeply, in through my nose and out my mouth, attempting to calm my raging nerves. This shouldn't bother me this badly, and yet it does, which only pisses me off more.

The guy pulls his phone out of his pocket, glances at the screen briefly, and then puts it away, like he's hiding something.

Or he's being polite, the angel on my shoulder says.

I want to tell it to fuck off, but it has a point. This guy would be an idiot for focusing on his phone instead of the beautiful woman sitting next to him.

A waitress approaches, a tray of oysters in her grasp. She sets it on the table and I rapidly press the volume button. London is a vegetarian, whose fucking brilliant idea was it to get oysters as an appetizer?

"Can I get you anything else?" she asks the table, her voice coming in faintly over my speakers. There's chatter from everyone in the restaurant but I can hear her enough.

"Let's go ahead and order," Leo announces, and clears his throat. "I'll have the steak, rare, potatoes. The lady will have a grilled chicken salad with the house dressing on the side." He hands the waitress his and Grace's menus, and I can't help but wonder if they discussed this beforehand or if my brother just became even more of an arrogant prick.

The waitress turns her attention to London and whatever the fuck that guy's name is. "And for you?"

"We'll do the same," the guy tells the waitress.

My mouth drops open. "Are you fucking kidding me?"

"Actually," London interjects. "I'll have the butternut squash ravioli. And a side of fries." She pauses and adds, "And another one of these." She holds her almost empty cocktail glass up.

Grace speaks up, "Scratch the salad, I'll have the same thing she's having." She winks at London and a weird sense of pride fills me at seeing these two defy the disgusting male egos sitting at their table.

It's one thing to order for a woman, but to take it upon yourself to make the decision that they need a salad is something else entirely. You figure out what your woman likes, and then you order for her, to be a gentleman, not a controlling asshole.

Moments like this make me embarrassed to be Leo's brother.

"Anyway," the guy says once the waitress is walking away. "Dig in." He puts an oyster onto the plate in front of London but she doesn't move toward it.

"Maybe I failed to mention it, but I'm a vegetarian."

The guy looks at her for a long moment and shrugs. "It's an oyster, that doesn't count."

London's hand, which was resting on the table, carefully and ever so subtly puts the tiny little fork they give you for oysters into her palm, and she tightens her grip around it. I lean in, watching with bated breath at the possibility that she might stab this guy for being so fucking ignorant. Maybe letting London go out on dates isn't an entirely bad thing after all. But when she loosens her grip, that lovely mental image floats away.

"It counts," is all she says, reaching and tipping back the rest of her drink. "Where is that waitress?"

I settle into my seat, hating myself for having given in but not able to turn back now. I've already gone against her wishes, I might as well see this thing through.

"So, Austin, Leo tells me you're in logistics. What does that entail?" Grace says to Austin, the guy who won't stop reaching over and putting his grimy hand on London's back and shoulder.

If looks could kill, he'd be dead from across this screen.

"You know, this or that. Keeps me busy," Austin replies vaguely.

"Could you be any more evasive?" London straight-up asks him.

"Excuse me?" Austin says to her with a tone that sets my nerves ablaze.

My jaw tenses as I reach for my phone, transferring the feed over to it as I make my way toward the door. I keep my eyes on the screen, popping in an AirPod and grabbing my keys off the table. I know I should stay here, not react, but my gut is sending out blaring warning signs that I need to be closer to her just in case something happens.

"I said what I said," London continues. "You're being evasive. She asked you a question and you didn't even attempt to answer it. Why?" London takes the drinks the waitress brings over, offering her a brisk thank-you before turning her attention to Austin again. "I'm waiting."

"You're a feisty one, aren't you?" Austin looks to Leo. "Didn't tell me how disobedient this one was."

I slam the door to my apartment shut and jog down the stairs and into the parking garage as fast as I can. I shove my phone onto the front mount and don't even bother to put the helmet on or wait for my bike to fully warm up.

"You have some fucking audacity, don't you?" London says, but I don't catch it happening on the screen.

I'm too focused on bolting out of the parking garage, ignoring the oncoming traffic as I dart out in front of it. My front wheel comes off the pavement and I throttle through it with perfect control. If I don't stop at any of the lights or Stop signs, I should make it to the restaurant in four, maybe five minutes. I drive onto the sidewalk, blasting past stunned pedestrians, and back onto the street, slamming on my brakes to avoid a car, the back wheel coming up this time before I twist the throttle and leave them behind.

My gaze flickers down to the screen, the engine of my bike and blaring horns making it hard to hear what's going on. I twist the throttle more, not a care in the world other than getting to her as soon as I can. There's no telling what kind of shit Austin will pull, especially now that I place his name as one of the criminals Leo is friends with. I forgot he existed, nothing special about him other than the fact that he works with my brother. And even that isn't much to brag about.

Leo is successful, I mean, we all are, but every single one of us, me included, are notorious criminals. August might be the best one out of us, but even that is a stretch. Ivy, on the other hand, she's a saint, and the fact that she puts up with the rest of us should grant her a special place in heaven if I believed in that sort of thing.

London's voice comes through my headphones. "Don't you fucking talk to me like that."

I push the bike harder, taking the last corner so fucking fast that the back tire kicks out, and it takes all my strength to keep the bike from completely losing it. I pull up to the restaurant, manage to shove the kickstand down, and hop off without tipping the bike over, ignoring the valet as I march straight toward the entrance.

My phone rings and I push the button on my AirPod to connect it. "Yeah?"

"Archer," London says, catching me completely off guard.

"Yeah?"

"Can you come and get me?"

"I'm already here." I stomp past the hostess and go in the direction I can only assume London is.

"Wait, what?"

I lay my sight on her the second I'm through the door, her red head scanning the crowd to find me. We lock eyes and then I home in on *him*.

My hands are at his collar the moment I reach him, lifting him from his seat. "The fuck you think you're doing?" I yell in his face.

Austin's eyes go wide, along with everyone else's in this place.

"Archie, c'mon, man," Leo says.

I release one arm from Austin to shove it into Leo's chest as he approaches me. "Don't you fucking start with me." I shove him away and return my attention to Austin. "You think you can talk to her like that?" I slam him against the wall, knocking a picture frame loose. My vision darkens, and my pulse sort of slows down at having him exactly where I want him. "I will fucking kill you."

"Archer," London calls out from behind me.

"Say something." I force Austin against the wall, his stature not much smaller than mine.

He grips my arms and tries to pry himself free but it's no use, my rage is calling the shots now.

"Let me go, you fucking psycho," Austin pleads.

"I'll show you a psycho." I tighten my grip on him and wonder how many people are about to bear witness to this.

"Archer," London says, her voice stern and piercing. She places her hand on my back and every inch of me softens. "Let him go, Archer."

I stare at the excuse of a man standing in front of me, his gaze darting back and forth between my eyes, his brow moist with sweat, his upper lip quivering. In a swift movement, I release him and take a step away, his body dropping the couple of inches I had been holding him up.

Austin runs his hand over his collar and catches his breath. "You need to get your bitch in check," he mumbles.

Everything goes red, and without giving it another thought, I reel my arm back and slam it into his face, his nose breaking the second my fist hits it. He cries out and I hit him again, grabbing him by the throat to hold him in place. I land two more blows before Leo and someone else peel me off Austin, who collapses to the floor, blood covering his face.

My chest heaves and I turn around to find the entire restaurant gawking at the show I gave them.

London plants both hands on my shoulders, steadying me toward her. "Archer, look at me."

I comply, her bright green eyes desperate in their attempt to calm me down. "Are you okay?" I ask her. "Did he touch you?"

She shakes her head. "I'm fine. I called you as soon as things got bad."

"I'll fucking kill him," I whisper so only she can hear, the words meant for no one other than her.

"I know." London trails her hands up to my neck, cupping under my chin. She runs her thumbs along my jaw, her touch soft and soothing. "I know."

"I ruined your dinner," I tell her, something apologetic in my tone.

"That's okay." London keeps her hands on me, her eyes on me, and for a second, it feels like we're the only ones in the room, and damn if I wish that were true.

As much as I don't want to, I break away from her, focusing my attention on everyone around us. "Out," I say loudly. "Everyone out." I scoot my hands in the air at the crowd, who for a split second I'm not convinced will listen to me. "My last name is Sin, and I am telling you all to get the fuck out." My gaze scans the tables, wanting to make sure I touch every person with my glare.

A few couples get up, my warning resonating now that they know who I am, or well, at least what I stand for, and this seems to spark the rest of the patrons to do the same.

An employee rushes over to me. "Sir, what can I help you with?"

"Get everyone out of here. Clear the table. Get those fucking oysters out of here. And so help me God, do not bring the steaks out." I take a breath and continue. "Bring her another drink." I turn around, Austin still resting against the wall. "Get the fuck out of here before I change my mind."

Austin bolts, not giving me a chance to say another word, and leaves the rest of us. He pushes past other people trying to get out and I grow a little disappointed in not ending him right here and now.

"Are you done yet, Brother?" Leo says to me while leaning against the wall. "You sure do like making an entrance, don't you?"

"And you don't?" I take in Grace, who's been seated at the table this entire time. "I'm sorry to ruin your evening, Grace. Let me make it up to you."

She nonchalantly shakes her head. "It's fine, honestly. It brought a bit of excitement."

Employees make quick work of clearing the table off, getting the last of the patrons outside, and closing the restaurant to just the four of us.

"Sir," the employee who greeted me a moment ago says. "In place of the steaks, what else would you like prepared? We have a lovely salmon and—"

"Nothing with meat," I tell him. "I don't care what it is, only bring out vegetarian options."

"Any dietary restrictions?"

I glance at the rest of my party and tell him, "No."

"Very well, sir. And what can I offer you to drink?"

"I'll have whatever she's having." I point to the drink London had been gulping down, reminding me that she's already two drinks in. I'll have to keep a close eye on her so she doesn't get too intoxicated. I can't have her falling off the back of my bike on the way home.

"You didn't have to do this," London says as she approaches.

I reach out, defying every ounce of self-control within me, and cup her cheek with my hand. I lean in close, my mouth just against her ear, and mutter, "If you want to go on a date so badly, let it be with me."

CHAPTER TWENTY-THREE

London

I'm so fucking mad at Archer right now but he's making it hard as hell to stay that way when he's this close to me.

I know damn well that he was stalking me, that he went against my one fucking wish of giving me some space. I'm not sure how he does it, whether it's something on my phone or he put a tracker on me, or maybe he found cameras inside the building, but he somehow knew that Austin was being a pretentious dick and that he ordered steak.

Yeah, he must have a bug on me somewhere.

Part of me wants to slap him in the face for disrespecting me, but then the other half wants to hug him for being here when I needed him. I didn't expect to actually call him, and yet the second shit started going further than I was comfortable, my hand was reaching for my phone and dialing his number. I wasn't even fully aware it was happening until his voice came through the speaker and then he appeared out of thin air.

Austin was a terrible date. I was only doing it as a favor to Grace and to get a chance to spend some more time with her. Sure, the idea of being wined and dined was nice, I just don't like blind dates. I thought since it was one of Leo's friends, that he would keep decent company, and boy was I wrong. I can't quite get a good read on Leo either. One minute he's a perfect gentleman, and the next there's *something* off about him, like he's scanning everyone around him, looking for a better option, or maybe just so they pay attention to him. He's conceited, that's for damn sure. And I mean, I get it, Leo is so gorgeous he could have been plucked straight out of a *GQ* magazine. But it's a hair too much, like he's trying too hard to be something that he's not.

I guess that might have to do with growing up in the foster system, and never having anything of your own. Perhaps I shouldn't fault him for something he might not have much control over. Still, there's this little thing called therapy he could try out to get past that big ego of his.

As long as Grace is having a good time, that's all that matters.

I return to my seat, the memory of Archer's voice whispering in my ear lingering in my mind. His breath on my neck is so fresh, I can almost still feel him. I hate that I had only been gone less than an hour, and I was sort of missing him already. I shouldn't, especially now that I figured out I'm the reason Archer is cold and shut off. What kind of person would I be if I pursued something with him after finding out his girlfriend was dead because of me? And it's not as if I could tell him. I don't want to reopen a wound that's clearly still bleeding.

Archer slides into the seat next to me, the one Austin was sitting in only a little bit ago. "I'm not exactly dressed for the occasion," he says.

"You look great," I tell him truthfully. Archer always looks great, no matter what. Even when he's at home, rocking sweatpants and a fitted tee. And now, with him in black jeans and a black button-up rolled onto his forearms, he's especially sexy. Something about the way he barged in here and took control of the situation has me *almost* forgetting that I'm mad at him, that I'm supposed to be keeping him at arm's length.

I take an unhealthy swig of the cocktail the waiter brings me, ignoring a glare from Archer.

"So," Grace interjects, a lovely break from the awkwardness filling the space. "Tell me how this baking gig is going." She reaches for her glass, sipping a bit of the sparkling liquid and returning it to the table, one pinkie out the entire way.

"It's good," I respond. "Mostly learning the ropes at this point, nothing too crazy. What's been keeping you busy?"

Grace sighs. "Planning this big charity event. We're about two months out and it's a lot of back-and-forth with vendors, making sure everything is on order and doesn't fall through. We've sent out invites, but it's been slower than I'd imagined with donations."

"Is this the Children's Gala?" Leo chimes in, his arm over the back of his chair, the other hand fidgeting with his whiskey glass.

"Yeah." Grace turns toward him. "You familiar?"

"I'll buy a table," he tells her.

"A table?"

"Did I stutter?"

"A table is two hundred thousand."

Leo shrugs. "Do you want me to buy two of them?"

Her eyes narrow like she's not quite sure if he's joking.

"I'll buy one too," Archer adds, his tone unserious. Both of them act as if they're purchasing a ten-dollar sandwich at the local deli.

Grace breaks out into a smile. "Okay then."

I lean closer to Archer. "Are you being serious?"

"Yeah, why?" He reaches for a piece of bread in the basket on the table, ripping a piece off and popping it into his mouth.

I glance at Grace and throw my hands up. "I can't afford a table, otherwise I'd get one too."

"I could buy you one?" Archer says without hesitation.

Grace laughs. "I think your generosity is enough, Archer. Anyway, won't you need a date?" She side-eyes Leo, and I wonder if he's going to get the hint or if he's going to be a dumb boy.

He clears his throat, picking up on it easily. "Will you be my date, Grace McCallister?"

"Hmm." She taps at her mouth. "I mean, I guess a date would be nice..."

"What's a man gotta do? Get down on his knees and beg?" Leo all but puts out his bottom lip and pouts. It's sort of cute watching them flirt, but I can't help but feel like something is *off* with them. It's too forced, too fake, too inauthentic.

She has more chemistry with Seven, even if she claims she hates him. Although I'm sure she'd never admit that because she and Seven are truly opposites. Not like Archer and I, but to a more extreme level. Everything that Seven is missing—common decency, empathy, kindness, a moral compass—Grace has in heaps. Things between them would never work. Although I imagine their sex life would be fueled with fiery passion.

My mind floats back to Archer, his mouth on my center in the parking garage, the sensation of his hands on me a distant memory, begging to not be forgotten. I adjust in my seat, my cheeks reddening.

"I'd make you beg," Grace finally says. "But there's no one here to witness it, and what fun would that be?"

"I'd find enjoyment out of it," Archer adds, his gaze doing a double take on mine. He pauses and comes closer. "You okay? We can get out of here."

I force a smile. "I'm good."

My feelings are too fucking conflicted, and they're starting to get on my nerves. Can't my mind, my heart, and my vagina decide what they want with Archer before I internally combust?

Under the table, Archer slides his tattooed hand onto my leg, resting it near my knee, his touch setting my skin on fire. "You'd tell me if something was wrong, right?"

I swallow and nod. "Mm-hmm."

His eyes dance back and forth as he tries to see through what I'm hiding from him.

I place my hand on top of his and give it a gentle squeeze. "Everything is fine, big boy."

"There's my little tornado." Archer's cheeks turn up into a grin and he winks at me, my entire body igniting with a passion I cannot do a damn thing about other than snuff it out.

Three waiters approach the table, providing an escape from Archer's torture he doesn't even realize he's inflicting on me. They set various plates around the table, pointing and going into brief detail about which is what, and somehow, I don't hear a single word of it. I just smile and nod politely and wait for them to leave, my head ringing and my core tightening.

Archer scoots his chair in, and I find myself doing the same, copying him without meaning to. He leans in again, this time right next to my ear. "Do I have your permission to touch you?"

I blink at him, confused by his question. "Of course," I respond.

Slowly, he returns his hand to my knee, sliding his inked fingers under the dainty fabric of my dress.

Grace and Leo place some of the food onto their respective plates and dig in, chatting among themselves, probably finalizing details about their gala date, or curing cancer for all I know. I can't be bothered, not with Archer's hand tracing a trail up my thigh.

My breath catches as he stops at my panty line, only I'm not wearing any, and he must have just come to this conclusion.

I reach for the glass of water near my cocktail, busying myself with taking a sip while Archer traces his finger along my wetness, teasing my entrance. I stifle a moan when he slips a finger in, my pussy clenching around him, my heart picking up its pace at being this exposed, this intimate, in a public setting.

With complete fucking composure, Archer takes his left hand to reach for one of the appetizers, placing it into his mouth. "This is good," he mutters, grabbing another one and extending it toward me. "You should try it."

My eyes meet his, never leaving them as I obey, opening my mouth and my legs just slightly. Archer carefully places the appetizer into my mouth and shoves his finger in farther, twisting it to apply pressure to the softness of my G-spot. He lingers his thumb over my lip and watches me chew while slowly rocking his hand so discreetly that neither of our table guests seems to be aware that he's fucking me with his hand.

I let out a soft moan, the sound easily passing for satisfaction with the flakey, gooey thing I'm currently chewing. But Archer and I both know my suppressed sounds are for him, and him only.

"You want another one?" he asks me, and I can't quite make out what exactly it is he's referring to. "This is such great finger...food." Archer pops another one of the bite-sized pastries into his mouth. "These are good, right?" He points to the plate, commanding the attention of Grace and Leo, his other finger gliding in and out of my pussy.

The two of them mumble something and motion to the other things on the table that I don't care one bit about.

"I'll take another one," I blurt out, and scoot down, doing everything I can not to ride his fucking hand right here and now.

Archer smirks, feeding me once more, only this time, shoving another finger inside of me, too. He positions his hand to cup my pussy, with his thumb resting just along my aching clit, dying for him to apply pressure and finish me off.

I move my hips, trying not to draw too much attention to myself but still devouring the pleasure he's giving me. I have half a mind to unbutton his pants and sit on his lap, filling my pussy full of him instead of his fingers, and come undone around his cock, not a care in the world for who bears witness. But luckily, I'm a tiny bit more reserved than that, and this isn't exactly the time or place for exhibitionism, no matter how badly I want him.

I'm just glad our seats were positioned ever so perfectly to give him the right amount of access to finger-fuck me under the table without anyone knowing.

"Archer, Leo tells me you two used to work together," Grace says, her voice threatening to pull me from my daze.

"Yeah," Archer responds, sending me right back to it with his smooth cadence. "Few years ago. It's been a while since then..." With each word, he strokes me, moving his fingers in a decadent rhythm that's sending me closer, and closer...

Until Archer stops abruptly, his fingers still buried but unmoving.

"I have to use the restroom, if you'll excuse me." Archer removes his hand, leaving me practically panting with want. He gives me an extended look before leaving the table.

"I hope it wasn't something I said," Grace says.

"He's always getting his panties in a bunch about something," Leo tells her. "Don't worry about it."

I clear my throat. "I'll go make sure everything is okay." I go after Archer, following him into a dimly lit hallway, my sight losing him once I'm down it.

A firm hand catches my waist, spinning me around. Archer pins me against the wall, his body pressed along mine.

Letting out a gasp, I relax into him, my hands tugging at his sides, my mouth desperate to be on his.

Archer holds my face in his hand, skimming his thumb over my cheek. He runs his palm over my neck, his entire grip around it, tilting my head to give him room to leave a trail of his lips behind. I shudder under his spell, aching from head to toe with carnal lust.

"Archer," I whimper.

He returns his hand to my center, hiking up my dress to grant himself access. Archer wastes no time, spreading me open and dipping his fingers in again. "You're so fucking wet."

Clumsily, I reach for the waistband of his jeans in my attempt to unbutton them. "Fuck me, Archer. Please?"

Archer pivots out of my way. "Not here."

I loosen a breath and settle for stroking him through his pants, his cock aching through the thick material. At least I know he *wants* to fuck me, even if he won't.

"Taste yourself," he says, pulling his hand from my center and grazing his fingers over my lips. He pops them into my mouth and I swirl my tongue around them and wish it were his cock in my mouth, not his fingers.

I moan against him and he groans in response, pulling his fingers out of my mouth and putting his tattooed hand around my throat again, no doubt making one hell of a necklace. He applies pressure and I press against his grip, desperate for it to be tighter as our lips meet, our tongues frantic in their embrace.

Out of breath, Archer breaks away and drops to his knees in front of me. "If you're going to come, it's going to be on my tongue, little tornado." He blows warm air on my pussy and I tense in anticipation for what's next.

I dig my fingers into his hair, my head leaning on the wall when his mouth meets my wetness.

Archer sucks on my clit and my legs shudder, the edge so fucking near. With one hand on my thigh, he nudges my knees apart and shoves his fingers back inside of me, spreading me open and filling me full of him. He doesn't bother teasing me anymore, yet instead fucks me so hard, his knuckles rattle against my entrance. My clit aches with relief on the horizon, and I hold on to his hair tighter, yanking him into my pussy as I climax hard and abruptly, biting down on my lip to suppress the scream I want to let out.

He moves his hand until my orgasm settles and I release the hold I have on him. Archer presses a few soft kisses on my pussy before slowly removing himself from inside of me. He licks my slit one final time, like he's making sure to lap up every bit of my juices, and fixes my dress for me. He rises to his feet, his gaze dark through the shadowy hallway as he brings his hand to his mouth and sucks on his own fingers.

In a moment of pure fucking bliss, I move out from under Archer and push him against the wall. "Let me return the favor." I settle my hands over his waistband but don't go any further, not if he truly doesn't want me to.

"I didn't do that for a favor. I did it because I wanted to, and because you needed it."

"Maybe I need this too." I lick my lips. "Please?"

"How am I supposed to say no to that?"

I grin and unbutton his pants, pausing just at the zipper. "Is that a yes?"

"Are you asking for my consent, little tornado?"

"I am." I blink up at him.

He cups my chin in his hand. "You have my consent, now and always."

Something flutters in my chest and I ignore it, focusing on his approval. I go to work, reaching into his jeans and gripping his thick cock, careful to not react to just how fucking big he is. There's no way I can fit him in my pussy, let alone my mouth. Still, that doesn't mean I'm not going to try.

I take him into my hand and lower onto my knees, not caring about the dress that's no doubt ruined by now. Looking up at him, he smooths my hair away from my face and gently holds on to my cheeks.

"Don't be afraid," he tells me. "You can take me."

His reassurance somehow gives me the confidence I need, so I inch closer, resting the tip of his shaft on my lips, swirling the precum. I let his cock spread my mouth open, my tongue guiding him in as he groans and grips my cheeks tighter.

My pussy throbs with want, but she's already had her turn, and right now, it's his time to be pleased.

Archer stays still and allows me to ease him into my mouth, inch by inch. His cock hits my throat and I try again, holding on to him and driving more of his length inside of me. My eyes water and I push through, opening my throat and angling myself better, hungry to swallow every bit of him I can.

"You're doing so fucking well." Archer pivots his hips, fucking my face slowly at first. "So. Fucking. Well." With each word, he picks up his pace, and I welcome it wholly, my greedy mouth salivating.

A dish breaks in the distance, stopping us for only a split second before he rams his cock down my throat.

I moan against him, the reverberations making him grow even harder in my already so fucking full mouth. Taking both hands to wrap around the base of his shaft, I twist them around and bob my head up and down on him, my eyes wet but my pussy wetter. I want to stand, to bend over in front of him and take the wrath of his cock inside of me, to let all the emotions and angst we've been building for each other this past month and finally let them come to fruition, but Archer keeps his hold on my face, not giving me a chance to let go.

He throbs, moans, and runs his thumbs along my cheeks. "Look at me, little tornado. Look at me when I come down your throat." Archer bucks his hips and pulls me into him, our eyes locking onto one another.

I squeeze his cock and relax my throat as he pounds into me, the noises of him fucking my face not for the faint of heart. How no one has come down this hallway yet, I have no fucking clue, nor would I care at this point.

With one final thrust, Archer makes true to his word, filling my throat with his orgasm. I keep stroking him all the way through it, the same hunger I have for taking all of him no doubt the same he felt for me just moments prior. His entire body quivers and I smile around his cock at having made him, Mister Grumpiest Man Alive, climax.

His hands relax and his chest heaves, his sight still locked on me. "I'm so proud of you." Archer carefully pulls himself from my mouth, my jaw unsure of what to do with all the space he leaves behind.

I swallow him down and lick my lips, somehow still lusting for more.

Archer hooks his hands under my armpits and helps raise me to my feet. "Are you okay? What can I do for you?"

Drunk on our climaxes, I shake my head, my vision a bit blurry from the tears still silently spilling out of my eyes. "I'm great."

He wipes away the rogue waterworks that stream down, not even paying attention to his cock still hanging out of his pants. "Did I hurt you?"

I blink up at him, my senses starting to come around. "I'm fine, big boy. Don't ruin the moment." I trail my finger along the length of him. "You should probably put your cock away, though."

Archer rolls his eyes and fixes himself up, the two of us no doubt looking like we're up to no good. "You said *cock*."

I raise a brow at him. "Am I not allowed to say *cock*?"

"Only when you're referring to mine." He presses a brief kiss onto my lip, and before I know it, he's slid his hand into mine and is guiding us away from where we were. "Let's get you cleaned up first."

I go along with him because what other choice do I have, but I can't help the strong realization that none of this should be happening. His kisses. Our lust. The implication that we might be a thing. I was supposed to be strong, to withstand whatever uncontrollable pull we have toward each other.

This has to end here. We can't take this any further, and I have to be strong enough to not let it happen again.

Only, I don't know if I have the willpower to stay away from him.

CHAPTER TWENTY-FOUR

Archer

It's been a week since London and I hooked up at the restaurant, and things are back to being awkward and tense. She's quiet, reserved, and if I'm not mistaken, she's hiding something, but I'm just not sure what.

I thought things went great. I thought we connected again. I thought we might be able to see our way through this and here she is, icing me out again.

I guess it isn't entirely bad. It just isn't what I wanted from this. I want her to want me the way I want her. If life has taught me anything, it's that we don't always get what we want, and right now, I'm going to have to settle for what I can get, because the thought of anything less makes my chest ache.

If simply existing in the same space as London is what I get, I'll accept that, even if it hurts a little bit, too.

"Hey," she calls from the kitchen. "Do you want to split this bagel?"

I shrug and keep my eyes glued to the screen in front of me, typing away at some code to strengthen the security at August's headquarters. It's been a while since I've reinforced things, and if he found out how much I've dropped the ball recently, he'd have my head. "You can have it," I tell her.

London doesn't respond, and I don't expect her to.

Except, once a few minutes pass, she comes over and places a plate next to me, half of a bagel with cream cheese on it. "Here."

"Thanks." I look up at her, her glowing green gaze locking onto mine and reminding me of her watery eyes as she was swallowing me down. I reach for her when she walks away, catching her hand gently. "Hey."

She stops, her back still to me. "What's up?"

"Are we good?" I ask her, but the second it's out of my mouth I realize how stupid and insecure it sounds.

What's wrong with me?

London clears her throat. "Yeah. Why wouldn't we be?"

"For starters, you'll barely look at me."

Slowly, she turns around. "I'm looking at you right now."

"Because I said something about it."

"Say what you want to say, Archer." She chews at her lip and crosses her arms, a dead giveaway that she's trying to put a barrier between us.

I stand from my computer chair and step toward her, her neck tilting up to keep her eyes on me. My hand grazes her cheek and tucks her red hair behind her ear. "Why do you keep pretending like there isn't something between us?" I whisper, still caressing her face.

She swallows harshly.

"You drive me fucking insane, London. But I don't want it any other way. The thought of you with another man..." My jaw tenses and my heart pounds harder at the image of anyone else touching her. I wanted to keep things platonic with us, but how can I do that when I want to kill anyone who breathes the same air as her? "I can't deny this anymore. Tell me you don't feel the same and I'll let it go, but until then, I'm not going to stop pursuing you, pursuing us."

"Archer...it's not that simple."

"It doesn't have to be simple." I skim my thumb over her soft skin and linger my sight on her lips. "Nothing worthwhile ever is."

"It's too complicated. You don't even know me, not the real me."

"You're right," I tell her. "But we've lived together for five weeks. Spent every single day together. We've had meals and fights and intimate moments. That must count for something. I know how you like your coffee and I've picked up your little quirks, like how you don't wait for your food to cool down before you eat it, how you can read a book in record speed, how you insist on doing things yourself, how you pretend everything is fine when there's a tornado brewing inside here." I place a gentle kiss on her forehead. "I've seen you battered and bruised, and polished and put together. I adore both versions of you, all versions of you." I take a breath and continue. "It doesn't have to be forever, I'm just asking that you give me a chance. A date, a real one. Let me take you out. Just the two of us. Let's forget about everything else and just focus on us. If you hate it, if you don't feel anything, we can go back to the way things were before, no harm, no foul. One chance, what do you say?"

London takes a long breath in, her bottom lip trembling ever so slightly. "What if we can't go back to the way things were before?"

"Would that be such a bad thing?" I ask her, and withstand the urge to quiet her mind with my mouth on hers.

"One date," she says, and pokes my chest. "But nothing fancy. I'm serious. I want something simple, like pizza on the roof."

"Do you want me to stand outside your window with a boom box, too?"

"I'm not impressed by money, no matter how materialistic you think I am."

"I don't think you're..."

But she cuts me off. "I'm going to stop you there, big boy. One thing I don't tolerate is lying. Don't lie to me. Ever. I don't care how bad you think it will hurt my feelings. Tell me the truth."

I shake my head. "No lying."

"Now eat your bagel," she instructs me, that adorable playfulness I've been missing returning in full force.

I glance at my watch. "Family will be here around noon for

lunch. What do you say I pick you up at your place around seven?"

"Tonight?"

I nod a bit too enthusiastically. "Too soon?"

London rolls her eyes and walks away, her jeans hugging her ass in all the right ways.

***

When I open the door to let my siblings in, Ivy homes in on me immediately. "Why are you smiling?"

"I'm not smiling." I step out of the way to let them enter.

Ivy's heels clatter on the hardwood floor. Leo pushes past her to get in, walking right by and plopping down on the couch, his phone glued to his hand. August finishes up a call, his face pinched like he's annoyed by something, and Seven drags his feet, quite literally, his entire body sluggish as if he doesn't want to be here at all.

"Brother," I say to Seven, and wonder if I'm going to have to swing on him again today.

He slaps me on the shoulder, his glassy eyes meeting mine. Seven is already drunk and it's barely noon. Part of me worries for him, but the other half, the more rational side, recognizes that he's a grown-ass adult who can make decisions, and mistakes, on his own. My only hope is that they don't impact our family and everything we've built. One bad move and Seven could crumble our entire empire. Perhaps I could care more after all.

Ivy scans the apartment and I follow her over to the table, where she drops a bag of food and takes the other one from under August's arm. "Where's the princess?"

"Excuse me?"

"London. Where is she?" Ivy drags out box followed by box of Chinese food, the one meal we can all agree on.

"She's in the bathroom, is that okay with you, Sister?"

Ivy continues getting the food out of the paper bag.

"Something's off about her, Arch. I just know it."

"Something's off about all of us, doesn't mean it's a bad thing."

She stops and looks directly at me, her gaze daring me to understand. "I'm not wrong about this."

"Maybe you are, have you considered that?" I walk away, go into the kitchen, pull out plates, forks, and napkins, and bring them back to the table.

"What are you two going on about?" Leo says, his attention split between his phone and us.

"Get over here and help us, you lazy shit," Ivy teases him, and glances over at Seven, who's wandering toward where I keep my liquor. "God damn it." She breaks away to go over and redirect him. "You're already piss-drunk, Sev. Can't you go one meal without getting hammered?"

Seven pouts but otherwise complies, letting Ivy push him into the dining room and onto a chair. He slumps there, his mood more subdued than usual.

"What's he on?" I ask Ivy quietly.

"Beats me." She shrugs and plops a container of food in front of him. "Eat this. Sober up."

Seven shoves it, pouting like a child and folding his arms over his chest. "I'm not hungry."

The door to the bathroom opens, London darting out a second later and going into my bedroom. I close the distance between us in a few long strides and lightly tap on the door, my other arm pressed against the frame, waiting for her.

London peeks her head through the doorway. "Yeah?"

"Come on. Eat with us."

"Enjoy your time with your family. I don't want to intrude." London averts her gaze like she's looking past me but at nothing in particular.

"You're not intruding." I pause then add, "And besides, when has that ever stopped you?"

London doesn't laugh at my joke, and I worry I may have ruined things before they even started. I just got her back; I can't lose her already. "I don't know," she says.

"Don't know what? I want you to eat with us. Please?"

London sighs, tugging her bottom lip into her mouth. I want to reach out and make her stop, but we aren't there yet. Not when things are too up in the air between us.

"Fine," she says finally. "I'll be out in a minute."

"You promise?" I ask, that desperation in my tone I wish I could get rid of.

I'm a fucking simp and I can barely hide it.

"Yes, Archer, I promise." London closes the door and I return to my siblings, all four of them now at the table.

"Nice of you to join us," Leo mouths off. "Where's Little Miss?"

"She's coming, don't worry."

"I'm sure that's not the first time she's come for you," he replies.

I stare directly at him, my cheeks no doubt turning red from his out-of-place remark.

He throws up his hands. "I'm just saying, you two came back to dinner pretty flushed the other night."

Ivy stops scooping noodles onto her plate. "You went to dinner? Without me?"

"It wasn't that kind of dinner, sis. More like a double date." Leo grabs an egg roll out of the sack and holds it in front of himself.

"And who was your date?" she asks him without realizing the weight of the answer that's to follow.

"Grace," he says without skipping a beat.

I narrow my eyes, preparing for the outburst from Seven, only when I settle my sight on him, he's doing nothing but staring directly at Leo. Typically, he'd have reacted by now, and I don't know if that should concern us more or not.

"You and Grace went out on a double date with Archer and

London?" Ivy points between us like she's trying to make sense of it all.

"Well, originally, London was on a date with Austin, but Archer stormed in and threatened him. Naturally, of course. And then he demanded everyone in the restaurant leave and took Austin's place. Even made the waitstaff clear the table and wouldn't let them bring out any meat." Leo takes a bite of his egg roll, his expression smug.

"Austin was being an asshole," I add. "Leo failed to mention that part."

Ivy pinches the bridge of her nose. "This just keeps getting more complicated." She turns toward me. "Are you two a thing or not? You said you weren't. You said she was a means to an end. You said you couldn't stand her and wanted her out. What is it, Brother?"

If London hadn't already heard all this, I'd be more pissed at Ivy for speaking so loudly, but I know damn well she's doing it on purpose to stir shit.

Ivy aggressively points at Leo. "And you. You know Seven has a crush on her, why would you take Grace on a date? What the fuck is wrong with you?"

"Seven has a crush on everyone," Leo blurts out. "He can't call dibs on everyone. Plus, *she* asked *me* out. What was I supposed to do, say no? That's not very gentlemanly of me."

"Since when are you a gentleman?" August chimes in, and sets his phone on the table. "What did I miss?" He stands, removing his suit jacket and hanging it over the back of his chair, then rolls his sleeves up.

Seven wipes at his nose. "Grace and Leo are fucking, and London and Archer are fucking. Ivy is losing her mind about it because no one told her, and I'm the embarrassment of the family."

The door to the bedroom latches shut and London walks over, stopping a few feet from the table. "Archer and I aren't fucking, for the record."

Not yet, I think. The way our bodies gravitate toward each other, I'm not certain how much longer we can withstand the tug-of-war.

"And Grace and I haven't hooked up either," Leo adds, and eats more of his egg roll.

"And I'm not losing my mind." Ivy sighs heavily and sits in her chair. "I just wish you guys would talk to me instead of shutting me out. I feel like I'm the last to know everything."

August reaches out and pats Ivy's shoulder, her body seeming to relax at his touch.

London takes the open seat next to Ivy, which happens to be the one next to Seven, too. I clench my teeth at him being that close to her. Why wouldn't she have sat next to me? Maybe she's trying to get on Ivy's good side and show her that we aren't as close as she thinks we are.

Ivy sits up, reaches for a box of food, and puts it in front of London, almost like a peace offering. "This is vegetarian."

"Thanks," London says, opening it up.

The room goes quiet aside from everyone's chewing. It's awkward, although I'm not sure any of our family dinners aren't weird in some capacity. I don't enjoy them, but it makes Ivy happy, and despite her making me mad from time to time, I do love her and want the best for her. We all do, that's why we have these silly family meals.

"So tell me about your parents," Ivy starts, looking directly at London.

"They're dead. What about yours?" London knows damn well that we're orphans who banded together and vowed to be stronger than blood, and yet she asks anyway, no doubt to get under Ivy's skin.

"Probably dead too."

London chuckles. "Hey, at least we have that in common."

"Yeah. I guess so."

"What happened to them?" Ivy persists. "If you don't mind me asking."

London swallows the bite of food in her mouth and pats her lips with her napkin. "Well, my dad killed my mom when I was three. And he died not that long ago."

"Damnnn," Seven drawls out. "That's brutal." He leans forward, placing his tattooed arms on the table and resting his head in his hands. "How did he do it?"

"Seven," I command. "Knock it off."

"Yeah," Ivy agrees. "You don't have to tell us the details." She glares at Seven. "You know better than that."

Seven slams his fist on the table. "You get to pry, but I can't? How is that fair?"

"Because I know where the line is, Seven," Ivy tells him. "You have no filter."

"Whatever," he scoffs, leaning back in his chair. "Can we leave yet?"

"What's your hurry?" August asks him. "Do you have work that needs to be done?"

"No, I'm just fucking bored." Seven motions toward Ivy, his hand going dangerously close to London. "Sis won't let me drink, what else am I supposed to do?"

"Not everything is about you," Leo says. "You can suffer through a meal like the rest of us."

"Excuse me? Suffer?" Ivy sucks in a deep breath, and I wonder if she's going to explode. "Torture? Is that what this is? Spending time with your family? How fucking self-centered and selfish of you." She turns to August. "Do you feel this way, too?"

"I didn't say anything." August flinches like she's about to hit him and he's bracing for it. For such a large, brutal man, he sure is afraid of such a tiny person. Ivy has always been a spitfire, though, especially since she has to put up with us. We've trained her well over the years, teaching her how to fight, defend herself, and shoot guns—giving her all the tools she requires to keep herself safe when we aren't around. She's deadly despite the small package she comes in and the sweet exterior.

"Why don't you leave then, huh?" she huffs at Seven, and turns to Leo. "Fucking leave if you don't want to be here."

"I don't have to take this shit," Seven says. "I didn't want to come in the first place." He stands from the table so quickly, his chair goes shooting out from behind him.

I react without thought, rising to my feet and readying myself to tackle him if he takes one step toward London.

"The fuck do you think you're going to do about it, tough guy?" Seven shoves my shoulder.

"Don't start with me," I say through gritted teeth.

"Why can't we make it through one fucking meal without one of you fighting the other?" Ivy shakes her head. "This is disgraceful."

Leo snatches a box of food off the table. "I'm out, you coming, Sev?"

"Don't pretend like you're my friend, you arrogant prick." Seven stumbles in his spot, his body swaying under him. Whatever he's on must be fucking with his balance. "You knew I fucking liked her and you took her out anyway. You're lucky I don't come over there and snap your fucking neck."

I extend my arm, preventing Seven from advancing any further. "Dude, really? He's your brother. Don't say shit like that."

Seven's mismatched eyes meet mine. "I'd kill you all and not think twice."

"Get the fuck out of my apartment," I tell him, the rage in me building.

"My fucking pleasure." He looks down at London. "Call me if things don't work out with this douchebag. I can fuck you better than he can."

"That's enough." I grab his shoulders and all but drag him from the table, not stopping until I reach the front door and shove him through.

He shakes me off him and straightens his shirt. “You’re just mad I’m right.”

“You’re so high, I doubt you could get your dick up, Seven. Go home. Sober up. You’re fucking pathetic.”

“You wanna fucking go?” He shoves me, his hand slipping off my shoulder, his entire body falling. He struggles to catch himself from hitting the floor, lowering himself completely and slumping against the wall.

“You’re the only one calling yourself an embarrassment, Seven, and nothing you’re doing is proving to us otherwise. Get your shit together.”

“Must be nice to be the golden child,” Seven says, his words slurring.

I stop in my tracks as I’m walking away from him, his statement digging in like a knife. I turn around slowly and attempt to carefully choose my response, a million things I want to say fighting for their path out of my mouth. “Me? The golden child? Seven, you’re a fucking lunatic. Leo is an arrogant, self-centered prick, and August? He’s so fucking calculated and always right, it makes me sick. There’s no room to be anything other than out of the way. I can’t afford to go off the rails like you. Who else would hold this family together? Huh? I ask for a little privacy while I grieve, and it’s met with cleaning up mess after mess from you. I’m supposed to be taking time away from this business to figure shit out.”

“You’re not the only one who lost someone.” Seven looks up at me, something broken in his stare. His eyes are glazed over but not from whatever he’s on, but because he’s near tears. I’ve never seen him this torn apart, and despite wanting to do right by him, there’s nothing I, or anyone else, can do for him. Not until he truly hits rock bottom. You can’t help someone who doesn’t want to help themselves; they’ll only pull you down with them.

I kneel beside him. “I love you, Seven. I really do. But I don’t like you very much anymore." I leave Seven behind in the hallway and return to my apartment, a heavy weight following me like a shadow, cloaking me in his sadness and despair. I hate that he's hurting and there's nothing I can do about it.

Passing Leo on the way in, I ignore him and continue toward the table, my chest not relaxing until I lay my sight on London. It's not that I don't trust my siblings, but they are a little off the hinges and I don't want them to ruin whatever slim chance I have with her before I get the opportunity to see it through myself.

"Everything okay?" Ivy says to me once I reach the table.

"Yep." I slip into the seat next to London, not realizing it wasn't the one I was sitting in before until I'm already there. I run my hands through my hair, tugging it tightly. "Everything is fine."

London gently places her hand on my shoulder, rubbing it ever so slightly. "Do you want to talk about it?" Her voice soothes me unlike anything I've ever known. I don't want her to have this effect on me, this power over me.

But I especially don't want Seven to have the ability to ruin my day—not one when I intend to take London on a date later.

August clears his throat. "He's going to be fine. Just needs some time."

"How much time?" I ask him. "He's been this way his entire life. There's something wrong with him. He needs professional help."

Ivy shrugs. "He won't do it. I've tried. And the few people that he's gone to, they've turned him away after a couple of visits. He's out of control."

"He needs to be institutionalized," I suggest. "I don't even mean that in a condescending way. I just don't know what else can be done."

"He's too dangerous," Ivy says. "He'd kill them all." She catches what she says the second it's out of her mouth, looking over to London to gauge her reaction.

I watch her carefully too, unsure how she'll respond to us speaking so candidly about our fucked-up brother.

But London remains there, no surprise hidden in her features but very cognizant of our conversation.

"I'm sorry," she announces. "Do you want me to leave the room so you guys can talk privately?" London goes to stand up but Ivy puts her hand out to stop her.

"No, it's fine. You've already seen his outbursts. There's no denying his true nature now." Ivy leans back in her chair. "I hate to say it, but he's a lost cause."

My heart aches for her—only being able to imagine what it must feel like to have a blood brother, one that I shared a womb with, who acts so incredibly opposite in all the worst ways. She does everything she can to defuse him, and still, he's a ticking time bomb that's set on exploding. And the more she makes it her problem, the more it consumes her life. She deserves better than that, we all do.

I can't fathom this is fun for Seven either. I know he doesn't choose to be like this, but there has to be some tipping point for him to want to change, to be better, if not for himself then for his twin sister.

CHAPTER TWENTY-FIVE

London

After the very dysfunctional yet entertaining family meal with Archer's siblings, Archer has busied himself on his computer and has left the apartment a few times, being cryptic in his reasoning for leaving, something no doubt to do with our date tonight.

It's cute to watch him get nervous, and under any other circumstances, I would dive pussy-first right into him, but I can't get past the truth—that I'm the reason the love of his life is dead.

I want to tell him, I really do, I just can't. Not when so many things are uncertain, and I don't have another place to live yet. I can't imagine he'll want me to stay, or even remain in his life at all. I wouldn't.

I shouldn't have given in when he asked me on a date, but Archer is persistent, and a week of him asking me out finally wore me down, along with the speech he gave me earlier. It made me feel things I've never felt, and I hate myself for not being able to control my desires.

I like Archer. He's sexy, intelligent, protective, and incredibly entertaining to annoy. He's loyal to his family, and despite them not being able to get through a meal without fighting, I admire what they share. I've never known what family meant, not when my sperm donor did nothing but torture me my entire life, starting with killing my mom. I've never really had close friends, either. It was dangerous, not just for them, but for me too. My dad hated anyone and everyone, trusted no one, and destroyed every good thing that came near me, because by extension, it could hurt him in some way. He was paranoid, and that paranoia consumed all the good things.

Even in death, I hate him endlessly.

But what worries me more is that someday I might turn out

just like him.

I stare in the mirror, applying one final layer of lipstick, and pinch my cheeks for some color. Butterflies stir in my stomach, a strange nervousness consuming me unexpectedly. I live with Archer, and I've spent every day for over a month with him, so why am I anxious all of a sudden?

A soft knock thuds against the door to Archer's bedroom, the same room I've spent almost every night in since I arrived here. Archer has made a home on the couch even though his bed is plenty big enough for us to share. For a hardened criminal, he sure is a gentleman.

I stand from the vanity Archer had built for me a week ago and smooth out the dress I'm wearing. It's a little black thing I picked up a couple of days back, not knowing where I'd wear it, but once Archer asked me out, I knew exactly why it called to me. The top half is a corset style with beautiful lace, and the bottom is a short, tightly fitted mix of spandex and nylon. It hugs all my curves and is surprisingly comfortable, which is hard to find in women's clothing.

Walking to the door, I swallow down my nerves and hope I don't puke on him when I open the door. I'm not one to get worked up over a date, or a man, and yet here I am, my palms sweating. But the second I lay my sight on him, everything settles, and my heart skips a beat.

"Hi," he says, his eyes lit up unlike any other time I've seen him.

"Hi." I take him in, his black slacks, his short-sleeved black button-up, a few of them undone at the top, revealing his tattooed chest. I would jump him right now if I lacked self-control, but unfortunately, I'm a bit more reserved than that. "You clean up nice," I tell him.

"And you look radiant as always." Archer holds out his hand. "Shall we?"

I slip my fingers into his palm, ignoring the heat of our touch and letting him guide me out of the room. I don't bring my purse, or my phone, because tonight is about him, about us, and I don't want any distractions, especially knowing this might be our only time together. I can't let things go past tonight; I have to draw the line there. I'll make up some excuse as to why things can't work and insist we have to go back to being friends, no matter how difficult that may be. If he knew the truth, he'd never want to date me, and since I'm not willing to confess, I must put that boundary in place for both of us.

Archer leads me to the front door, opens it, and motions for me to step out. He places his hand on my lower back and I remind myself to keep my fucking cool. Ever since we hooked up at the restaurant, I haven't been able to get the thought of his hands on my body out of my mind. I want him, all of him, so badly, it hurts.

We walk in silence, my heels clicking on the hallway floor on our way to the elevator. He pushes the button, it dings a long second later, and we step inside, the space around us pulsing with tension.

"What happened to you not trusting elevators?" I ask him.

"It didn't change, but I'm trying to be romantic, and making you walk up a few flights of stairs isn't exactly romantic."

The doors close and I fight the urge to be closer to him than I already am.

"It's taking everything in me not to kiss you right now." He stares forward, his eyes meeting mine in the reflection on the elevator door.

"Why don't you?"

"Because this is our first date. I'm supposed to wait until the end to kiss you."

"Such a rule follower..." I tug my bottom lip into my mouth. "Tell me what you would do."

Archer's jaw tenses before he turns toward me, his hand on my waist as he moves me back, against the wall of the elevator. "First, I'd touch you here." He skims his fingers along my cheek, not quite making contact. Archer leans in close. "I'd pull your body toward me, like this." Swiftly, he tugs me into him, our bodies melting into one another's, the desire palpable. "I'd run my nose over yours." He does exactly what he says, his mouth just a breath away from mine. He whispers, our lips almost touching, "And I'd kiss you until you went weak in the knees."

The elevator dings, and neither of us moves as the door opens. Our eyes dart back and forth, daring the other to make the move, to do everything he just said.

But instead, Archer softly kisses my cheek and steps back, air filling the space between us. "Something like that, maybe." He winks at me and I die a little inside at knowing this is temporary, that it can't last. Why does this have to feel like more than a visceral attraction? Why do I want the one man that I can't have? And why does he have to be so fucking hot?

"Yeah, something like that would work." I kick off from where I was leaning and exit the elevator.

Archer takes my hand, my fingers fitting perfectly in his, and escorts me down the hall, to a doorway for stairs. We go up those and are met by a solid door that leads onto the rooftop of his apartment complex.

My eyes go wide as I take in the string lights covering the entire space and the candlelit table with an ice bucket and a bottle in it.

"Archer," I mutter in disbelief at how he could make such a simple request turn out so beautifully.

"Do you like it?" he asks, his hand still in mine, only now he's cupping mine between his other hand, too, like he's afraid I might slip out of his grasp if he doesn't hold on tight.

"Like it?" I glance over at him, my head tilted upward because even with four-inch heels, he's still significantly taller than me. "I love it."

Archer grins, and it might just be the best thing I've ever laid my eyes on. "Good. I'm glad." He motions toward the table. "Want to have a seat?"

We walk over and Archer pulls out my chair for me, every action tonight being more chivalrous than the next. It's hard to believe he's a murderer when he's so damn sweet to me.

He leaves me behind to walk over to a table, where a strange metal thing sits on top. He opens the small door and pulls out a pizza box, returning to our table a moment later and setting it between us. "You asked for pizza, you get pizza." Archer flicks the top open, revealing a steaming cheese pizza from one of the best pizza shops on the entire East Coast. How he managed to get it here while getting all these lights up and everything else, I'll never know.

I'm sure Archer's endless bank account had something to do

with it.

"Champagne?" he asks, pulling a bottle of Dom Perignon out of the bucket.

"Wow, you went all out, didn't you?"

"This is nothing. If you're not going to let me take you out and spoil you, I have to make do with what I can."

"I don't need you to spoil me," I tell him honestly. Sure, I may have grown up with money, but I don't expect it from anyone else, especially a guy. I've lived under the thumb of the cruelest man who ever lived, I don't want to ever do that again.

"I know you don't. I want to. There's a difference there, little tornado." Archer winks at me before uncorking the bottle and pouring us both a glass. He settles into the other seat and takes his glass into his hand.

"What are we cheersing?" I ask him, raising my glass too.

"The beginning of something beautiful," he responds, my heart skipping a beat again. If he keeps this up, I might need to seek medical attention.

We clink our glasses and take a sip, the taste almost like toasted bread with a hint of vanilla, maybe caramel. I've had Dom in the past, but none of them are as rich and complex as this one.

"This is good," I say while setting the glass down. "Really good."

"I'm pleased you approve." Archer grins, reaching for a slice of pizza and setting it on the plate in front of me, then going back for one for himself. "*Bon appétit.*"

"Can you speak French?" I raise an eyebrow at him at having potentially unlocked something about him I didn't already know.

"*Oui je peux, petite tornade. Peux-tu*?"

I hold out my fingers, pinching them together to signify a small amount. "*Pas beaucoup.*"

"What about...*j'ai envie de verser ce champagne sur ton corps et de le lécher, goutte à goutte, jusqu'à en obtenir chaque morceau?*"

My core tightens at hearing the French roll off his tongue so easily, despite having no idea what he's saying. It's sexy either way. "I got the *I want to* and *champagne*, and *drop by drop*. What else was it?"

"Maybe you should brush up on your French," he teases, and

takes a bite of his pizza slice. "Good call on the pizza," he mumbles.

"You have to admit, this is better than going out." I eat some of my pizza, too, the cheese melted perfectly, and the sauce has the best balance of sweet and garlicky.

A horn blares in the distance, and the lights of the city pollute our view, and still, I'd rather be here, with him.

"I'm not mad about it," Archer says, his intense stare meeting mine. "So tell me, Miss London, what brings you to New York?"

I smile at him. "Is that what we're doing, pretending we don't know each other?"

"We're on a first date, that's a first-date question."

"Mmm." I swallow the bite in my mouth. "Well, I come here for work. You see, I'm a traveling magician. Gigs all over the country. I'm just passing through, really. Won't be here long."

"A magician, ey?"

You have something I could make disappear, I think, my perverted nature getting the best of me.

"Why did your cheeks just flush?" he asks me, seeing right through my facade.

"My mind was in the gutter," I admit.

"Let me guess..." Archer puts his finger to his chin, tapping it before continuing. "Were you thinking about making something disappear?"

My mouth drops open. "No fair. Can you read my mind?"

He laughs and I can't help but laugh too, everything about him contagious. "No, but that's hilarious."

"Are you sure you can't read my mind?" I persist, unsure how he knew with such accuracy.

"I can't. I'm just perceptive, that's all. I pay attention...to you."

"You pay attention to everything." I take another bite of my pizza.

"I do, but I watch you a little closer."

"Tell me something then, what do you see?"

Archer's expression darkens and he readjusts in his seat. "I see a woman who's strong, but afraid. Broken, but whole. Someone who's hiding something, because she's afraid if someone saw her for who she really is, they would leave, because that's what everyone else has done. They've left. Viciously loyal and hopelessly romantic, whether she'd admit it or not. She sees the best in people, even when they don't deserve it. She has her walls up, understandably. Surprisingly optimistic if not a bit cynical. You're a paradox in the best way."

I hate how transparent I am, that he was able to pick up on all of that in a month of living together. I know I'm not exactly a mystery, but I thought I was leaving something to the imagination. Archer got me spot-on with everything, even the things I haven't been willing to admit to myself.

"At the end of the day," he says. "We all want to be seen, to be validated. It's human nature."

I shrug, trying to play it off like he didn't completely call me out. "I mean, you're not completely wrong."

"You're saying I was wrong? About what? I'd love to know." Archer takes a drink of his champagne. "This ought to be good."

"Okay, fine, you weren't wrong. Is that what you want to hear?" I blurt out.

A huge smirk breaks across his handsome face. "Was that so hard?"

"Painful, actually. Don't let it happen again."

"I'm not often wrong."

"And neither am I." My heart sinks at the reminder that what we're doing here, no matter how good it feels, can't last. I should tell him this, go ahead and rip the Band-Aid off. But there's a stronger part of me that wants to see this evening through and pretend like it can last, if even for one night.

"Now that we've established you're a traveling magician who wants to make something disappear, tell me more about yourself."

"Hey now, since when do you get to ask all the questions?"

"Kill a man for loving to hear you talk."

"You wouldn't like it if I started yapping, trust me."

"I'll be the judge of that." Archer eats more of his pizza, waiting for me to continue.

I roll my eyes. "Only child, I think. Knowing my dad, though, I might have a sister or two out there."

"Why not a brother?"

"Because if I had a brother, my father's one goal in life would have been accomplished. He wanted an heir. I didn't count, being a girl and all. We're worthless aside from what we can offer with our bodies."

"That's...that's terrible, London. I hope you don't believe that."

"I mean, considering I heard it nonstop my entire life, it's hard not to think it from time to time." I chew at the inside of my lip, a million thoughts wanting to come out of my mouth. I've never spoken candidly about my father and the true relationship we had. I've mentioned it here and there to the people who know me, but no one *really* knows what he did to me, what he forced me to endure. It's enough to drive a person mad.

The thought of Seven comes to mind, the way he acts, the carelessness to his actions. If I were wired differently, perhaps that's how I would have become. From the little I've heard about Archer and his siblings, there's no telling the torment that Seven went through. Maybe his actions are justified because of the trauma he's experienced. Maybe it's a cry for help because he doesn't know how to process his emotions otherwise. He's quite unlikable, but it's hard to hate him with everything considered. We might be more alike than we are different, and that alone scares me.

Archer reaches forward, latching his hand onto mine. "Hey." His voice is soft and reassuring. "I think you're the most beautiful woman I've ever laid eyes on, and I am so attracted to you, it hurts at times. But I don't care if we never get intimate again, I value you way more than what you can offer me with your body. This isn't transactional, London. Do you understand?"

I nod and will my eyes not to water any more than they already are. "I understand." I say those two words despite struggling to wrap my head around what he's telling me.

This entire date was such a bad idea. The more I get to know him, the more I want him, and not in a temporary way. I can't begin to count how many times our entire life has flashed before my eyes. Us annoying each other every single day, him washing my hair in the sink, me making sure he eats, stealing kisses in the kitchen, walking hand in hand to the grocery store, no longer ignoring the passion and chemistry between us.

He rubs his thumb in a circle on my hand, letting out a breath before releasing me. "If you ever want to talk about it, I'm here to listen. Don't feel obligated. I'm here for you, in whatever capacity you need me to be."

We spend the rest of our dinner talking about lighter subjects—music we like, movies we've seen, places we've traveled. It's strange how many times our paths have crossed and yet we never met until now. I'm sure there would be even more connections if he knew who I truly was, but I'm not ready to cross that bridge yet, so I keep that information to myself, locked away for a time when I'm ready to let him go. I'm not convinced that day will ever come.

I eat two large slices of the pizza and Archer finishes off the rest of it, making sure to offer me the last slice at least eight times before taking it for himself. I sit back, holding the flute of champagne, the bottle almost empty and my body warm from the buzz. I'm nowhere near drunk, but I feel good.

"Oh, I have one," Archer says, snapping his fingers. "Would you rather have no taste or be colorblind?"

"No," I say loudly. "Both of those are terrible. Ugh, I guess be colorblind. What about you?"

"Colorblind for sure, I still want to be able to taste you." He winks at me and it makes me tingle more than the champagne already was.

"Let's take this up a notch..." I tap my finger on the table. "Would you rather give or receive?"

Archer scoffs. "That's easy. Give."

I picture his hands on my thighs, his face buried at my center, his tongue caressing my entrance. "Would you rather sleep with someone on the first date or wait for six months?"

"You skipped me, little tornado. You're bad at this game." Archer licks his lips. "Six months is a long time..."

The implication of his answer hits me in full force, my mind reeling at how far I'm willing to take things. I've wanted him since the very first frustrating moment I saw him, but I don't want this to go further than anything we can come back from. Sex complicates things, and things are already so fucking complicated between us.

"It is," I say, unsure of what to do next.

"Would you rather always have sex with the lights on or off?" Archer asks me, picking up where I left off.

"Lights on."

"Would you rather have sex in the bathroom or the kitchen?"

"Both?"

"Would you rather have sex in the bedroom?"

"Or what?"

Archer stares at me for a long moment, the wheels in his head turning so much, I can practically see them. If only I knew what he was thinking. "Tell me what you want, London." His chest rises and falls at a quicker pace.

"What?"

He stands, comes around the table, and leans against it with one tattooed arm. "Tell me what you *want*." The last word is almost a growl, my pussy clenching with desire.

"I want you," I whisper. "I want all of you."

"I'll give you anything you want."

"What happened to you not wanting to be intimate? What happened to valuing me more than what my body can offer?"

He looks at me so intensely, it's like he's staring right into my soul, his eyes hauntingly dark. "I worship you, London. If you say no, I'll drop it right now. You call the shots, not me."

I stand from the table, making him take a step back as I come toward him. "Then take me."

"Are you sure?"

"Are you asking for my consent, Archer Sin?" I smirk, teasing him the same way he did me when I asked for his permission to go down on him.

"I wouldn't have it any other way. I might be a bad man, but I need to hear you say it, little tornado."

I rest my hand on his chest, tilting my head up at him. "I'm sure, Archer. I want you. Please?"

"You don't have to beg, not yet."

"What are you waiting for?" I ask him, being far more assertive than I typically am. But this push-and-pull thing we've had going on for the past month has done nothing but fuel the excessive longing I've had for him.

"I'm not going to fuck you out here." He nods toward the exposed rooftop. "I want you all to myself." In one fluid motion, Archer swoops down and pulls me into his arms.

I wrap my hands around his neck and fight the giant smile that threatens to appear on my face. He can't know how eager I am even more than what's showing.

Ever since I took him into my mouth, I've been fantasizing about what he would feel like stretching me open. I'd be lying if I said his size didn't scare me and turn me on all at the same time. I've never been with a man as big as Archer, and I'm not entirely sure if it's possible. Either way, I can't wait to find out.

Archer leaves the mess we left behind and carries me across the roof, opening the door with ease and kicking it out of his way.

I giggle and bury myself in him to make it easier to carry me down the stairs. "I can walk, you know."

"And I can carry you." Archer pushes the button to the elevator, and it dings a second later, the door opening for us.

"Put me down," I tell him, something stern in my voice.

He complies immediately, setting me inside the empty elevator.

"Now kiss me," I command.

Archer hesitates for only half a second before pressing his lips to mine, the touch both warm and aggressive at the same time. Our tongues meet, something entirely too ravenous about their embrace. He slams me into the wall, with one arm wrapped around my waist and the other pinned above my head. He moans into my mouth and I nearly lose it.

Does he know he has this effect on me?

Our kiss deepens and Archer, with one arm, lifts me into the air. I wrap my legs around him, hooking my feet behind his back, not daring to break from his mouth.

The elevator stops abruptly and the door opens. Panting, we rest our foreheads together as a throat clears.

"Shit," I mutter against him. "Someone's out there." I peek around him to find Camille standing just inside the elevator like she's not sure if she should come in or not.

"I'm interrupting. I can totally take the stairs. Yeah. I'll take the stairs," she blurts out.

"No," I call after her. "Sorry, we—we were just leaving."

Archer turns around so my back is to her, my ass no doubt exposed from the minimal fabric I was wearing to begin with. He keeps one hand down there and I hope it's enough to cover me, since I'm not wearing any panties.

"Sorry, Cami," Archer says while stepping around her and out of the elevator. "Have a good, uh, night."

"Oh my God," I mutter, still in Archer's arms. "That was embarrassing. I'm pretty sure my ass is out."

"It's not," he reassures me, and goes to his door, unlocking it with one hand and crossing the threshold. He tosses his keys onto the counter with a bit less regard than he usually pays them. Archer is typically uptight and overly tidy, but right now, he doesn't seem to mind. "Where were we?"

I run my hands through his long hair and meet his gaze. "I think you were about to fuck me."

"Such harsh words from such a pretty mouth."

"Yeah?" I lick my lips. "What else do you want from this mouth?"

"I think you know." Archer backs me into the wall, his eyes meeting mine before he crashes into me with his body, his lips.

We kiss, both of us moaning into each other, desperate to be closer, to feel more.

I keep one hand in his hair and drag the other down, tugging at the collar of his button-up. His cock hardens in his pants and I grind against him, wanting, lusting, begging for it. I reach for him, feeling him through the fabric, moving my hand up and down.

He groans and I unbutton his pants to shove my hand inside.

"Fuck me," I whisper against his mouth. "Fuck me right here."

"I don't have a condom."

"I don't care."

"Are you on birth control?"

Each question and answer is said between heated kisses.

"I'll take a morning-after pill. Just fuck me, Archer."

"I need to make you come first."

I break away, looking him dead in the eye. "You said I can have whatever I want, big boy. Now, I said *fuck me.*"

Archer stares at me for a long second, questioning my demand, and finally giving in. He holds me with one arm, my body still pinned against the wall as he grabs onto his cock, sliding it along my eager entrance. "You're so fucking wet, little tornado. Are you ready for me?"

I nod expectantly, a bit nervous.

"Say it," he growls.

"I'm ready," I pant.

Archer lines himself with my hole, his gaze on mine as he pushes gently into me. "Keep your eyes on me."

I moan loudly when he penetrates and spreads me open, inch by inch until he can't go any farther. "Fuck, you're so big."

"You're taking me so well." He slides out, slowly, and enters me again, repeating this countless times, getting my body familiar with his. "You're so tight, you feel amazing."

I tense around him, my pussy reacting to his praise.

"You like when I tell you you're doing good?" Archer rocks his hips, moving in and out of me a little quicker this time.

I nod and he narrows his eyes at me.

"Yes," I tell him.

He smirks and his cock hardens, filling me even more. "Am I hurting you?"

"No. I like it. I want more."

"More?" He thrusts into me. "Like that?"

"Yeah." I moan, this angle rubbing against my clit, heightening my pleasure. "I'm so close."

Archer drops his face, planting his lips on my neck, kissing and sucking the tender skin. He keeps hold of my waist and lifts me up and down onto his shaft. "Come for me. Come on my cock, little tornado." He fucks me harder, my orgasm nearing with each thrust.

I dig my nails into his hair, squeezing tightly, my entire body tensing as I near the edge. I scream out, my pussy pulsating around him. He fucks me all the way through it, not daring to stop until I loosen my grip on him. Breathlessly, I say, "That was intense."

He plants a brisk kiss on my lips. "That was just the beginning." Still buried inside of me, Archer carries me over to the couch he's slept on for the past month and lowers me onto my back. "I'm going to fuck you in all the places I've imagined fucking you."

I grin at him and shake my head. "How many places?"

"You'll find out." He kisses my lips and slams into me, taking me off guard in the best way. "Is that too hard?"

"Not at all," I breathe into him. "Give me all of you."

Archer lifts my leg, putting it over his shoulder, and pounds into me, my dress ripping from this new position. "I'll buy you a new one, don't worry."

"I wasn't worried." I slide my hands under his shirt and dig my fingers into his back, pulling him closer to me.

Our mouths meet, desperation and desire fueling our kisses.

"You feel so fucking good. This feels like heaven," Archer says into my mouth, and drives his tongue against mine. He brings his hand up my chest, squeezing my boob before putting his fingers around my throat. The pressure is light but divine.

My pussy clenches and my hips rock into him. I place my hand on his, my grip firm, silently giving him approval to tighten his.

"You like it when I put my hand around your throat?" His brown eyes stare into my green ones even though he already knows the answer to that question.

"I like everything you do to me," I tell him.

He slides his hand up my chin, his thumb dragging over my bottom lip. "Open up."

I comply, eagerly waiting for what's to come.

Archer hesitates while still thrusting into me. "Say it."

"Spit in my mouth," I tell him, and part my lips.

He smirks and does exactly that, spitting right into my fucking mouth, making all this that much hotter. "You know I respect you, right?"

I narrow my gaze. "Yeah?"

"Because for the next few minutes, it might seem like I don't." He slows his pace, reaching down to grip the base of his shaft. "You need a safe word."

"I don't need a safe word," I say. "There's nothing you can do to me that I won't like."

He stops completely and I ache for him to continue. "Do you want this to keep going?"

"Yes." I sit up on my elbows.

"Then what's your safe word?"

I rack my brain, words failing to come to mind, my only thought how badly I ache for him. "I don't know."

"That's not a good choice, little tornado." Archer carefully glides out of me, leaving my hole empty and ravenous. He strokes his cock with my juices coating him.

"Bagels," I blurt out, my cheeks reddening from that being the only thing I could come up with.

"Bagels?"

"Yes. Bagels. Now, are you going to fuck me or not?" I reach between my legs and rub my clit, hungry for another release even though I just had one.

He snatches my hand, pulling it away. "You touch yourself when I tell you to." Archer steps back and points to the couch. "Now get on your knees."

My heart skips a beat and I lick my lips, moving without question and getting on my knees, my back to him. I glance over my shoulder as he watches me, his eyes scanning my body.

Archer hikes my dress up my back, exposing my ass more than it already was. He grips it tightly then gently smacks it.

I arch into him, the tip of his cock pressing against me.

"Remember what I said." Archer slides up and down my pussy, pushing into my hole but not entirely. "Okay?"

"I remember."

"What did I say?"

"That you respect me." Part of me wishes he would disrespect me, though.

"That's my girl." He lines himself up with my entrance. "Now grab onto the back of the couch."

I grip the edge loosely and he slams into me, sending me forward. I reposition, holding on tighter as he wraps his hands around my thighs and drags me onto him with force.

It takes me a second to adjust to his wrath, but the second I do, I push into him, both of us moaning, his coming out more like grunts, each sound hot as fuck.

"Fuck," I pant, struggling to keep hold while he fucks me hard and fast.

He reaches down, moving my leg to spread me wider, each thrust more intense than the last.

I take every bit of it, not wanting it to stop but aching for a release.

"You're such a slut for me," Archer groans. He rubs my ass before smacking it, this time harder. He smooths his hand over the spot and hits me again.

I respond by slamming into him and arching my back more.

"You like it rough, don't you?" Archer smacks me again, my ass no doubt welting.

"I do," I can barely get out.

"Give me your hands."

I don't even think about it, I just sit up a bit straighter and extend them toward him.

He stops fucking me for a quick moment to grip them both in one of his hands and turn me so my body is horizontal with the couch. Archer shoves my face into the cushion, one of his legs now up on the couch as he holds my hands behind my back and fucks me hard.

My vision blurs and I turn my head, gasping for air, moans leaving my mouth.

Archer rubs my ass, smacking it again, hard, before sliding his thumb over my asshole. He pushes until the tip has penetrated me.

Not for a second do I consider using my safe word, my mind and body desperate for more of whatever he's willing to give me.

"Have you had enough?" he says through grunted thrusts.

"No," I whine.

He shoves into me harder, my face dragging against the cushion. Keeping hold of my hands, he spits onto my ass, rubbing his thumb over my hole and putting it back inside. Archer applies pressure and changes his tempo, fucking me slower, but deeper, slamming into me. His body smacks against mine and I revel in the sensations, all of them so much at once.

I bite down on my lip as an orgasm builds without warning and throws me over the edge. A copper taste fills my mouth, and I tense, but not from the climax still rattling through me.

"What is it?" Archer asks, softening his blows.

"I'm bleeding on your couch." Suddenly, I feel overwhelmed with panic, like he's going to be mad at me for real instead of this play pretend he's doing right now. "I'm sorry."

Archer removes his hands, letting mine fall to my sides, flips me over and picks me up, all of it happening so fast, I can barely keep up. He looks into my eyes before sucking my lip into his mouth, my blood now on his lips. "It's just a couch, I don't care." He slides me onto his cock while holding me. "Can you take more or are you done?"

"I'm not done until you are," I tell him. "You need to come too."

"That's the least of my worries." Archer bucks into me once, stiff and hard, and sets me back down on the couch, pulling himself out of me. Slowly, with his heavy gaze on me, spread-eagled on the couch, he unbuttons his shirt and slides it over his broad shoulders, dropping it onto the floor. He unzips his pants the rest of the way, dragging them over his ass and kicking off his shoes. He stands there, stark naked, covered in ink all over.

"God damn you're sexy," I say, my mouth practically hanging open.

He extends his hands and I put mine into his. Archer helps me up and turns me around, ripping what's left of my dress off. "Shame about the dress," he says, but I know damn well he doesn't care about the dress.

I'm now in nothing but the heels I've been wearing all night. Archer runs his fingers through my hair, along my back, and kneels to continue down the length of my body. "On your knees," he commands.

Completely obedient, I plop onto the couch, expecting him to fuck me from behind again, but instead, Archer leaves a trail of his tongue up my thigh and to my core. With his hands spreading me apart, he licks at my center, tasting the lust that's been building for him for so long. Archer dips his tongue into my pussy and cups it, licking me with force. I tense, every bit of me sensitive from what he's already done to me, my mind wondering how much more I can take, and how much he's willing to give.

Every inch of me is eager to find out.

Archer shoves two fingers into me, not even easing them in. He thrusts them hard, burying himself knuckle deep. He keeps licking me, his tongue dancing perfectly over my aching core. Rocking his inked fingers, he moves like he's spent his entire life dedicated to finding out what I like.

I bend over, arching my back for him, and moan. "Oh fuck, Archer. Right. Fucking. There."

He thrusts another finger into my hole, filling and stretching me, but nothing like his cock had done. Archer keeps finger-fucking me, aggressively and so fucking good, until I'm tensing around him.

But this time, Archer doesn't let me come; he stops abruptly right before I'm about to dive over the edge. He pulls his hand out but leaves his face there, tilting it from side to side, licking all over my pussy. He sucks my labia into his mouth and buries his face in me.

"Archer," I pant. "Please."

I can practically feel him smile against my pussy, giving it one last lick and breaking away. Archer stands, gripping his hard cock in his hand, stroking the length of it. "I don't think you're ready yet, little tornado."

"I am." I nod too enthusiastically and reach between my legs, my clit aching against my fingers.

Archer halts mid-stroke, dropping his cock. "What did I say about touching yourself?"

I continue anyway, not caring what he has to say. If he won't finish this orgasm, I will. He's given me two others, what's so different about this one?

"Put your knees together," he demands, and because I'm desperate for him to please me, I do it. With one leg, he leans onto the couch next to me, one hand on my back and another on my ass. "Remember your safe word, little tornado?"

"Yeah, I remember it." I hold on to the back of the couch and look at him, wondering what's next.

"Good, because you're going to need it." Archer rubs his palm over my ass, smacking me a second later, harder than he has before.

I flinch, but only from surprise, not from the pain. No, the pain is fucking delectable, and I want more. "Is that it?"

He hits me with more force, the sound rattling my ears.

A smile breaks across my face and I pucker my ass in the air for him. "I'm waiting."

"Very well." Archer moves, his target no longer the entirety of my cheek, but now his aim is dead center. He swirls his palm over the skin, smacking me, my pussy lips included.

"Oh, fuck," I moan, both agony and pleasure battling to take the stage. "Again."

He hits me again, and again, and again, each one making my body tense in so many ways. Archer moves his hand from my back, bringing it under to pinch my nipple in between his fingers. He rolls it around and releases it to give the other one attention while skimming his palm over my ass and pussy. His next hit almost sends me into orgasm, but I fight it back, wanting more.

I've never had sex this rough before, but I don't think I ever would have wanted it from any of my past partners. There's something about Archer that makes me feel safe even though he's absolutely destroying me.

"That's enough," he says after he smacks me one more time, almost like he's annoyed I hadn't given in.

I'm not sure there's anything he can do to me I wouldn't allow him to, not when the tension has been building between us this long, and knowing that it can't happen ever again, no matter how badly I want it to.

Archer spins me around and picks me up, holding on to my legs as he carries me over to his desk, setting me down on the cold surface. "Lie back."

"What about your computer?" I start to lean but hesitate.

"I said lie back."

"Gosh, Mister Groucho." I lower myself completely so I'm flat on his desk as he stands between my legs.

He glares at me. "How many times am I going to have to tell you I'm not grouchy?"

"You're just in denial," I tell him, and watch him fist his cock, pointing it at my hole, sliding it up and down.

Archer doesn't take his eyes off my pussy when he glides into me, slow at first and then all at once, slamming deep and hard. "You frustrate me, you know that?" He brings my knees up, pushing his chest against them, and fucks me with a passion that tells me exactly how frustrated I make him.

I reach for him but he's too far away, my hands dropping to my sides.

"Touch yourself," he orders. "Pinch those nipples for me."

I run my hands up my body, my eyes on his as I do what he says. "Like this?" I moan when he shoves into me.

"Harder." Archer drives himself further, rattling something off his desk and sending it onto the floor. "Pinch them as hard as you'd want me to."

I squeeze them so tightly it hurts, and my pussy throbs at being beaten by not just his cock but his hand too. "Fuck, Archer, I'm so close. Please. Please let me come."

"Beg for it." He drops one of my legs, letting it fall to the side, giving him access to my clit. Archer hovers his hand right above it and stares right at me. "Beg for it, little tornado."

"Please," I whimper. "I'll do anything." I cup my tits in my hands, grabbing them firmly. "Let me come. Let me come for you. Let me come on your cock. Fuck, Archer. I need this. I need you."

Archer spits onto my pussy and applies pressure to my clit, giving me exactly what I want, my entire body rattling with pleasure and pain.

I come hard and fast and it lasts so fucking long, I'm not sure it will ever end. Archer rolls my clit through the entire thing, his cock slamming in and out of me, slowing its pace once I'm done.

Panting, I open my eyes and meet his.

"Next time keep your eyes on me," he says with a straight face. "Or I'll stop mid-orgasm."

Archer slides me off the desk, his cock still buried inside of me. I cling to his sweat-glistened, decadently tattooed body as he carries me into the kitchen. He lowers me onto the floor by the counter and pulls himself out of me. "Turn around and bend over, little tornado."

Unsure of how much more of this I can take, I do what he says and stretch my body across the cold counter. This isn't the first time my body has been horizontal on this surface, but the other times were when he was washing my hair, his hands gently scrubbing my scalp. There's nothing gentle about what he's doing to me tonight.

Archer nudges my legs apart with his foot and runs his left hand up my back while guiding his cock with his other. He moans as he penetrates me and goes easy for a second, slamming into me the next.

I brace myself on the counter and revel in the fullness. My pussy aches in the best way, and I spread my legs a little wider for him, tensing around his rock-hard shaft.

"You feel so fucking good, little tornado. Your pussy was made for me. You were made for me." He continues thrusting, his hands gripping my hips, his fingers digging in. "Tell me you were made for me."

"I was made for you," I struggle to get out.

"Is this too much for you?" he asks, the tone of his voice like he's breaking character because he's not sure if I'm okay.

"No," I tell him truthfully. "I want you to come."

Archer smacks my ass and continues to fuck me, hard and deep. "I don't think you're ready for that yet." He changes his rhythm, thrusting in at an angle, a new bout of sensations consuming me. "I think I could make you come again. What do you think?"

I clench around him and moan loudly.

"You keep making those noises and I might come for you." Archer slows down but keeps fucking me deeper, rocking his hips in such a heavenly manner. "Don't be shy. Let me hear you. Moan for me."

I don't hold back, letting every bit of pleasure course through me and to my mouth, moaning like no one is listening. Desperately searching for something to grip, I push back onto him and wonder how it's possible another orgasm is so fucking near. A man has never been able to make me come, let alone this many times. It's like I've died and gone to orgasm heaven. Archer unleashing sweet hell on my pussy.

"That's it, baby." Archer's cock throbs inside of me, and it's enough to send me over the edge, screaming out as I shatter around him.

My vision blurs again and my entire body shakes, my pussy convulsing like it's trying to milk his fucking cock, this one more intense than the last.

Archer carefully pulls himself out of me, leans down, and presses a kiss on my back before kneeling behind me and playing with my still-aching pussy. "You're throbbing for me. So fucking wet." He moans. "You taste so good." Archer skims his finger along my soaked skin and dips it inside, stroking gently. He licks at my hole, sliding his tongue in and out, over and over a few times.

I hate that everything he does is so fucking good, making me want him even more, despite thinking I've had my fill. I guess if there's a way to die, I'd settle with being fucked to death by Archer Sin.

Archer stands, his hand on my pussy, his fingers penetrating me. "You think you can come again, little tornado?"

Breathless, I shake my head.

"Is that a challenge?" Without looking at him, I can hear the smile on his face. Archer continues to stroke me with his fingers, gliding them in and out, all around, hitting every nerve ending he can. He presses his thumb against my asshole, applying just enough pressure to make me tense. "You have a few more in you, baby. Don't deny me."

Still reeling from my last orgasm, I can barely catch my breath as he builds another. I've lost total control over my body and I'm not entirely sure if I'm mad about it at all. There are worse things than a drop-dead-gorgeous man making you come uncontrollably.

"When I'm done with you, you won't even remember your own name," he says with his fingers buried in my pussy. "That's it." His voice is rough but reassuring.

"Archer," I moan. "Fuck."

"Say my name. Keep saying my name." He shoves another finger inside of me.

"Archer...Archer..." I bite my lip.

"Don't stop," he tells me.

"Archer..." I whimper, and buck against him. "Fuck me, Archer."

He slams his fingers into me and I come undone, crying out for him.

Archer removes his hand, quickly pulling me off the counter, turning me around and lifting me into the air, setting me down onto his cock, my orgasm still rattling through me.

I wrap my legs around his waist and moan against his neck, my teeth dragging along his flesh.

"I love when you come around me," Archer whispers. "I can't get enough of your tight pussy." He holds me close to him and carries me to the bedroom, still maintaining his grip as he lowers me onto the bed ever so softly. Archer stills, his dark eyes meeting mine. He tucks my damp hair behind my ear. "You're so beautiful, London."

The way he says my name sparks something in my chest. I swallow and move my hands up his back, to his neck, to his face.

Archer leans in, grazing his nose against mine before placing a kiss on my lips, nothing aggressive about him this time. He keeps kissing me, the movements growing passionate, but not forceful. Ever so subtly, he pushes his cock into me, his thrusts considerate. We stay like this for a while, kissing and fucking, fucking and kissing, only, after some time goes by, I'm not sure we're fucking at all, and that is somehow hotter than I would have expected it to be.

I spread my legs and push against him, my moans mixed with his, our mouths not daring to break apart until finally, Archer pulls away and looks into my eyes.

His cock hardens and his breath goes ragged. "I want to see your eyes when I come inside of you." He cups my face in his hand, his thumb rubbing my cheek, so much love in every single thing he's doing.

My pussy aches, and despite not thinking it was possible, I find myself so fucking close from how loving he's being. "I'm close," I tell him.

"Come with me, London. Let's do this together."

"Together," I breathe, my gaze locked on his.

With one final deep thrust, I feel him quiver, setting my orgasm off, too, the two of us climaxing at the same time, his cock spilling over into me, my pussy pulsating around him.

It's more intense than I imagined, and I'm not entirely convinced I'm going to be able to walk once we finish.

Archer melts his mouth onto mine, kissing me with a renewed passion, our tongues dancing along each other's as he fucks us both through our orgasms. With a grunt, Archer stops completely and rests his forehead on mine. "That was intense." He collapses onto his side, taking me with him as his cock is still buried in me.

I lie there, panting and reeling from orgasm after orgasm, my body all but glued to him with the sweat coating both of us.

We stay there in silence for a few minutes, Archer holding me like he never wants to let go. He presses soft kisses on my forehead, his cock throbbing in my pussy. "Are you okay?"

I nod.

Archer rises onto his elbow, taking a better look at me. "Are you okay?" he asks me again.

"Yes," I tell him, my voice cracking. "I'm okay."

He breathes a sigh of relief and traces the outline of my face. "Are you sure?"

I roll my eyes. "I'm sure, big boy."

Carefully, as if I might break completely if he makes the wrong move, Archer slips his cock out of me. He sits on his knees and scoops me into his arms.

"What are we doing now?" I question, and consider using my safe word if he has more in store for me.

"*We* are going to take a shower. But *I* am going to do all the work. You've done enough, London. It's my turn to take care of you." Archer carries me from the bed toward the door.

"You just made me come how many times, and you came once. It's safe to say I have a little more work cut out for me," I respond.

"That was my plan all along." He kisses my forehead and takes me into the bathroom, somehow holding me in one arm as he turns the shower on, giving it a chance to warm up before bringing me inside. "I know you like it hot, but we're going to have to compromise." He sets me on the bench in the shower, turning some of the faucets to where they're hitting both of us at the same time. He grabs the showerhead and rinses my body, the stream both warm and comforting, but not as much as he is.

I didn't expect to feel so vulnerable once we hooked up, and now here I am, wondering why I did this to myself to begin with. I thought this could be a one-time thing, that maybe sleeping with Archer would get him out of my system, but I'm afraid all this did was make things worse, my desire to keep him in my life somehow stronger than it was before.

But I can't keep him, I know this, not when he'd hate me if he knew the truth.

"Archer..." I say, not quite ready to tell him but knowing I can't wait much longer. Not when he was kissing me like he loved me, touching me like he needed me, and especially not now, taking care of me like I'm the only girl in the world.

"Shh." Archer runs his fingers through my hair and lets the water hit it. "Don't waste your energy. I've got you."

Tears well in my eyes and I'm grateful that we're in the shower and I can easily disguise them. I sit here, allowing Archer to continue to do with me as he pleases, my throat aching to say my safe word, finally hitting the limits of what I'm capable of taking.

He washes my hair, this time because he wants to, not out of obligation like in the past. Archer lathers up a washcloth, cleaning every inch of my body, being extra gentle in all the sore spots. He kisses me, and for a split second, I enjoy how he's pampering me, each time reminding myself that it can't continue, that it won't last—I can't let it.

Once he's done, Archer showers quickly, and I watch him, admiring every inked spot on his body. I hadn't noticed that his back was covered in a giant skull surrounded by roses. It's sort of poetically beautiful in a cynical kind of way, but I can't help but wonder how painful it was, and what provoked him to get it. Or all his tattoos, for that matter. It takes a special sort of dedication to get one tattoo, let alone as many that could cover most of your skin. His body is a stunning canvas I want nothing but to explore, one night not long enough to navigate every inch of him.

Archer rinses himself and shuts the water off, stepping outside of the shower to retrieve a towel. He comes back, dabbing my damp skin and wrapping it around my body, not a word spoken between us, and still so much being said. He secures one around his waist before scooping me into his arms and setting me on the bathroom counter. Archer brushes my hair, and even goes as far as to apply lotion to my body, and the special one I use for my face. He hands me my toothbrush and pops his into his mouth, both of us brushing our teeth together, the thought of doing this forever crossing my mind.

I hop off the counter to finish brushing my teeth, my legs a bit wobbly underneath me. I ignore the pain in my ankle at not being completely healed just yet, the cast borderline taken off prematurely but not something I'd ever admit out loud.

"I can walk," I tell Archer as he comes toward me, no doubt to pick me up again.

He narrows his gaze at me. "Let me take care of you."

"I am," I admit. "But I can walk. It isn't far." The truth is that I'm not sure how much more I can stand to be in his arms if it won't last another night.

But maybe it could. Maybe I could find a way to make it all make sense. Maybe I could explain to him that my father was a disturbed man, and I tried, I really tried to save her, the love of Archer's life. I know damn well that's not the truth, though—I could have tried harder. I could have done something, anything, to save her, even if it meant dying alongside her. That's what should have happened. I shouldn't have bargained for my life; I should have bled out at the hands of Ricardo Gardella—only if I did, I wouldn't have been able to help Cora. And if I hadn't helped Cora, then my father might still be alive, and his torturous reign wouldn't have died with him.

"What's on your mind?" Archer tells me as he pulls back the comforter on his bed and fluffs my pillow for me.

"Nothing," I lie, climbing into the spot he makes for me. "You're staying, right?" I blink up at him, unsure of the words that come out of my mouth.

"Do you want me to?" He covers me up, his dark eyes meeting mine.

"More than you know."

"Okay." Archer turns off the light in his room before coming back. "Scoot over. I want to be closer to the door."

I fight the urge to smile at him and comply, barely giving him space and settling into his warm body once he's positioned himself horizontally. My head fits perfectly on his chest and only adds to the struggle I'm facing at not wanting to let him go.

At least for tonight, maybe I won't have to.

Archer lets out a sigh, holding me to him and kissing my forehead. "You sure you're okay?"

"I'm okay," I breathe into him. "Right now, I'm perfect."

"I was rough with you."

"I liked it." I kiss his bare chest. "I promise."

Archer keeps me close to him, his arms tight around me, all night, occasionally pressing his lips to my face and head throughout the night. I doze in and out, never quite able to fall completely asleep, not wanting to miss the chance of enjoying what I have while it's right here.

Hours pass and I drift into a nightmare, jarring myself awake abruptly.

"Shh." Archer rubs circles on my back. "You're safe. I'm here," he murmurs, lulling me to sleep.

I wake sometime later, a vibration on the nightstand disturbing us both.

Archer kisses me and reaches blindly, his hand hitting the tabletop a few times until he locates the source of the ringing. "It's Ivy," he says, his voice ragged. "I should answer this, she doesn't often call this early."

My eyes adjust to see the time, two after six in the morning. I could use a few or thirty more hours of cuddling Archer.

"Hello?" he says into the receiver.

"Check your email." Ivy is clear and straight to the point.

"What?" Archer clears his throat and sits up, reaching to cover my shoulder with the blanket.

"I said check your email. Right now. It's urgent." Ivy pauses and adds, "I'll stay on the line."

Archer sighs dramatically. "Can't this wait?"

"No."

He grunts and shimmies out of bed, going over to his dresser to pull out a pair of boxers, sliding into them sloppily, almost falling over as he keeps the phone pressed between his ear and shoulder. "This better be good, Ivy."

I can't make out what she says, not from my spot in bed. My heart races at what could have prompted her to demand this from Archer, none of it any of my business.

Archer slips out of the room, and I follow the sound of his footsteps quietly across the hall until I lose them near his desk. He types onto his keyboard and lowers himself into his chair, a sound I've gotten familiar with in the course of my time here with him.

Curiosity consuming me, I slip out of bed, too, and throw one of his shirts over my head, tiptoeing out, not trying to distract him from his family matters.

But when I settle on Archer's figure, he's tense, tenser than he ever has been, his phone held tightly in his grip.

I go behind him, wrapping my arms around his shoulders and glancing at the screen, my pulse pounding wildly in my ears, threatening to give out completely, my arms going slack as they untangle from around him.

My picture. My face. My driver's license from California.

My real name glaring back at me.

London Gardella.

My birth certificate loaded next to it, Ricardo Gardella's name listed as my father's.

"Ivy," Archer says cooly. "I'm going to need to call you back." He drops the phone onto his desk, his chest heaving.

"I—I can explain."

Archer whips his head toward me. "What do you mean, you can explain?"

"I mean, I only just found out. Not that long ago. I wanted to tell you. I tried to tell you." But that's a lie, because if I was going to confess, I could have done it a million times over by now. No, I was being a selfish asshole and keeping this secret to myself. It's my fault he's staring at me the way he is right now, like I'm a fucking stranger to him, someone that he didn't just share an epic night with.

Archer lowers his head into his hands, rubbing his temples. "I don't understand. You're Ricardo Gardella's daughter?"

"Not by choice," I blurt out, tears streaming down my cheeks. "I hate him as much as you hate him, especially for what he did to Madison."

Archer's eyes dart up to meet mine. "You knew about this?"

My mouth falls open, unable to find the words to make this right.

"You fucking knew about this?" Archer rises to his feet, and for the first time since I've known him, he holds all the cards to hurt me, to really fucking hurt me. And the sad thing about it is that I wouldn't blame him, not one bit. His nostrils flare and I sense the end before it even happens. "Get the fuck out."

"Archer, please...let me explain."

His hand balls into a fist and he looks at me like he's never looked at me—like he hates me, but not in a cute and annoying way, like he truly wouldn't be bothered whether I lived or died.

"Get the fuck out of my apartment right now before either one of us does anything they regret."

"Please," I protest, my voice smaller than it's ever been. In all the times I begged my father for my life, I've never been this desperate. I reach for Archer, but he yanks himself away.

"Get the fuck out of my apartment, London." His jaw tenses as if he's choosing his next words carefully. "I never want to see you again."

My heart rips in two, both from having something so wonderful and losing it, and from knowing there's not a single thing I could do to ever fix this. A sad reality that I'm going to have to learn how to face, even if it takes me forever.

CHAPTER TWENTY-SIX

Archer

Two weeks have passed since things ended with London, and everything still feels as fresh as the moment I saw that email pop across my screen.

I wanted to keep some kind of anonymity between us, let her bury her secrets in the depths of hell like mine. Of course, there was this dying urge to know her, but I thought things were better off this way. I had my demons, and she had hers.

I just never imagined her demons would have anything to do with the man who killed Madison, the girl I loved more than anything. I gave up everything once I lost her, because the idea of living in a world that killed her killed me more than I could bear. That's why I left it all behind, or, well, at least that's what I've tried to do, only my family and their criminal past have their claws in me deep, and there doesn't seem to be any escaping the things that haunt me the most.

My phone rings, and despite not having answered it six times already, Ivy keeps trying me anyway.

Reluctantly, I answer. "What?"

"Well, hello to you, too, Brother."

"What do you want, Ivy?"

"Not even a hello back. Not even a happy birthday?"

"Happy birthday."

"Say it with a little emotion."

"Ivy. I love you. And I want the best for you. But right now, I can't. I can't handle your patronizing *I told you so's* and your condescending *get over it's*."

"Give me the phone," someone calls out from a distance on

Ivy's end. "Arch, buddy, hey, it's Seven, your favorite brother."

"You're my least-favorite brother," I tell him, not entirely sure if it's the truth or not. I'm not fond of any of them at the moment.

"I'm going to pretend like that didn't hurt my feelings."

"You don't have any feelings. You're a sociopath." I stare at my computer screen, clicking through the same few tabs I have for the last couple of weeks. It's pathetic that despite not wanting to see her ever again, I can't stop keeping tabs on her. I guess Silver's voice keeps appearing in the back of my mind, that it's my responsibility to keep her safe, regardless of how badly she hurt me.

"Oh, right," Seven says. "It's my birthday. I'd say it's only fair you're nice to me today. Humor me and come out. Please. Don't make me beg."

"I'm not leaving my apartment."

"He said he's not leaving his apartment," he yells to someone else. "Come on, Arch, what do I have to do? Do you want an escort? I can get you one. Name your flavor, I'll make it happen."

"I don't want an escort."

"What do you want?"

"I want you to leave me alone." I hang up the phone, not caring to hear another word from him or any of my other siblings. Sure, it might be the twins' birthday, but they have one every year, and maybe next year I won't be this fucking numb and hurting all at the same time.

I should have known the first person I'd open up to would rip my heart to shreds.

CHAPTER TWENTY-SEVEN

London

I've been crashing with Grace for the last three weeks, and if I stay another day, I might go insane.

Her father is a narcissistic, controlling prick, and he shows up unannounced whenever he wants, demanding the most outrageous things from Grace, as if she's his personal errand runner instead of his daughter. He reminds me too much of my father, and that alone sets my nerves on edge every minute that I remain here.

Despite saving most of the money I've earned at the bakery and working every available shift they will give me, it still isn't enough to cover the deposit to get Camille's place. I thought it would be my saving grace, but instead it's just a temptress I can never have because my father left me nothing other than trauma.

"How are you dealing?" Grace asks me from overtop the mug in her hands. Aside from her disturbing dad, she's been a fantastic friend, letting me sleep on her couch and cry on her shoulder. She's let me tell her the parts I've wanted to and hasn't pried when I've been vague about things. I don't know how she does it, because I know damn well I'd be asking for more information to fill in the blanks and make sense of things. There's a small part of me that wishes she would, that way I could have someone help me rationalize what happened and tell me what to think about this entire situation.

"I'm fine," I lie. "How are you? How are things with Leo?"

She rolls her eyes. "Leo is great, really. But it's like every time we're out, I can't help but think he's scanning the crowd to see if there's someone else better out there. Does that make sense?"

"It does. I can see that."

"Right? Okay, so I'm not being paranoid." Grace bites the corner of her chocolate croissant.

"Not at all. I mean, I can see where you have fun with him. Not to mention he's super-hot. But he seems like a playboy through and through. Maybe he's not looking for anything serious."

She swallows the mouthful and continues, "But here's the thing. I don't think I am either. Don't get me wrong, the idea of having a boyfriend, a partner, sounds great, but it also sounds suffocating. I have too much going on, a career to focus on—I don't have time to worry about whether someone is cheating on me. I don't know why I'm so pressed when I wouldn't even know what to do if he wanted to be serious. Maybe this is a blessing in disguise."

"A self-aware queen, I love it." I raise my coffee mug to her. "Cheers to that."

She grins and clangs her mug against mine, the front door to her apartment blasting open a second later, both of us almost dropping our coffees.

"You haven't changed yet?" her father says the second he's through the door, his gaze trailing up and down the two of us.

I cross my arms and cover my chest, hoping it will conceal me from his prying eyes.

"Don't bother," he tells me. "You're not my type." Mr. McCallister continues into her apartment, taking the croissant she was eating and snatching it off the table. "You're going to gain weight if you eat like this." He tosses it into her kitchen trash can and continues around the space. "This place is a disaster. What did I tell you about keeping tidy, Gracie?"

Grace stands from the table, folding over the robe she's wearing and hugging it tightly. "What can I help you with, Father?"

Mr. McCallister snaps his attention at her, walking directly toward her and backhanding her. "Don't take that tone with me, young lady."

I bite my lip to hide my reaction, my breath catching at witnessing him be so blunt. If he's willing to treat her like this in front of me, what's he capable of when no one is around? Still, nothing good ever came from me voicing my opinion, so I keep my mouth shut and stay firmly in place.

Grace holds her cheek, her eyes welling with tears.

"And if you must ask, you must not be very good at your job." Mr. McCallister breathes deeply and exhales. "This gala. I need your support. This election is coming up, and I can't afford to lose any votes, especially not because of my *darling* daughter. That wouldn't bode well for the family, would it? You want me to keep footing the bill for this place." He motions around the room. "Then I suggest you consider your options." He flits his attention to me only briefly, then back to her. "You do love charity, don't you?"

The rhetorical question goes unanswered as he leaves without another word, enough of them lingering in the air in his absence.

I rush to the freezer and grab a frozen bag of peas to give to Grace. "Here. Put this on your face."

She takes it, wincing as she presses it against her cheek, and doesn't say anything.

"You don't have to be embarrassed," I tell her. "My father was worse than yours."

Grace scoffs. "I doubt that."

I raise the corner of my shirt and show her the scar from the time he almost took my life. "See this here. That was him." I point to another one. "And this." And then another. "This." I lower my shirt and sit in the chair next to her. "Remember the casts when we first met?"

"That was him too?"

I nod. "Twenty-three years of torment. Countless broken bones."

"Is that why you're hiding out here?"

"Sort of," I tell her, unsure of how much I'm willing to admit. "He's gone now, dead. But not before he made sure I'd have to hide forever."

"He sold you to someone."

"Yeah."

Grace chews at her lip. "He wants to do the same thing to me."

"What?" I ask her, shocked by her response.

"He claims it will be good for his political career. That I'd be doing the family a favor. That it isn't asking for much. That it's standard of a politician's daughter and that I should be grateful I have a father looking out for my best interests."

"Your best interests?"

Grace chuckles dryly. "It's funny how he twists things around to make it seem like I'm the bad guy. That I'm doing something wrong."

I reach out and grab her forearm. "You know that's not true, right?"

Grace shrugs, and it's strange to see her this way. She's a strong, independent woman, not afraid to call a single man out on their shit, but when it comes to *him*, her father, she folds completely. I guess she and I aren't that different after all, the only difference is that my oppressor is dead and hers is tugging her strings like a puppet master.

"It's not true," I tell her, hoping she understands the weight of my words. "Your life is yours. Your body is yours. I don't care what kind of favor he thinks he's doing you; he isn't. You get to call the shots, not him."

"It's not that easy," she says, a million things hidden within the depths of those words.

"I know." Because things were never easy with my father either. Every single time I thought I found my way out, he would sink his claws back in and drag me to the depths of hell with him. There was no escaping him, not really. Even in his death, he still has his hold on me, both with Joe Vito thinking I'm his bride and Archer Sin hating my guts. Neither fate is one I can ever escape from. I'd offer to help Grace, but the thought of Madison lying there, bleeding out, comes back in full force. All I wanted to do was help her, and yet I was too late, the maid getting rid of her body before I ever got a chance to say goodbye, to tell her I was sorry for letting her down.

"Thanks for being here," Grace tells me. "It's been fun having a friend around."

"It has, hasn't it?" There's no denying that I have enjoyed staying with Grace, but it's been a strange kind of terrible, too, bringing back far too many memories that are way too fresh for me not to feel completely exposed. Her father is too much like my own, and every single time that front door opens, it's like I'm getting whiplash, never knowing if it will be her dad or mine that walks through that door. It's the most uneasy I've felt in a long time, and despite how things were left with Archer, I'd be lying if I said I didn't wish I was back there, living under his thumb and having him watch every step I took. At least I felt safe there, with him, even if I had no privacy.

But living with Archer is a thing of the past, and there's no coming back from how badly I hurt him, and if I'm honest, how much he hurt me too, when he threw me out without even giving me a chance to explain the situation. I didn't know when Silver sent me there that things would unfold the way they did, and maybe I handled them poorly, but still, he could have given me a chance to process and think things through.

You had a chance, my mind reminds me, knowing damn well I had time to come clean between finding out and that fateful night. It's my fault things ended the way they did, and I have to accept that, even if it kills me in a way my father never could.

"I should probably get ready for work," Grace announces, wiping a tear that rolls down her swollen cheek. "Throw this back in the freezer for me?" She hands me the bag of peas.

"Yeah, of course." I take it and return it to the freezer, the very least of what I could do, since she's let me crash here for three weeks. I never expected I'd find such a good friend when I came to New York, but I'm grateful our paths crossed. I just hope I can repay her someday, no matter how long it takes.

Once I've thrown the bag into the freezer and returned to the table, Grace is in the bathroom, turning the faucet to the shower on. I scroll through my phone, my finger clicking on the text thread with Archer that ended what feels like yesterday and years ago. I hate how much I miss him, how I'd give anything to see him one last time and at least tell him I'm sorry. For the lies, for the truth, for everything I put him through. I'd like to think that I would have done things differently if given the chance, but it would have ended the same regardless, and if that's what it took to give me that momentary heaven with him, I'd probably do it again just for the same outcome.

I read through the texts until they hurt worse than they bring me relief, and scroll mindlessly through some other apps, never quite finding what I'm looking for to scratch the itch I can't seem to appease.

That's when a text notification pops across the top of my feed, my heart skipping a beat thinking it might be from Archer but my brain knowing better that he'd never reach out to me.

CAMILLE

Hey, sorry it took me so long to get back to you. Timeline changed. Apartment is yours when you're ready.

Nausea courses through me. Not only can I no longer afford that apartment, but it's right next door to Archer. What kind of person would I be if I moved in next to my...I almost call him my ex, yet things were never serious enough for us to even have a label.

I read and reread her text at least a dozen times, noting the use of *when* and not *if.* Maybe it was a typo, or maybe I'm reading far too into it.

I thumb a response, deleting it over and over, unsure of what it is I want to say. I decide to go with part of the truth.

ME

Hey, Camille. Thanks for thinking of me. Unfortunately, things changed and I can no longer afford the rent. I'm sure you'll have no issues subleasing, though. Best of luck!

I hit Send and shut the phone screen off, not wanting to see the dots appear if she decides to reply. I steady my breath and glance around Grace's lavish apartment, desperate to find something to distract me from the reality that I'm forced to face.

But my phone dings, vibrating on the table and drawing my attention.

CAMILLE

Archer paid through the year. Didn't he tell you?

CAMILLE

Shit, I hope that wasn't supposed to be a surprise.

CAMILLE

OMG, if it was, I totally didn't tell you.

CAMILLE

My bad.

CAMILLE

But yeah, let me know when you're ready and it's yours. I'm leaving town later today, but I can leave the keys with Archer if you're not free.

My jaw drops open, unsure of how to process what she's telling me. There's no way. Archer would never do such a thing, not when he hates me as much as he does. Unless...unless he did it before things went bad. Which wouldn't quite make sense either, since he was such a control freak in wanting to keep me close and under his constant watch. There's no way Archer would willingly pay for me to move out of his apartment, let alone for the entire year.

Only...what if Archer didn't want me there to begin with? He did tell Ivy that I was a means to an end and that he couldn't wait for me to be out of there. Perhaps Archer was only trying to make his life easier, and I never meant to him what he meant to me.

For the first time in weeks, I feel something other than sadness—I feel anger. Anger laced with betrayal. How could he have fooled me so badly that I thought I mattered to him? That I wasn't just some random hookup?

But when I think about his hands on my body, his mouth on mine, the way he looked at me, cared for me, loved on me...how could I have been so fucking wrong?

CHAPTER TWENTY-EIGHT

Archer

I open my refrigerator and stare at the empty shelves, closing and opening it a second later, like maybe something will appear that wasn't there already. A half-eaten container of cream cheese stares back at me, no doubt growing mold, considering it's been in there since London left. I haven't been to the grocery store in weeks, and if I don't go soon, I may have to resort to eating the contents of a ketchup bottle.

Running my hand through my hair, I sigh and slam the door shut. It's only a few blocks away, but the last time I was there, London was with me, and I know if I show up alone, Ruth is going to ask questions that I don't want to answer, not now, not ever.

I could go somewhere else, but that would involve me having to find another store, deal with a different clerk, and potentially be farther away from my apartment than I'd prefer. Ordering delivered groceries is off the table; the people never get my order right to begin with and I don't exactly want expired produce.

I just need a few things to get me by, it shouldn't take too long, and I can be back in the confines of my apartment where no one can bother me.

Rummaging through a pile of semi-clean clothes, I throw a T-shirt over my head and sniff a pair of jeans, deciding that they will suffice for the time being. I glance toward my computer and consider stalking London to see what she's up to, to make sure she's okay, to keep tabs on her, but according to her schedule at the bakery, she should be there, and if I stop to watch her, there's no telling how long it will take to pry myself away.

My stomach growls and I know that I must seize this opportunity before it's gone.

Slipping out of my apartment, I make sure the door is locked, tugging on it three times. I turn on my heel, starting toward the staircase, when I hear voices coming from downstairs. I freeze but remind myself that it's okay, that I can handle strangers. I don't have to look at them or talk to them or do anything other than walk past and complete the task I've set out to do.

But when I'm a bit closer and those voices come into focus, I realize I've made a grave mistake.

"Archer," Camille says once she's at the top. "Hey." She walks straight toward me, the person she's with stopping dead in their tracks.

My attention flutters to the other person, my heart thudding in my chest. *Fuck.*

Our eyes meet at the same time and I'm overwhelmed by a million thoughts and feelings at once. My cheeks flush and I wipe at my brow.

"Hey," I reply, my voice catching. I clear my throat. "What's up?" I internally kick myself for not having checked on London, that momentary lapse in judgment costing me this entire awkward exchange.

Camille throws her thumb in the direction of London, who remains firmly in place. "Was just giving London keys to the place, making things official."

I blink once, twice, not fully processing the information she gave me.

London crosses her arms, doing everything she can to put whatever she can between us.

I hate it, every bit of the distance, but I hate that I hate it more, ashamed that even though I said I never wanted to see her again, I haven't been able to keep true to that word. There hasn't been a single day that has passed since I pulled up some kind of feed to check on her. I'm sick in the head and can't stop.

I should hate her, and I do, but that doesn't mean it's the only emotion I feel for her.

"Nice," I say, unable to come up with anything else. Of course London is moving into Camille's...I paid for a year of her rent, and staying with Grace was probably always meant to be temporary, like her stay with me.

How fucking fortunate that Camille's place is right next to

mine. I used to think this was a good thing, but at this rate, I'm never going to get her out of my system if she's living there for the next year. I'm going to have to develop some fucking self-control if I stand a chance.

"Yeah, so anyway. I was going to show her around and give her the keys. Do you want to come in with us?" Camille asks me, clearly having no clue that things are the way they are between me and London.

"No. I'm okay, I was just heading out." I point in the direction London is standing, needing to go past her to get downstairs. Even if I wanted to use the elevator, I'd still have to pass her. "Maybe another time." I start toward her, noting how London doesn't budge.

Camille walks toward her apartment, shoving the key into the lock. "It was good seeing you, Arch."

"You, too, Cami."

She slips into the apartment, leaving London and me there in the small space together.

"So much for never seeing you again," I tell London as I stop in front of her, my tone coming across more aggressive than I intend, although I'm not sure what I expected, given my entire statement was rude as fuck to begin with.

"Shouldn't have paid the rent if you didn't want me living next to you," she retorts.

"It was before I found out the truth."

London shrugs. "You should move, then."

"Excuse me?" I stare down at her.

"If you don't want to live next to me, if you don't want to see me ever again, you should move."

I don't say anything for a long minute, my brain trying to comprehend her words, her tone, her body language. "Don't flatter yourself," I tell her. "We were never that serious anyway."

"Yeah?" London narrows her gaze and leans in closer. "Then why are you so nervous right now?"

"I'm not nervous," I lie, although I'm not convinced *nervous* is what I'm experiencing. *Utter hell* might be more accurate. To be this near her and not be able to figure out whether I want to kiss her or kill her is torture unlike any I've ever gone through. "You're nervous."

"I feel nothing for you, Archer. Not love, not lust, not even anger. *Nothing*. Living next to you is going to be like living next to a ghost."

"If you feel nothing, then why are you talking to me?" I ask her, knowing damn well she's lying as much as I am. I'm not entirely sure what I meant to her, but even if it was a fraction of what I felt for her, it's still more than nothing.

"Because you're in my way."

I step aside and motion for her to continue. "Be my guest. Don't let me stop you."

"You couldn't make me do anything," she mouths off before walking past me and into the apartment she's now calling home. London shuts the door, almost slamming it, but not quite. I'm sure she's being reserved because Camille is around, and she doesn't want to make a bad impression on her first day of having the place.

I take a deep breath in, exhaling it and coming to terms with the fact that I survived my first encounter with her since our big fight. If I'm being honest, I wasn't sure if I'd ever see London again, and despite those being my last words to her, that I never wanted to see her again, that doesn't exactly mean I wanted that to happen.

In that moment, one hundred percent. I was pissed. I had just found out she was lying to me. That she was the daughter of the man who killed Madison. Even if I could look past the fact that she was his daughter, how can I forgive her for knowing this and not telling me the truth? No matter how much I wish things could be different, I'm not stupid enough to think I could look past her deceit, especially after lecturing me that honesty was so important to her. She made me promise that I'd be honest, and how do I get repaid? By her lying to me about something that utterly destroyed me.

Madison's death was the catalyst that made me retreat into myself and realize that everyone I care about is put in danger because of my family's association with the criminal world. It's not enough that every single one of us is a killer, but everything we touch is tainted and compromised.

Loving anyone with the last name Sin is a death sentence where no one makes it out alive.

I rush out of the apartment complex, glad to be breathing air that she isn't once I'm outside. A body slams into mine, or maybe mine into it, and I steady their shoulders. "Shit, I'm sorry," I blurt out.

"Fucking prick," the guy mutters, brushing off his sport coat and side-eyeing me. He adjusts his collar, and I consider snapping his neck just for being an asshole.

My fingers dare me to move them, to snake them around his throat, squeezing until there's no life left in him.

He must realize I'm considering his demise, because he does a double take and then darts away as if he could read my mind and see the images I was envisioning of him lying on the cold, hard pavement.

Ignoring every other person around me, I continue to the corner store and hope that Ruth will take it easy on me for not bringing London. There have been a few rare occasions that I've popped down without her, but this time is different, and Ruth will see right through it.

"Archie, honey, how are you?" Ruth tilts her head from the register to look past me. "Where's my girl?"

"She, uh, she had work to do, so she won't be joining me today." Somehow, I feel more guilty lying to her than almost murdering that man on the sidewalk.

"You've been saying the same thing for weeks," she tells me, and puts her hand on the counter, leaning on it. "What's really going on?"

I grab a basket, holding it in my arms and wondering why I'm folding like a limp dick to this random store clerk. "We had a fight," I confess while moving into an aisle to avoid the glare she's no doubt giving me.

Ruth moves out from behind the counter and follows me. "You can't say that and expect me not to ask questions. Is she okay? Are you okay? What happened? Why haven't you apologized yet?"

I reach for the bagels, my hand stopping in midair. "What makes you so sure I did something wrong?" I throw them in my basket, ignoring the thoughts that bubble up...*bagels...London's safe word, and one of her favorite foods.*

"Because it's always the guy's fault. Haven't you learned anything about women?" Ruth stays like a shadow, calling me out without even knowing what happened.

Mindlessly, I continue around the store, tossing things in and trying to get out of there as quickly as possible.

"For someone who doesn't think he did anything wrong, you sure do seem to have a lot of the things she likes in this basket." Ruth pulls each item out and places them into a bag. She doesn't ring them up, because she never does, and regardless of her giving me a total, I pay her in cash anyway, always more than what it would have been.

This started years ago when I moved in, and some guy tried to rob her place. I took care of it and vowed to offer my protection, making sure everyone knew who was claiming this territory, a Sin brother. Since that day, no one has dared step foot into this store to cause trouble, except when I brought London in for the first time—that man sent from the Manor brothers trying to stir up shit. If only I could prove it, then maybe my older brother would take me seriously that they're a bigger threat than they let on. I shouldn't concern myself with such issues, but it's hard when I care about my family more than I care about myself. I don't want them to suffer just because I'm down in the dumps.

"Fine. If you don't want to talk about it, I understand." Ruth sets the bags on the counter, scooting them toward me. "You might not have asked for my advice, but I'm going to give it to you anyway." She stares right at me. "You need to fix this. I don't care what happened. What was between you two is rare. You want to miss out on that because of some fight? Life is too short, Archie. Don't let love pass you by. Don't be that stubborn."

I slide a couple hundred-dollar bills across the counter and take the bags. "Thanks, Ruth." I leave the store without another word, hers ringing in my head and making me wish I had never left my apartment to begin with. I wouldn't have run into London and I wouldn't have gotten lectured by Ruth.

Maybe I needed both of those things to happen. Maybe I need a wake-up call. Or maybe I need to be more like Seven and not give a fuck about anyone other than myself.

***

A week of living next to London feels more like an eternity in hell. I don't leave. Not once. I don't even poke my head out of my apartment, not to check the mail, not to get groceries, not to get a breath of fresh air. I've kept my blinds drawn and my lights dimmed, and I wouldn't be surprised if I have a vitamin deficiency at this point.

My computer dings, alerting me to a feed I had been trying to hack into, the code finally going through. I scan the screen, watching Joe Vito walk into the massage parlor he's been frequenting lately. His belly is round, and in the past month I've been surveilling him, he's gained even more weight, his complexion uneven and the bags under his eyes darkening. He doesn't appear well, like he has an underlying medical condition or something severely stressing him out. Not that I care either way, although I wouldn't be mad if he dropped dead, making my task of keeping London safe permanently complete, the one person who's after her buried in the ground. I'd do it myself if he weren't such an untouchable man.

I hate that word—*untouchable*. It implies my inability to kill someone, but it has nothing to do with whether I could pull it off, yet the implications that would follow in his death. If it were natural causes, no one is to blame, and there would be an investigation to make sure that's what happened, but if someone were to kill him, it would mean things worse than death for anyone who associates with the killer. Joe is part of a powerful family. As was Ricardo. Their influence is passed down generation after generation, giving each fresh blood more authority than they deserved, never really earning it themself, unlike my family. We're new to this criminal world, the first in the Sin syndicate, which is what intimidates so many—the fact that it wasn't passed down; that we did, in fact, earn every bit of fear exuded when someone utters our name. It wasn't easy, and I'm not proud of everything we did to get here, but we came from nothing, and I think there's something to be said about someone who can build an empire out of jack shit.

My phone rings, Ivy's face lighting up the screen. I hit ignore, letting it go to voicemail, knowing damn well she's not going to leave one. How many times will she call before she gets the hint that I don't want to talk? I've already told her countless times, but she keeps insisting I'm worth trying to get through to. I understand she wants to help, but the fact that she's the one who brought this to my attention makes me relive the moment of finding out London lied to me over and over.

I silence another call from Ivy, keeping my attention on the screen, begging myself not to get curious and click on another feed I keep nearby, too...the one of London. I thought with her living next door, I'd be able to stop watching her, but I can't, and no matter what I do, I can't withstand the urge to check on her.

Letting my impulses get the best of me, I pull up the feed, holding my breath as London appears in my line of sight. She's talking to Grace at the bakery, only she's sitting at a table, maybe on break or off the clock. I should know her hours by now, but every time I figure them out, they change again. I'm not mad at her for being unpredictable, because that alone is what could keep her from some creep that isn't me stalking her.

"Don't turn on the audio," I tell myself, hovering my finger over the button. "Don't do it." I sigh and push it anyway, hating myself for my lack of control.

"You're coming to the gala still, right?" Grace asks London, and takes a sip of her latte.

"I mean, I want to, yeah." London rubs at her neck like something is bothering her. "I don't know if I can."

"Why? The bakery is closed then, right? What else could you be doing? Come on. Don't leave me hanging. I will totally guilt-trip you, and I won't even feel bad about it."

"You're ruthless," London tells her.

"I know. Need not mention how we're no longer roommates, and that was devastating enough. You're not going to leave me with

Leo, are you? Come on, who cares if the grumpy brother is there? Don't let that stop you."

I lean in closer, my breath hanging on their every word, wondering what London is going to say next. It's like a fucking car crash I can't peel my attention away from.

"It has nothing to do with *him*."

"I'm not going to let it go until you give me a reason. I deserve that much." Grace bats her eyelashes dramatically at London.

London sighs. "I don't have anything to wear."

"Is that it?" Grace laughs and shoves London's shoulder playfully. "We can go shopping this weekend."

London doesn't add that she can't afford to go shopping, because I know damn well she isn't going to use the black Amex of mine that she's still in possession of, and she isn't exactly rolling in cash at her bakery gig. I've checked the charges almost every day, and she hasn't spent a dime of my money.

Not bothering to witness any more of what their conversation entails, I throw on the cleanest clothes I can find and slip out of my apartment, marching straight into the store London went to on her first outing when she arrived here over two months ago.

"Welcome to Charlotte's," a woman calls out to me from her spot stocking a shelf. "Can I help you with anything?"

I point to the dress in the back corner, the one London had her eye on the second she came here, passing on it because it was way more than she had at the time. "I'll take that. And whatever shoes go with it. A size seven."

"Oh, you're serious." She drops the sweater she was folding and darts around the table. "It's eight thousand."

"I don't care." I slide my Amex out of my wallet and hold it out to her. "Here."

She goes to work zipping a garment bag around the dress and taking it off the hook. "Special occasion?"

"Something like that," I tell her, not quite coming to terms with the fact that I'm here at all, spending thousands of dollars on a woman that hates me, and that I sort of hate, too.

"I have these open-toed stilettos that would look great with the Lorenzo. What do you think?"

"That's fine." I glance in the direction of the door, hoping like hell London doesn't get some random urge to come in here right now. According to her schedule, she's supposed to be at work. Perhaps she was meeting with Grace before and will be clocking in afterward.

"Can I help you with anything else today?" the store clerk asks me.

"No, thanks." I turn toward her, tapping my card on the screen as it flashes nine thousand something due. I made more money in the two hours I was drifting in and out of sleep last night, this is nothing.

"I'll put my card in the bag. If you ever need any assistance, I'm happy to help." She pauses and adds, "I'm Charlotte, by the way."

I force a smile and take the items from her, slipping out of the store and making my way back to the apartment complex. A window across the street catches my eye and I dart in front of traffic, not quite caring if they hit me or not.

A doorman holds his hand out to stop me. "Excuse me, sir. Do you have an appointment?"

"No. I don't need one." I stare at him, contemplating murder yet again. "Get your fucking hands off me."

"Sir, I'm going to have to ask you to calm down." He puts both of his hands on my shoulders.

I react without thinking, taking my free hand to grab and twist his, positioning it behind his back in the blink of an eye.

He yelps and drops to his knees. "They don't pay me enough for this, really. Let me go, please."

"Sorry about that." I release him instantly, helping him to his feet. "Let's start again."

The doorman dusts off his legs and shoots a look into the store, no doubt hoping no one saw that happen.

"I'm Archer Sin. I don't have an appointment. Could you please check and see if they have an opening for me?"

His eyes widen and he averts his gaze, turning toward the door and unlocking it. "I'm sorry, sir. I had no idea. Please, come on in. Someone will be right with you." He pushes a button on the walkie-talkie attached to his collar. "Archer Sin is here, team. Please be advised."

By the time he's unlocked the door, four salespeople greet me inside, one of them taking the bags from my hands and another offering me a glass of champagne.

"I'm not thirsty," I tell him, and scan the other clerks. "You." I settle on a rather timid, short female, not appearing quite as ravenous as the other three. "The rest of you, leave us be."

She blinks a few times and swallows harshly.

I snap my fingers at the person who has my bags from the other store. "Those stay."

The guy circles back, dropping them onto the counter before slipping into another room, out of sight.

"What can I help you with, Mr. Sin?" the woman who remains says.

"First, call me Archer. Second, I'm not going to hurt you, so whatever they told you in the twenty seconds it took to get me in the door, forget that. Third, what's your name?"

"Faith," she tells me.

"Well, I have faith that you're going to help me, Faith." I point to a display that catches my eye. "This here. Do you think it would go with this?" I grab the garment bag, unzipping it to reveal the dress I purchased for London.

"I think that would be a fine choice," she says reluctantly.

"Be honest, Faith. I won't be upset." I try to keep my tone even but I'm not exactly great with talking to other people.

Faith walks over, tapping on the glass. "This is a great piece, it is. But I think with the necklace and fabric choice, you'd be better suited with something else...something like..." She scans the displays until she finds what she's on the hunt for. "This."

I settle my eyes upon the case, knowing damn well I made the right choice when I picked her to assist me.

There, in all its glory, is a beautiful necklace fit for a princess.

"Tell me about it," I say, not knowledgeable about jewelry at all but confident this is the one I'm going to get.

"This is the Flowerlace necklace. It is rhodium-plated

eighteen-karat white gold with over four hundred stones, totaling over twenty carats. With the lace and silhouettes of flowers, it combines nature and couture for a timeless look."

"I'll take it."

"Sir, I must mention that it's two hundred twenty thousand dollars." She holds her breath like I might die at hearing the price tag.

"Yeah, that's fine. What else do you have that would go with it?" I peer into the case. "What about that ring and earrings, too? Oh, wait, do you have any bracelets?"

"Yes, we do." She pulls the items out of the case for me to take a closer look at, not quite realizing that I've already decided to buy them all. "There isn't a matching bracelet for this collection, but there's one I think would go lovely with it..." Faith goes to another case, pulling out a bracelet that sparkles brighter than anything in this room. "Over thirty-six carats."

"I'll take that too."

She clears her throat softly. "It's more expensive than the necklace."

"How much?"

"This piece is three hundred ninety-seven thousand."

"Oh. That's fine. I thought it would be more." I pull my phone out of my pocket, checking the time and notifications littering the screen. "If you don't mind, I'm rather in a hurry."

"Of course, sir. I'll get those together for you. If you'll give me a moment." Faith carries everything into the back, leaving me out here alone with every camera in the building focused on me.

I'd take offense to it, but I can only imagine the shit these people would be in if I robbed the place. I have no issue paying for it on my own; I'll leave my sticky fingers to the people who deserve to be taken from.

Faith returns a long moment later, a large bag in her grasp and a male sales associate on her heels. He's older, at least twice her age, and I hate how fucking close he is to her, her body language tense like she doesn't like it either.

He sets a small device on the counter. "Good day, Mr. Sin. I expect Faith has taken great care of you?"

I step toward him and he flinches. "Do you work on commission?" I tilt my head in Faith's direction.

"Why, yes, Mr. Sin. All sales associates at Van Cleef & Arpels do," the man confirms.

"What's your name?" I ask him.

"Ransom, sir."

"Ransom," I repeat, inching closer. "Do you know who I am?"

He nods stiffly, his entire body tense.

I keep my voice low. "Then you know what I'm capable of, right?"

He nods again.

"If Faith doesn't make her entire commission, I'm going to hunt you down for a little visit. Do you hear me?"

"Y-yes, sir."

I allow some space between us, giving him a chance to alter the course of his future.

He chooses the right path, taking the device into his palm, pushing a sequence of buttons, and handing it to Faith.

"That'll be seven hundred fifty thousand, one hundred forty-eight dollars and seventy-five cents." She lays the thing on the counter while hiding a grin.

I tap my black Amex, my phone ringing a second later. "Hello?"

"Mr. Sin, this is Gretchen from American Express calling. We flagged potential suspicious activity on your account."

I cut her off. "That's me. I'm purchasing a gift for a friend. Approve the purchase, please."

Typing on a keyboard comes through the speaker. "I have approved your purchase. Thank you, and have a great day, Mr. Sin."

The line disconnects and the card reader dings, alerting us to the transaction going through.

I focus on the man again while reaching for my bag. "And stop standing so close to her. It's making us both uncomfortable." I leave the store, shoving everything into one arm to bring my phone back out to check London's whereabouts.

Her location pings at the bakery still, giving me a little more time for one more task.

CHAPTER TWENTY-NINE

London

I pace the confines of my brand-new apartment, stewing in a plethora of emotions and thoughts I'm not sure what to do with. I got home from work late, never turning the lights on for long enough to see anything, plopping down into the bed Camille left behind.

It wasn't until I woke up this morning, the light of day spilling in, that I saw someone had broken into my apartment and left me presents.

There was no note, not a single word giving away the culprit, but I know exactly who it was—my stalker, the man I love to hate... Archer Sin.

I huff, mumbling under my breath and considering my options. I could pile everything up and leave it on his doorstep, bang on his door and throw it all inside, or I could keep them, not acknowledging his generosity at all. Each one has its pros and cons, and not even one of them makes me any less angry that he continues to violate my privacy.

He knew I wanted that dress, the one I saw when I went shopping the first main day I was here.

He knew I told Grace yesterday that I didn't have anything to wear.

I open the garment bag, tracing my fingers along the delicate fabric, sighing at how fucking beautiful the dress is up close and personal. Popping the top of each jewelry box, I gasp at how shiny and expensive they look.

I drag out my phone, doing a quick internet search, my mouth dropping at the price tags.

Did Archer spend over six hundred thousand dollars on someone he can't stand? Someone he claims he wants nothing to do with. Someone he threw out of his apartment because he couldn't be bothered to hear their side of the story.

Pushing a button, I dial Grace, because I can't be responsible for making this decision on my own.

It rings twice before she answers, her voice the sound of angels. "Hey, babe. What's up?"

"I need you to come over, *right now*. It's an emergency." Okay, maybe I'm being dramatic, but it feels like an emergency of some sort. "I'm not, like, dying or anything."

Grace laughs. "I was just grabbing coffee. I'm next in line, want something?"

"This calls for something stronger than coffee."

"Got it. Getting out of line now. I'll pick up a bottle of wine on the way over. Give me five."

We hang up and I stare at the boxes until a soft knock hits my front door. I peer through the peephole to find Grace on the other end, two bottles of wine in her grasp.

I open the door and all but drag her inside. "I need your help."

"I have never felt more important in my entire life," she says. "Good thing I got screw tops." Grace sets one of the bottles on the counter, carrying the other over and into my kitchen, rummaging through the cabinets to find two glasses.

I'm no help. Even if I wasn't stewing in my thoughts, I haven't really gone through the apartment that well to know where things are located. Camille gave me the place fully furnished, telling me it was easier on her that way, and I wasn't exactly protesting, considering I came to New York with just the clothes on my back.

Grace hands me a glass of red and takes a long swig of hers. "Okay, so what kind of help do you need? Makeup? Boys? Hide a dead body?"

"You'd help me hide a body?"

She shrugs. "Hey, what are friends for?" Her gaze catches on the bags sitting in my dining room. "Um, did you go shopping without me?" She marches right over, her hand on her hip. "Is that Van Cleef?" She flips the top on one of the jewelry boxes, stifling a gasp. "Oh. My. God." Grace slowly spins on her heel. "You robbed the fucking Van Cleef store?"

I chug some of my wine, ignoring the way it warms my chest

and empty stomach. “I did not rob the Van Cleef store.” I lick my lips and try to make sense of the situation. “I woke up and this was here.”

Grace stares at me, blinking a few times. “What?”

“I mean, it was either here when I got in last night, or someone came when I was sleeping.”

“Someone? Like whom? Santa Claus?” Grace helps herself to the rest of the things, shaking her head as she explores all the stuff Archer bought me.

“You know who it was, we both do.” I settle onto a stool in the kitchen, near the bottle of wine, refilling my glass when I empty it a second later.

Grace comes over, topping hers off, too, and sits down. “You think he broke in here?”

“I mean, I didn’t give him a key. How else would you explain how it got in here? I sleepwalked to Van Cleef and went shopping? I don’t have that kind of money.”

“You said you had his black card, right? It’s not impossible.”

That’s when it dawns on me, I do still have Archer’s American Express. I had forgotten all about it, buried in the bottom of one of the handbags he had gotten me. I should probably pay it more consideration, since it’s capable of purchasing six hundred thousand dollars’ worth of stuff. Unless he paid cash, then that’s an entirely different story altogether.

“I didn’t use his card. This was him, not me.” I drink more of the wine, not caring about the taste and focusing on how it makes my body tingle and loosen up at the same time.

“It’s kind of hot,” Grace admits.

“What?”

“Don’t get me wrong, breaking and entering is definitely a criminal activity. But it’s weirdly romantic. Isn’t that the dress you’ve been wanting from Charlotte’s, too? He pays attention, it’s sweet.”

I glare at her. “Grace. Don’t encourage him, he’s probably listening right now.” I crane my head all around the apartment, feeling entirely too vulnerable.

Grace hops off her chair, sets her wineglass down, and goes over to the window.

"What are you doing?" I ask her.

"Trust the process." She lowers each of the blinds, the place getting darker and darker until she shuts off the lights, leaving us in almost pitch-black.

"What the hell," I blurt out, bracing myself on the counter like the world might topple over now that I can't see.

Grace pulls out her camera and hits Record, panning the kitchen, dining room, and living room. She walks back over, how she can find her way I'll never know, and hits Play next to me. "We're looking for a red dot. It's hard to find them with the naked eye, but if there was a camera in here, this video would pick it up."

We watch it three times, and nothing indicates that there are any hidden cameras in here.

"Let me check your other rooms. Is that cool?" Grace waits for me to give her my approval before continuing.

"Yeah, of course."

She leaves me there in the quiet darkness, returning a couple of minutes later to show me the screen. "I think you're good, babe." Grace flips the kitchen light on and I squint at the bright assault, my eyes taking a second to adjust.

"Why do you even know how to check for cameras?" I ask Grace, and swallow down the rest of the wine in my glass.

"Politics, babe." She climbs onto the stool. "It's hard to know who to trust."

"Isn't it a conflict of interest? You dating Leo, a known criminal."

"Meh. It is what it is."

"You're only doing it to make Seven jealous, aren't you?"

Her mouth drops open, and I almost applaud her acting skills. She'll never willingly admit she has a thing for Seven, but I can't say I blame her. He's a fucking lunatic. Leo is gorgeous, and much better suited for her, considering he has some semblance of human decency. But there's no denying her chemistry with Seven, even if she refuses to acknowledge it.

She smirks while refilling our glasses, my head swimming with the wine buzz. "What are you going to do?"

"What should I do?"

"Well, you could confront him, or not. If you confront him, you get the satisfaction of arguing with him, which I know you absolutely love. If you don't, you deny yourself of that but will probably drive him crazier than if you said anything at all. I guess it depends on what your gut is telling you. Both are viable options."

I want to let it go, to allow him to stew in the mystery of my nonresponse, but I don't know if I have the self-control not to march over there and rip into him for breaking in here. Sure, it was thoughtful, that much is true. And now I have something to wear, along with some of the most beautiful accessories I ever could have imagined. I love everything he picked out, I just wish he would have given me a choice in the matter, or maybe a heads-up before he broke into my apartment. He might mean well, but it was an invasion of my privacy and I'm not sure how that makes me feel.

Slipping off my chair, I chug my wine and wipe the droplet that rolls down my chin. I leave the empty glass on the counter and turn to Grace. "I'm going over there."

"Oh, like now?" Her eyes widen and she follows suit, drinking her wine and following me over to the door, not daring to convince me to stay put and think through what I'm about to do.

We're out of my apartment in a flash, storming over to his door, Grace hanging back as I pound my fist against the hard surface.

It takes twenty whole seconds before Archer opens up, barely cracking it as if he's hiding something inside. I hate the jealousy that arises at the idea that it might be another woman. Was he able to move on that quickly? Even after buying me all that expensive shit?

"London," he says, a hint of surprise in his tone.

"Archer." I try to look past him, to see into his apartment, but he keeps it blocked with his wide frame and tall stature.

"What do you want?" His gaze darts from me to Grace, who remains firmly behind me, her arms crossed over her chest. "Grace." He nods at her.

"Grace?" a voice calls out from farther within his place, the person attached to it gripping and pulling the door open to reveal the rest of the Sin family. Seven pushes past Archer, throwing his arm over Grace's shoulders and tugging her close.

"Ugh, gross. You reek of booze, Seven." She attempts to shrug him off but he keeps ahold of her.

Archer sighs and steadies his attention on me. "See what you've done?"

"What I've done?" I glare at him. "I think we should talk about what *you've* done."

"Have you been drinking?" he asks me, and leans closer, sniffing my breath. "What the fuck, London? Are you drunk?"

"Get out of my face, Archer. You don't get to have a say in my life." I back away from him, stumbling over my own feet.

He reaches out to steady me, his touch warm and firm. I hate that I enjoy it more than I expected I would. I'm supposed to hate him, not want his skin on mine. But I guess just like Grace and Seven, we can't help who we're attracted to.

Maybe I should try Leo out and see if it will distract me from Archer. I wouldn't mind dating the playboy brother if it meant getting over the grumpy one.

"Get inside." Archer guides me into his apartment and I don't bother convincing him otherwise. "You need to sober up."

"You need to sober up."

"Good one." Archer shuts the door behind Seven and Grace, Seven's arm still slung around her shoulders.

She pokes him in the side, causing him to flinch and break his hold on her.

"What's going on here?" Leo comes over, putting his hand on Grace's lower back, asserting his dominance over Seven, a dangerous territory I'm surprised he's willing to explore.

Leo might be dangerous, but Seven has made it clear he doesn't care who it is; family or not, he'd kill them for crossing him.

Grace melts into Leo, hugging his torso and kissing his cheek. Aesthetically, they look damn good together, and if they reproduced, their babies would no doubt be supermodels straight from the womb, every diaper brand desperate to get their faces plastered on the side of a diaper box. But they're almost too pretty, like if you stared too long, you'd lose your eyesight, as if you were staring into the blazing sun.

Ivy stands from her spot at the table, August sitting in the chair next to her, busy doing something on his phone. "London."

"Ivy." I glare at her, endless bad thoughts running through my mind, since she was the one to expose me to Archer before I had gotten a chance to do it myself. I hate her for ruining what we had before it even began, but I sort of applaud her for doing something I don't know if I'd ever have been capable of doing.

A month later and the entire situation feels as fresh as that fateful morning, when things felt so right, only to end so badly.

I never want to see you again, the final words Archer spoke to me, the ones that sealed our fate permanently.

"Didn't realize you'd be joining us today," she says.

"I came over to have a chat with your brother." I slap Archer on the shoulder, his muscles tense under his shirt. "Isn't that right, big boy?"

Archer's jaw clenches and his nostrils flare slightly.

"We have no secrets," Ivy announces. "What you need to say to him, you can say to the rest of us." She comes around the front of the table like she's daring me to make a move so she can finish things off.

Rationally, I know I should be afraid, not just of her, but every person in this room, but how can I be when the worst is behind me? Nothing they could do to me could ever be worse than anything I've already been through.

"Fine." I turn toward Archer. "Do you want to tell your siblings what you put in my apartment?"

Archer moves quickly, grabbing my shoulders and navigating me away from earshot. "Okay, fine, we can talk alone."

"What, I thought there were no secrets?" I blurt out loud enough so they can hear me. I don't give a fuck if they find out their brother is a stalker who broke into my apartment and left me hundreds of thousands of dollars' worth of gifts.

"Bedroom, now." Archer shoves me through the door, kicking it shut once he's through. "You have a big mouth, don't you?"

I spin out of his grasp and fold my arms over my chest. "What the fuck, Archer?"

"What?" He mimics my stance.

"What do you mean, *what*? Are you really going to pretend like you didn't break into my fucking apartment?"

"I don't know what you're talking about."

I narrow my gaze. "You're telling me you didn't? You swear to me it wasn't you."

He pinches his brow and exhales dramatically. "Why do you have to be so difficult? Just say thank you."

"No, absolutely not." I shake my head. "That was a violation of my privacy. Not to mention how you watch my every move. How did you even know I wanted that dress, Archer? Huh? How did you know I didn't have anything to wear? How could you have possibly known those things unless you were watching me, listening to my conversations?" I tap my shoe on the floor. "It has to stop, Archer. It's uncalled for. There's no reason for it. You said you never wanted to see me again. Remember? You're telling me you're a liar?"

"You're one to talk," he scoffs.

I point my finger at him. "That's not fair. You didn't even give me a chance to explain."

He steps closer, his presence nearly suffocating me. "You don't deserve a chance to explain."

"Fine. Whatever. If you don't want me to, I won't. But you have to stop fucking stalking me. It's not romantic."

"I wasn't trying to be romantic." His dark eyes meet mine and I can't help but linger my gaze on his lips, reminiscing on the way they felt pressed against my body.

"You're confusing, you know that?" I swallow harshly and keep looking at him.

"There's nothing confusing about this. You're reading into something that isn't there." Archer is the first to break away and walk to the door. He hesitates, his hand on the knob. "What we had died that day, London. There's no coming back from that."

I hate the way his words slice through my heart. I hate that I care at all. I hate that I wish I could turn back the clock, but that's not possible and there's nothing I can do to change his mind. And even if I could, he's not the only one who got hurt—the way he threw me out of his apartment, the way he tossed me aside as if I never mattered to him, that isn't something I could forgive, either. What we had might have been powerful and passionate and life-changing, but it was fleeting and I have to come to terms with the fact that it's gone.

Only, I wish he would, too.

Maybe living next to each other really was a bad idea.

***

I adjust my dress in the back of the limo Grace had sent to my apartment complex. It fits perfectly, as does every piece of jewelry Archer had bought me.

"You look beautiful," she tells me, and fixes her makeup in a small compact mirror. She pinches it shut and tucks it into her clutch.

"So do you." I take her in, her blond hair slicked back into a pony, the ends in perfectly soft curls. Her dress is a buttery gold, long gown with sequins and frilly ends coming off the shoulders and bottom half. It's stunning, and I wouldn't be surprised if it was custom-made for her body. The neckline plunges deep and shows just enough of her chest not to be too revealing.

"You both are hot as hell," Leo says from his spot next to Grace.

He's wearing a dark navy cashmere suit from Louis Vuitton with a handkerchief that matches Grace's dress. Everything about him screams *I have money*, and I can't help but wonder what people are going to think about my outfit, considering I didn't pay for a damn thing. I can't even claim my panties, since I'm not wearing any.

"Thanks, Leo. You clean up nice, too," I say, dancing around the awkward fact that he's Archer's brother. They're not even blood-related, but every time I see Leo's face, it reminds me of Archer.

I chew at my lip and stare out the window, the cars passing by in a blur.

"What are you nervous about?" Grace taps me with her stiletto to get my attention.

"Nothing."

She tilts her head. "Don't lie to me."

I let out a sigh and wish Leo wasn't here so I could talk more candidly.

"I don't think he's coming," Grace tells me. "I mean, he bought a table, so he has every right to, but he didn't RSVP. I had my team follow up a few times."

I avert my gaze, fidgeting with the purse I brought with me. I can't tell if I'm relieved or disappointed.

"How long has it been since you talked to him?" Grace slides her hand on top of Leo's when he sets it on her leg.

"Four weeks."

"That's a month, sweetheart," Leo says.

"It will be a month on Thursday," I correct him, regretting it the second I blurt it out. How psycho do I sound, counting the days since Archer and I last spoke? We've been apart longer than we were together and yet it still won't ease the ache in my chest every time I think about him. I already made it through denial, anger, and bargaining, so I guess that leaves depression and acceptance. The only silver lining is that eventually I'll be over him, and that can't come soon enough.

I'm saved by the limo stopping in front of the massive building Grace secured for this event, my heart racing at the flashing lights that appear when the driver opens the door. I step out first, taking the man's hand to assist me, and do everything I can to be as poised as possible.

Cameras snap, people talk loudly, and I ignore the "Who is she?" and walk with my chin up, my shoulders back, across the red carpet leading to the entrance. I don't let out the breath I was holding until I'm through the chaos, waiting for Grace and Leo, who should be behind me any moment now.

"Welcome," a woman says to me, her eyes bright and a tablet in her grasp. "London Smith?"

"Yes," I confirm. "I'm with Grace McCallister."

Grace and Leo come through the door, noise from the crowd blaring and fading out once they're fully inside. They're smiling, and I'm almost convinced they like each other, but they're both biding their time until something better comes along. There's nothing wrong with having some fun while it lasts, though. Something I wish Archer and I would have spent more time doing instead of the push and pull we did for the month leading up to getting together.

I bite the inside of my lip, punishing myself for thinking about him at all. Tonight is about Grace and the work she's done for this charity, not Archer and our temporary fling that meant nothing.

"Ms. McCallister, it's a pleasure to see you." The woman greets her with an even bigger smile than she gave me.

"Tori, hey. How are things going?" Grace comes up beside her, glancing at the tablet as Tori points to a few things.

"Everything has kicked off without a hitch. There was a minor hiccup with catering, but it was dealt with. I assure you a flawless evening."

"Perfect." Grace glances at me and Leo, who are standing in wait. "Let's get in there."

Leo holds both of his elbows out to us. "Come on, help a man out by walking in with the two most beautiful women here tonight."

Grace is the first to latch onto Leo, taking a look back at me. "What the hell. Come on, London."

I grin at her and hold on to Leo as he escorts us through the main double doors and into the stunning hall filled with tons of other people. Music is playing softly, and chatter fills the space.

"Drinks?" Leo says, shifting his attention to both of us.

"Please," I'm the first to respond. "Stronger the better."

Grace nods, and he kisses her cheek before leaving us to head toward the bar. I gravitate toward Grace and consider how mad she'd be at me for dipping out of here when she's distracted.

"Don't even think about it," she says, as if she can read my mind.

"What?" I ask her.

"You're about to pull an Irish goodbye."

"Am not," I lie.

Grace slips her arm through mine and glares at me. "I know you better than that, London *Smith*."

A lot has changed in the last few weeks. Not only am I improving at the bakery and learning how to better budget my money, but my friendship with Grace has deepened to the point that I've confided my true identity to her. I hadn't planned on telling anyone, but with the way things went down with Archer, I couldn't afford to lose Grace, too, and I trusted that she'd keep my secret safe. I've never had a friend like her before, I couldn't gamble with fate that it would last if I couldn't be honest with her. It was hard, at first, to find the right way to tell her things, but once I started, I word-vomited my history with my father, the events that transpired, and even the fact that I'm the reason why Madison, Archer's old love, is dead. I spared no details, giving Grace the ability to ask questions, answering them as best I could without shutting down from having to relive those torturous moments of my past. It was strange being able to finally talk about what happened with someone, like a huge weight was lifted from my shoulders at not having to bear it all myself. Grace didn't judge me and wasn't all that shocked, which didn't surprise me one bit, considering how well she handled Archer's family and the fact that they're notorious criminals.

I'm honored to have her as a friend, and I can only hope to support her the way she's supported me, getting me through a time when I felt incredibly alone. I hadn't realized how much having Archer around helped me through the transition of losing everything and starting over until he wasn't there anymore. I wasn't just losing a lover; I was losing a friend, a confidant, too.

Leo returns a moment later, three glasses in his grasp. "Tequila old-fashioned," he tells us.

We each take one, clinking them together before giving them a taste. I swallow mine in one go, the liquid warming a path down my chest.

"Okay, then." Leo takes my glass from me and points to the bar. "Do we want another one, or would you like to hold off on embarrassing yourself just yet?"

"I'm not going to embarrass myself," I spit back, the two of us developing this sort of brother-and-sister banter throughout Grace and him dating. He's like the annoying older brother I never had, and despite him being Archer's brother, I do enjoy being around him.

"Oh, twelve o'clock, hot-dude alert," he says, catching me off guard. "Play it cool, champ."

I narrow my gaze at him and as nonchalantly as possible, turn in the direction he implied, a very attractive man in a black suit is shaking hands with an older man. We watch a woman approach, wrap her arm around his, and kiss his cheek.

"Oops." Leo winces like I might slap him, and I do, but teasingly. "I'll try to make sure the next one is single."

"You two be okay if I go mingle?" Grace asks us, focusing on me. "Don't let this one leave."

"I'll make sure to say goodbye if I do." I wink at her.

"We're golden, babe." Leo takes her hand and presses his lips to her fingers before releasing her to go do her job.

"You two are cute," I tell him, and steal his glass to drink the contents of his drink too.

He sighs. "That was mine."

"You'll survive." I nudge him with my elbow. "Don't ignore what I said, though."

Leo scans the crowd, nodding at a man who waves at him. "It's nothing serious."

"Do you want it to be?"

He tilts his head at me. "I don't do serious."

"I mean, that could change. Don't you want to be in a relationship? Know that you're coming home every night to the same person?"

"That sounds like my worst nightmare." He drops our glasses onto a tray a server walking by is holding. "Sex with one person for the rest of your life."

"It doesn't have to be forever. You can commit to one person without it meaning marriage. Have you ever had a girlfriend?"

"I've had plenty of girlfriends."

"Girlfriends, Leo. Not hookups. Not people you're dating just to fuck. I mean people who you've introduced to your family. People who know something deeper than surface level about you."

"Grace has met the family."

"That doesn't count. She met the family before you guys started sleeping together."

Leo stops his scan of the crowd. "Grace and I haven't slept together."

"What?"

"She didn't tell you?"

I search until I find her, my sight settling on my best friend, who never mentioned to me that she and Leo weren't fucking. I feel like that's important information that could have been brought up at some point.

"Huh. That's interesting." Leo adjusts his suit jacket. "Yeah, we aren't. Not for lack of trying. At first, our schedules didn't allow for it. Now we've just sort of become friends who attend events with each other. Don't get me wrong, Grace is wicked sexy. I'd have sex with her right now if she wanted to go fuck in a coat closet."

I fold my arms over my chest, my bracelet almost catching on my dress. "And you're okay with this?"

Leo shrugs. "We've talked about it. We aren't exclusive. We can see other people."

"How very mature of you." I never would have assumed Leo would be the communicative type. He's an arrogant asshole, and somehow the most mature out of all the Sin brothers.

Leo raises his brows at me. "I mean, if you want to upgrade brothers, let me know. I'm sure Grace wouldn't mind."

I shove him again, this time a bit harder than before. "Shut up. You're disgusting."

He brushes off where I hit him.

"You aren't the brother I'd trade for, anyway," I tease him, knowing damn well I wouldn't mess with any of the others. Seven is crazy, and August and Ivy have an unspoken thing going on that I'm not sure if either of them is aware of. They're supposedly siblings, but they have chemistry like they're secret lovers.

Leo gasps and holds his hand to his chest. "You hurt me, London." He presses his finger to his chin. "Let me guess, August. You have a daddy kink, don't you?"

"Please. He's, like, thirty-something."

"I believe big brother is thirty-six. And you're what, twenty?"

"Twenty-four, get it right."

"That's a pretty big age gap."

"Aren't you two the same age?" I ask him, despite being well aware that Leo is a few years younger. I just like giving him shit and doing anything I can to injure his ego.

"That's fucked up, London. I'm thirty-two. Arch is barely two years younger. You're hurting my ego." He pauses and continues. "Wait a minute, you're telling me you'd go for Seven over me?"

"What can I say, I have a thing for bad boys, and for the record, I think your ego will be just fine." I survey the crowd, attempting to find someone to distract me from thinking about Archer. I'm having a good time chatting with Leo, but he's still his brother and that will never go away.

"Archer is a bad boy...Seven, he's a psycho." Leo sighs like he's holding back something he isn't willing to say.

"What's with that? Has he always been that way?"

Leo nods. "Yeah. It's gotten worse over time, though." He clears his throat. "Enough about my family. Let's dance." He holds out his hand to me and starts walking backward to the dance floor where only a few people are dancing. He wiggles his finger upward to entice me and I shake my head at him. "Aw, come on. Don't leave a guy hanging."

Reluctantly, I go after him, because what other choice do I have? Sure, I could get another drink from the bar and drown my sorrows until I forget about Archer, but there's no telling if the alcohol would make things worse.

Leo latches onto my hand, spinning me into his chest. I slam against him with a thud and we both laugh.

"One dance, then another drink, deal?" I say to him, intending to get a drink regardless of what he has to say.

"Deal." Leo twirls me again, this time away from him, and puts his hand on my waist, leading me beautifully.

The last time I danced was with Archer, but I shove that thought away, enjoying this moment here now.

"Admit it," he says. "You're having fun." Leo dips me, holding on to my back and preventing me from hitting the floor.

I stare up at him with an involuntary smile on my face. "Fine. It's not a terrible time."

He pulls me back onto both of my feet, more people joining around us as the music starts to fade.

"One more," I tell him. "Then we can get a drink."

He winks at me, and we dance through the next song, Leo

twirling and spinning and dipping me here and there—this dress, this jewelry, this entire night making me feel like a princess, the only thing missing is my knight in shining armor.

The song stops and I do too, a bit out of breath.

"I think I'm ready for that drink," Leo says to me, his cheeks flushed, somehow making him even more handsome than he was before. With his hand on my lower back, he guides me across the dance floor and over to the bar, putting his finger in the air to get the bartender's attention.

"Listen, don't let it go to your head," I tell him. "But every woman in here is looking at you."

He grins and orders our drinks, turning his back to put his elbows on the bar while we wait. "Come here with one woman and leave with another. That wouldn't be very gentlemanly of me."

"Then why are you scanning the crowd searching for your next victim?"

"Victim?" he scoffs. "Any lady would be lucky to go home with Leo Sin."

I take the drink the bartender brings, grateful I've commandeered Grace's rich date. It isn't that I don't want to contribute to the charity, I just don't have as much disposable income as the rest of the people in attendance. Luckily, they picked me up on their way, otherwise, I might not have been able to cover the Uber to get me here.

"What made you guys choose that last name?" I ask him while stirring my almost third tequila old-fashioned.

"How much has Archer told you?"

I breathe deeply through my nose. "Do you *have* to say his name?"

Leo takes a drink out of his glass and puts his other hand in the air. "Geez, didn't realize you were so sensitive."

"I'm not sensitive."

"Whatever you say." He does another glance around the room before giving me his attention. "Long story short, we all changed our names when we aged out and collectively agreed with Sin, since that's what we built our freedom with."

"With sin?"

"Yeah, I mean, you know, pride, greed, wrath, so on and so forth. We weren't exactly virtuous. It just sort of fit. It felt right, so we went with it." Leo catches sight of something and his whole body tenses. "Shit." He pivots to try to block his view with me. "Hide me."

"What?" I glance over my shoulder, catching sight of a round, old man who's approaching. "Uh, I think it's too late."

"Mr. Sin," the old man croaks. "It's me, George Bannon."

Leo sighs and throws on his best poker face. "Mr. Bannon, hello. Pleasure seeing you here. It's been a while."

"I've been contacting your office," George tells him. "Your secretary keeps saying you're out, and I keep thinking *what a busy man, that Mr. Sin*."

Leo fakes a laugh. "Yeah, that's me." He wraps his arm around my shoulders. "Let me introduce you, Mr. Bannon, this is London Smith. London, George Bannon, owner of Bannon Gaming."

I shake George's hand and he barely gives me a second glance as he focuses on Leo. I zone them out, not wanting to be a part of whatever *that* is, and assess the growing crowd of people mingling here and there. Through a massive set of doors, the tables are being set, dinner no doubt on the horizon. Grace had informed me there would be drinks and socializing, then dinner, speeches, then after-dinner cocktails with the hopes of getting donors intoxicated enough to pledge more before they're done.

A couple dances in the distance, the man stepping on the woman's feet so many times, she finally stops and breaks away from him, leaving him there red-faced and unsure of what to do. A creepy older man stands just along the dance floor, his eyes roaming every single woman in eyeshot range of him. He focuses on a tall blonde wearing a black dress hugging each one of her curves. I wander from Leo a bit and watch the creep watch her, my attention splitting when a jet-black-haired woman approaches him from behind, bumping into him and offering him an apologetic embrace. I almost buy it as an accident until I see her slip his watch off his wrist and tuck it into her palm, the move so fucking slick, I'm impressed. I keep my sight on her as she lands three more unsuspecting targets, securing a pair of cuff links, another watch, and a wallet. I sip my drink and consider going over there and befriending her, but when I glance over at Leo, I lose the mystery girl altogether. She was right there, and it's like she vanished into thin air. Maybe I dreamed her up entirely, my mind doing something to entertain itself while Leo is talking business with his friend.

"Yeah, we'll be in touch," Leo says while patting Mr. Bannon on the shoulder and walking past him, putting his hand on my back and ushering me away from there. "Keep walking, don't stop, please." He doesn't let up until we're a safe distance away.

"What was that all about?" I ask him, searching for the mystery girl from this new angle, her robbing four people the highlight of my entire evening. I have no intention of telling anyone about it, because I support both women's rights and wrongs, and if stealing from the rich is what she does for fun, I say more power to her.

Leo downs his drink and takes mine out of my hand, swallowing down what's left of it too.

"Hey, what the hell!"

"Now we're even," he tells me. "By the way, thanks for checking out back there. I could have used your help."

"You were doing just fine without me, plus, that guy wasn't interested in me one bit. He had his sights on you."

"He's been begging me for years to merge with his company."

"And? What's so bad about that?" I chew my lip and wonder how expensive the drinks at the bar are and if I could afford to get us another round. I rummage through my bag, sifting through the dollars to find something more substantial. That's when I spot Archer's black Amex sitting at the bottom, staring up at me like it has a flashing sign. No, things between us have finally settled, I shouldn't stir the pot by using his card. Although...if he didn't want me to use it, he would have asked for it back. Maybe he shut it off, that would explain why he hasn't said a word about it. I guess there's only one way to find out...but on the very likely chance that he did, I'm not sure if I have enough cash on me to foot the bill.

"His business is clean," he tells me. "To merge with mine, that would be suicide. Now, if he died, I could acquire it at a low cost, expand my market, and pinch out the competition. You get the gist?"

"You're going to kill the old man?"

"Moments like this, London, I see what he sees in you." Leo stares right at me and I could punch him in the throat for implying what I think he's implying.

"Can I borrow twenty dollars?"

With a sigh, Leo pulls out his money clip, sliding off a thick stack of hundred-dollar bills, licking his thumb and pulling a few off. "Here." He shoves them into my hand.

"I said twenty, Leo." I pause. "Actually, no, it's fine, I'll take your money." I shove it into my purse and clasp it shut. "I'm getting us another round. I'll be right back. Stay out of trouble and don't kill anyone until I get back." I leave him there, heading straight to the bar without giving him a chance to follow me, because if he did, then he'd see me pull out Archer's American Express and try to use it. I don't particularly care if he knows, but I don't want to lose face in front of him if it gets denied.

I go up to the bar and squeeze through a spot in the chaos, the last bartender who helped Leo coming right up to me.

"Two more tequila old-fashioneds?" He's already reaching for the ingredients without giving me a chance to interject, not like I would have anyway.

I tend to stick to the same thing once I get started out of fear of getting a gnarly hangover. It won't get rid of them completely, but it does lessen the likelihood of it happening.

"Please," I tell him, and reach into my purse, latching onto Archer's black Amex, the weight of it gaudy in my grasp.

"Did I hear that right?" the guy next to me says. He's attractive, with his long-on-the-top, short-on-the-sides dark hair and bright blue eyes. He's pretty in an annoying kind of way, like God decided to favor him a bit more than the rest of us. "You're getting an old-fashioned with tequila? Never heard of such a thing." He points to the guy. "I'll have one of those, too."

I force a smile and keep looking ahead, my brain taking far

too long to realize that this man is attempting to talk to me and I'm blatantly ignoring him. "Sorry, I'm being a total bitch." I turn toward him and extend my hand. "I'm London, and yes, it's a weird combination, but it's really good. Trust the process."

He smiles, exposing his excessively white and perfectly aligned teeth. "Blake Manor." There's a sort of twinkle to him that makes me uneasy, but I'm not sure if I should blame him or the entire environment itself, all this feeling a hint too on the nose for what I'm used to back home. And here I am, an impostor among them with barely two pennies to rub together.

We shake hands and his touch lingers longer than normal.

"Miss," the bartender says. "That'll be thirty-seven even. Sir, yours is eighteen fifty."

"Allow me," Blake chimes in, putting his hand out to stop me from reaching forward with the card in my hand.

My lips part to stop him, but I don't out of fear it wouldn't work anyway. With the money from Leo, I would have had plenty to cover it, I just didn't want to deal with the awkwardness of what-ifs.

"Thanks," I tell him, and take the two drinks that belong to me. "I'm over here, with a friend." I point in the direction Leo is, our eyes meeting from across the way, his expression shifting when he spots me, his feet moving away from the couple he's talking to without hesitation.

"You're here with Leo Sin?" the man asks while sipping the old-fashioned.

"Yeah, you know him?" I walk a few steps away from the bar, Blake coming with me as Leo approaches.

"Blake," Leo greets him with not even a hint of friendliness in his tone.

"Leo." Blake remains cool and collected, neither of them letting on that they probably want to kill each other right here and now. If I had to guess, they're rivals of some sort, but I doubt either of them is going to confess the truth, not to me.

"Are your brothers here?" Leo takes one of the glasses from me.

"Here, there, you know how brothers are." Nothing about what Blake just said made sense, and I don't bother questioning him because it's none of my business and I don't actually care all that much. "And yours?"

"Oh, you know, the same."

"Can you two be any vaguer?" I scan the floor for Mystery Girl again, the music picking up and playing a faster-paced ballad. I chug my drink, shoving my glass toward Leo. "Here." I shift my attention to Blake, grabbing his hand and guiding him away. "Let's dance."

"London, don't you—" Leo gets out, but it's too late, I've already made my mind up, and even though he claims there's nothing serious going on between him and Grace, he isn't willing to ruin her night by making a scene.

"I thought you'd never ask." Blake grins and spins me into him, his chest broad and strong. His hand finds my waist and he guides us farther into the crowd, and I'm grateful that Leo disappears from my line of sight with his judgmental glare. He was helping me hunt for a distraction, what's wrong with Blake? He seems like a perfectly suitable choice.

"Are you married?" I ask him, the question so out of line.

He chuckles and continues dancing, not for a second hesitating. "No. I am not married. Are you?"

"I am not."

Blake tilts his head in the direction we came. "And Leo Sin, are you two dating?"

This time it's my turn to laugh. "No. He's dating my best friend, Grace."

He raises a brow. "Grace McCallister, as in, the senator's daughter?"

"I'd argue that she's much more than the senator's daughter."

"Oh, my apologies. How dare I assume." He extends his hand, twirling me around and back to him. "Interesting friends you keep."

"What about you? You come here alone? Where are your friends?"

"I have friends all over." He leans in close. "Maybe you'll be one of them."

A chill runs up my spine, and I can't decipher whether it was poorly timed with him saying that or if my intuition is trying to tell me something. The alcohol coursing through me can't be bothered, not when my mind is finally distracted.

"Are you always vague?" I hold on to him, his body swaying with mine, everything about us in sync with each other.

Blake stares down at me, something about it reminding me of Archer, my brain not wanting to let it fucking rest. "What do you want to know, love?"

"How do you know Leo?"

"We're business associates."

"Why are you here tonight?"

"To support a great charity."

"What did you eat for dinner?"

"Steak and lobster."

"How many people have you killed?"

"I stopped counting." The words are out of his mouth before he can take them back, his grip on me tightening, his expression darkening. "That was a joke, obviously."

"Obviously," I scoff, and keep dancing, because what other choice do I have? I could push him away, cause a scene, or finish the song and part ways. I have to act unbothered and pretend like he didn't just admit to being a murderer. I'm no stranger to killers, but I prefer to know mine a bit more so I can determine whether I'll be added to that list.

But I don't get a chance to finish the song, and neither does he, because something catches my attention from behind him. I settle my gaze on Archer fucking Sin barreling toward us like he might slaughter everyone in this place.

My mouth drops open and I freeze in place, unsure of what to do. I don't want to ruin Grace's night, but all I see is Archer and his hands balled into fists.

"Get your fucking hands off her," Archer says through gritted teeth, putting his hand between me and Blake, breaking us apart.

Blake matches his energy. "Don't touch me, Archer."

They glare at each other, not quite drawing an excessive amount of attention toward themselves, but the kettle brews and is at risk of boiling over any second now.

Leo rushes over and grabs Archer's shoulder. "Hey, buddy, simmer down."

Archer shoves Leo, hard. "I'll deal with you later."

"Deal me with? What the fuck did I do?" Leo rubs the spot on his chest Archer hit.

"Stop it," I announce. "All of you. You're being dramatic."

"You know this guy?" Blake looks at me but points to Archer. "He your boyfriend?"

"No" I say at the same time Archer says "Yes."

I whip my head at him. "Excuse me? You fucking wish."

"London, now is not the time or place," Archer tells me.

My eyes go wide. "Oh, it's not? You barge in here acting like some tough guy, and *I'm* the problem?"

"I'll deal with you later," Archer says, the same thing he said to Leo, but this time, to me.

"You're not serious," I blurt out, ready to punch Archer for being such an asshole. I thought Leo was the arrogant brother, not Archer. "You're such a fucking child, you know that, Archer?" I glare at him before turning on my heel and storming away. They can figure their shit out themselves, it's not my problem and I won't be a part of it.

"Where are you going?" Leo calls after me.

I don't stop, I keep going, not even when I can hear footsteps trailing behind me, my fist forming and ready to land on whoever is following me out. But once I'm through the doors, I'm met with flashing lights, the camera people hungry to take photos of anyone walking out those doors. I squint and shield my eyes, marching past them and onto the sidewalk in front of the gorgeous building where Grace is hosting her gala. "Shit," I mutter, realizing I never got a chance to say goodbye. I promised her I would, that I wouldn't ghost her, but Archer and his scene sort of forced my hand. Hopefully, she'll understand that.

"London, wait." Archer reaches out and grabs my arm, causing me to halt to a stop, his grip firm. He releases me the second I'm no longer moving away from him, like I might catch him on fire.

I spin toward him, crossing my arms over my chest. "What do you want?" It's then that I see Leo and Blake hot on Archer's heel. The two of them shove each other. "Children, all of you."

"Get your hands off me," Blake tells Leo, and pushes him aside, stopping next to Archer. "Are you okay?"

"Don't pretend like you care," I say to him. "You probably knew about me and Archer the whole time, just trying to get under his skin." I point at Leo. "And you, if you don't get back in there and support Grace, I'll hire someone to kill you."

Blake raises a brow and clears his throat.

Archer shoots him a dangerous glance. "Not a word out of you."

"Don't speak over him," I tell Archer. "You have no right."

"I don't think I should leave yet." Leo scratches his chin and motions to Archer and Blake.

"Your families have some kind of agreement, correct?" I tap the toe of my heel impatiently.

"Yes," Archer is the first to say.

"Then it's fine." I shoo Leo. "Leave. Now. Tell her I'm sorry."

Leo sighs like he's disappointed he's going to miss something and leaves us be. He collects a few photographers who are lingering and gets them to give us some privacy.

"Listen, I don't care if you two rip each other's throats out, but I need a ride home, so who's it going to be?" I steady a glance between them, knowing damn well I'm not going to go home with Blake, but not wanting to go with Archer either. I guess I could use the cash I took from Leo to pay for a cab, but that doesn't sit well with me either. Suddenly, a chill rattles through me, the night breeze nipping my exposed skin.

"Here, you're cold." Blake unbuttons his jacket. "I can take you home."

Archer slams his arm into Blake's chest. "Over my dead body."

"Don't tempt me with a good time," Blake tells him. "You keep putting your hands on me and I'm going to make damn sure of it."

"It's fine," I say. "Archer's going in my direction anyway. Thanks, though." I reach toward Blake, patting his shoulder. "I appreciate it." It's not lost on me that Archer's jaw tenses at witnessing me touch Blake, but he maintains his composure, probably because I admitted I'd leave with him.

"Are you sure?" Blake asks me, his eyes staring into mine, something so dangerous and unsettling about his gaze.

"I'm sure," I lie, not being sure of anything at all, especially right now, with Archer hovering like he's going to kill anyone who even looks in my direction.

With a final sigh, Blake decides he doesn't want to take things further tonight and leaves me and Archer behind, my chest tightening at being this close, this alone with him. I rub my arms and avoid Archer as if he might disappear if I don't settle right on him.

He unzips his hoodie, sliding it off and revealing a black T-shirt and his tattooed arms. Archer doesn't even bother asking for my permission as he drapes it over my shoulders and shoves each of my hands through the sleeves.

I don't fight him because I am cold, and there's something about the way the fabric is still warm from his skin that does something to me.

Archer chuckles, almost to himself, but it's enough I can hear it.

"What's so funny?" I ask him.

"Nothing."

"No, what is it? Share it with the class."

Archer's jaw tenses and he speaks. "You ruined my birthday."

"What?"

"Today, it's my birthday. I told you you could ruin it, you know, since I ruined yours. And you did without even realizing it. It's just kind of funny."

"Oh," I say. "I, uh, I'm sorry. I didn't know."

"It's not a big deal." Archer pauses. "Come on," he tells me, putting his hand on my back, but not too low, and guiding me back in the direction we came.

I stop, his feet coming to a halt, too.

"What is it?" he asks, his tone the softest it's been all night.

"I don't want to go home with you," I admit.

"You're not going home *with* me, London. I'm taking you home. There's a difference."

I continue walking, each of the photographers dropping their cameras upon our approach, Archer shooting each of them a threatening glance. We reach a motorcycle and that's when it hits me that Archer got here so quickly because he was on his stupid bike.

"I'm not getting on that thing, it's a deathtrap," I protest.

"You don't have a choice, London."

"I always have a choice, Archer."

"That's not what I meant, and you know it." Archer runs his hand through his long hair and grabs the helmet off the hook in the back, releasing it and spreading the straps wide. "I'm going to put this on your head, little tornado, and then I'm going to take you home. Okay?"

I motion at my dress. "Not in this. It'll get ruined."

"I'll buy you another one."

"There's only a few of them made."

"Five," Archer corrects me. "I'll buy the other four if it really matters to you."

"Fine. Put the damn helmet on." I stare at him as he does. "You should wear one of these, though. It's not fair that I have to and you don't."

"Would it make you feel better if I wore one?"

"Would you if I said yes?"

"I'd consider it." Archer tightens the strap under my neck and shuts the visor before throwing his leg over the bike and turning on the engine. It roars to life and I contemplate running away, but I know Archer would catch me quicker than I could get away.

I breathe in, hike the dress up, and step onto the back foot peg, using Archer's hand to help me climb onto the back seat. "These aren't exactly the right shoes for this," I tell him.

"Wrap your arms around me." Archer glances back. "Hold on tight."

I do what he says, using his instructions as an excuse to feel his body against mine. I hate that even after two months, I still hate and want him the same. I would have thought all that time would have made it fizzle out, but it's done nothing to ease the ache in my chest at how things ended.

Archer slides a pair of clear glasses onto his face, shifts the bike into gear, and eases onto the throttle. He slips us into the traffic around the gala with great caution and only drives a few miles an hour over the speed limit the entire way back to the apartment complex we both live in. He pulls us into the parking garage, and I have to remind myself that we've stopped and that I can take my arms off him. He helps me off the bike, removes the helmet, and pats down my hair.

His eyes meet mine and I regret ever leaving with him.

"I'm so fucking mad at you," I whisper.

"Good, then maybe that means there's still hope for us."

CHAPTER THIRTY

Archer

I answer my phone, not because I want to, but because Leo has called me seventeen times and if I don't answer soon enough, he's going to show up to my apartment to bother me with whatever it is he wants. He doesn't call just to talk; Leo calls because he needs something, this time being no different than the last.

"What do you want?" I put him on speaker and continue typing away on my keyboard, hoping I can get this over with and be done with him.

"I need a favor."

I laugh. It's short and blunt, and the sound almost surprises me. "No."

"Archer, please, listen."

"No," I cut him off. "You listen to me. You're lucky I don't shoot you in the leg for what you did last night. You pretend like you care, like you're my brother, and you let her get that close to *him*."

The image, replayed in my mind, makes me want to rip my fucking hair out. The Manor brothers are our enemy, and he knows this. Why would he be stupid and let him near her? Unless he's dumber than I give him credit for.

"She was in no danger, Archer, you're being dramatic."

I laugh again. "Dramatic? The guy you're trying to get a favor out of? Why don't you call someone who actually cares, Leo, because I can't be bothered. You don't deserve my help, and honestly, I'm sure whatever it is, you had it coming."

"Listen, Arch, I'm sorry, okay? Is that what you want to hear? I'm fucking sorry. I fucked up. I should have kept a better eye on her, but I'm telling you, the situation was under control. The second I saw him next to her, I went over there."

"I saw you on the fucking camera, Leo. It took me less time

to get across town on my fucking bike than it did for you to walk across the room, and you only did it when I showed up and handled things myself. Don't pretend like you were on top of shit, you fucking prick." I hover my finger above the red button, ready to disconnect the call.

"Archer, I wouldn't ask if I had another choice. I got robbed."

I set my hand on the desk and stare at the phone. "What?"

"Yeah, this girl I went home with last night, she stole my—"

"Hang on," I interrupt him one more time. "You didn't go home with Grace, you know, your fucking date?"

"Grace and I aren't exclusive. She's cool with it. But yeah, I went home with this girl last night, woke up, and she fucking robbed me. Can't you do that thing you do and find her? She was there at the gala, jet-black hair, tiny little thing, black dress."

"I'm hanging up now." I press the button and hang up on Leo, not wanting to hear another word that comes out of his mouth. If he would have gone home with Grace, none of this would have happened, and if he hadn't let Blake Manor get close to London, she probably would have been there to advise him against fucking some stranger. It's his fault he got robbed, and knowing him, it's something that's easily replaceable. Between all of us siblings, we have enough money to buy anything we could imagine, except the pride he lost when his date got the best of him. If anything, more power to the mysterious woman who got the upper hand on my asshole brother.

I drag my hands through my hair, annoyed that I let Leo interrupt what I was doing and taint my already frustrated mood. I can't quit thinking about Blake, his hands on London as she danced with him at the gala in the dress I bought her—the dress that was meant for me. I've never been a possessive man, but with her, I find it hard to be anything else.

Rising from my computer chair, I go to the kitchen, open the fridge, which is pretty fucking bare, and close it again. I distract my mind with a glass of water, chugging it down and washing the cup, returning it to its home in the cabinet before wiping the water droplets out of the sink.

I stare at the wall separating me and London and wish like hell I could see through it. I've wanted so badly to break in again and install cameras, but I knew if she found them, she'd never forgive me. She's caught on to the fact that I've surveilled her, but hasn't figured out the specifics, and if she did, she might go out of her way to avoid the things I can track.

"Focus, Archer," I tell myself, steadying my hands on the counter and bowing my head. "Think of anything *other* than her."

I had been doing so fucking well, avoiding her every chance I got, timing when I left my apartment so I wouldn't run into her. I'm still watching her, but only to make sure she's safe and that nothing has happened to her. With Joe Vito still alive, there will always be a threat to her life, and it's my job to keep her safe. I never intended to interrupt the gala last night, even though I was supposed to be London's date, but when I saw her with him, I couldn't allow her to get tangled up with such a man. It's already bad enough she was involved with me; I couldn't let things get worse.

I didn't mean to say yes when Blake asked if I was her boyfriend, but when the question came out, the answer followed, taking us all by surprise. Maybe in a different world it would have been true, and London wouldn't have reacted the way she did when she heard me admit it.

A scream lets out from London's apartment, my heart almost lurching out of my chest quicker than I can move. I rush out of my front door, not caring that I'm not wearing a shirt, my jeans and boots hopefully being enough for whatever threat is on the other side of the door. I twist the handle to London's door and the second I realize it's locked, I hike my foot up and kick her door with enough force to blast it open, then barge into her apartment.

She yelps again, clinging to the towel around her body, her hair wet and hanging in loose ringlets on her shoulders. "What the fuck, Archer?"

I do a quick sweep, ready to snap the neck of whoever might be in here, only I don't find anyone other than London, who is gawking at me like I'm the intruder.

"Who's in here?" I ask her, my gaze still roaming her apartment.

"You are."

"I'm not messing around, London. Who the fuck is in here?"

She steps toward me, her hands clenching her towel. "Archer, you idiot, you're the only one in here. And you broke my front door."

It takes me far too long to conclude that London is telling me the truth. "Then why did you scream?"

London sighs and pinches the bridge of her nose between her fingers. "Because of a spider." She motions around the space. "One of which you probably scared into hiding with all the commotion. My door, really? You couldn't pick the lock; you had to kick it in? What's wrong with you? Are you out of your mind?"

I close the space between us, not because I want to, but because I can't control myself. I need her more than I've ever needed anything, and I hate myself for it. "Do you ever shut up?" I ask her, my hand hovering next to her face.

"Make me," she says, her eyes looking up at me through her lashes.

I tuck a strand of her wet red hair behind her ear, her skin so soft and smooth. "Are you sure that's what you want?"

"Kiss me before I change my mind," she tells me.

It's just the approval I require to erase any remaining air separating us. My lips come crashing down onto hers, and they're just as greedy as mine. London doesn't hold back, reaching up to put her arms around my neck, her towel slipping off her body, her bare chest pressing against me. I lift her into the air, wrapping her legs around my torso and backing us into the front area to kick the door shut as best I can, not for a second breaking from our kiss. She moans into my mouth and the sound goes straight to my aching cock. My hand roams her body, and hers tangle in my hair—tugging, pulling, driving me fucking wild. She reaches for my waistband to unbutton my jeans and slides her hand into my pants, gripping my dick.

"Fuck," I mutter against her, and swirl my tongue along hers, desperate to feel her, all of her, as much as she'll let me. I move us to the wall, her body pressed on mine, her hand stroking me.

She breaks away first, breathless. "Fuck me, Archer."

"I want you to come first," I tell her, and roam my mouth over her cheek, down her neck, and suck along her collarbone, biting the sensitive skin gently.

"I said *fuck me.*" London grabs a fistful of my hair and drags my lips back up to hers, parting them with her tongue.

I keep hold of her with one arm and take my cock into my palm with the other, sliding it over her wet pussy, teasing her a few times before shoving straight into her, watching as her head tilts back and her eyes close, her mouth making the sexiest sounds.

London relaxes onto my shaft as I pump into her, hard and deep, her tits bouncing between us. "Fuck, Archer," she moans, and tightens around me.

"Touch yourself, little tornado." I hold her hips, letting the wall support her back, giving her a bit of room to put her hand between her legs. "Show me how you like it."

She complies, her fingers gliding over her clit and around my cock that's pounding in and out of her. London bites her lip, and I fuck her slower, not wanting this to end. I shouldn't be enjoying this as much as I am, but I didn't realize how badly I missed her until I was buried in her pussy, a place I'd like to die in, as morbid and terrible as that sounds.

London glances up at me, her eyes staring straight through me. "What are you doing?"

"What do you mean?" I ask her, unsure of what she's referring to. "I'm fucking you."

"No, you're not. You're making love to me. Stop."

I slow my pace even further.

"That, right there, you're looking at me like you love me. Stop." London continues to circle her finger over her clit, her pussy tensing around me, enjoying this even if she isn't willing to admit it herself.

"I don't know what you're talking about," I lie.

"Bagels," she blurts out.

I stop moving immediately. "Did I hurt you? What's wrong?"

With one arm still draped over my shoulder, she tugs at my hair. "I told you to fuck me, big boy. Now, either fuck me, or put me down."

I take a steadying breath and consider her words carefully, and the boundaries she's put in place, choosing the only option that ends in her satisfaction. "Fine." I thrust into her, hard and deep, repeating the motion until we're both panting and covered in sweat, my cock spilling into her as she climaxes on it, her pussy throbbing. I fuck her all the way through her orgasm, milking every last quiver that rattles through her body.

She exhales and lays her head on my shoulder, kissing my chest gently. "That was unexpected."

I hold her against me, one arm around her waist, the other gripping her thigh, my forehead resting on the wall. My cock twitches in her tight, soaked pussy, and I wish I could remain here, not just inside her, but with her, where I can make sure she remains safe and out of harm's way.

"Sorry about the spider," I tell her. "I can look for him and kill him."

She breaks away immediately, her hands cupping my cheeks. "You will do no such thing."

"What?" My brows pinch together.

"Never ever kill a spider."

"I'm confused. I thought you were afraid of them."

"I mean, yeah, who wouldn't be, with all their creepy legs and creepy eyes. That doesn't mean they deserve to die, though. If this is ever going to work, we must be a catch-and-release household."

My heart skips a beat, and my eyes dart up to meet hers.

"I didn't mean it like that," she blurts out.

"What did you mean?"

"I, uh." She wiggles her body. "Put me down."

Carefully, I slide my still partially hard cock out of her and lower her onto her feet. "What did you mean, London?" I button up my pants as she rushes over to get the towel that fell off her body, covering herself up like I didn't just fuck her a minute ago.

"I hope you're going to fix that." She points to the door.

"I will, I promise." I shove my left hand into the pocket of my jeans. "Are you going to ignore my question?"

"I need you to do me a favor," she says, catching me off guard.

"Anything," I tell her, hoping she understands the lengths I would go to for her.

There isn't anything I wouldn't do for her—I'd kill for her, hell, I'd die for her.

"I need you to stop stalking me." Her request renders me speechless, my mouth parting but words not coming out. "You have to stop following me, watching me, tracking me. Whatever it is you do, Archer, it has to stop."

I shake my head slowly at first. "No."

"You said you'd do anything for me." She hugs the towel tighter around her body.

"Anything but that." Is she out of her mind? I can't quit, because the second I do, something could happen, and how could I live with myself if I was the reason Vito finally got to her? Things have been tame since she's been here, but that doesn't mean it won't change. But I guess I could spend more time tracking him and less time on London. I could still check in on her and somehow respect her wishes to be left alone. What she doesn't know won't hurt her...

How can she ever trust me if I go behind her back?

But how much does her trust matter when things are already broken beyond repair?

CHAPTER THIRTY-ONE

London

I cover the last of the dough and set it in the giant commercial refrigerator at work, dusting my hands off and silently congratulating myself for not fucking anything up today. The mistakes have become fewer and farther between in the time I've been employed, but every time they happen, I worry it'll be the one to end my career here.

After I wash my hands, I check my phone, skimming my missed text messages, none of which are from Archer.

The guy I went on a date with yesterday called and left me a voicemail to let me know he had a good time and wants to do it again, but I delete it, not being able to ignore the fact that despite him being a perfect gentleman, something was off. I thought the date would have spewed some kind of reaction from Archer, all the other times doing exactly that, but this time he didn't show up, didn't reach out, didn't do anything. Maybe he's finally started to respect my wishes, something that I should be okay with, and yet I'm not.

I slide my phone into my back pocket and approach the office in the back of the bakery, peeking my head around the corner. "Hey, you need help with anything else?"

Andrea looks up from her stack of papers, her hair a mess, her mouth hanging open. She blinks at me a few times. "Actually, yeah."

I come a little closer. "What's up?"

"I forgot to tell you, but we got a call this morning for a baking gig. Is there any way you can do the consultation? I'm up to my neck in paperwork from the health department that just came in, and I can't peel away." Andrea turns her wrist to check her watch. "If you leave now, you should be able to make it there in time. I'll order you an Uber. Please, I'm begging you."

"You want *me* to do the consult?"

"Don't act so surprised, London. You know all the cake variations we make, the quantities of cookies and brownies and muffins. You've taken orders over the phone without having to check the notes. You're ready for this, really." Andrea adds, "Plus, I'm desperate, so what better time than now to throw you to the wolves?" She winks at me, and I fight the urge to panic.

When I got this job, I had quite literally zero formal experience, both with baking and working in general. I've tried hard to prove to myself, and everyone here, that I belong, but I guess it only hit me just now that maybe all the faking has gotten me somewhere. If Andrea trusts me to pull this off, I must trust myself, too.

"Okay," I tell her. "I'll do it."

Andrea lets out a sigh of relief. "Thank God, I thought I was going to have to beg." She pulls out her phone. "Let me order you an Uber now." She pushes a few buttons and drops her phone onto her desk. "It should be here in three minutes. Look for a black Kia, license plate starting with SKP. Seriously. Thank you."

"Don't thank me yet." I grip the doorframe and say, "Let me know if you need anything else," before leaving her office and making my way to the front of the store, navigating past coworkers and customers. Once I'm outside, I stand on the sidewalk, watching the cars pass and keeping my eyes peeled for mine.

It arrives just as she said, pulling up in front of the bakery behind a white Range Rover. The driver rolls down their window. "Andrea?"

"Yeah, that's me," I say, sliding into the back seat. "Or, well, I'm not Andrea, my boss is. She ordered it."

"Totally understandable," the woman tells me, and pushes a button on her dash to turn some music on.

I thank the universe that I don't have to make awkward small talk with her and settle into the seat, bracing myself for the consultation I'm about to go through. Andrea is right, I do know all the cake variations, along with icings that travel well and don't, and every single small item we offer. I've been on the opposite end of a sales transaction plenty of times, what's so different about being the person doing the pitch for a change? Plus, if they were calling to request Andrea's baked goods, they've no doubt tasted something of hers before, and that alone should be enough to convince them to order anything from our bakery.

Glancing out the window, I attempt to locate where we are, this side of town farther than anywhere else I've been since I've arrived in New York. My heart picks up its pace as my safety net disappears, Archer somewhere in the distance, no longer watching me intensely like he had been doing. I suddenly regret asking him for space, but the second I pull out my phone to text him, we stop in front of a beautiful historical house on a large plot of land, with trees and overgrown shrubs all around it.

"Here we are," my driver says, putting the car into park. "Have a good day."

"You, too," I tell her, and step out, closing the door behind me.

She leaves, turning down an alley and disappearing out of sight. The street is empty of passing cars, not a single soul in sight. I take a steadying breath and turn toward the house, marching right up the sidewalk and knocking on the door.

"Come on in," a woman's voice calls out. "It's unlocked."

I grip the handle, glad it was a woman who answered instead of a man, my nerves already settling.

But once I'm inside, that peculiar feeling hits me again. I reach for my phone, thinking that if I just let Archer know where I am and what I'm doing, he'll do whatever it is he does and keep an eye on me. Only, I don't get that chance, because instead of making contact with my phone, a hand grabs onto my wrist and snatches it from me, their other hand pressing a rag over my mouth and nose.

Fucking chloroform.

I try to withstand the way it makes my vision blur, but the man holding it against my face is too strong, too much in control. I reel up my leg and kick him in the shin, causing him to falter and loosen his grip. With his hand exposed, I bite down hard, the skin of his finger breaking under my wrath.

"You bitch," he blurts out. "You fucking bit me." The man hits me with the back of his hand, knocking me onto the floor.

I scoot away from him, desperate to regain my footing, but I can barely make anything out, my vision still fucked up from the shit he was making me inhale. See, that's the thing that movies always get wrong. Sure, it can make you pass out, but depending on how much is inhaled, that's not always the immediate effect.

Trust me on this, I grew up with a fucking lunatic of a father.

He kicks me in the stomach, sending me onto my back, my lungs gasping for air. Tears well in my eyes and I can't help but wonder how much damage he re-inflicted that I had healed from following my time with said father. Just when I thought I was fully on the mend, another dickhead man hurts me. I cough and hold my side as he grabs a fistful of my hair and yanks me a few feet into the house.

Is this the way I die—at the hands of some guy I have never met in my life?

"Tie her to the chair, you imbecile," a familiar voice orders him.

The man complies, dragging me onto the wooden surface and securing my arms to the rungs. He backs away and sets my phone on the table by the door, his form disappearing and the woman stepping into my line of sight a blur. I blink, trying to clear my vision, unsure of what I'm seeing, almost like she's a ghost materializing in front of me.

She traces my face with the gun in her hand, tilting my head up toward her. "London," she says with a grin.

I stare at her, those big brown eyes, that mud-colored hair. The last time I saw her, she was bleeding out on the floor in my father's study. She was pleading for her life. She was dead.

"Madison," I respond, uncertain whether I've finally had a psychotic break or not. There's no way she's standing in front of me alive and well. "I watched you die."

"You saw what I wanted you to see," she tells me, smacking my cheek with the barrel of the gun. "Funny, you did the same thing, didn't you, London girl?"

My nostrils flare, and before I know it, I'm leaning back and spitting in her face. "How fucking dare you."

Madison pinches her eyes shut and wipes at her face. "That was uncalled for."

"You're supposed to be dead."

"So are you." She taps the toe of her stiletto against the wood floor. At least it isn't covered in plastic, then I'd be really concerned. But what Madison has in store for me today isn't to kill me, it's to send a message, I'm just not sure what it is yet. If she intended on killing me, the room would be covered in plastic, making for an easy cleanup. No one wants to scrub blood out of a wood floor, never quite getting it all out of the nooks and crannies. I hate that I know this but find comfort in it all the same.

"I think you owe me an explanation." I fight the haze in my eyes and focus on her, confirming that she really is real.

"I don't owe you shit." Madison pauses and adds, "But I'd say a thank-you is in order. I guess we were both liberated when you killed your dad."

"I didn't kill him," I tell her.

"You were complicit, and to me, that's all the same."

"This is a fucked-up way of saying thank you." I tug at the ties around my forearms and they dig into my flesh.

"How did you do it?" Madison asks me. "I heard there was a fire."

"What do you want, Madison? What's the real reason you brought me here?" I don't mention that I'm sure it has something to do with Archer, because why else would she have some weird fucking vendetta against me?

"It's funny, you know. The same man that helped me get away is the man who thinks you're dead." She hits my face with the gun again and I wish like hell I could get free of these confines so I could shove the barrel in her mouth and pull the trigger, ending her life once and for all. Twenty minutes ago, I would have been glad to see her alive, but now, now I'm fucking pissed.

"You're boring me, Madison." I sigh. "Get to the point or shoot me and get it over with."

"You think I won't? Is that it?" She drags the cold metal across my face, pressing it on my forehead.

I lean into it. "Get it over with, bitch."

Madison pulls her arm back, hitting me across the face with the gun, my lip splitting open, blood filling my mouth.

I smile, red coating my teeth. "Is that all you got?" I spit again. "You forget who my father was, Madison. You can't fucking hurt me."

"You talk a lot of shit for someone tied to a chair." Madison taps her toe, clearly getting annoyed that I can't be bothered.

I stare up at her, raising my brows, daring her to fucking try me. "Either tell me what this is about or put me out of my misery. Why are you here? Why now? What's the connection to Vito? Stop beating around the bush, it's not cute. You don't do the whole hostage thing well, babe, sorry."

Madison huffs. "I'm here because you pissed off the man I owe a favor to. It's funny, really, because you might have gotten away with it. You were this close." She holds her fingers up, showing what little space she can make between them. "I hear Ricardo is dead, so I come out of hiding. I pay Vito a visit, thank him for helping me escape, and he tells me Ricardo made a deal with him before his downfall, that you were to be his bride, but you had succumbed to your injuries. And I mean…" Madison brings the gun to her chest, pressing her fingers to her heart. "I was saddened to hear the news. I always felt a sort of kinship with you. I hated to hear that Ricardo took you with him."

I watch her feign sadness and hope she spits out the point to this story before she bores me to death.

"I'm not sure if you know this, but Archer and I have a *history*. So it was truly shocking when I did a little research to find out how he was doing, that I saw *you* in the photos the private investigator sent me. It was like seeing a ghost. A beautiful gold mine of a ghost." Madison tilts her head, smiling at me. "I thought it was going to take me years and years to pay off the favor I owed Vito, and here you are, landing right in my lap. Perhaps it was fate that brought us together after all. Of course, I had to come take a look myself, I had to be sure. I couldn't get his hopes up."

Madison kneels in front of me, resting the gun on my thigh, pointing it at me, her finger on the trigger.

"What do you want, Madison?" I ask her, understanding the connection now but not the point.

"I want what you want, London girl. I want my freedom, and I want Archer."

I clench my jaw and try to figure out which part makes me more furious, the fact that she keeps using the nickname my father gave me, or the fact that she thinks she's going to walk away from this with Archer at her side. As tortured as he was, he'd never forgive her for what she did, and considering the way he looks at me now, there's no way he'd come to terms with her killing me. Hell, I'm not positive he'll ever be able to look past me being Ricardo's daughter, the man who supposedly killed the love of his life.

"He'll never love you," I tell her.

"What makes you so sure?" Madison drags her bottom lip into her mouth. "I can be quite convincing." She smiles, a sadistic grin. "I'll tell him I was forced into hiding, that it was all against my will, that the only thing that got me through each day was the thought of him." She bats her lashes. "What do you think?"

"Ask him yourself," I say.

Madison furrows her brow. "Oh, you doubt me?"

"Not at all." I shake my head. "I'm just sure he'll be here any second."

"What?" Her dark eyes meet mine, a hint of genuine concern lining them.

"Archer, when you two were together, did he not have OCD? Did he not put trackers on you? Did he not follow your every move? Oh, just me? Must mean he cares more about me than he did you." This time, the smile is on my face, not hers, satisfaction rolling through me at unsettling her despite having no idea whether Archer is on his way or not.

I hear the gun before I feel it, the sound rattling in my ears, my torso, my entire body. I'm warm and cold all at once, and when I lower my head, I realize Madison pulled the trigger, and when I meet her gaze, I see she's just as shocked as I am. "You shot me," I mutter.

Madison rises to her feet, gawking at the gun in her hand like it went off itself and she had nothing to do with it. "This isn't over," she tells me as she backs away. "This isn't fucking over."

Blood pools around my shirt as Madison continues to back her way toward the door and slips through it.

"You're just going to fucking leave me here?" I shout after her, but it's no use, she continues until I hear the door slam shut. "Fuck," I blurt out, and scan the room to find anything to get me out of this. Telling her Archer was on his way was severely useful in getting under her skin, but I didn't think she was going to fucking shoot me. And since Archer didn't show up during my date, I highly doubt he'd be watching me now. I'm in this alone, and if I don't do something quick, I might die here.

That's when I spot my phone sitting on a table across the room.

"Hey, Siri," I speak into the space, waiting for her to respond.

A long pause leads to more silence. I must not be close enough, loud enough, clear enough, for the phone to pick up what I'm saying.

"Hey, Siri," I say, louder this time, holding my breath in anticipation.

Nothing.

I take in the way my arms are secured to the chair, tugging harder than I had before, not making progress on freeing myself. I could attempt to slam backward and break the wooden chair, but if I don't get it exactly right, I'd end up more stuck than I already am, ensuring that I die here. I do the only thing I can think of, lift my body into the air and try to scoot even a fraction of an inch toward the door.

I grunt, the pain in my side growing by the minute, but I muster every bit of it into a rage that carries me, slowly, in the direction I need to be. Pausing only a few inches away from where I started, I even my breathing to call out once more, "Hey, Siri."

Nothing.

With everything in me, I force the chair to move and my body to cooperate. I once hated myself for what I allowed to happen to Madison, and now I hate her for what she's done to me. Funny how the tables have turned in a split second.

"Hey, Siri," I say, my vision blurring, my eyes welling.

"Mm-hmm?" she responds like an angel answering my prayers.

I do the one thing I shouldn't but the only thing that might get me out of here. "Call Archer."

It only rings one time before his voice comes through the other end. "London?"

"I've been shot," I say, not sure how much time I have left.

"I'm on my way, hang on, I'm on my way." His voice cracks. "Stay with me, little tornado. I'm coming."

CHAPTER THIRTY-TWO

Archer

I ride my motorcycle harder than I ever have, speeding across town and risking my life to get there to save hers. The engine roars and I push its limits, begging it to go faster, to not waste another moment.

Skidding to a stop in front of the house where her phone pings she's located inside, I hop off the bike, not bothering to even put the kickstand down before I rush inside, flinging the door open so aggressively, it buckles on the hinges.

"London," I call out, my chest tight, my fist clenched. I don't have a single weapon but I will kill anyone that stands in the way of getting to her.

She doesn't answer, and that only terrifies me more. What if I didn't make it in time? What if this was a trap and I walked straight into it?

I poke my head around the corner of one room, not finding her, and moving on to the next, searching frantically for her.

My sight lands on London, tied to a chair, her head hung loosely, blood covering her shirt. I run over and kneel in front of her, my stomach coiling into knots. "London," I whisper, tilting her head up.

Slowly, her eyes flutter open. "Archer?" She blinks a few times. "You're really here?"

"Of course I'm here. You think I wouldn't come for you?" I make quick work of freeing her arms, my anger rising at the marks that remain once she's untied. I hate that this happened. I hate that I wasn't here to stop it.

London's head sways and she rubs at her forearm. "Let's get out of here." She tries to stand but falls right back down, her hand going to her side. "Oh, right, I got shot."

"Let me see." I reach for her shirt, lifting it up, having to peel the fabric from her blood-soaked skin. The bullet went through low and to the side, a clean shot through and through. There was a lot of initial bleeding, but it appears to have coagulated. I force myself not to focus on the bruise forming on her face and logically assess the situation. "I need to get you to a hospital. London, can you look at me?"

She stares right into my eyes, hers red and watery. "Hi."

"Hey, baby." I grab her hands. "I'm going to help you up, okay? I'd carry you, but I don't want to put too much pressure on that wound until we know for sure what we're dealing with." If it were up to me, I'd scoop her into my arms and run the entire way to the hospital, but that isn't an option, and I can't afford to be careless, not with her.

"Okay." She squeezes my hands, a good sign that she still has strength left in her. London might be small and fragile, but she's resilient as hell, and she has a will to live more powerful than anyone I've ever met. She'd have to, considering Ricardo Gardella is her father.

Was, I remind myself. Ricardo is dead and I refuse to let him haunt me any longer.

With London's assistance, I guide her out of the room and through the house. I leave her leaning against the porch as I rush to pick up my bike and turn it on, riding it up as far as I can and helping her the rest of the way.

"I'm going to lift you onto the back, okay?"

She nods, releasing her hand on her side and wincing when I pick her up and set her on the back.

I unhook the helmet attached to my bike and slide it over her head, securing the strap faster than I ever have. I climb on the front, careful not to hit her, and turn toward her. "All I need you to do is hold on to me. Can you do that for me, London?"

She leans her head against my back and wraps her arms around me, holding on tightly.

I tap her hands, letting her know I'm going to take off, and once I do, I keep a firm grip on her while driving with one arm. I navigate through the desolate streets until I get to the closest hospital, riding all the way to the entrance and through the giant double doors. I don't stop until I'm idling in front of the registration desk, people from each direction rushing toward us.

A man with a security badge is the first to speak. "Sir, you can't be in here on that. You need to leave immediately."

I glare at him and slip my leg off the bike, not giving a single fuck what he has to say. I ignore him while helping London off the back, sliding her arm over my shoulder and doing everything I can not to make things worse for her.

"Gunshot wound to the abdomen," I tell the woman at the desk. "She needs to be seen immediately."

She hops out of her chair. "I can take her back, but you have to move your bike, sir. This is a hospital, not a parking lot."

"Do you want to keep your job? My last name is Sin."

The security guard who spoke to me puts his arm out to stop another one that rushes over, clearly unsatisfied that the first one didn't do his job. "Brandon, let him through," he tells the man.

"Right this way," the lady at the desk says. She presses a button on a walkie-talkie-looking device. "We've got a level one coming in." She releases the button and looks at me. "Which brother are you?"

"Archer," I tell her.

She brings the device back to her mouth. "Patient is related to Archer Sin. Send in any and all available staff."

Part of me strongly dislikes the weight my name carries, because we gained it from doing terrible things, but in times like this I'm grateful for the destruction that led me to have this power.

London's body goes rigid, and she looks up at me.

"What is it?" I ask, terrified that something even worse has happened I haven't yet discovered.

"I don't have health insurance."

"Shh. You don't need to worry about that. Not anymore." When she doesn't seem to soften her resolve, I scan her face. "What's wrong?"

"I don't want a male doctor."

I nod and reach out to the lady from the desk leading us back. "No male staff. That's an order."

She doesn't question me, she simply gets on her radio and makes sure London's wishes are met.

From there, the next hour is a blur of doctors and nurses coming to and from the room as they check London over and patch her up. The final workup is that she'll be fine in a few weeks when she heals. Most of the damage is superficial with minor internal injury. It appeared a lot worse than it really was, and for that, I am grateful.

I sit next to her in a hospital chair, holding her hand between mine, never having left her through all of this.

"You don't have to stay," London tells me, the color returning to her cheeks after going through what must have been such a traumatic event.

"Do you want me to leave?" I ask her.

London shakes her head. "No."

"Then I'm not going to." I lean down and press my lips to her fingers. "Can we talk about what happened?"

She licks her dry lips and uses the controller next to her to raise the hospital bed. "Yeah."

"Who did this to you?"

London clears her throat. "You're never going to believe me."

I steady my breathing, trying my best to maintain my composure. If it were up to me, the person responsible for hurting her would already be dead, having suffered at my hands and shown no mercy. I want to rip the flesh from their bones, cut them a thousand times over until they beg for my mercy, and just when they think I'm finally going to grant them reprieve, make them suffer even more. At the very least, they deserve that.

"You can trust me, London. I'm sorry I made you feel like you couldn't. I know things are messed up between us, but I still care about you, I always will." I keep hold of her hand, silently begging her to understand how much she means to me even if I don't know how to articulate it myself.

"I don't even believe it," she says, something strange in the cadence of her voice.

"Walk me through what happened, then. We'll make sense of it together."

"I was at work. Andrea was in her office. I asked her if she needed anything else. She told me there was a customer that needed a consultation, and she wasn't going to make it in time, something about paperwork that came through from the health department earlier today. Anyway, she ordered me an Uber to the house. I was supposed to do the sales pitch and hopefully take their order." London breaks, her eyes darting off in the distance like she's recalling what went down.

I wait patiently for her to continue.

"I knocked on the door, a woman called out that it was unlocked. I went in. I had a bad feeling. I was reaching for my phone to text you to let you know where I was, and that's when the guy came out of nowhere and pressed a chloroform rag to my face. I fought him off and kicked him in the shin. He hit me, knocked me down."

Anger consumes me but I keep it at bay and listen to the rest of the story.

"That's when she told him to tie me up, and he did."

"Who told him? Who was it?"

London looks at me, tears welling in her eyes. "Madison."

"Madison?" I pinch my brows, unsure of what she's implying.

"Madison."

"Madison, who?" I ask her.

"*Madison* Madison."

"That's impossible, Madison is dead."

London shakes her head slowly. "Madison isn't dead, Archer. I thought she was, too, but she's not. She's alive and well."

"I don't understand."

"I don't either, but I promise you, I'm not lying."

I rub circles on her hand, desperately trying to put the pieces of the puzzle together. I want to believe her, I do, but how can I when Madison died three years ago? I'm sure of it. What reason would she have to lie to me now? But why would Madison fake her death when she was in love with me? We had a future together, why would she throw that away? And why would she out herself, after all this time?

"Archer." London draws my attention. "I'm sorry." She squeezes my hand. "Not just for this, for everything. I should have told you sooner. I can't change what happened between us, but I need you to know how sorry I am. I never meant to fall for you. I had no idea who you were when Silver sent me to you. We were both caught by surprise."

"You should rest," I tell her, and pat her hand. "We'll talk about this later. Get some rest."

I remain there with her while my mind wanders a million different places, attempting to rationalize the situation, to come up with some kind of logical explanation for what happened to London, to Madison. But nothing makes sense, and the more I ruminate, the more frustrated I become by everything. I hate that I can't figure it out and I hate that I never saw it coming—any of this. I was under the impression Joe Vito was the one I had to be watching out for, not Madison—someone I never expected to come back from the dead. And since it wasn't Vito, why would Madison kidnap and shoot London, unless she's working with Joe? Maybe that's why I didn't see him coming, because he was working in my blind spot. But why would Madison be working with someone as sinister as Joe Vito? What could he have against her that would make her turn her back on me? I would have done anything for her, and I thought I made that damn clear. Maybe she didn't love me the same way I loved her. Maybe I didn't know her at all. Because if I did, I would have suspected this, even in the slightest.

Once London dozes to sleep, I pull out my phone, swipe through a few apps, and touch base on a few work-related things. I do what I can to make sure Joe Vito is still in California, but the brunt of my feeds is on my computer at my place, and I'm stuck to limited resources on my phone. The thing buzzes in my hand, Leo's stupid face popping on the screen. I grow furious with him but answer it anyway.

"What do you want?" I ask him quietly.

"Archer, please. I'm begging you. I need your help."

"I'm not going to help you."

"Arch, bud. It's my birthday, help a guy out."

"It was my birthday the night of the gala, Leo. Did you forget that? You let Blake fucking Manor dance with my girl on *my* fucking birthday."

"I—I, uh, I didn't know."

"You don't give a shit about my birthday, why should I care about yours?"

Leo sighs, knowing damn well I have him backed into a figurative corner. "I didn't know she was your girl, Arch. I thought you didn't want anything to do with her."

"I'm not talking to you about this."

"Why are you whispering?" Leo asks me.

I almost don't dignify him with a response but decide to anyway. "I'm at the hospital."

"Hospital? Are you okay?"

"I'm fine," I tell him. "London was shot."

"Holy shit, are you serious? By whom?"

"I'll talk to you later." I hang up the phone, not caring at all that I left him on one hell of a cliffhanger. He can't help me figure out the truth, he's only pretending to care because he wants me to solve his problem, and I can't be bothered with pointless shit like some random hookup stealing something from him. He had it coming and that has nothing to do with me. If he doesn't want to deal with the backlash of a scorned one-night stand, then he shouldn't have had one.

***

London is discharged the next day, told to rest, stay on top of her pain with medication, and take it easy. Typical for a gunshot wound that didn't hit anything vital. I haven't slept a wink, and despite being fatigued, there's no way my mind will be quiet enough for me to find any peace.

Nothing makes sense. Not things with London, my family, and now Madison.

She's supposed to be dead.

A week ago, if someone had told me she was alive, I would have been thrilled. Still in disbelief, but grateful she wasn't dead. But now, knowing she's the reason London is in the condition she is, and that she's working for Joe Vito, I can't wrap my head around it. I want to be happy, but I can't find it in me. I have to see her with my own eyes and talk to her, otherwise this is going to consume me.

Seven is leaning against his Rolls-Royce when we step through the hospital doors. He pushes his black shades up his nose and kicks off the ground to come toward us. "Hello, beautiful people!"

I eye him. "What are you on?"

"I'm high on life, baby," Seven says as he comes closer. "How's our girl doing?" He walks beside me and London.

"*Our* girl?" London glances at him. "When did I become yours, too, Seven?"

"Oh, you know, you're like family now, firecracker." Seven rushes forward to open the door to his car.

"I'm not even going to ask what that nickname is all about." London winces and climbs into the back of his Rolls-Royce, scooting into the seat.

"Give me the keys," I tell Seven. "I'm driving." I reach into my pocket and pull out a key. "Here, this is to my bike, it's parked in the emergency room."

"Whoa, you rode your bike into the hospital? That's sick." He swaps the keys without questioning me, which only adds to the weirdness of the situation. Seven is usually much more unhinged and uncontrollable. Today he's almost...agreeable. "See ya at your place." He slaps my shoulder and takes off in the direction we came from, and because I don't want to deal with figuring out what he's on, I go around to the driver's side and get in.

I go slow, driving the speed limit and braking easily, to not disturb London too much. Peeking back at her every so often, I grow more furious about things, and even more angry that I can't figure it out. I'm well aware I'm like a broken record at this point, but I'm not often caught by surprise, and it unsettles me to my core. Maybe if I can make sense of *something*, I won't be struggling this badly.

Slowing the Rolls-Royce to a stop, I park in front of our apartment complex and hop out.

Seven sits on the ledge of the steps, dangling his feet with his arms behind him as he leans toward the sky. It's like he's enjoying the sun for the first time in his life. He hops off the spot and rushes over. "Dude, what took you so long? I already parked your bike in the garage like ten minutes ago."

"Precious cargo," I tell him, and go around to let London out. I pass him his keys, expecting him to leave, but he follows us into the building and up the stairs. I take a quick look at him as I help London into our apartment and onto the couch in the living room. I kneel beside her. "What do you need?"

London draws in a deep breath, wincing halfway through, and swallows harshly. "I'm fine," she lies.

Seven plops onto the far end of the couch and I glare at him.

"Seriously?" I say.

"What?" Seven shrugs and pulls out his phone, scrolling on it like he's not planning on leaving anytime soon. "Oh, hey, has Leo called you?"

"Only about a hundred times," I tell him, and go to the kitchen to get London some water. I fill a glass, bringing it to her a moment later.

"Yeah." Seven brings his foot to rest on his other knee and throws his arm over the back of the couch, his hand dangerously close to London. "He got robbed."

"What? No way," London says, her interest piqued. "By whom?" She repositions herself in Seven's direction and I settle into the chair beside her, my entire body aching to be the one sitting on the couch with her.

"Some chick from the gala." Seven sets his phone down and crosses his arms. "Serves him right."

London takes a drink of the water I brought her. "Wait, what? He didn't go home with Grace? Man, I'm so out of the loop."

"You haven't heard?" Seven says, like he's the queen of gossip.

"Um, no, tell me. I need all the tea." London settles into the couch, fully preparing herself for whatever he has to say.

It's strange to witness them getting along, and I hate that I kind of like it. Seven is a fucking lunatic, but he's still my brother, my family, and that means something to me, even if I want to kill him at times.

"Leo went home with this girl from the gala. Didn't get her name. *Typical.*"

"What did she look like? Any identifying features?" London asks Seven.

He shrugs. "He told me she was hot."

I clear my throat, somehow ready to be nothing like who I am as a person and add to the gossip. "He told me she had jet-black hair."

London cackles, like straight out-of-pocket laughs, and I have no idea what I could have said that was so funny.

"I know exactly who it is. Or, well, sort of." London grins. "There was this woman there, I only saw her briefly, but she was *stunning*, like gay-panic kind of gorgeous."

Seven cuts her off. "You're gay?"

"Aren't we all?" London gives him a vague answer and continues, "But anyway, I saw her pickpocketing people, snatching wallets and watches. It was glorious, really. They had no idea." She covers her mouth. "Sorry, this isn't very girl's girl of me."

"Why didn't you tell someone?" I ask her out of curiosity, not that I really care someone was there stealing from the rich.

"Well, the first guy was a total creep, so I wasn't bothered. And then once she hit a few more targets, I was impressed. Then she disappeared into thin air, and I never saw her again." London pauses to catch her breath. "Everyone in that place had far more than they needed, I didn't think she was doing anything wrong."

"That's my little firecracker." Seven raises his fist and London bumps it with hers, the two of them bonding over crime.

"That's fair," I tell her. "Honestly, that's what I told Leo, that he had it coming, that he probably deserved it. Plus, I thought he was with Grace, which only made it more fucked up that he was asking me to help him find this mystery woman."

"He and Grace aren't exclusive," London says.

"They aren't together at all," Seven announces, and that's when it hits me, the reason why Seven is floating on cloud nine. He has no chance with Grace, but if Grace is with Leo, it means she's off-limits. Now, she's back within reach, and he thinks he might have a shot of getting with her. He's a strange sort of predator—his sight locking on to someone and not letting up until he's gotten what he wanted. Grace is one of the only women who has ever turned Seven down, making her possibly his biggest challenge, and that means he'll never stop pursuing her.

"Man, what the hell, I feel like such a bad friend, I had no idea." London turns toward me. "Where's my phone?"

I reach into my back pocket, pull it out, and hand it to her. "Here."

"Shit." London scrolls her finger along the screen, no doubt catching a glimpse of what she missed while she was in the hospital. "Yeah, I have three missed calls and a few texts from her. They definitely broke up."

Seven's smile grows, reaching all the way to his eyes. I don't think I've ever seen my brother this happy, not even when he murdered six men and was covered in their blood. That image is forever ingrained in my memory, speckles of red on his face, his filed-down teeth showing in his toothy grin.

"Is she okay?" I ask London.

"Yeah, I'm sure she's fine. Grace is resilient. Plus, I don't think things were ever serious between them."

"Probably because she wants me." Seven is so full of himself that it hurts to witness.

"I doubt it's that," I say, not trying to hurt his feelings, not that he has any of those to begin with.

"I should probably get going." London braces herself in her attempt to stand up.

"What do you mean?" I rise to my feet. "You aren't staying here?"

She shakes her head. "I need to go home, Archer."

"You are home."

Seven makes a hissing sound. "Oh, sounds like trouble in paradise."

"You know what I mean, Archer." London ignores him.

"Stop saying my name like that," I spit out, unsure why it is annoying me so much.

"Like what?"

"I don't know, like you're talking to me like I'm a child." I hate how each word slips out of my mouth without first going through my brain to process how insane they are.

"Archer..."

"London, so help me God." I motion to the kitchen. "Stay for a few days, at least. I can cook for you. You shouldn't be alone right now. You need someone to take care of you."

"I don't need anyone to take care of me." She glares at me like she wants to set me on fire, and I can't say I blame her. London never seemed to be the type of person to ask for help, not really. Sure, she showed up on my doorstep needing a place to stay, but that was different, that was life or death.

Life or death...Madison pops back into my head along with all the unanswered questions surrounding everything London told me.

"Do you think you could give us some privacy?" I stare right at Seven, hoping he'll get the hint to get the fuck out of here.

"Whatever, man." He hops up from his seat. "I'm not going to let you ruin my mood." Seven lowers his fist to London. "Firecracker, it was a pleasure seeing you. Get well soon."

"Don't tell me what to do," London teases him, and bumps her fist against his.

Seven chuckles and nods at me before heading toward the door and slipping out of here, not staying to protest or throw a fit about being asked to leave.

I lower myself onto the couch a few inches away from London. "Will you please stay?"

She looks up at me, her eyes darting back and forth. "Where were you?"

"What?"

"Where were you, Archer?" She pauses for a split second. "You're telling me you saw every date I went on, you knew what dress I wanted, heard conversations that were private, but when I *actually* needed you, you weren't there?"

"I'm sorry" is all I can get out, because she's right. I did see every date she went on, even the one the night before. It fucking killed me to watch her with another man, to see him make her smile, hold her chair out for her, and walk her to the car. Fuck, just the fact that he got to have a conversation with her was enough to make me go insane. That's why I hesitated the next day, that's why I wasn't watching her every move, because if I had to witness her meet him again, or kiss him, I'd lose my fucking mind. But the self-control

I thought I had was quickly squashed, and when I checked her location and saw her on the other side of town, I irrationally hopped on my bike and headed in that direction, only by the time I reached her, it was almost too late.

London sniffles and looks away, and I want to kill myself for making her feel this way.

I should have been there. I failed her. I lost her trust.

CHAPTER THIRTY-THREE

London

Five days have passed since I've been at Archer's, and I'm recovered enough to almost be able to get around like I wasn't shot in the stomach by his evil ex. I've had my fair share of injuries before, and this was nothing compared to some of the worst ones, especially when I showed up here almost four months ago. It's strange to think that it's been that long since I arrived in New York.

On one hand, it seems like forever, and on the other, a blink of an eye. I knew things would be weird as I got adjusted to my new life, but I never imagined it would have gone down like this. That I would have accidentally developed feelings for the grumpy billionaire tasked to keep me safe. That a woman I thought was dead because of me would appear in my life, shoot me, and tell me she was coming for the guy I had a crush on, who happened to be her ex-boyfriend. That the people around me would be the most notorious crime family in the state and merely muttering their last name causes everyone around them to tremble and bow down.

Archer stops typing on his computer and stares at the screen, the silence distracting me from my rampant thoughts. Something is wrong, I can tell from the way his body is tense from head to toe.

"What is it?" I ask him, unsure if I want to hear the answer. I've been waiting for the shoe to drop ever since I agreed to stay here, and so far, I've been lucky, but it appears my luck has run dry.

He swallows and doesn't turn toward me. "He's on his way."

"Who is?" I rise from the couch and walk over to Archer, planting my hands on his shoulders as I take a look at the screen, a flashing dot on a map indicating whatever Archer is referring to.

"Joe Vito. His private jet left LAX about a half hour ago. The flight itinerary is for LaGuardia. He should be wheels on the ground in less than six hours."

I rub his shoulders even though he's not the one in danger, I am.

"I need to talk to Madison," Archer announces, making me stop moving completely.

This is what I was worried about. Not Joe Vito, but Archer's ex coming back and finishing what she started.

"No," I tell him, despite having no control over what he does. We aren't together, and even if we were, Archer is a grown-ass man who decides his own fate. I couldn't stop him if I tried, although that's not going to prevent me from doing exactly that.

"I need to know what their deal is. I need answers, London." Archer spins in his chair and pulls me onto his lap, wrapping his arms around my waist. "You don't have anything to worry about."

This is the closest we've been since we hooked up in my apartment three weeks ago. Not counting him helping me when I was shot, other than a small touch here or there, that's been the brunt of our intimacy. I thought what we had fizzled out, that Archer was only keeping me around because he felt bad for what happened. But the way he's holding me now unravels feelings I didn't realize were still there.

"I have everything to worry about," I confess. "The love of your life came back from the dead. I can't compete with that."

"This isn't a competition," Archer tells me, but it does nothing to settle my nerves.

Madison was different. More vindictive than I remember, something terrifying and cruel in her eyes that wasn't there all those years ago. Faking her death changed her, and not for the better. Even if she doesn't have feelings for Archer, that won't stop her from taking him from me just because she can.

He tilts his head up toward me, his beautiful eyes meeting mine. I fight the desire to kiss him, not sure if that's what he'd want anyway. I haven't been sure of anything for weeks, especially what's going on between us. One minute he's hot, the next he's cold. And I'm not confident I know what I want anyway, all I know is I feel safe with him.

That simple fact scares me more than anything.

***

Five hours and twelve minutes after Archer first saw my betrothed's private jet taking off from an airport in California, his phone rings, no number showing on the screen.

He answers it, putting it on speakerphone but not saying a word.

"Archer Sin." Vito's voice comes in clear and sends a chill up my spine.

"Joe Vito." Archer stands from the couch and paces the small space in front of me.

"You know who I am."

"Not by choice."

"I hear you have something that belongs to me."

"And what's that?" Archer asks him, knowing damn well I'm what he's referring to.

I chew on my lip and recall Joe's awkwardly shaped body, his foul-smelling breath; and how he lingered his gaze on my chest despite me being in a hospital gown the last time I saw him. He reminds me of my father with how he thinks everything and everyone belongs to him. They say women are often attracted to the same kind of man as their father, but I couldn't be any more repulsed by Joe Vito.

"Is she there, right now, my London girl?"

I hop to my feet and lean toward the phone. "And what if I am? What are you going to do about it?"

Archer widens his eyes and tilts his head, pushing the Mute button. "Really?" he whispers, even though Joe can't hear him.

"What?" I say. "What's he going to do, show up here and demand I go with him?"

"I mean, maybe, I don't fucking know."

Once Joe finishes laughing, he continues, "There's that London girl of mine."

I could slit his throat just for using the name my father used to call me. Every time, it grated my nerves knowing there was not a damn thing I could do about it, but with Joe, there's nothing that will stop me from ending his life if he thinks he can take me away from here. I don't care how fucking untouchable people claim he is, I don't give a shit about that. He's already taken more from me than he realizes, making me completely start over in a new city and leave everything behind. Do I blame my father? Yes. But do I blame Joe Vito too? Without a doubt.

I push the Unmute button, Archer yanking the phone from my reach and lightly smacking my hand.

Joe clears his throat. "I'm glad you two are together. Tell you what, I'll meet you at your place, say...ten minutes, depending on traffic. Don't bother leaving, I have the place surrounded, a bullet in both of your heads if you leave. Don't worry, all I want to do is chat, you have my word. See you soon." He hangs up without giving either of us a chance to respond.

Archer calmly sets his phone on the desk next to his computer and runs his hand through his hair as he blankly stares out the window.

"What are you doing?" I ask him.

"Thinking." He inhales deeply and nods to himself, turning on his heel and marching to the bedroom.

I follow him in, not sure what he's rummaging through his closet for.

"Put this on." Archer stands with a vest in his grasp, putting it over my shoulders, the weight of it heavy but not too unbearable. He returns to his closet and pulls out a hooded sweatshirt. "And this on over it."

A minute later, I'm swimming in Archer's hoodie and he's tilting my face up toward him. "Stay behind me, please. If I move, you move, okay?"

"Only on one condition," I tell him.

"Name it."

"Kiss me."

Archer's eyes dart back and forth between mine, almost like he's considering whether the risk outweighs the reward, finally settling on an answer as he presses his mouth to mine, our lips brushing for the softest kiss. "Come on," he says, running his hand down my arm to grab ahold of my hand.

"What now?" I go with him because what other choice do I have? "And why don't you have one of these vests on?"

"Because I only have the one." Archer doesn't stop until he's at his computer, lowering himself onto the seat and pulling me into his lap. He manages to reach past me to type on the keyboard while still holding me close, countless screens popping up and closing, all of it not making much sense.

"What are you doing?"

Finally, a set of camera feeds pops up on the screen.

"Surveillance." He points to one of them. "This is out front." And then another. "Side of the building." And another. "Back. And this one is the other side. You see this?" He zooms in on a black car, and then a black SUV. "I think Vito was telling the truth about having the place covered."

"Can't you, like, call your brothers or something?" I wrap my arm around his neck and watch the screen as he flits in and out of tabs.

"I'm not talking to Leo, and August has his own issues to deal with." Archer exhales. "And Seven's insane. He'd probably cause more trouble than he's worth. I don't trust Vito, but men like him, they're big on their word."

"So you're going to talk to him?"

"I don't have another option, London. I knew he was coming but I didn't know he was coming *here*. I'm unprepared and unequipped for this. I'm not going to let him take you, though, if that's what you're worried about. I'll die before I let that happen."

I skim my fingers through the hair on the back of his head. "That's what I'm worried about, Archer. Not what he'll do to me, but what he'll do to you."

His gaze meets mine, something so intense in the way he's looking at me that it rattles my core. "Don't worry about me, little tornado." Archer's attention splits from me to the computer, the computer taking his full focus as he clicks on one of the tabs. "There he is."

Joe Vito steps out of a black car, matching the ones that Archer had pointed out. He takes a long glance around before climbing the stairs alone.

"He won't try anything if he's by himself," Archer tells me, a sense of comfort coming from his words.

The buzzer to Archer's apartment rings and I jump in his lap, startled by the loud sound even though I should have expected it.

"Remember what I told you, London. Stay behind me." Archer nudges me off him and steps around me to walk toward the door to grant Joe Vito access to the building.

I want to tell him not to, to tell him that we could stay here forever, living off the remains of whatever is in his fridge and never leave here ever again, but I know that isn't realistic and that it would never last. Joe would find some way into the building, and once he did, he'd finish us both just for making him wait. But Joe won't be the only untouchable man in this room, and I have to remember that when being forced to confront him.

It takes Joe almost two minutes to get into the building and up to the second floor, whether he took the stairs or the elevator is lost on me. His knuckles pound against the door and I hold my breath as Archer opens it slightly and puts his foot in front of it.

"Archer," Joe says, his voice raspy but not in a sexy way, in a disgusting way like he has too much phlegm built up and he needs to cough any second.

"Are you alone?" Archer asks him.

"You, me, and the breeze, baby." Joe pauses. "You going to let me in or leave me in the hallway like the trash?"

Archer hesitates before stepping out of the way and letting Joe enter, my heart skipping a beat once he's in here. I thought I was ready to face him, but now that he's this close, I can't help but feel like my father's ghost came in with him, too. There are parts of my past that I miss, but this isn't one of them.

"Ah, there she is." Joe looks directly at me but makes no attempt to bridge the space between us.

Archer closes the door and quickly moves to position himself better, acting as a barrier.

"So hasty," Joe teases him. "Are you in love with my bride, Archer Sin?"

"How much do you want?" Archer cuts straight to the point, not answering the question Joe asked him.

Joe runs his grimy finger along the edge of the table near the door, walking farther into Archer's apartment. I eye him cautiously, the weight of the vest providing the tiniest comfort, lingering in

Archer's shadow giving me more. "Funny thing," Joe says. "How we buy and sell things, people, as if it's normal practice." He points to the couch. "May I?"

"Sure." Archer continues to position himself between us.

Joe unbuttons his suit jacket, the bulge of his stomach nearly making it come undone prematurely. He groans as he sits down and pats the spot next to him. "Have a seat. Both of you."

Archer glances back at me and nods to the chair beside the couch.

I slip onto it and Archer rests against the arm of it, staying as close to me as possible.

"I'm going to keep things short, because I have another meeting to attend to while I'm in town." Joe coughs, barely covering his mouth, spit flying out.

It's everything I can do to not let my disgust show across my face.

"There is no price. I was promised a bride; I want a bride. Not any—the one I was guaranteed. I know you're well-off Archer, your whole family is. I understand I could profit quite nicely from you, given how you've bonded with her. Unfortunately, money isn't what I'm after, so I cannot be paid off. I'm also aware that I cannot simply put a bullet in your head and take what's rightfully mine, because of the hell that would unleash upon me. I'm afraid that puts us at a stalemate." Joe pauses like he's done, but then he opens his mouth once more. "But what you're missing is one key detail. I'm not much for gossip, although when it benefits me, it's hard not to indulge."

My fingers dig into the fabric of Archer's sweatshirt, waiting for Joe to spit out whatever it is he's hinting about, the thing that's supposed to seal my fate.

"I know, Archer," is all he says, his gaze boring right into the man sitting next to me.

"Is that supposed to scare me?" Archer doesn't fold to his vague threat.

Joe grins and it unsettles me, something wicked in him, unlike most men in this industry. The last time I saw a look that similar was when my father was beating me nearly to death.

"Oh, Archer, you naive boy. You think you have it all figured out, don't you? You think you can break a treaty *and* get the girl? You're mistaken, because if you think for a second that you got away with what you did, you're wrong. And see, that's where this little match of chess goes into checkmate, because I don't have to be the one to put a bullet in your head, the Manor brothers will do it for me when they find out the truth. And that's when I'll swoop in and not only take your girl, but I'll come after everything your family ever had a claim to. The Manor brothers won't stop with you, Archer, they'll end your entire family, and I'll be there, waiting with a big fat *I told you so*. Think long and hard, boy. Is she worth the price you'll pay?"

Archer remains firmly planted next to me as Joe rises to his feet, reaching to button his jacket.

Joe continues. "I'll offer you a one-time deal. Hand her over to me in two weeks, and the secret remains buried. Fail to do so and I'll take everything you hold dear. Either way, you lose the girl, so consider how much you're willing to risk." He focuses on me instead of Archer for the first time since he sat down. "And don't worry, London girl, I'll be a better provider than he ever could. I thought I lost you once, I won't let that happen again." His eyes darken. "Don't try to escape me, I'll find you. I'll always find you."

Joe makes his way toward the door, stopping once he's at it to give a few parting words. "Two weeks from today, I'll be at The Branford, room 423. If you don't show by noon, I'll consider that your answer." He smiles again. "I do look forward to your response either way." He leaves a second later, Archer's apartment suddenly feeling so fucking small as Joe sucks all the air out of it with his departure.

"Archer," I whisper.

He stands slowly and takes a few steps away from me. "London, I need you to go into the bedroom and turn some music on."

"What?" I reach for him but he pulls his arm from my grasp. "Why?"

Archer's entire body tenses. "Because I'm about to get very angry and I don't want you to be in here when I do."

Tears well in my eyes and despite fighting them off, one slips down my cheek. "It's okay, everything is okay. We'll figure this out.

We have to."

Archer turns around to face me. "You don't understand, do you, London? There is nothing to figure out. There is no getting ahead of this. Joe was right about one thing, he has me in checkmate, and there's not a damn thing I can do about it."

"There has to be something," I tell him, despite having no idea what it could be. "Tell me what happened, maybe I can help. Let me help, please?"

Archer drags his hands through his hair and mutters under his breath, "Fuck."

"Talk to me, Archer, please. I'm begging you."

"I hacked into The Manor, the stupid hotel that is supposed to be a safe haven for us criminals, the one in California. I'm the reason there was an explosion. I'm the one who was responsible for it." Archer shakes his head. "I should have never fucking done it, it was stupid. I can't believe he found out. My hacking is untraceable. Unless Silver told him..."

"Why would Silver do that? That doesn't seem like something he'd do." Granted, I didn't get the chance to get to know Silver, but he doesn't cross me as someone who would out someone on such a thing.

"It's irrelevant at this point, something to figure out later. Regardless, Vito holds all the cards with this information."

"What's so bad about the Manor brothers finding out? Can't you just pay the damages to the hotel or whatever?"

Archer takes a long breath in. "You really underestimate how badly our families hate each other. We've been looking for something to prove they violated the treaty every day since it was signed. But until that happens, touching one of them would be like signing your death warrant. That goes both ways. It's not just me they would come after, either; they would take out each one of my siblings and anyone close to them. Our empire would crumble and nothing could be done to stop it."

"I didn't know it was that serious, Archer. I never would have danced with Blake if I knew. It's a little late for apologies, but I am sorry." I'm not even sure why I'm saying it now, but with the clock ticking until our demise, he needs to hear it.

Archer stares blankly past me, his gaze flickering like he's processing a million different things at once. Always the problem solver, and now he has the ultimate complication to navigate. I don't blame him for ignoring me, not when there are much more important things to focus on. The only solution is the one that I've been trying to avoid.

I fold my arms across my bulletproof chest. "I have to turn myself in, Archer. We're out of options."

"No." He still doesn't meet my gaze. "I won't let that happen."

"We don't have a choice," I tell him, because it's true. Each possibility ends with the same fate, and if I want to stand any chance of minimizing the damage I've already done to him and his family, I must give myself to Joe Vito.

Giving Archer up is how I keep him alive, even if I lose myself in the process.

CHAPTER THIRTY-FOUR

Archer

My eyes burn from the lack of sleep, but I refuse to let myself rest until I come up with a solution that doesn't result in losing anyone I care about.

Nothing makes sense, and the more I try, the more unsettled I become. If I don't find clarity on something, anything, I'm going to drive myself insane.

I hate that it's come to this, but I don't have any other choice. I'm going to make London mad, but that seems impossible to avoid.

I clear my throat, preparing for the argument that's about to happen.

"Why are you looking at me like that?" London asks me from her spot on the couch.

"Because I know you."

"No, you don't."

I tilt my head and wonder how I got here. For as long as I can remember, I have been feared, I have killed many, I have lived a life full of crime and zero remorse—and here I am, a foot taller than this woman, afraid of how she's going to react.

"Just spit it out," she says when I don't speak.

"I located Madison. I'm going to meet her. Seven is on his way here to sit with you. He should be here any minute. I'm not going to argue with you, I'm not going to change my mind. I need to do this. I need closure. You have nothing to worry about." I spit out the words like if I don't get them out quick enough, this whole place will explode.

London stares at me for a long moment and I hold my breath, waiting for her to say something, anything, to give me any indication of what she's thinking.

"I don't need a babysitter," London mutters, crossing her arms. "I'm not a child."

"He's not a babysitter, he's a bodyguard. Those are two different things. If anyone's babysitting anyone, it's you babysitting him."

London shrugs. "Whatever."

"If he tries anything..." I hold out a switchblade, offering it to her. "Pull this on him. I don't care if you kill him, just try not to ruin the rug."

London takes it, flipping it open and pricking her finger along the blade. "Sharp."

"Be careful, please."

"Why not a gun?"

"What?"

"Why didn't you give me a gun?"

"Oh," I say. "I don't know. Guns are loud. I don't need the neighbors calling the police on you."

London narrows her gaze. "I'm your neighbor, big boy. Did you forget?"

I kneel in front of her, my hand on her knee. "What do you say, when we figure this out, you and me, we go away together? Anywhere in the world, you name it."

"Not London," she says with a smirk. "Anywhere but there."

"Anywhere but there or here." I pause. "You're okay with me going?"

"No, but I don't have a choice, so what's the point in arguing about it?" London exhales. "Don't be long."

"Why, going to miss me?" I grin at her this time, doing anything I can to lighten the mood.

"Something like that." She leans forward. "Kiss me."

And so I do, bridging the gap between us and pressing my lips on hers, my heart burning at not having found a way out of this yet but determined to pull off the impossible. I refuse to accept that there's nothing I can do to save us all.

***

I walk into the hotel that I found Madison was staying at. She's using a fake name, but once I ran her picture through the facial recognition software I developed, it was a piece of cake locating her. I'll never forget the way my stomach turned seeing her strut across the hotel lobby floor as if nothing ever happened, as if she hadn't faked her death and left me to mourn the loss of her.

Combing through my thoughts, I try to reconcile what it is I want to say to her, but the only thing I can settle on is *why*. Why did you deceive me? Why didn't you tell me you were alive? Why did you leave me?

I pound my fist on the room she's inside and cover the peephole, obstructing her view out.

Like a fucking idiot, she answers, disappointing me somehow even more than she already has.

Madison's eyes go wide, and before she can shut me out, I grab hold of the door and force it open, stepping inside and slamming it shut behind me.

I take her in, my heart pounding, my mind unable to comprehend that this is real, that London is telling the truth. There must be some kind of logical explanation for Madison faking her death, and that's what I'm here to gather.

Only when I go to speak, that's not what I ask her.

"Why are you working with Joe Vito?" I go into the room, looking around and making sure no one else is in here. I had been damn sure of it during my investigation, but if recent events have taught me anything, it's that sometimes I'm wrong.

"Archer, I—I can explain."

"I'm waiting." I fold my arms and lean against the wall.

Madison's eyes dart from me to the door, back to me. She does exactly as I anticipate and makes a dash for it, but she's not as quick as she thinks she is, and I latch onto her arm and yank her away from it, throwing her onto the bed. She gasps and shuffles to scoot onto her elbows. "Archer," she mutters.

I wrap my hand around her throat, not so hard that it'll leave a mark, but enough she'll get the fucking point. "I'm not the same man you remember, Madison. He died when you supposedly did. Anything good you think you know about me, you need to fucking forget. I came here for the truth, and if you don't want to give it to me, I beg you to remember the bad parts of me, because that's all that's left. I will get it out of you one way or another. Now, you have a choice. Which would you prefer?"

She blinks up at me, a false sense of fear in her eyes. It took me until this moment to realize the moments I shared with her were fake, that it was all an act. Nothing about us was real, because if it were, she never would have left me the way she did. That's not what you do when you love someone.

"That doe-eyed look isn't going to get you anywhere, Madison. Cut it out." I shove her and step away, giving her a moment to compose herself and decide the path we're going to go down. "I don't care that we used to fuck, that means nothing to me. *You* mean nothing to me."

"Fine," she finally says. "But I want you to know, I did care about you."

"Did. Past tense. Let's leave it there and move on. Tell me what I want to know and I won't snap your neck." I have never hurt a woman in my entire life, but Madison crossed too many lines to not have it coming. First, when she betrayed me, and second, when she shot the woman I'm in love with.

My heart stutters, my breath catching. It was only a thought, and yet it still stunned me.

Love. I shake my head. I'm sleep-deprived, I must be losing it. I have feelings for London, but that doesn't make it love.

"Fine, fine, I'll talk. Don't get your panties in a bunch." Madison sits up and fixes her shirt. "You look worse for wear, Arch. You having trouble sleeping?"

"Don't be concerned about things that don't concern you."

"For the record," she begins, "I never meant to hurt you."

"You didn't," I lie, and lean my back along the wall in this hotel room that seems to be getting smaller by the moment. I don't want to be here, not with her, not when London is across town and with someone else. I trust that Seven will keep her alive. He enjoys killing too much to let the opportunity pass if anyone tries to pull anything. Aside from me, she's honestly probably in the best hands. Seven might be out of his mind, but right now, he's the only brother I'm willing to bother with something this serious.

"Let me start at the beginning," Madison says, and lets out a big, overly dramatic breath.

I hold out my hand. "The short version, Madison. Stop wasting my time."

"The short version is that Ricardo Gardella bought me. I was to be his baby-producing pet."

I cringe at the thought of that man coming anywhere near her, or any other woman for that matter.

"He and Joe were friends, or, well, business associates, whatever. Anyway, Joe came by one day and offered me a way out. Said he would vouch for me, that we had to find the right opportunity. I didn't see it coming until it was too late and Ricardo nearly killed me, but it was the perfect out. Ricardo thought he succeeded, and I had to make it believable, which meant leaving everything and everyone behind. I couldn't involve you, otherwise he would have found out. You have to understand that I didn't want to leave you, Arch. It hurt me as much as it hurt you. I loved you, I really did."

"Not enough, apparently, because if you did, you would have known that you could have come to me, Mads. I would have helped you figure it out. Why didn't you tell me?" I hesitate and decide I don't want an answer. "Never mind, forget I asked. I couldn't care less. So that's why you're working with Vito, because he did you a favor and now you owe him one?"

Madison licks her lips and nods. "What else was I supposed to do, Arch? I thought he was going to kill me, to kill you. I had no other option."

"There's always another option."

"You don't get it. I mean, how could you? You don't know what it's like."

I glare at her, the idea of snapping her neck quite literally crossing my mind. I hate myself for how badly I've let her corrupt me, making me into somehow even worse of a man than I already was. "You have no idea what I've been through. I would have done anything for you, Madison. But now? Now I don't care if you live or die."

I nearly completely abandoned my family because I thought my involvement with the crime world was what resulted in her death. I gave up everything when she died, in some twisted way to try to right the wrong that was no one's fault but my own. Little did

I know she was the one who put herself in danger, and she was the one who chose to solve the problem without involving me. She took that choice away from me and because of it, lost me forever, and here she is, ready to force London into the same life she was destined for.

"It's a little hypocritical, don't you think?" I ask her, not sure if she realizes it fully.

"What do you mean?"

"London faked her death to get away from Vito, the same thing you did to get away from Ricardo. And now you're stripping that away from her." I tap my finger on my crossed arm. "What's the connection between you two, anyway?"

Madison sort of stares past me like she's recalling a memory. "Part of me feels bad about it, since she was the one who almost died trying to save me. Man, he gutted her good as she begged for her life, for mine."

My nostrils flare as she tells me the part of the story I had no idea about.

That scar on London's torso, the one she won't talk about, it had to have been related to this, to what her father did to her. I can't believe I ever got mad at her for lying to me about Madison. How could she have told me when the entire thing was such a traumatic experience for us both?

"London bought it, too," Madison says. "You should have seen her face. It was like she saw a ghost. Kind of like what you looked like when you walked in." She smiles as if she's proud of herself for fooling us.

"You're sick, you know that, right?" I shake my head slowly. "What happened to you? You weren't like this before."

Madison shrugs. "You weren't the only one who changed, Archer."

"How did you find her?" I ask, trying to make sense of the gaps in the story.

"When Ricardo died, I finally gained my freedom. Well, the part that Joe didn't still have a hold of. I came out of hiding and Joe made it clear I still owed him a favor." She rolls her eyes. "You guys and your favors." She uncrosses and recrosses her legs. "He had told me about London, and I have to admit, I was sad to hear about her death. Totally unrelated, I guess I got a little curious about how you were doing, so I started checking in on you, to see what you were up to. Lo and behold, I find footage of the two of you together, and that same look that was on your faces, it was on mine, too. Little London girl pulling a Houdini act in Manhattan with my ex. I had to come to verify it for myself." Madison chuckles. "I wondered how I was ever going to repay Joe for what he did, cash in that favor that felt impossibly hefty..."

"And you didn't care you'd be giving her up in the process? That you'd be ruining my life all over again?"

"With London out of the picture, maybe we could try again." She looks up at me and bats her eyelashes. "What do you say, Arch? For ol' times' sake?"

"I'd rather chew on glass, Madison." I kick off from the wall and stand completely up, taking her in for what I hope will be the last time. I came here for closure, and I received that and more, the very presence of her making me wonder what I ever saw in her to begin with. I can't believe I ever cared for her, loved her, mourned her.

"That's hurtful, Arch." Madison hops off the bed and I snap toward her, daring her to move another fucking inch.

"Choose your next words and move wisely, Madison. My patience is wearing thin and I can't be held responsible if you push me over the ledge. I don't want to be the one to end your life, but that doesn't mean I won't do it." I stare at her for a long moment, almost hoping that she tests me, my nerves needing something to take the edge off.

But when she doesn't speak, doesn't move, I know things are done here.

CHAPTER THIRTY-FIVE

London

"I need a gun," I say to Seven, knowing he might be the only person to help me.

Archer will do everything he can, but there's only so far he's willing to go, and at the end of the day, I have to take care of myself.

"What kind?" Seven drinks straight from a container of orange juice and puts it back in Archer's fridge.

"I...I'm not sure."

"What do you need it for?"

"To kill someone." I swallow harshly. Is he going to judge me? Is he going to tell Archer the second he's back?

"Cool." Seven lowers his elbows onto the island in Archer's kitchen and taps his tattooed finger to his chin. "Something small, probably. Are you trying to conceal it?"

"Yes."

"Let me see your hand." He reaches out, grabbing hold of my palm and examining it. "Yeah, you're going to need a .380. No way you could handle much more than that on a whim. I'd opt for a revolver, too, so you don't have to worry about the slide getting stuck on anything. But...if you want a hammerless one, I'd opt for a 38 Special. Pretty sure Smith & Wesson has one. When do you need it by?" Seven looks up at me, running his tongue over his sharpened canine tooth.

"When can you get it?"

Seven shrugs. "Today, probably."

"Archer can't know about it."

"I figured, otherwise you'd be asking him." Seven leans back, his arms across his chest and tugging his dark, faded T-shirt up, revealing even more tattoos on his stomach.

"Why would you help me?" I ask him.

"You caught me on a good day."

"Thank you," I tell him, truly meaning it. I'm not convinced I'm going to go through with it, but if I do, I need a weapon that is deadlier than the switchblade Archer gave me.

"Put in a good word for me," Seven says. "With Grace."

"She's never going to go out with you." I shouldn't be saying this to him right now, but he has to know the truth.

"Doesn't mean I'm going to stop trying." Seven grins at me. "I'm a rather persistent man."

"Seems like everyone in your family is."

"It's not often we don't get something we want. When you grow up with nothing, you end up getting greedy. What about you, firecracker? Did you grow up with nothing?"

"Actually, the exact opposite. My father was wealthy, but he was a sick bastard."

"Ah, right. The dead dad who killed your mom."

"Yeah."

"Sounds like you had nothing, too, then."

I guess I hadn't thought about it that way until Seven pointed it out. I may have had access to money, but I never knew family, not really. I never have, and with the way my life is going, I never will. Ricardo made damn sure of that. I was born alone, and I will die alone, especially if I do nothing to stop the pattern of being owned by a man. If it's not Ricardo, it's the next sad sack of shit who thinks he has a claim over me. I'd rather die than live another day under the thumb of a man.

"Who was he?" Seven asks. "Your dad."

I meet his gaze, not sure which eye to focus on, the blue one or the green one. "Ricardo Gardella."

"You're fucking with me."

I shake my head. "I wish I were."

"Damn, that sucks. I thought I had it bad. That man was a sick fuck."

"You knew him?"

"He's tried to merge with us over the years, wanting to get a foothold on the East Coast. We never did. August would have never allowed it. Especially after Ricardo killed Archer's girl. August is the moral compass of us all." Seven rolls his eyes. "Uptight prick, if you ask me, but no one did. He's the decision maker, having the final say in anything we do as a whole. But hey, he's usually right, so whatever."

It's interesting to hear Seven's perception of his brothers, since I've already heard some from both Archer and Leo. Grace has had her input, but she only knows them from the outside.

"What about Ivy?" I ask him.

"Uh, my annoying sister." Seven goes to the cabinet where the alcohol is, taking a look and closing the doors, grabbing a bag of chips from the pantry instead. "She keeps us all in line, me more than them. She's August's right-hand woman and the face of our empire." Seven pops the bag open and shoves a few chips in his mouth, pausing and holding it out to me.

"I'm good," I tell him, and hope he continues. Typically, he's in more of a manic state, but today he's articulating himself well and doesn't appear to be as unhinged as he usually is. It's refreshing, honestly, but I have a feeling it won't last. The second he finds out Grace is dating or even talking to someone, he'll probably revert to psycho Seven.

"Your dad, though, that sucks." He finishes chewing and barely swallows before starting again. "Come to think about it, I think I heard from him, like, six months ago. Something about a deal, he was trying to sell something..." He zones out for a moment. "Oh, right, a daughter. He was trying to marry her off to the highest bidder."

I force a smile and wave my arms. "And here she is."

"No shit, that was you?"

I nod slowly. "In the flesh."

"Wait, I think he said she was a virgin. He kept saying it like it was his selling point."

This time, it's me who rolls my eyes. "He was just a disgusting pig who thought that would help him get more money."

"It wasn't true?"

"Not that it's any of your business, but no, and my father knew this. He killed the guy I lost my virginity to when he walked in and found us getting dressed after hooking up."

"Brutal."

"Yeah. He killed the next guy, too."

"Shit, that's ruthless." Seven eats another handful of chips, his mouth still full when he says, "This dude you're wanting to kill, he's the one who bought you, isn't he? That's why you're here, hiding out with a fake name."

I can't quite tell whether Seven is asking for confirmation or simply stating that he's pieced it together. Still, I give it to him anyway. "Yeah, but if you don't mind, I'd like to keep it a secret a little longer."

"I'm good at keeping secrets," Seven announces, and taps his head. "It's like a vault in here."

"Would you like another one?"

"Would I? Are you kidding?"

"She's not dead."

His brows pinch together. "Who's not?"

"Madison—Archer's girl." Calling someone else Archer's girl turns my stomach, but I have to come to terms with the fact that I can't keep him and that I can never be Archer's.

"You're shitting me."

"Nope. That's where he is right now."

Seven's eyes widen. "You let him go? What the hell is wrong with you?" He tosses the bag of chips on the counter and latches onto the countertop, staring right at me. "Dude was so heartbroken, he abandoned his family, and you gave him permission to walk out of here and be with her? You're either wickedly confident or completely out of your mind."

Archer told me not to worry, but it's hard when Seven is freaking out the way he is.

"I don't control Archer," I tell him.

"Not for long." Seven rocks his head back and forth. "I never liked her."

"Why?" I wait anxiously for him to give me dirt on Madison to hopefully settle my nerves about Archer being with her.

"Oh, man, where do I start? Let's go with the fact that she was sleeping her way around The Manor, looking for anyone to bunk up with to *take care of her*." Seven uses air quotes on the last four words. "Thought we were going to go to war with the Manor brothers back then. Madison was doing this back-and-forth shit with Blake and Archer. God, it was fucking nauseating."

"Blake Manor?"

"Yeah, what other Blake would I be talking about? Keep up, firecracker."

I want to ask him more questions, uncover more of what Madison was like with them, because I only knew the version of her that was involved with my father, and the one that shot me in the fucking stomach, but before I get a chance to, the door to Archer's apartment opens and Archer steps inside.

Seven slaps the counter next to me on his way past, and whispers, "I'll keep your secret, don't worry." He moves into the open space and approaches Archer. "How's my favorite brother?"

"Don't start with me, Seven. I can't handle your shit right now." Archer walks right past him and into the kitchen, opening a cabinet, getting a glass out, and filling it halfway with water. He drinks it, not even acknowledging me until he's done. "Hey."

I sit there, in the same place I was having a conversation with Seven, and attempt to not let my mind consume itself with all the things Archer isn't saying. Like how it went with Madison. If they're getting back together. If he's choosing her over me.

But even if he did, it doesn't matter, because I'm choosing me over him, and if he knew that, he'd hate me more than he already does.

Seven leans against the wall, his arms crossed over his chest, one leg kicked out behind the other. "You done being an asshole yet?"

Archer sighs and leaves his glass on the counter, a sure sign that he's distressed. "You're right. I'm being a dick. I need your help."

"Holy shit, I never thought I'd see the day when Archer fucking Sin was asking for my help." Seven grins from ear to ear, showing both of his sharpened canines. He winks at me and starts toward Archer. "What do you need, big bro?"

He follows Archer over to his computer, where Archer drops down into his chair.

"I need anything you can find on Joe Vito. I need dirt. Not who he's fucking, but who he's fucking over. I want a list of all his enemies and his closest friends. I'll work on combing through his business dealings. I need you to handle anything you can think of that would provide me with even the slightest bit of leverage. I don't care who you kill to get it. I know we've beat this Manor brother thing to death, but I need something on them, too, preferably against the treaty." Archer rubs his temple. "And I need it, like, yesterday."

"I make no promises, but I'll do my best." Seven glances at his watch. "I'll be over tomorrow with anything I can find."

"Can you stay sober that long?" Archer leans back in his chair. "Sorry, I have to ask."

"You're a real prick, you know that?" Seven leaves it at that and walks across the room, offering me a parting nod as he slips out the front door.

I climb off the stool and go over to Archer but keep a little bit of distance between us. "For the record, he looked right in the liquor cabinet and chose a bag of chips instead."

"Really?"

"Yeah. And he was making coherent sentences the entire time he was here. I don't want to assume I know anything about him, but I think he was sober today."

"That's good." Archer runs his hand through his hair and intertwines his fingers behind his head. "That's really good."

"Are you going to tell me how it went, or do you enjoy making me beg for information?" I hate that I want it but I can't stand not knowing the truth, regardless of how things end up with us.

"Right, sorry." Archer doesn't meet my gaze, instead, he stares off blankly into the distance. "It was so weird seeing her. It was like seeing a ghost."

"Yeah, it was." *A ghost that shot me.*

"She explained why she did it. Said she never meant to hurt me."

I chew on my lip, waiting for something to give me a fucking clue as to where his head is at with all of this.

Archer releases his hands and scoots his chair forward to grab me and pull me into his lap.

"What are you doing?" I ask him skeptically.

"Why didn't you tell me?" Archer wraps his arms around me and looks into my eyes.

"What?" A lump forms in my throat.

He slides a hand up under my shirt, his touch warm against my bare skin. Archer traces his finger along the outline of the jagged scar on my stomach, the scar left behind by my father when he fully intended on killing me—when I thought he killed Madison.

My lips part but I can't find any words.

"I should have never held you accountable for your father's actions. I should have stopped to think about how difficult it was for you to live with that monster." Archer's gaze darts to my lips, back to my eyes. "I don't blame you for not telling me, London. Especially not now, after knowing the truth."

"She told you what happened?"

"Some version of it. I don't know how much was real or not, and I don't know if I want to make you relive it just to fact-check her."

My mind races, the memory flooding in without my consent. Chest tightening, I hate that Ricardo still has this effect on me, even in his death.

"How are you so strong?" Archer tucks a strand of hair behind my ear.

"I'm not strong."

"You lived your entire life with him. London, you're covered in scars, and I can only imagine the ones that don't show, the psychological warfare he put you through. It isn't right. I'm sorry you ever had to go through that." He pauses. "Never again. I promise you, never again."

"Don't make promises you can't keep, Archer."

Archer runs his thumb over my cheek and cups my face in his hand. "If it's the last thing I do, London, I swear to you, I will not let your father haunt you. I will not let Vito take you. I will die before that happens."

"How are you going to keep your promise if you're dead?"

"Just trust me, please." Archer leans closer, putting his lips to my forehead, kissing softly, then pressing another on my nose, each cheek, and finally, my mouth. "Trust me, London. I've got you."

I kiss him back, knowing damn well I'm being selfish. Archer might think he can handle this situation, but there's a reason the Joes and the Ricardos of the world get away with shit like this, and no matter what he does, the only way out of this is if someone dies.

I just haven't figured out which one of us that is yet.

CHAPTER THIRTY-SIX

Archer

"Talk to me, give me good news," I say to Seven, hoping like hell he's going to give me some kind of leverage against Vito so this shitstorm can be behind us once and for all.

"I've got good news and I've got bad news," Seven tells me as he steps into my apartment. "The good news is that Joe Vito has a ton of enemies, the bad news is that it's pretty much everyone he comes into contact with. No one likes the guy. Literally. Not a single person he's in business with has a good thing to say about him. I wouldn't be surprised if the guy hates himself, too."

"Fuck," I blurt out, and go back to my computer to keep combing through his financials, looking for anything I can use. Joe has terrible spending habits, that's for sure, but it's nothing out of the ordinary for your common criminal with money.

He blows money on drugs, escorts, bottle service, private jets—the typical shit that only raises the IRS's red flags, not mine.

"Where's London?" Seven asks me, my attention turning to him.

"Why?"

"I wanted to see if she's talked to Grace."

"Oh." I don't know what I expected him to say, but that checks out. "She's in the bedroom. Knock first."

Seven goes over, actually listening to me and alerting London before barging in. Whoever this person is that is possessing my psychotic little brother, I hope they stick around.

I lean back, trying to think of any possible angle I can use to my advantage, hating myself for taking so fucking long to come up with a solution that doesn't end in my entire family being murdered because I fell for the wrong girl.

There's that fucking thought again—*love.*

I don't want it to be, the last girl almost ruined me for good when she broke my heart, but how can I ignore the feelings that won't seem to stop growing? If I can just solve this fucking problem, then I could process what it is I feel for her and figure out what it is. Maybe we could go on a proper date and get to know each other for who we really are, not the select few parts of us we chose to share. For the brunt of our relationship, London was hiding her entire identity from me, and I wasn't exactly being truthful with her about who I was, either.

I want to start over, but how is that possible when so much has already happened?

How can we begin when we've already been sabotaged?

***

Another day goes by and I'm nowhere closer to figuring out how to fix what's been done.

I can't erase what I did to the Manor brothers, and there isn't anything I can offer Joe to get him to give up his pursuit to take what's mine. I even reached out to Silver, asking him to use his contacts out West to try to come up with something to help me save everyone.

That's when it hits me, maybe I don't have to save *everyone*.

"Archer?" London says from the doorway of the bedroom in our apartment.

I look up from my computer, where I had been staring blankly anyway. "Yeah?" I clear my throat. "What's up?"

"It's late. You should try to get some rest."

I can almost barely make out her words from across the way, so I get up and walk over there, my eyes still burning from lack of sleep.

"I'll go to bed soon," I tell her.

"Will you come to bed with me?"

"What?" My brain is slow to process what it is she's asking me.

"Not for sex. To sleep. *Please*. Sleep with me instead of on the couch."

I rub my neck and glance back at the computer, afraid that if I don't keep searching, the answer will slip right through my fingers. But with that, I realize I've already come up with what I have to do, I just haven't come to terms with it yet, and if I'm going to follow through with my plan, I should enjoy what remaining time I have left with London while I have it. Because once this is said and done, I'll never get that chance again.

London tugs on my shirt. "Archer, please."

"Okay."

I let her pull me into the room and strip out of my clothes, tossing them onto the chair in the corner, not giving a shit about folding them. That's the least of my worries at this point. I climb into bed next to her in nothing but my boxer briefs and hold out my arm for her.

London settles right into the spot between my collarbone and jaw, and I know with one hundred percent certainty that I'd be okay dying like this. She puts her arm over my chest, her leg between mine. I turn, our bodies entwining perfectly, with no indication of where I end and she begins. I almost suspect that this is what heaven is, being with her, so intimately yet so innocently. I'm going to miss this most, holding her, right where she belongs, safe in my arms. Maybe in another life we could get our happily ever after, because this one is destined for tragedy.

"I like it here," London mutters into me, her breath warm on my bare skin.

"Me too," I tell her, never speaking anything more truthfully.

Under different circumstances, I wonder how things between us would have ended up. London and I are polar opposites. I'm a clean freak, she's a mess. I grew up with no money, she had it all. She's a spitfire and I'm reserved. She's stronger than I am. If I would have had to endure everything she did, I would have given up long ago. I admire that strength, but I hate that she ever had to go through it. Sure, it brought her here to me, but at what cost? If I had to give up this pure bliss just to save her from a shred of the trauma she's been through, I'd do it in a heartbeat. I'd go back to my life of misery and solitude just to make sure she got the life she deserved, not the one she was forced into.

But these are the circumstances we were dealt, and the only thing I can do now is free her from the shackles her father placed on her the day she was born.

And as I press her fragile body into mine one last time, I savor this moment, because tomorrow I'm going to do something for possibly the first time in my life.

I'm going to accept responsibility for what I've done.

I'm going to turn myself in to the Manor brothers and confess to breaking the treaty.

It's the only way to save London, to save my family.

I must sacrifice myself.

CHAPTER THIRTY-SEVEN

London

I float in and out of sleep, my body wrapped around Archer's all night long. I wake just enough to confirm he's still there and drift out again.

He stirs, holding me tighter and kissing my head. I feel him sigh and I wish we could stay like this, forever together, out of harm's way and ignoring the troubles of the world.

But I know come morning, reality will sink in and we'll be forced to face the impossible situation I've brought into his life.

So I allow this momentary and fleeting opportunity to entertain what will never happen again, because I've decided that the only person who can save me is myself, and I can't let a man cloud my judgment ever again. I only regret that I didn't do it sooner and end my father's life before he had the chance to ruin mine.

"I love you," Archer whispers, and moves once more.

I reach for him, but sleep still has its hold on me, and I can't maintain a grip on him. I must have imagined Archer saying that, in the hypothetical fairy tale I fabricated to commit to memory so I never have to come to terms with the truth.

The truth that as soon as the opportunity presents itself, I'm going to betray Archer once and for all.

I'm going to kill Joe Vito.

***

I wake sometime later, gasping for air as I open my eyes to find Seven sitting on the bed beside me instead of Archer. "Jesus Christ, Seven. You scared the fucking shit out of me." I scoot up and away, clutching at my chest. "Are you trying to give me a heart attack?"

He reaches for me, his fingers out. "You have some drool right there."

I smack his hand away. "No, I don't." I lick my lips and wipe my mouth just in case.

"Whatcha wanna do today?" Seven says, repositioning himself more comfortably.

I rub my eyes. "Where's Archer?"

"I don't know." He shrugs. "He was being all weird and cryptic. Asked me to come babysit."

"I don't need to be babysat," I groan, and slip out of bed, Seven staying there as I grab clothes to change into. "How long is he going to be gone?"

"I don't know, firecracker. A couple of hours, probably." He examines his hands. "Will you paint my nails?"

I stop and look right at him. "What?"

"My nails, will you paint them?" Seven drags his legs off the bed and comes over to me, holding out his tattooed fingers to me. "What do you think about black?"

"Why don't you just go get them done at a salon, Seven?"

"Because I don't like people."

"I'm people," I tell him with my arms full of clothes.

"Nah, I like you, firecracker." He rubs my head, messing up my hair more than it already was.

"I'm honored." I roll my eyes and turn on my heel to march toward the bathroom, Seven close behind me. I come to a stop before the bathroom door. "Um, excuse me, a little privacy?"

"Geez. It's nothing I haven't seen before." Seven throws his arms up as I shut the door in his face. "You never answered me," he says loudly through the door. "I'm bored, what do you want to do? You wanna get some food or something?"

I make quick work of peeing, changing out of my clothes, and brushing my teeth and hair. I splash my face with water and throw on some makeup, deciding that today calls for winged eyeliner—channeling my inner Taylor Swift. With a final glance in the mirror, I apply an auburn lipstick and tuck my hair behind my ears. I force a smile, the memory of the first time I looked in this mirror coming back to me. I was a different woman then—battered and bruised and terrified of my haunted past. Today, I fully embrace the fact that I'm going to face it head-on, no longer willing to live in the shadows caused by a man. I hate that I have to risk everything, but my freedom has to count for something. I can't continue to put everyone else first, I must consider what's best for me.

"Damn," Seven says when I open the door.

Marching past him, I continue into the bedroom and kneel beside the bed, reaching my hand in until I find what I'm searching for. I pull out the gun Seven gave me when Archer was distracted, and check the barrel to make sure it's loaded.

Seven leans in the doorway, his tattooed arms across his chest, a smile creeping across his face.

I tuck the gun into my waistband. "Take me to The Branford?"

Seven doesn't question me, he doesn't inquire about what we're doing. All he does is say, "Let's go."

I follow Seven through Archer's apartment and pause at the door to leave my phone on the table Archer keeps his keys. I'm well aware that he's been using it to track and spy on me, and in the past, I've allowed it to happen, but today, I don't want Archer to stalk me, not when I'm about to betray him in a way we'll never recover from.

Taking in his apartment for the last time, I draw in a breath and leave, my stomach in knots at the idea that I'll never be close to him again, feel his skin on mine, his body pressed against me.

I love you, his voice calls out to me, but it was only a fever dream. It wasn't real. None of this was.

Then why does my heart hurt so badly?

I ignore the ache seeping through me and reach for the handle of Seven's car, but he gets there first.

"I'm not being a gentleman; I just don't want your fingerprints all over it." Seven opens it for me and closes me in, the smell of new car somehow still present despite him having this at the very least since I've known Archer.

I settle into the seat and fight the urge to change my mind, to turn back while I still have a chance. There's still time for Archer to come up with a solution, to figure a way out of this, but what if he doesn't and this is the only opportunity I have to get to Vito without Archer stopping me? I can't risk the possibility that my fate is sealed, I have to end this once and for all.

Seven pokes through some music as he maneuvers us into

traffic, finally choosing nothing, the silence filling his Rolls-Royce. He speeds through town and darts around cars carelessly like he didn't just give me shit about putting fingerprints on the door.

It takes twelve awkward minutes to get to The Branford Hotel. Seven pulls up front and puts the car into park, completely ignoring the other vehicles coming and going.

"You ready to do this?" Seven glances over at me and reaches for his door handle.

"I need to do this myself, Seven." I clear my throat. "Plus, you'd make him suspicious. I have to go in alone."

"Archer's going to kill me," he says as if I didn't already know that, but I can't let it deter me, not when I'm this close.

"For what it's worth, he'll probably kill me too." I drag my bottom lip into my mouth and imagine how angry Archer is going to be, both at me and Seven. Me for killing Vito and dooming his entire family, and Seven for allowing it to happen.

"What do you want on your tombstone?" Seven asks me, his train of thought so random at times.

"I don't know. Think of something cool for me." I put my hand on the door handle, my gaze focused on the hotel and not on Seven, because if I look at him, I might change my mind. Sure, he's a fucking lunatic, but he's become a friend over the last few weeks, and I'm betraying him too.

"How long do you think it'll take?" Seven asks me, causing me to pause.

"You don't need to wait, I'll find a way home." I leave the vehicle before he questions me about anything else I don't have an answer to and march right past the valet and into the hotel lobby.

The lights are bright and borderline blinding, but I keep on because I have no choice. I can't turn back now.

"Checking in?" the woman at the desk says to me when I approach, a soft smile on her plain face.

"Actually, I'm here to see a guest. Joe Vito. Room 423. Could you let him know I'm here?" Hotels like this don't allow random people to access the elevators. You need a room key, and I don't have one of those. I'd love the element of surprise with him, but this will have to do.

"What's your name?" she asks me.

"London Gardella." It's the first time in a while that I've truly acknowledged my name out loud, and I have to say, I was quite getting used to being London Smith, the orphaned girl trying to start over in a new town. I hate having any association with the man who ruined my life. My father.

"One moment." She picks up a phone and pushes a few buttons. "Hello, sir. This is the front desk. You have a guest here, London Gardella." After a long pause, she extends the receiver to me.

I hold it to my ear, the time for backing out fully expiring now that he knows I'm here. "Hello," I say while trying to keep my voice from cracking.

"My London girl. What a pleasant but unexpected surprise. Have you come alone?"

"Yes."

"And where's your lover boy, Archer?"

"I don't know."

"Interesting." He goes quiet for a minute. "I'll meet you by the elevators. I'll be down momentarily." Joe hangs up and I give the phone back to the woman, who pretends to be busy on her computer.

"Thanks. He's going to meet me," I tell her. "Where are the elevators?"

She points behind me. "Through that walkway."

I step out of the way, giving the man waiting in line a chance to be helped, and make my way in that direction, swallowing my nerves in hopes that I'll be able to accomplish what I set out to do here. I can't think about the consequences, for me, or for Archer, because the only important thing to consider is gaining my freedom for once in my life. I already have my story planned out in my head. I went up to meet him and he forced himself on me. I grabbed a weapon he had up there and used it as self-defense. Seven told me it was untraceable, and I can't imagine he would have lied about that. I highly doubt someone as experienced as Seven would make a mistake that massive. I try not to let the gun bother me while walking through here, the cold barrel rubbing against my bare skin, but too many prying eyes and cameras are on me, otherwise I'd adjust the way it's sitting in my pants.

The wait feels like an eternity and a blink of an eye, and every time the elevator dings, my stomach turns a bit more.

I rehearse this over and over in my head, but nothing prepares me for the cold that sweeps over me when Joe Vito steps out of the elevator toward me. My lips part and suddenly I shrink, my entire body going stiff at the weight of the situation. I'm not prepared for this, I'm not ready.

"London girl." Joe stalks toward me, turning and putting his hand on my lower back and guiding me in the direction he came. "I'm so happy to see you." He keeps his grimy palm on me as he pushes the Up button, the elevator doors springing open for us.

I go in and remain composed, not wanting to fuck things up just yet. I have to get him into his room. I can't do this here, even if I really fucking want to get it over with.

"You're so tense." Joe comes up to my rear and puts both hands on my shoulders, rubbing harder than he should, like he's trying to assert his male dominance in some weird way.

The light goes from the first floor to the second to the third, and dings at the fourth. I take a big step away from him and move toward his room, hoping like hell he doesn't put his hands on me again but very aware that's exactly what he intends on doing once we're behind closed doors.

Joe is much larger than me, significantly heavier, and no doubt stronger. It wouldn't be hard for him to overpower me, even with a gun trained on him, and I don't exactly wrap my head around that until we're on the other side of the door inside his hotel suite.

"Let me get you a drink." He goes over to the minibar and yanks the cork out of a whiskey bottle, pouring two glasses with three fingers' worth. "Cheers to us." Joe gives me no choice, clinking his glass against mine and keeping his stare on me as he gulps down his drink.

I swallow the golden liquid, ignoring the burn as it ripples down my throat and warms my belly.

"What made you change your mind?" Joe takes my empty glass from me and sets it on the counter next to his.

I pretend to explore his suite to put some distance between us.

"Archer had nothing to do with this. I didn't see a reason for him to suffer." I manage to keep my composure pretty well, considering I'm screaming on the inside to get the fuck out of here. My nervous system hasn't felt this high of an alert since my father was alive.

"Hold that thought." Joe picks up the hotel phone and pushes a button. "Yes, I'd like champagne and strawberries sent up." He mumbles something else I can't quite make out over my heartbeat pounding loudly in my ears.

"Can I use your bathroom?" I ask him.

"What's mine is yours, wife." He pokes his finger toward a closed door. "Through there."

I bolt quickly, but not so quickly it raises suspicion, into the room, closing the door shut behind me. I let out a breath and rush over to the sink, turning the water on and lifting my shirt to adjust the gun pressing into my flesh. Staring at my reflection, I consider how I got here, almost actually escaping this man if it weren't for Madison blowing my cover. I hate her for what she did to me, what she did to Archer. And I hate myself for doing the same fucking thing. I shake my head because I can't think like that, I can't let his feelings come in the way of my own. I have to choose myself—I'm the only person who ever will. I cannot rely on a father, a man, or anyone to save me. I have to do it myself.

When I'm sure I've been in here almost long enough, I flush the toilet and pretend like I'm washing my hands. I wipe them on a fresh towel under the sink, not trusting the one sitting on the counter. Joe is gross and there's no telling what he did with it.

"I figured we could celebrate," he tells me once I've returned. "We're going to have a great life together, London girl. I'll arrange the jet to fly you home tomorrow, and I'll join you as soon as I've finished my meetings. Don't worry about your belongings, I'll get you brand-new everything. You won't want for anything." Joe comes closer, so close I can smell the whiskey on his breath struggling to mask the stench of the cigars he must have been smoking earlier. "And soon enough, I'll put a baby in you."

It's everything I can do not to vomit, my lips pressing together.

A knock sounds on the door and my heart nearly leaps out of my chest.

Joe smiles, plaque buildup on his teeth showing. “Must be our dessert.” He winks lazily at me and heads to the door, peeking through the peephole.

I reach into my pants, taking hold of the gun and putting it behind my back while he isn’t paying attention.

Joe opens the door, the hotel worker bringing in a tray on wheels, the man’s head hung low to avoid eye contact.

“Over there,” Joe tells him, and pulls out his money clip, sliding a twenty off and tossing it onto the rolling table. He grins at me and the tug of the ticking time clock blares that my moment is coming and if I don’t act quickly, I’ll miss my chance.

But when the hotel worker notices that someone else is in the room, their head snaps up, their eyes locking onto mine—eyes that have stared at me far too many times to be mistaken for anyone else’s.

Archer’s brows pinch together, genuine concern and surprise lining every beautiful inch of his face.

Joe takes far too long to realize it’s Archer, but it doesn’t matter, because my arms move, pointing the gun in my grasp right at Joe’s fucking chest.

“Sit the fuck down,” I blurt out, and rush toward him, my grip trembling.

Joe laughs and lowers himself onto the couch, throwing his arm over the back of it. He doesn’t seem the slightest bit concerned, and that alone concerns me. How can he be so cocky when I’m training a loaded gun right at him?

“London, put the gun down,” Archer tells me.

I shake my head. “No.” Tears well in my eyes because there’s no way out of this, no way that I won’t kill Joe Vito with Archer witnessing my betrayal. I was supposed to do this myself, not have him here to see it.

“London,” Archer says again.

“Stop,” I yell. “You’re not going to talk me out of this. You weren’t supposed to be here. Why are you? Did you follow me? I told you to stop stalking me.” I don’t know why I’m blurting out words instead of shooting, but I am, and I know once I pull the trigger, there won’t be time for questions, because I’ll have to get out of here before Archer kills me for ruining his life.

"I wasn't following you, London. I came here to talk to Vito myself."

I blink a few times, the tears in my eyes clouding my vision. "That doesn't make sense." None of this makes sense. But it doesn't matter. "I don't care why you're here," I tell him. "I have to do this, Archer. You don't understand. I won't live like this. I can't do it again."

Joe tilts his head as if he's trying to comprehend what I'm saying. "So let me get this straight. Archer didn't know you were here, and you didn't know he was coming." His brows perk up and he nods. "Great communication you two have there." He licks his gross lips. "Archer came here to talk, and you came here to what, shoot me? Oh, sweetheart, you and I both know you're not going to do that. And neither is Archer, so whatever your grand plan is, you should give up without making things worse."

"No." I sniffle and inch closer, Archer moving in my peripheral vision.

"London. Please. Just give me the gun. You don't want to do this."

"I do. I have to do this, Archer." His name on my tongue is like acid burning me to my core. I don't want to hurt him, but I have to, it's the only way out of this for me. "I'm sorry."

"After everything we've been through, you're really going to go through with this?" Archer's voice breaks and I feel the defeat in his every word deep in my bones. "I thought we had something special, London."

"Listen to him, London girl," Joe says plainly. "Do you want him to suffer because of your actions? Do you want Archer and his entire family to lose everything, including their lives?"

My heart pounds wildly and I keep my aim on Joe, who sits there, not bothered at all, and it only infuriates me more that he thinks he's going to get away with this, that he's so fucking sure I won't kill him.

Archer moves closer and I ache to close the distance and fall into his arms, to apologize profusely for even considering doing this to him, but I can't. I have to see this through, I have to.

"Don't do this, little tornado," Archer speaks low, almost a whisper.

I steady my finger on the trigger and stiffen my grasp on the gun. I look directly into Joe's eyes, eyes that I never want to see again for as long as I live, even if that's a short while.

But the only thing I can think about is Archer this morning telling me he loved me. It might have been a fever dream, and yet it felt real, so real that it weaved its way around my heart and swallowed me whole.

And the next thing I know, I'm lowering the gun and wiping the tear that rolls down my cheek, because as much as I want to, I cannot betray Archer, not when he's the only person on the planet that I've ever truly cared for, that I've ever actually loved.

Archer moves fast, snatching the gun out of my hand and pushing me away from Joe. "What were you thinking?" He shakes his head and I realize the damage has already been done. I might not have gone through with it, but I've hurt Archer in a way I can never come back from.

"'Bout time you got control over that bitch," Joe spits out from his spot on the couch, crossing one leg over the other.

"The fuck did you just say?" Archer turns toward him, the gun slack against his side, still pressed in his grip.

"Don't get all feminist on me, Arch. You and I both know she's only good for one thing." Joe coughs, phlegm rattling in his chest. "Why don't you grab a drink and we can talk about it?" He nods his head toward me. "We'll put this bitch in the bedroom where she belongs. Don't worry, we can take turns. I'll go first. I'm sure she won't mind."

I recoil, slinking back slowly against the wall, the weight of his words too heavy to bear, my hatred growing for him with each passing second. I regret not pulling the trigger while I had the chance, and now I've lost it forever. I've lost myself forever.

Archer's arm moves and the entire room and everything in it

is engulfed in a slow-motion picture playing out in front of me. He trains the gun on Joe and pulls the trigger before either of us has a chance to react, the bullet going straight through Joe's stomach and another through his chest. Archer shoots again in Joe's torso and I clamp my hands over my mouth to suppress the scream that escapes me, not because of Joe being shot, but because I wasn't the one to do it.

Joe gurgles up blood with his eyes wide and heavy, the realization that he was in danger all along hitting him. "You're going to pay," he struggles to get out. "You're going to—"

But Archer doesn't let him get his last word out, because he shoots Joe one final time, straight through his forehead, Joe's body slamming back and coming to an abrupt stop, lifeless and bleeding out.

I can't control the tears as they roll down my cheeks and I look from Joe to Archer, his back to me, everything about him stiff and threatening. I want to move, to go to him, but I can't. I'm frozen in place.

"Archer," I mutter. "What have you done?"

CHAPTER THIRTY-EIGHT

Archer

My palms sweat and my stomach is twisted in knots, but not because I just killed Joe Vito.

I wipe my brow with my arm and try to keep the world steady beneath my feet.

"I had it figured out," I whisper. "I had it all figured out."

"Archer," her voice calls out and slices through me like a dagger to the chest.

"Don't." I turn toward her, the sight of her making all this somehow worse. "How could you?" If I thought what Madison did to me stung, that was nothing compared to this. London was supposed to be different. What we had was supposed to be real.

"Archer, please, you have to understand. I didn't do this to hurt you." London comes toward me, her hands out as if she's going to touch me but she isn't quite sure if she can.

"Don't touch me," I tell her to make it abundantly clear, my heart aching at the finality of everything. The moment she stepped foot in here with a gun given to her by my own fucking brother, that sealed both of their fates. I want nothing to do with either of them, not now, not ever.

She lowers her arms and silent tears stream down her cheeks.

God, it fucking kills me to watch her cry, but there's not a damn thing I can do to stop it, not when she's already made her decision.

I sit on the armrest of the nearby sofa chair, the gun still in my grasp, my head hung low. "I had it figured out," I say again, this time louder.

"I didn't know, Archer. I didn't know. I'm sorry." London remains where she stands, where I snapped at her not to touch me. "I didn't think I had a choice."

I look up at her despite it unleashing another bout of agony raging through me. "That's the thing, London. You *always* had a choice. And you made yours. You couldn't be bothered to talk to me, to trust me. I told you I'd figure it out. I gave you my word, did that mean nothing to you?"

"It did, I promise you, it did, but I still thought we were in too deep." She wipes her cheek, her chest sputtering from the tears she can't control. "I couldn't give myself to him, you have to understand what that would be like. You heard him, what he was planning on doing to me." Her lip quivers. "But even as badly as I wanted to, I couldn't go through with it." She shakes her head. "I couldn't do that to you."

"But you did, London. You had every intention of killing him when you came here with this." I shove the gun into the air between us, causing London to flinch. "You trusted Seven, but not me?" I slump my head once again, trying to make sense of everything.

"I don't trust Seven over you, Archer. I just knew he had no moral compass and would help me. I manipulated him because I knew I could, that was it."

"Is that what you've been doing to me?" I meet her watery gaze. "Manipulating me?"

"Never," she says, her voice barely a whisper. "I wouldn't do that to you."

"I don't believe a word coming out of your mouth."

"Then kill me." London spreads her arms wide, inviting me to end her life. "I'm going to lose you either way. Just do it."

I scoff. "I'm not going to kill you, London. I don't care how much I hate you. I could never kill you." I couldn't even bring myself to kill Madison, although the thought crossed my mind, and I don't know what that says about me, about my character. "I wish you would have talked to me first, told me what you were planning on doing. I wouldn't have stopped you; I just would have asked for more time." I pause, my mind going a mile a minute. "That's what's fucked up, you know? I understand why you did it. But it doesn't make it hurt any less. After everything we've been through, after telling you what Madison did to me, you went and did the same thing. Only, this is worse, because I actually loved you." The words slip out of my mouth before I have a chance to stop them.

London inches forward hesitantly. "Archer." She drops to her knees next to me, her hands on my leg, her head tilted up at me.

"Don't say it, it's only going to make this worse."

"But..." Her eyes dart back and forth between mine as if she's trying to telepathically communicate with me, and as much as I hate it, I can read her mind.

I can feel how sorry she is.

I can sense every bit of love she's begging me to understand, but it doesn't matter—it doesn't change anything.

If she loved me, truly, she wouldn't have done this.

"Why are you here, Archer? If you weren't here for me, why were you here?" London changes the subject and I'm grateful, because I can't stand to think about everything we lost when she came here today.

"To kill him," I tell her truthfully.

"I'm not following." London stays at my side, her hands practically burning their way through my pants and into my body.

"I guess we were both here for the same reason." I swallow the lump in my throat. "You came here to choose yourself, and I gave myself up to choose you."

"What do you mean, you gave yourself up? To whom?"

"I went to Blake Manor, I confessed to hacking into The Manor, I told him I was the reason for the breach. I figured my only choice was to take away the one advantage Vito had over me."

"You didn't come here to talk to Joe?"

"No, I already told you, I came here to kill him." I lift my shirt to reveal the gun I had tucked up under my waistband, never needing it since London brought her own. It was cake hacking into the elevators and granting myself access, and Vito did me a favor when he ordered room service, giving me the perfect opportunity to get into his room. He was a careless and overly confident man, and because of it, I was able to come in nearly undetected, until I spotted London inside the room and that changed literally everything.

"But if you told Blake, that means you..."

"Confessed to breaking the treaty," I finish when she doesn't. "I took full responsibility for it, sparing my siblings' lives and businesses. Blake was thrilled but reasonable, accepting my life in exchange for payment."

"Archer, no." She shakes her head as if she's realizing the

magnitude of the situation and the lengths I went through to save her life. And that's what makes it worse, because I traded my life for hers and she did nothing but stab me in the back when I wasn't looking.

"What's funny," I say, not a hint of humor detected in my voice. "Is that I negotiated my freedom and his silence."

She blinks up at me, her confusion completely appropriate given what I've filled her in on so far.

"One thing I forgot to mention," I tell her, "is that Blake Manor was in love with Madison, too. That's why it upset me seeing you two together at the gala. This whole thing, it's like I've been reliving it over and over." I draw in a breath and focus on the point I'm trying to make here. "He was convinced Madison was dead, too. I told him she was alive, and that I'd disclose her location if he held up his end of the bargain. Oh, the things a foolish man in love will do, even forsaking his oath to his family to chase after a woman who couldn't care less whether he lives or dies."

"I..." London struggles to find the words, and I don't blame her, but I can't continue to be in the same room as her, otherwise I might do something I regret more than what I've already done.

I stand from the spot where I was sitting, brushing London's hands off me and not even glancing in Joe Vito's direction, his fate sealed long before we stepped foot in this room. If it weren't London or me, it would have been someone else he crossed in his incessant rampage to gain power from places he didn't belong. I'll never live down the fact that I killed him, and sure, there will be consequences for my actions here today, but I've already lost everything once, and I don't really care if I have to do it all again.

"Come on," I tell London, and make my way to the door. "We're going home."

"Home? Together?"

I keep my back to her, every muscle in me going rigid, my mind fighting with my broken heart. "We're neighbors, London." I pause. "Plus, I don't trust Seven to take you home."

"Oh." She follows me to the door and watches as I tuck the gun she brought here under my shirt. "What do we do about that?"

"It'll be dealt with." I open the door, holding it for her to walk through, and walk behind her to the elevator. "This way." I guide her to the stairwell and descend the stairs, all too late remembering that I came here on my bike and that our entire ride is going to be her body pressed against mine. I detach my thoughts from my body and pretend this is any other time when I put my helmet over her head, secured it, and helped her onto the bike.

I ignore her arms around me, her legs hugging my sides tightly, the warmth of her seeping into my entire body. I focus on her deceit, how selfish she was in choosing herself over me, how she trusted Seven and plotted behind my back. I remind myself that I hate her, that I have from the moment she stepped foot on my doorstep, and that the only reason she's here is because Silver needed my help. She disrupted my life, my family, my every waking thought. London is a tornado, wrecking everything in her path, not a shred of remorse in her at all.

Holding on to that, I zip us through town, darting through traffic in a mindless state. It isn't until we're in the parking garage that I break the silence. I help her off the back of the bike. "Don't feel obligated to move. Your rent is paid up. I'll sell my apartment the first chance I get. In the meantime, I'll respect your privacy as long as you respect mine." I hook the helmet onto the bike and don't bother taking in the tears that still line her eyes because I don't know how much more of it I can take. I leave her there and jog up the stairs, desperate to put as much space between us as possible, my heart being ripped to shreds with each step away from her.

It kills me to leave her, but it would kill me even more to stay.

***

An entire week passes and I don't hurt any less today than I did then.

I haven't checked London's location and I haven't looked up a single surveillance feed to show me what she's doing. I can't bring myself to see her because if I stand any chance of getting over her,

I have to move on, as much as it pains me. Part of me wishes she would have died that day, because at least then I would have had something to mourn instead of the betrayal I can't seem to stomach.

Madison gave me that—her death—something to hold on to and attempt to process. London left me with nothing but her hair in my shower and the scent of her remaining on my sheets. I can't do anything without being reminded of her, and despite my efforts, I can't help but think I'm leaving my apartment in a shambles just to pretend like she's still here, haunting me in her wake.

My phone rings and I want to ignore it, but Ivy is persistent, and if I don't answer soon, she'll show up at my apartment.

I swipe the button and connect the call. "Yeah?"

"Arch, hey, finally."

"What do you need, Ivy?"

"I wanted to call and check in, see how you're doing."

"I'm fine," I lie. "Now, if that will be all..."

"Don't hang up on me," she blurts out. "Aren't you going to ask me how I'm doing?"

I sigh. "How are you doing, Ivy?"

"I'm great, thanks for asking."

"Fantastic. Glad we got that out of the way."

"I'm worried about you, Arch."

I fidget with my phone on my desk, my computer screen blinking with the few open tabs of nothing in particular. I haven't gotten much of anything done lately, and it shows, because our finances have started to decline, and I don't have the will to figure out how to fix it. Even when Madison *died* I wasn't this out of sorts, and I don't know what to think of that. I was with Madison for six years and London and I were never truly together. Surely, I should be over things by now, but every time I glance in the direction of London's apartment, a pain jabs me in the chest.

"You have nothing to worry about," I tell Ivy.

"Why don't you just talk to her? Make up? She's not dead, Archer, but you're acting like she is."

"Do you need anything else?"

"I need you to listen to me. This family needs you. *You*, Archer, not the ghost of you, not some shell of a human pretending to be him. We need you."

A knock ripples through my apartment. "Ivy, I've got to go, someone's at the door."

"Don't lie to me, Archer."

"I'm not lying." I grab the phone and head in that direction. "I'll talk to you later." I hang up and toss it onto the table near my door, right next to the one that London left behind. I have half a mind to give it back to her, but I'd be too compelled to track her and I don't want the ease of making that happen.

I open the door, not bothering to check and see who it is first, not caring at all if it's the fucking Grim Reaper ready to take me away.

London is standing there in fitted black jeans, tall heels, and a tight corset-looking top with lace. She's wearing a tan trench coat and holds a boom box above her head, with the song "In Your Eyes" by Peter Gabriel playing quietly. Her gaze meets mine and she steps forward, my body almost immediately reacting by moving back, but I stay in place.

"London, this isn't necessary," I tell her, not wanting her to make a spectacle.

"Archer, please, hear me out." London sucks in a breath as if to prepare herself for the speech she's about to make. "I don't have money, not like you do. I can't shut down a restaurant or redirect traffic lights. I don't know how to hack into your phone and track you, or pull up camera feeds to figure out everything you want or desire. I've been racking my brain on what to do, some grand gesture, to tell you, to show you, just how sorry I am. I've wanted to march over here so many times, to bang on the walls, just to see if you're still there. I hate that I hurt you. I hate that I can't make it right.

"There isn't anything I wouldn't be willing to give up to change what happened. I'm sorry, Archer. From the bottom of my heart. I have regretted what I did every single second. I made a mess, and it's up to me to clean it up, to repair what I've broken. I can't sleep. I can't eat. There isn't a thought in my head that doesn't involve you. What you did for me? No one in my life has ever put me first. I didn't know what to do with that. But I do now. If you'll give me a chance. I'll do anything to fix this, just please give me a chance." Her eyes glisten but she keeps the tears at bay this time.

I watch her carefully, her words coursing through me as I process everything she said, coming to the same realization that I have for a week now. I can't do this. I can't be with her. Not when it hurts this fucking badly just to be near her, to see her, to breathe the same air she is.

"I'm sorry, London. Some messes can't be cleaned up." I shut the door without another thought, closing myself off to her forever.

CHAPTER THIRTY-NINE

London

The five days following my embarrassing gesture to Archer are filled with mostly self-loathing and ignoring my responsibilities. I call out of work, using the excuse that I'm still recovering from the gunshot wound, some aches and pains lingering that prevent me from going in. Grace doesn't buy it. She shows up anyway, and despite my best efforts, she forces herself into my apartment with the key I gave her and pokes around.

"You can't live like this," she says while turning up her nose. "This place is a disaster." Grace uses a pair of tongs from the kitchen to pick up a shirt hanging on the back of a chair. "Where's your hamper?"

"I don't have a hamper." I plop onto the couch, not caring at all that she's disrespecting my personal space. With Grace, those things don't matter, and I don't exactly have it in me to put up a fight.

"You're going to shower." Grace goes over to the bathroom, turns the faucet on, and then goes into my room. "Don't you have any clean clothes? Ah, there we go." She has a pile of my belongings in her grasp as she goes back into the bathroom, returning a minute later to drag me from the couch. "I'm going to order Chinese food, and you're going to wash your ass. When I get back, we're going to make a plan, an actionable one. A how-to of sorts."

She shoves me into the bathroom but I just stand there as it fills up with steam.

Grace groans and comes inside, reaching for the hem of my shirt.

I smack her hand. "I can undress myself, Grace, I'm not completely helpless."

"Could have fooled me." She makes her way to the door, turning around to face me. "I'll be back in half an hour. I've let you mope enough. This ends today." Grace shuts me in and I know if I don't do exactly as she says, she'll bathe me herself and never let me live it down.

So I strip out of my clothes, tossing them into the pile heaped on the floor, and step into the piping-hot water. Closing my eyes, I'm grateful my tears have a place to escape as they're washed down the drain. I wash my hair, breaking momentarily here or there to sob, my back against the wall. I do what I can to clean my body well, not wanting to leave it to Grace to verify I followed through. Once I'm done, I sink onto the shower floor and bring my knees to my chest, hugging my body tightly. The hot water spills onto me and I lower my head, considering what it would take to accidentally waterboard myself to death. It's not that I want to die, I just don't exactly want to be alive, not when everything reminds me of the life I gave up when I finally had it all. I was an idiot for thinking what I was risking was worth it, and by the time I realized it, it was too late. Too late for me, for Archer, for us.

A loud knock fills my bathroom, but I don't move. If it's Grace, she'll use her key, and if it's anyone else, I can't be bothered to find out what they want. The only person I want to hear from wants nothing to do with me, and I can't even blame him. I lectured Archer about telling me the truth and then I went behind his back to put his entire family in danger. He has every right to hate me, and honestly, I'm surprised he didn't kill me just to make sure it never happens again. I can't get the image of him out of my head, shutting the door on us forever after baring myself to him in a way I never had with anyone ever. I've relived that moment over and over, and reworked that speech a million different ways, but each one ends with the same outcome—Archer shutting me out.

Why couldn't I make him change his mind? Why couldn't I fix what I had broken? Why couldn't I just make him love me?

But Grace is right, I have to move on from what can't be changed, because if I continue to sit in this state of misery, I'm going to go completely mad.

I wipe away my tears and climb out of the shower, towel-drying and throwing on the clothes that she had picked out for me—nothing special, a pair of jeans I bought the first week I lived with

Archer and a fitted black top. I slide my palm across the steamed-up mirror and take a look at myself, my eyes red and puffy, my hair in wet ringlets on my shoulders.

A booming sound rattles my walls and my first instinct is to reach for my phone, to call Archer, but those days are behind me, and I have to figure out how to move on without him in my life, even if I'd prefer nothing less. Not to mention I haven't gotten a phone since I left mine at his place, and I haven't had it in me to figure out where to even do that. I'm sure Grace would help me, but I don't want to, not yet, not when I'd have to step out into a hallway that we share, walk down steps we walked together, exist in the world without him.

What we had was temporary, but it was the first real thing I'd felt in my entire life, and I let it go up in smoke because I was too afraid it would consume me like everything else had up until that point.

I follow the rattling that fills my apartment, stepping out of my bathroom with caution, another blast crackling loudly. The hung pictures shake and the glassware rattles in my kitchen cabinets. Is this an earthquake? We had plenty of those on the West Coast but none of them were quite like this. Maybe this is how they are in New York, something else I'm going to have to get used to if I'm going to be living here.

I guess I hadn't thought too much past getting free of Joe. Now that I regained my name, I could return home to California and be London Gardella once again, that name feeling so foreign despite spending my entire life living as that person.

Another bang shakes me to my core and I gasp as a piece of drywall goes flying, the wall separating my apartment from Archer's quite literally being torn to shreds. With my hand to my chest, I gawk at the sight unfolding in front of me, a sledgehammer blasting the wall apart and Archer stepping through in a cloud of dust particles.

With my eyes wide, I take him in, his chest heaving, his tattooed muscles bulging his shirt more than they ever have.

"What the fuck, Archer?" I blurt out because that's the only thing I can think of. I didn't exactly pay it, but I won't be getting the security deposit back on this place anytime soon.

"You," Archer says as he catches his breath. "You didn't answer the door."

I blink a few times and process what he just said. "I didn't answer, so you busted the wall down?" I point at my wet hair. "I was in the shower."

He nods and shrugs. "Right, yeah, that makes sense."

"What if I wasn't home?"

"I, uh, I guess I would have waited until you came back."

"Waited for what? You told me you never wanted to see me ever again." Even saying it out loud reopens the wound I keep trying to mend. "What is this about?"

"I need to talk to you." His eyes frantically roam my body and suddenly I'm exposed and vulnerable, even more so than when I was holding that stupid fucking boom box over my head and confessing my feelings for him.

"You couldn't have called? You had to break the—"

Archer cuts me off. "Will you please shut up, for one minute?"

"Fine, sorry, by all means, the floor is yours." I sigh at the mess he made but realize I've done far worse and yet he's still here, standing in front of me, a beautiful ghost from my recent past. My heart aches and I'm not sure how much more I can take of his rejection.

"I have been in that apartment, rotting every single day since I last saw you, and every day before. I can't tell you the last time I slept, not deeply, and when I have, I dreamed of you, waking up in a cold sweat because it wasn't real. I have thought of and played things over and over in my head. I have theorized what happened, and I have done everything I can to shut it off, to shut you off. I stare at this fucking wall, and at this point, it's like it's been talking to me, taunting me, daring me to tear it down."

Archer pauses to loosen a breath and I take one with him like I had been holding it that entire time.

"I don't know what else to do. I can't keep this up. My work is suffering. My family is suffering. *I* am suffering."

He takes a cautious step, barely moving at all.

"I hate you, London. I hate your father, I hate what he did to you, what he did to me. I hate everything you stand for. I hate how you never shut up and how you leave destruction in your wake everywhere you go. I hate that your hair is all over my apartment, tangled in my laundry and clogging up my drain. I hate how the scent of you no longer remains on my sheets. I hate how you fight with me over everything and I hate how you think you're always right. I hate that you never listen to me, and you're so fucking hardheaded. I hate how independent you are and that you never really needed me. I hate that I have no idea what you're doing, or who you're with, and I hate that you've been living this close to me. I hate that I don't trust you, and I hate that despite hating you, you consume every single one of my thoughts. And I think the thing I hate the most is that I don't hate you at all."

Archer drops the sledgehammer and it thuds against the floor.

My heart stutters and I freeze, unable, unsure, unwilling to move.

"What I'm trying to say, my little tornado, is that I love you." Archer comes closer. "I can't stand another second without you in it. I don't know how to fix what's been broken, but I refuse to waste another moment not trying to figure out how."

He bridges almost every shred of distance between us and looks down at me. "Say something," Archer whispers. "Say anything."

I stare up at him, my heart pounding and settling all at once, everything I hoped and wished and prayed for coming to fruition in this very moment. "What took you so long?" My eyes well and I grow tired of the tears that won't seem to stop now that they've begun.

But this time, I have Archer to wipe them from my cheeks, his hands cupping them, his thumbs rubbing gently. "I'm so sorry, London. For the things I said, for the way I treated you, I'm sorry."

I shake my head. "You could have done worse and it would have been justified. I was the one who messed up, Archer. It's me who should be apologizing."

"You already did," he reminds me. "With a boom box."

I pinch my eyes shut, hating the memory that follows—him shutting his door and breaking my heart one final, but well-deserved, time.

"For the record," he adds. "It was the single most romantic thing anyone has ever done for me." Archer presses his lips to my nose, kissing me gently. "I wish I had reacted differently. I wish I realized then how much you mean to me."

I open my eyes and stare up at him, my heart beating evenly in my chest, all this feeling so fucking right despite how hard it was to get here.

"You can wreck my life anytime, my little tornado."

"Shut up and kiss me, big guy."

Archer grins before doing exactly that, his mouth meeting mine, something so drastically different in the way he touches me, the way our bodies melt into each other's, the way I want nothing more than to get closer to him, not out of the undeniable chemistry we've always shared, but because of something much deeper this time, something that I can only assume is love.

He backs me straight into the wall, my body hitting it with a thud. Archer's arm wraps around my waist and my hands slide up his neck and into his hair. He lifts me from the ground, his body pinning me there, the heat of us becoming one. We stay that way for a few minutes, not quite getting enough of each other, until the door to my apartment opens and the sound of it shutting pulls me away from the sexy man grinding into me.

With Archer still holding on to me, I settle my sight on Grace, who is holding a brown sack of food in her hand, her eyes wide.

"Well," she says. "Um. I see that I'm interrupting something here." Grace walks farther into the apartment and drops the bag on the counter. "I'm just going to leave this here, for when you two are *finished*." She puts her thumb and pinkie finger to her face, mimicking a phone, and mouths "Call me later," and slowly backs away, slipping out the door she entered through, not even waiting for an explanation.

I laugh into Archer's neck and sigh, taking him in. "Oops."

His dark eyes meet mine. "You hungry?"

"Not for what's in that bag."

Archer swallows and asks me, "What are you hungry for?"

"You," I tell him, not even a second passing between his question and my answer. "We've spent more time apart than we have together, and I don't want to waste another moment. I missed you, Archer. So fucking badly."

"Do you remember your safe word?"

"Bagels," I confirm.

"Good." His gaze scans my face. "Do I have permission to make love to you?"

I inhale and consider his words carefully. The last time we hooked up I told him not to, but it wasn't because that isn't what I wanted, it's because I was afraid of what things would turn into if we got too deep. But here we are, surviving the worst, finally showing up authentically for each other.

"I give you my permission," I mutter finally, no longer afraid of my feelings for him.

Archer's cheeks turn up as if he was afraid I might have a different response, and he continues holding me as he carries me into the bedroom and sets me on the edge of the bed. He kneels in front of me and unbuttons my jeans, guiding them over my ass and off my legs. He trails his hands up my now exposed skin, up my thighs. "You're so fucking beautiful, London." Archer shakes his head. "I can't believe you're mine."

I press my foot to his chest, stopping him. "Your what?"

His brows bunch together.

"Ask me, big guy."

Archer sighs dramatically but then clears his throat, standing completely up, holding my foot in his hands. "London, will you grant me the immense honor of being your boyfriend?"

"Hmm." I squint my eyes. "I mean...I guess so."

"You guess so?" Archer narrows his gaze. "You're really out here trying to break my heart, aren't you?"

"Archer," I say, no longer wanting to tease him, at least not like this. "Be my boyfriend."

He winks at me. "If you say so, *girlfriend*."

I release my leg and pull my shirt up over my head, tossing it onto the floor, no doubt driving him insane by my lack of tidiness. I reach for his waist, undoing his pants as he takes his shirt off to reveal his tattooed, chiseled stomach. My nipples perk at the sheer sight of him and I skim my hands up his chest, feeling the ridges of his abs, then going all the way down to grip his cock. I take him into my fists and lick his tip, looking up at him. Swirling the edge of him over my lips, I spread them and guide him into my mouth, moaning when he hardens against me.

Archer holds on to my head, his tattooed fingers in my hair, sliding me along his growing shaft. He takes a big breath and bucks his hips before saying, "Lie back on the bed."

I scoot on my elbows, my eyes never leaving his as he climbs onto the mattress with me and skims his fingers up my thigh and to my core.

"You're already so wet for me." He positions himself beside me and slips his fingers into my soaked hole, rubbing his thumb on my clit.

I turn toward him, keeping my legs apart and grabbing hold of his cock to take him into my mouth again. I moan onto him and revel in his thickness, and the way his hand rocks waves of pleasure over me. Hungrily, I suck every inch of him I can and whimper, my hips moving, my pussy clenching.

"That's it, baby. Fuck my fingers." Archer curves them upward and it's my undoing, my climax coming hard and fast and out of nowhere.

I stop sucking, his cock still in my mouth, and focus on my orgasm as it consumes me whole.

Archer moves away to climb between my legs, grabbing them with his tattooed arms and lowering his head to my center. With my body still shaking, he licks my pussy, his tongue dipping into my hole and trailing to my aching clit. He pinches it between his lips and releases, dragging his tongue all over it until I accidentally orgasm again, the second one beginning where the first one ended, with almost no break in between. He smiles against me and blows on my throbbing center before finishing his journey up my body.

"Fuck," I blurt out with my entire body quivering.

"Yeah?" Archer lines his cock up with my hole, sliding the tip around and pushing into me, slowly at first, and then all at once. "You were made for me, little tornado." His voice is thick and gravelly and I want nothing more than to hear him tell me all the ways I was made for him.

"Keep talking," I pant, and reach for his face.

He kisses me, his tongue darting into my mouth, one of his hands holding him up and the other braced on the side of my face. Archer breaks away. "You like hearing someone other than yourself talk for a change?" He rocks his hips, in and out, slow and steady, the buildup painfully decadent.

"Mm-hmm," I moan.

"Your body is mine, baby. Your mouth." Archer plants his lips on mine. "Your skin." He kisses my cheek. "Your tight little pussy." He groans and pumps into me. "Your every breath." He grabs my right leg with his left arm and spreads me wide. "Every fucking whimper, every moan, every desire, every dirty little thought, I want them all." His brown eyes bore into mine. "For as long as you'll have me, London. You are mine, and I am yours." He thrusts into me. "Do you hear me? Do you understand me?"

I nod and bite my lip, my fingers dragging down his chest.

"Say it," he all but growls.

"I'm yours," I say breathlessly. "I'm yours. All of me, I'm yours."

"God, I missed this." He looks down to watch his cock penetrate me. "I missed you." Archer turns his attention back to me and lets go of my leg. He grabs a pillow and positions it under my ass, pivoting me up toward him and leaning closer.

"Fuck, Archer, you feel so fucking good. I'm not going to last." I drag him toward me and dig my nails into his back.

"Then don't." He maintains his slow pace, almost slowing down even more, giving me a chance to truly feel every inch of him as he makes sweet fucking love to me, my heart just as full as my lustful pussy. "Come for me, little tornado. Come with me." Archer moans and crashes his mouth onto mine, desperately eating up every noise that escapes me as I pull him into me, his cock growing even harder as it spreads me open, the sensation both pain and endless pleasure.

Archer thrusts deeper, his cock spilling into me and my pussy clenching around him, our orgasms hitting us in tandem. I cry out into his mouth, and he moans loudly, his heavenly sounds making my orgasm somehow more intense.

I tremble under him and he pumps his hips slower and slower, until we're left there, glistening with each other's sweat and struggling to catch our breaths.

Archer rests his forehead against mine and kisses my nose. "I love you."

I tilt my head up, forcing him to look at me, my gaze darting back and forth between his eyes. "I love you, Archer Sin. I've never been surer of anything in my entire life. I love you."

I don't know what the future holds for us, I don't know if we can ever truly repair the damage that has been done, but I do know one thing for certain. As long as my heart continues to beat in my chest, it will belong to this beautifully grumpy man.

EPILOGUE

London

Archer and I have been back together three weeks and two days.

I mean, that's if I'm counting.

And I'm counting.

Because being with Archer is worth keeping track of, and for the first time in my life, I finally feel at home, at peace, and safe. With myself, with a man.

I never thought I'd find that, and I'm beyond grateful Archer gave me a second chance—gave us a second chance.

"What's got you smiling?" Archer asks me from his spot at his computer, his tattooed fingers resting on the keys.

"Nothing," I lie, and put my arm over the back of the couch, turning fully toward him. "What happened to the *no falling in love* thing?"

"What?"

"When I first got here, you set some ground rules. One of which was no falling in love."

Archer grins. "I guess some rules are meant to be broken." He returns to his task but I stay focused on him.

"Tell me how you do it."

"Do what?" His brows bunch together and because I can, I rise from my spot and walk over to him.

Before, when we were just roommates, I wouldn't act on those impulses, those urges to be near him. At least not in an unfiltered way. Sure, I gravitated in his vicinity, but not like this.

I'm his girlfriend now, so I'm allowed to invade his personal space.

Putting my arm around his shoulder, I nod to the computer. "How did you stalk me?"

"You're saying it like it's past tense," Archer scoffs and pulls me into his lap, his hand resting on my bare knee. His touch is warm and electric and sends a shock wave straight to my center.

I've never wanted a man as badly as I want Archer Sin—and boy am I lucky I can have him whenever I want.

"Come on," I tell him. "Show me."

Archer kisses the side of my head. "You really want to know?"

"Don't make me beg."

Archer sighs and leans forward to type a sequence of buttons I can't quite keep track of. A bunch of screens pop up, some loading, some with code still on them, and some with camera feeds. "Traffic cameras are cake to hack into. Those are everywhere. There aren't many dead spots in the city, so tracking someone is super simple. And most businesses have some sort of security or surveillance system that uses their Wi-Fi, which is child's play. Once you get the hang of how to get in, it's pretty easy. Some have audio, some are in black and white, some have color. It just varies depending on what they're using. I haven't come across anything I haven't been able to hack into. Anything with a Wi-Fi connection or a camera is fair game. Cell phones, smart TVs, computers, baby monitors, you name it, I can get access to it."

I watch in awe at the tabs displayed, wondering if there's anything I could ever hide from Archer if he truly wanted to find it out. He already knows the worst of my secrets, I guess there isn't anything I wouldn't be willing to share with him.

"And..." Archer clears his throat. "Since I'm being honest right now. There are trackers on almost everything you own. Your phone, your purses, your shoes." He swallows harshly like he's a bit embarrassed by what he's saying. "Some of your jewelry, too."

I breathe in deeply, my shoulders rising with it. "Well, I mean, that explains a lot."

"Are you mad?" He breaks his attention from the computer to look at me.

"No." I cup his cheek in my hand, my thumb running along his skin. "But you better not be stalking any other women. I draw the line at me. I know you're an untouchable Sin brother, but I will castrate you if you—"

Archer cuts me off, pressing his lips to mine, kissing me in such a passionate way that I lose track of my thoughts. He breaks away, resting his forehead on mine. "I don't want anyone other than you, London, I swear. I give you my word."

"Good." I give him a brief peck. "What else can you hack into? Can you get me some of the money my dad had tied up with the Feds when he died?"

"Let me see." Archer scoots us a little closer, going to work typing on the screen. It takes him two minutes to pull up five of my father's accounts, all of them frozen.

"I can't believe the bastard took everything with him."

Archer lets out a small chuckle. "Don't worry, little tornado, I've got this."

Ten minutes later, Archer has managed to pull all but a tiny amount of money out of each of the accounts, rerouting it to various offshore accounts and finally depositing it into another, totaling over twenty-three million dollars.

I blink at the screen, not quite following completely. "What did you just do?"

"I got you the money." He says it so matter-of-fact, like he expects me to understand what he just did. "Long story short, I ran his money through a few different businesses to legitimize it, made a fake will, put everything as payable to you upon death, and put it in an account with your name on it. It's yours now, legally. And because of the way I set it up, there are no state or federal taxes that need to be paid."

My mouth drops open at the zeros staring at me in my new bank account. "Holy shit, I have never been more attracted to you in my entire life."

"Yeah?" Archer squeezes my thigh and grins. "It's just twenty-three million, though, I can give you more."

"Shut up and kiss me, big boy." I shake my head and smile at him before crashing my mouth onto his, his tongue parting my lips.

He snakes his hand farther up my thigh and under my skirt. My legs part, desperate for him to keep going.

Archer doesn't stop. He keeps inching closer and closer until the tip of his finger hooks under my panties and is sliding over my wetness.

I moan into his mouth and wrap my arms around his neck,

kissing him deeper as he penetrates me. He obliges me by putting another finger in, curving them upward and rocking them along my G-spot. I nearly tremble under his touch, my body coming alive for him. I tighten around his fingers and quiver when he brushes his thumb over my aching clit.

Archer weaves his free hand up my back to my neck and grips a handful of my hair, dragging me away from his kiss. His eyes meet mine and I'm damn glad, because this means he's going to let me orgasm soon. If the last few weeks have taught me anything, it's that Archer loves to watch me come undone for him.

He tightens his hold on the back of my head and rocks his fingers inside of me like he's mastered the art of fucking me with every part of him. "Anything you want, London. It's yours." He continues to finger me. "You want money, it's yours. I'll take you anywhere, give you anything. You want the world to fucking burn, I'll light the match. You have me—mind, body, and soul—in this life and the next. A million times over."

My climax heightens with every word he speaks.

"My heart, my cock, my fingers...all yours." He tilts my head toward him as I gasp and moan. His nose grazes mine. "Now come for me, little tornado. Show me what a beautiful mess you can make."

He hits my clit and G-spot at just the right fucking angle to send me flying over the edge, my orgasm hitting so hard, I lose vision for a second as I shatter under his heavenly wrath. My legs shake and he kisses me, swallowing every one of my moans. He doesn't stop moving his fingers, not even while I tremble uncontrollably, pure bliss consuming me. Archer slows his movements and smiles against my mouth. "That's my girl." He carefully pumps his fingers in and out a few more times before withdrawing and sliding them around my throbbing clit. Archer tugs my panties back over my pussy and brings his hand to his mouth, tasting his soaked fingers. "The finest delicacy known to man."

I catch my breath and will my heart to stop racing and the world to stop spinning. Every time I think I'd be used to him making me come this intensely, but each time is unlike the last.

The second I'm almost certain I can return to somewhat normal,

I almost jump out of his arms when the door to his apartment flies open and Seven steps through.

"Shit," Archer mutters, and glances at his watch. "I lost track of the days."

"Smells like sex in here," Seven announces loudly.

I manage to hop off Archer's lap and stand without my legs giving out, forcing a polite smile at the rest of his siblings that follow Seven in. Dusting off the wrinkles in my skirt, I walk barefoot over to the kitchen and reach for the cabinet where the plates are, but Archer beats me there, swatting my hand away.

"Go sit down, little tornado. I've got this."

I fold my arms over my chest and glare at him. "I can help."

He presses a quick kiss on my lips. "I know you can, but that doesn't mean you have to." Archer gently pushes me. "Go sit at the table. I'll be right behind you."

"I wish you were right behind me." I wink at him and smile as a smirk forms on his handsome face. "I made you blush."

His eyes darken and I wish like hell I could read whatever filth that's on his mind.

"There's my firecracker." Seven interrupts us and slaps his hands on the counter. "How are we?"

I sense the shift in Archer and react accordingly, moving to get Seven away from him. Archer is still pissed at Seven, and at Leo, and despite reasoning with him, I can't quite get him to forgive them yet. I'm not even family and he gave me a second chance, I don't know why he can't do the same for them. Although, knowing those two, it's probably their five-billionth time stabbing Archer in the back.

Seven leans in close and lowers his voice. "You talk to Grace yet?"

"I'm working on it," I tell him, and guide him over to the table, pulling out a chair for him to sit in, at the far side where I know Archer won't be. "These things require finessing."

Seven shoves his bottom lip out, pouting like a damn baby.

"Cut that out. Grace wants a man, not a child," I tease him.

He immediately straightens in his seat and adjusts his black satin shirt, the top two buttons undone and showing off his tattooed chest. "How's this?" Seven shakes his head not even four whole seconds later. "Ah, who am I kidding?" He slumps in the chair and throws his arm over the back of the one next to him.

"I was almost impressed, Sev." I slap his shoulder and turn toward the rest of the family as they settle into their respective chairs.

"London." August nods a hello and thumbs something into his phone before setting it on the table and taking off his suit jacket. Does he not realize that family dinners don't exactly require formal attire? Unless that's all he owns. Suddenly, I can't picture August in anything other than suits, even when he goes to bed, or gets in the shower, or goes for a swim in a pool.

I bite down a laugh as Ivy's burning stare draws my attention. "Hey, Ivy."

"I see you two resolved things," she says, not even trying to hide her annoyance.

Archer approaches from beside her and sets a stack of plates on the table. "We have, which means you need to get that stick out of your ass, Sister."

She doesn't get a chance to respond, not verbally—with her eyes she speaks a thousand words at once, none of them nice—because Leo comes over and opens his mouth.

"London, hey, how are you?" He doesn't wait for an answer before turning toward Archer. "Arch, buddy, have you forgiven me yet? I could really use your help, please."

Archer, stone-cold, ignores him and passes a plate across the table to Seven. "Here."

"Oh, so you're talking to him but you're not talking to me?" Leo blurts out.

"A word?" I grab Leo's arm and tug him away from the table, ignoring the looks of everyone else as I take it upon myself to insert myself in business that probably isn't mine to deal with.

His muscles bunch under my touch but he complies, letting me lead him out of direct earshot. Leo fixes the collar of his white button-up, his entire aesthetic something straight out of *rich man Pinterest*. I hate how attractive he is, how attractive each one of the siblings are, especially because they're not even actually related. Well, Seven and Ivy are, but still, the point stands. How is it possible to have this good of genes between this misfit bunch? It's no wonder people are intimidated by them; they're nearly too pretty for their own good.

"You have to stop nagging him," I tell Leo, hoping he'll understand. "I know you guys are family and you have a way of doing things, but I don't think it's working, Leo. If anything, it's making him want to help you even less."

Leo sighs and runs his hand through his hair, the disheveled locks falling over his brow. "We fight. It's what we do. He's usually over it by now." He narrows his green gaze. "Then you had to come along."

I shove him playfully. "You were an asshole long before I got here."

"Touché." He chews on his lip and glances at the table. "I'll try to do it your way. But could you at least put in a good word for me?"

"What do you even want him to do?"

"Track down the woman that robbed me."

"To do what with her?"

Leo shrugs. "I just want to talk to her, that's all...and get back what she stole from me."

This time, it's me that glares at him. "You're rich, Leo. Replace whatever it is she took and I'm sure your ego will repair itself."

"You don't get it, she—"

"Everything okay over here?" Archer comes over and puts his arm around me like he's marking his territory.

I lean into him. "Leo was just telling me what he wants to get you for Christmas."

"Christmas isn't for another couple of months," Archer says.

"Trust the process, big boy." I pat his chest and hope he chooses to let it go. I don't want to watch him get into a fistfight with another one of his brothers. As hot as the whole bad-boy thing is, I draw the line at unnecessarily destroying his apartment again. Seven and Archer made one hell of a mess when they beat each other senseless.

Plus, the damage Archer made when he blew the wall out between my apartment and his, and we finally just got rid of all the debris in the aftermath of creating a doorway between the two. I still haven't figured out what I'm going to tell Camille, but that's a problem for another day, and Archer claims he'll handle it, since he's the one who tore it down. I guess that's one of the perks of having a seemingly endless supply of money—there isn't a problem you can't fix by throwing some cash at it.

Archer and I return to the table and slide into our chairs, him grabbing hold of the leg of mine and scooting me closer to him. He opens a box of noodles and puts some on my plate before giving himself some too.

I give him an egg roll and take one for myself, making sure to hand him a packet of the duck sauce I've come to recognize that he likes.

"Thanks," he says with a soft smile, taking it from me.

To be seen is to be loved, and boy is that all Archer ever does—sees me. When I'm mad, grouchy, hungry, tired, happy, sad, hyper, annoying...there isn't a version that has turned him away, not even the one where I betrayed him. That is a mistake I will never repeat. I am lucky Archer has forgiven me, I won't take that for granted again. He hurt me, too, but he was justified in what he did, meanwhile I was just being a selfish asshole.

August clears his throat and I don't think there's a single one of us that doesn't tear our eyes away from whatever we were focusing on to give him our attention. August is a man of few words, but when he speaks, he commands authority. Not like the rest of the guys do, in a threatening manner, but in a respectful way.

"I was contacted by a gaming owner, Leo. He wanted to set up a meeting to discuss a possible merger."

Leo shakes his head and I already know where this is headed. This is the guy who ambushed him at the gala Grace put on. The one that Leo said he'd never go into business with because of how *clean* he ran things. I passively suggested killing him, but apparently that wasn't a viable option.

"My secretary informed me that he has been quite persistent," August adds.

"Yeah, he calls nonstop. Shows up unexpectedly. Won't take no for an answer." Leo rummages through a few boxes of Chinese takeout, settling on some brown meat thing.

Archer, as if he can sense my energy, puts his hand on my knee.

I don't care if people eat meat around me, but I can't help the strange visceral reaction from time to time when I see it. Archer stopped consuming it completely, and despite reassuring him that it is okay, he insists that it isn't a big deal. Considering I eat most of my meals with him, that doesn't allow for much meat consumption. We've gone to dinner and have gone out with Grace, but Archer tends to make sure other people aren't around us. I sort of forgot what it was like to be around meat. Still, I can't help but think about that man my father dismembered and fed to a pig.

Archer's jaw tenses and I put my hand on his because I know damn well he's about to make a scene.

"It's fine," I whisper. "Really."

"Why don't you kill him?" Seven blurts out, not surprising any of us.

Leo chuckles. "That's what a friend told me to do, too." He shoots a quick glance my direction.

Seven shrugs. "We could do it right now. I don't have anything going on. We could be done in an hour. Two, tops. Tell me his name."

"Seven," Ivy snaps. "Seriously? Do you have no decorum?"

"I'm going to be real with you, baby sis. I have no idea what that means." Seven stares across the table at her. "Is that, like, a made-up word or something? You trying to act all smart? Make me look stupid? Is that what this is about? The fuck do you know about decorations."

Ivy doesn't soften her glare as she keeps her eyes on Seven. "Decorum."

"Potato, potahto."

"Can you stop talking about murder at the dinner table?" Ivy asks Seven.

"They can talk about it but I can't? How is that fair?" Seven pouts.

"When was anyone else talking about murder?"

Leo stands abruptly, holding his finger out to silence us. "I have to take this. Shut up for a second, guys." He puts the phone to his ear, his gaze frantically scanning at nothing in particular. "What do you mean? You can't be serious. What the fuck? How? When? Why am I just now getting a call? Are you fucking serious? I swear to everything holy, if this is some sick prank, I will have your— Yes, yes, I understand. Okay. I'll be right there."

Archer remains unfazed in his spot next to me, not wanting to give in that he's curious in the slightest at what that might have been about, but the rest of us, we're eagerly waiting for Leo to give us any indication of what's going on.

Leo lowers his arm, and for the first time since I've known him, he seems truly fucking haunted. "The casino was robbed."

"Isn't that what insurance is for?" Seven asks a pretty valid question.

"Not for what I had hidden underneath." Leo takes a deep breath, his eyes lingering on Archer, who still won't look in his direction. "Even still, you won't help me?"

Archer blinks a few times as if he's contemplating his response carefully, and I hate that I can already tell what is about to come out of his mouth isn't going to go over well, not with Leo, who clearly needs him. "I told you not to mess with the diamonds. I told you not to mess with the art." Archer rises from his seat, finally meeting Leo's desperate gaze. "I told you not to mess with the jewelry, the cars, the guns. What else, Leo? You never listen to me. And you have the audacity to beg me to help you? This is your mess, fix it yourself."

Leo keeps his face straight and slowly nods. He leaves the table and doesn't bother looking back.

"Leo," Ivy calls out. "Don't go. Let's talk this out, like a family."

Leo pauses at the door. "Seven, you with me?"

"Fuck this shit." Seven shoves his plate forward and takes off after Leo, leaving the rest of us behind in gaping silence.

I don't dare say a word, not because I don't want to, but because I know it's not my place. I've inflicted enough damage since I showed up here earlier this year.

My only option is to accept they'll figure this out on their own.

Leo takes one final glance over his shoulder at the door. His sight is trained on Archer as he says, "I'll remember this."

BONUS
Archer

Blankly staring at my computer, I realize I haven't done anything productive in the last thirty-seven minutes. The screen comes into focus, as do the camera feeds around my apartment building. London hasn't left today, and I don't know why I care, why I bother checking, why I can't stop myself from wondering what the fuck she's doing.

It's eating at me and driving me fucking insane.

I spin in my chair and take in the wall separating us. The few measly inches of drywall, some studs, probably electrical cables. That's it. I walk over to it, not really meaning to, and press my hand on the cold, hard surface. My heart aches and I want to rip it out of my chest so it stops reminding me of her.

I made my choice. I pushed her away. She lied to me. She betrayed me. How could I ever get past that? But how can I ever get over this if I can't get her out of my fucking head? I don't want her, but fuck, do I need her.

But the more I recall every moment with her, I'm not sure I don't *want* her, too.

She's frustrating. So much so, I can hardly stand her.

And somehow that only makes me more captivated, like she's the sun and I'm merely a pathetic planet stuck in her orbit.

I leave the wall separating us and go to my bedroom, plopping face down onto the mattress and letting out a muffled groan into the comforter. I take a deep breath, the bed no longer smelling of her, making me furious that I don't actually want to escape her. I pound my fist into the sheets and roll over, blinking up at the ceiling.

"Get it together, Archer. She's just a girl. This isn't the end of the world."

But then why does it feel like it?

The image of her standing outside my doorway with the boom box over her head comes back into my mind and I replay it over and over. As much as it pained me to see her, to hear her, it hurt me more to shut the door in her face. I didn't want to hurt her, to reject her, but how can I protect us both at the same time?

Maybe I made the wrong choice. Maybe I should have taken her into my arms and told her it was okay, that I forgive her, that we can get past this. But can we? How can we come back from something so fucked up? I let her in once and she broke my heart, what would stop her from doing it again?

Isn't that what love is all about? Putting yourself out there, fully knowing you can be torn to shreds, but taking it because the risk outweighs the potential reward? And as I lie here and trace the outline of the ceiling with my gaze, I can't help but wonder if I'm willing to gamble my heart for the possibility of getting my happily ever after.

Is it really a gamble when she's already stolen it anyway?

Being with her temporarily would be better than this misery of being without her.

I just hope it isn't too late, that I haven't pushed her so far away that I can't get her back.

"Fuck," I blurt out, and sit up, rushing out my bedroom and out the front door. I don't think for another second, I simply go straight to her apartment and pound on the door. When she doesn't answer, I hit my fist on it again, this time harder. "London, it's me. Please let me in. I need to talk to you." My heart thuds in my chest and my stomach knots at the finality of it all, that I may have actually lost her forever because I'm a fucking idiot and rejected her. I can't imagine how hard it was for her to put herself out there like that, and what did I do? I shut her out. Just like she's doing to me right now.

I rest my fist and my forehead on her door and consider kicking it open but remember the time I already did that, and came back after to reinforce it so it wouldn't come down so easily. How was I supposed to know that would come back to bite me in the ass? I push off the door, going down the hallway and into my apartment, slamming the door shut behind me. Rubbing my hand over my jaw, I consider my options. This can't be it. I refuse to believe that.

Marching straight over to the closet in the corner, I rummage until I find exactly what I'm looking for. A sledgehammer. I had used it to demo part of the apartment after I thought Madison had died, and left it in the closet just in case I ever needed it again. I say a silent thank-you to past Archer and grip the handle, dragging it out and toward the wall separating us.

Licking my lips, I size the wall up and attempt to process what I'm about to do.

"This is fucking crazy." I loosen my grip. "You're crazy, Archer." I drop the handle, letting it rattle onto the floor. "You're losing it, man. What am I thinking? I can't break the fucking wall down."

I walk away, putting some space between me and my stupid plan. But the farther I get, the more I realize this is what I have to do. I can't fucking stand having it between us. I can't be away from her. Not for another fucking second.

So I do the most insane thing I've ever done and grab hold of the sledgehammer, winding it up and slamming it against the wall. Debris flies everywhere and I come to terms with the fact that I cannot go back, not now, not ever. I reel back again, hitting it once more, and yank it toward me, ripping a section of the drywall with it. I thrust it sideways, blasting through some of the studs, wood flying all over, not a second of regret coming over me. I thought London was a mess, but she's nothing compared to this.

I keep at it, sweat forming on my brow, my chest heaving with adrenaline, my fingers digging into the handle as I swing and swing and swing until I create a gaping hole between my apartment and hers. I step through it in a cloud of dust, my gaze hazy as I settle my sight on her, on London, on my little tornado.

Desperate for her to speak, I worry that I did all of this for nothing, that I've taken things too far and there's no room for forgiveness in her heart. If only she'd say something, anything, to give me some kind of indication of what is going through her head, then maybe I can try to make this right.

"What the fuck, Archer?"

Usually, when I hack into things, getting in is the hardest part, but now that I'm inside her apartment, I realize this is the complete opposite of what I'm used to dealing with.

"You." I try to catch my breath. "You didn't answer the door."

"I didn't answer, so you busted the wall down?" She points at her wet hair. "I was in the shower."

I hadn't considered that, *oops*. I wasn't exactly thinking rationally. "Right, yeah, that makes sense."

"What if I wasn't home?"

"I, uh, I guess I would have waited until you came back."

"Waited for what? You told me you never wanted to see me ever again. What is this about?"

"I need to talk to you," I tell her, desperate for her to understand, to please just give me a chance to explain.

"You couldn't have called? You had to break the—"

I cut her off because if I don't, I'm going to explode with everything I need to tell her. "Will you please shut up, for one minute?"

"Fine, sorry, by all means, the floor is yours."

"I have been in that apartment, rotting every single day since I last saw you, and every day before. I can't tell you the last time I slept, not deeply, and when I have, I dreamed of you, waking up in a cold sweat because it wasn't real. I have thought of and played things over and over in my head. I have theorized what happened, and I have done everything I can to shut it off, to shut you off. I stare at this fucking wall, and at this point, it's like it's been talking to me, taunting me, daring me to tear it down."

I release a breath and swallow down the harsh possibility that all of this could be for nothing.

"I don't know what else to do," I continue. "I can't keep this up. My work is suffering. My family is suffering. *I* am suffering."

I take the smallest step, afraid to move too much and scare her away forever.

"I hate you, London. I hate your father, I hate what he did to you, what he did to me. I hate everything you stand for. I hate how you never shut up and how you leave destruction in your wake everywhere you go. I hate that your hair is all over my apartment, tangled in my laundry and clogging up my drain. I hate how the scent of you no longer remains on my sheets. I hate how you fight with me over everything and I hate how you think you're always right. I hate that you never listen to me, and you're so fucking hardheaded. I hate how independent you are and that you never really needed me. I hate that I have no idea what you're doing, or who you're with, and I hate that you've been living this close to me. I hate that I don't trust you, and I hate that despite hating you, you consume every single one of my thoughts. And I think the thing I hate the most is that I don't hate you at all."

I let the sledgehammer fall from my hands and it thuds against the floor.

"What I'm trying to say, my little tornado, is that I love you." Hesitantly, I move closer. "I can't stand another second without you in it. I don't know how to fix what's been broken, but I refuse to waste another moment not trying to figure out how."

I close the distance between us and peer down at her. "Say something," I whisper, my heart aching in her silence. "Say anything."

She takes far too long to say "What took you so long?" and her eyes well with tears.

I wipe them from her cheeks, my hands grateful to touch her again. "I'm so sorry, London. For the things I said, for the way I treated you, I'm sorry."

She shakes her head. "You could have done worse, and it would have been justified. I was the one who messed up, Archer. It's me who should be apologizing."

"You already did," I tease her. "With a boom box."

She pinches her eyes shut and I grow guilty of how long it took me to come to my senses.

"For the record," I confess. "It was the single most romantic thing anyone has ever done for me." I kiss the tip of her nose. "I wish I had reacted differently. I wish I realized then how much you mean to me."

She opens her bright green eyes and stares up at me, my whole world coming into focus.

"You can wreck my life anytime, my little tornado."

"Shut up and kiss me, big guy."

Relief washes over me, and I grow certain that everything is going to be okay, that we're going to be okay—even if it takes forever.

EXCLUSIVE BONUS PAPERBACK CONTENT

"SURPRISE"

London

I slip the black pleated miniskirt over my ass and secure it at my waist. A gift from Archer. But at this point, what isn't? Nearly every single piece of clothing, jewelry, or handbag in my possession is from him. For weeks, I tried to deter him from spoiling me senseless, until he convinced me that it made him happy, and who am I to deny him of that?

"You're really not going to tell me where we're going?" I ask, and settle on the gold Dior earrings he reluctantly bought me.

"*They're only $7,500, London,*" he had said, and then decided I needed the matching bracelet, necklace, and a purse to go with it.

Despite the fact that Archer managed to deposit over twenty million dollars of my dead father's frozen money into a bank account for me, he hardly ever lets me use it. I haven't quite processed the fact that my father is gone, his money is mine, and I am free of him for good. I've gone my entire life living under his thumb, and even after he died, I was still haunted by him. At least, until Archer put a bullet in Joe Vito and freed me.

Archer leans in the doorframe, watching me get ready like it's his favorite TV show. "I'm really not going to tell you. It's a *surprise.* Keyword *surprise.*"

"Can I have a hint?" I draw my bottom lip between my teeth and bat my eyelashes. "Please?"

Archer swallows harshly. "You keep looking at me like that and you won't ever find out."

"Like what?" I feign ignorance, turning toward the mirror, bending at the waist, and pretending to check my makeup.

"You know exactly what you're doing."

For a split second I'm not sure if Archer is going to bite, but he does, kicking off the wall and coming closer, his presence towering over me from behind. His hands find my waist—soft, gentle, firm. The same hands that have touched every inch of my body. He slides one up my back, the other tugging me into his groin.

Our eyes meet in the reflection, lust laced with every clipped breath, the inability to ever be satiated plaguing us both ever since we got back together.

He runs his fingers up my thigh, around my front, inching closer...closer...until he stops.

I inch my legs apart, daring him, begging him, to continue.

Archer clicks his tongue. "You're being a bad girl, little tornado."

I back into him, his cock throbbing against me but still concealed in his black dress slacks. "You going to punish me, big boy?"

Something evil glimmers in his eyes and he takes a small step back while keeping his hold on my body. He lowers onto his knees, dragging down my panties in one fell swoop, his mouth deliciously close to where I ache for it to be.

"What do you want me to do to you?"

"You know what I want, Archer."

"I know I do, but I want to hear you say it."

"Archer, please..." I all but pant.

He skims his nose up my leg, his tongue following where it leaves off, finding its way along my eager pussy.

My breath catches and I close my eyes, ready for him to make me climax on his mouth for what must be the millionth time this week. He slides his lips over my folds, parting them with his hot tongue and dipping inside of me. I whimper and lean against him, fucking his face slowly, him touching me exactly the way he knows I like. He holds onto my hips and guides me onto him, picking up his pace and moaning along my soaked pussy.

But just as my core tightens, the pleasure so damn good my vision blurs, he abruptly stops. Slowly, Archer drags my panties up and conceals my ever-aching hole, leaving a soft kiss where his mouth once was. He licks his lips, rises to his feet, and adjusts his cock in his pants. "What were you saying about punishment?"

My jaw drops. "You're not serious."

"Deadly." He winks at me in the mirror and wipes me off his cheek, sucking the remains off his thumb. "Come on, babe, we don't want to be late."

I want to protest, to throw a temper tantrum and demand that he makes me come, or threaten to do it myself, since he won't, but as much as I want the release, I know he'll follow through before the day is done. Archer gets off on getting me off, and he may be playing tough right now, but he'll have me screaming his name as he finishes me off soon enough.

Plus, the only thing he did mention about this surprise is that I would enjoy it, so maybe he's going to fuck me whenever we get there.

I've never been much for patience, but for him, I'd wait forever.

"Fine," I say while rolling my eyes and straightening my skirt. "But don't think I won't forget this." I apply a layer of Dior lipstick and blot my lips on a tissue, Archer keeping his eyes on me the entire time. "What?" I ask, and walk past him.

"You're stunning." He pauses and adds, "I could watch you get ready until the day I die."

"I don't take *that* long to get ready." My heels click across the hard floor of my apartment and to the gaping hole between his place and mine. I wait, because if I don't, Archer will scold me for not holding his hand while I step through, despite him having removed the debris and opened up the area more. We still haven't figured out what we're going to do about him destroying Camille's apartment, but that's a problem for another day.

Archer stands by the front door and crosses his tattooed arms over his chest.

I go into his kitchen, the bedroom, and traipse across his living room, not finding what I came over here for. I recall the night before, trying to retrace my steps and locate my missing purse.

He clears his throat and I ignore him, not wanting him to remind me that we're running late for whatever he has in store for me.

"London."

"Archer," I say, my back still toward him.

"Turn around."

"Why? Want to rub it in that I'm always making us late and that if I just put things back where they belong, I wouldn't have to search for them?"

I feel his presence without witnessing him move, his ability to be stealth-like no doubt concerning for anyone who isn't me.

"I tease you, London. Because that's what we do, we bicker and poke fun at each other. But don't you dare for a second think I'll ever tire from picking up your messes." He reaches around me, my bag outstretched in his giant palm. "Wreck my life anytime, little tornado."

I spin on my heel and let his arms engulf me while staring up at him. "I love you."

"I know." He grins and presses a quick kiss on my nose. "Now come on, we don't want to keep our company waiting."

"Company?" That perks me right up and slightly distracts from the fact that he didn't say it back.

Archer's hand finds the small of my back as he leads me to the door; the second we're on the other side, he slides his fingers around mine.

His driver nods stiffly at Archer once we're outside, and he opens the back door for us.

"Evening." I offer him a polite smile, and he doesn't return the gesture. Archer has told me time and time again not to take it personal, that he doesn't get paid to smile, but I'm determined to break through that thick facade eventually. He's never been mean to me; he just doesn't do anything other than exactly what's expected of him.

"I could pay him more to smile at you," Archer says, and settles into the seat next to me.

"I'd rather earn it," I tell him, and consider who we might be meeting. "Is it Grace and Leo?"

Archer perks up a brow. "What?"

"*Company.*"

"Oh." He chuckles. "No."

"Grace and Seven?"

"No. And for the record, I'm not speaking to either of them."

"You're going to have to forgive your brothers eventually."

"I'd rather not."

"Hmm." I press my finger to my lips. "August and Ivy?"

"Why do you say their names like they're *together*?"

"There's a definite vibe."

Archer narrows his gaze. "There is not."

I shrug because arguing with him about two of his siblings having the hots for each other is not what I want to get into right now.

He puts his arm over the back of the seat, his body shifting toward me, like two magnets that can't fathom being apart.

"Is it anyone in your family?"

"No."

"I give up, I don't know who it could be." I plant my hand on his thigh. "Wait, is it Taylor Swift?"

"It's not, but would you rather I see if she's available?"

"Maybe. Tell me who we're meeting first, and I'll let you know for sure."

"Trust me, I think you'll be satisfied."

"As satisfied as I was five minutes ago?"

He reaches out, his hand cupping my cheek. "I promise to make you orgasm later, okay? A few times, to make up for it."

My cheeks turn up into a smile. "What happened to punishing me?"

"It's no fun when it punishes me too."

The rest of the car ride to wherever we're going is uneventful. I give up on trying to guess who we're meeting and melt into Archer as I mindlessly scroll through cat videos on my cell. He catches up on something work related, my brain incapable of figuring out the code he's typing on his heavily encrypted phone.

We pull up to a place Archer has taken me twice before, an Italian restaurant in the cutest neighborhood. I try to hide my excitement, but it's hard when this outing involves wine and pasta.

He hops out first, coming around to my door, taking my hand, and helping me out of the back seat.

"Such a gentleman."

"For you, always." Archer doesn't let go of me, not even when we approach the building and a worker opens the door for us. He does manage to slip a hundred-dollar bill into the person's hand, and another into the palm of the hostess who greets us immediately.

The entire restaurant is empty except for the waitstaff and us, our dinner guests not here yet, either.

"Are we early?" I ask him. "I thought you said we were running late."

He pulls out my chair and pushes it in when I sit down. "We're on time. I told you we were running late so we weren't."

"What you're saying is I could have had that orgasm after all..."

Archer takes the seat next to me, leans over, and whispers, "In due time, little tornado," before planting a soft kiss on my cheek.

A young waiter comes over with a bottle of wine, extending it out to Archer and pouring some in a glass for him. Archer sniffs, swirls it around, and has a taste, deciding that it's good enough to be served. He gives him money, too—Archer's pockets endlessly deep.

I'm taking a long sip of the decadent wine when my eyes betray me, showing me someone from my past, someone I never thought I'd see again. My heart stutters, but not in the same way it did when I saw Madison, or when Joe Vito tried to ruin my life, but in a completely, utterly blissful kind of way.

"Cora," I mutter as I rise to my feet, rushing around the table toward her, both of us ignoring our boyfriends and wrapping our arms around each other. I hug her tightly, taking in her fruity perfume. "I...I can't believe it." Tears well, but I do everything I can not to destroy my makeup.

"London." Cora finally lets me go, holding me at arm's length. "You thought you could stay away from me? Never. I've been waiting for the right time, the safe time, to come and visit." She flits her gaze at Silver. "He kept telling me I couldn't, but that didn't stop me from nagging him every chance I got." She pulls me in again. "I'm so glad you're okay. And that you found someone hot." That last bit is a whisper meant only for us.

Archer and Silver shake hands, but I wouldn't care if they stripped naked and did cartwheels, because Cora is here. One of the only true friends I've had—one of the only people who understands what it means to escape the wrath of my father. We cheated the devil, and we did it together. That's not something you can ever explain to someone who didn't live through it themselves.

I glance behind her. "Are the other guys with you? Where are Alec and Miller?"

"Back home. They couldn't get away. You'll have to settle for me and Silver."

"You kidding? I feel like I've died and gone to heaven. I can't believe this...I'm so..."

"Surprised?" Archer finishes my sentence, a smug look on his handsome face.

My heart swells, adoration for him growing, the desire for him to return that *I love you* earlier erased, because sometimes, it doesn't need to be said. He shows it often, in every single caring and thoughtful gesture. He sees me, really sees me, and I can't fathom that he's the man I get to love forever.

And just in case I didn't know, didn't feel it, he mouths those three words anyway.

"London," Silver says, his voice stern and thick and aged like the fine wine we're drinking tonight.

I let go of Cora long enough to hug Silver, burying my face in his broad chest. "Thank you. For everything."

He pats my back, no doubt unsure of what to do with such a display of affection that isn't from his partner.

Not wanting to force him to endure it too long, I release him and return to Cora, weaving my arm under hers. "We have so much to catch up on. Come. Sit. Let's drink far too much wine and eat our weight in pasta. I need to know everything."

And that we do.

She updates me on the various buildings she's been consulting on, putting her interior design business on the map and drumming up interest from A-list celebrities. Cora is modest with each remark, and Silver follows up the rear to boast on her, his pride overflowing at his woman being so damn successful. She'd blush, tuck her blond hair behind her ear, and he'd squeeze her hand, or kiss her knuckles, or rub her back, anything to silently scream *this is my girl, and boy am I proud of her.*

She shows me pictures of the adorable puppy they adopted, and how she's been trying to convince her boyfriends that it needs a sibling. Cora informs the latest with her best friend back home, June, how she is and what her and her men have been up to. I ask how it is to navigate dating three different men, Archer clearing his throat and demanding that I don't get any ideas.

I understand Cora having multiple boyfriends. It works for her. Each one fulfills a need for her, and all of them get along. But for me, Archer is more than enough, and I can't imagine ever needing or wanting for anything or anyone else.

Cora has me explain from start to finish my life in New York since that fateful day that Silver helped me escape from. It doesn't take long, but with each follow-up question and pause for dramatic effect, she and I don't really give the guys much room to talk at all. Not that I think they mind.

The night progresses, more wine and pasta are consumed, and I grow more grateful that Archer gave me this, my friend, someone I wasn't sure if I'd ever see again. After what happened between us—the whole my dad trying to ruin her life, and her role in his death, I didn't know where we stood, not really.

"Wait, so, hold on, let me rewind," Cora says, holding her hand out. "His ex," she glances at Archer. "Your ex, who you thought was dead, wasn't dead, but instead is the entire reason that sick fuck ever found out you were alive? *And* she *shot* you?"

"Mm-hmm," I confirm, and take another drink of wine, the liquid warming its way down my throat and into my belly.

"Holy shit. Where is she now?"

Archer clears his throat. "She's Blake's problem now."

"He's one of the Manor brothers, right?" Cora asks him.

Silver nods. "Blake is one of the four, yes."

"Is he going to kill her?" Cora doesn't even lower her voice, and I kind of love that about her. She's blossomed from that soft-spoken people pleaser to someone who takes up space.

"Probably not." Archer shrugs. "He's obsessed with her. I don't care what happens to either of them as long as they leave us the hell alone."

"Can't believe she faked her death, escaped your father, and then tried to do the same thing to you with Vito. Speaking of him, what happens now that he's dead?" Cora rasps her fingers on the table, eating up every bit of the juicy gossip.

"I'm sure once word gets out about who did it, hell will follow, but until then, I dare them to step foot in our territory." Archer must notice the way my body tenses, because he puts his hand on my back. "It's nothing to worry about. You're safe."

"I'm not worried about me," I tell him. "Especially with your deal with Blake."

Archer turns his gaze to Silver. "I've been meaning to ask you. That favor you asked me to do a while back. Did you tell anyone about it?"

"No one that would say something to the wrong person."

"I wonder how Vito found out." Archer's eyes dart away like he's scanning for the answer to appear from thin air.

"You're one of the few people who could have pulled it off, especially that quickly. He might not have truly known. He could have been bluffing." Silver adds, "I wouldn't have asked you to do it if I knew what would come from it."

"It was fun," Archer admits with a grin. "Man, I hate the Manor brothers. I'd blow up every one of their businesses if it wouldn't come back on my family."

"How'd you get Blake to let you off the hook?"

"I gave him Madison's whereabouts and told him I owed him one."

Silver raises a brow. "That's dangerous."

"It's done." Archer reaches for his wine, downing the rest of it in one swig, and then refilling each of our glasses before he pours his own.

It's not lost on me that Archer never told me he gave Blake a favor to cash in at any time, or what it entails. And I can't help but feel like he isn't going to tell me, a strange sort of secrecy about whatever it is. Maybe it would put me in danger, maybe that's why he kept it to himself.

"Well, I, for one, am glad all of *that* is in the past. I'd apologize for tossing London on your doorstep, but it appears that worked out just fine too. You Sin boys really know how to make the best out of a shitty situation."

"Hold up." Cora looks at Silver. "You didn't let Archer know London was on her way?"

Silver chuckles and runs his hand over his salt-and-pepper beard. "Nope."

"Holy shit."

"Yeah, I forgot to mention that part of the story," I tell Cora. "Archer tried to kick me to the curb the first night I was here. He was *not* thrilled. But I slowly chipped away that grumpy exterior." Caressing Archer's cheek, I take him in, noting how sexy he is, my heart stuttering the same way it did when I saw him all those months ago.

"I knew you'd keep her safe." Silver glances between us. "Didn't know this would come out of it, but I had hope you'd break him out of his shell."

"I suppose thanks is owed, for finding me a safe haven and the love of my life," I confess.

"Speaking of owing someone something." He focuses on Archer. "I still owe you a favor for taking her in."

Archer brushes him off. "London is the single best thing that ever happened to me. It was my pleasure."

All the wine I've consumed tonight is nothing compared to the radiating love I feel for this man. Archer and I couldn't be more opposite, and yet we work. It isn't perfect, but it's worth fighting for, and I'd go to the ends of the Earth for him. No matter what comes our way, with the Joe Vito aftermath, the Manor brothers, and the issues with Archer's siblings, I'm certain that we will get through anything...or we'll die trying, because I'd rather be dead than live without Archer Sin.

My reunion with Cora and Silver doesn't last too much longer, Cora getting more wine drunk with each glass she pounds. Her words begin to slur, and Silver cuts her off—Cora pouting every time he puts water in front of her instead. Finally, Silver decides he needs to get her to their hotel, making sure to promise her that he'll do her entire skincare routine if she passes out on the way there.

"Pinky promise?" she stammers between hiccups.

They lock pinkies to seal their deal, and she breaks away to hug me. "I'm so glad you're alive, London."

"Ditto, babe."

"Oh, I know, let's exchange numbers." She fumbles with her dress. "I don't have pockets." Cora frowns but Silver hands me a cell phone.

"It's Cora's," he tells me.

I dial my number, waiting for it to ring, then hand it back to him. "There. Now, don't be a stranger, okay? We have rich boyfriends, so there's no sense in not visiting more often."

"We do, don't we." Cora smiles and leans her weight into Silver.

"I have a spare room. Come visit whenever you want. Bring all your men."

"I could rent out the Branford anytime," Archer adds.

"The," she pauses to hiccup, "entire Branford?"

"I better get her out of here." Silver holds on to her purse and wraps his arm around her waist. "Get ahold of me anytime, Arch. You name it, I'll be happy to help."

"I said I didn't—" But Silver cuts him off.

"Not a favor. As a friend."

Archer nods, and with that, Silver and Cora make their way to the door.

"You ready to get home, little tornado?" Archer goes over to pick his black Amex off the table and lays a fat stack of hundreds behind for the tip.

"Tonight was perfect," I tell him as we leave the same way our friends did, Archer's arm across my shoulders, tugging me into him.

"So, you were surprised?"

"Beyond."

Our driver opens the door to the car and I climb in, ready to be alone with Archer, even if it's in the back seat of a luxurious limo.

Once Archer settles into his seat, I climb right into his lap, straddling him and running my fingers through his hair. "Thank you. For tonight. For keeping me safe. For everything."

"London..." Archer whispers, his hands on my waist. "For you, anything."

I lean toward him, resting my nose against his, lingering just near his mouth.

And all at once, he kisses me—gently at first, but then deep and fast and full of passion.

I lower my body and feel his cock harden in his pants. Grinding on him, I continue to swirl my tongue with his, desperate to be closer, closer, closer. I wrap my hands around his neck and move my body up and down, my pussy aching to feel him inside of me. With one hand, I reach between us, fumbling with the button on his pants, unzipping them and wiggling just enough to free him, my hand gripping his shaft. I position him in front of me, rubbing his cock along my panties until I can't take it any longer, until I need him to be where he belongs.

Archer must feel the same damn way, because he snakes his fingers up under my skirt and yanks at my panties, ripping and tearing them off me.

I quit kissing him to reposition, putting his tip at my entrance and staring into his eyes when I sit on his cock. My eyes practically roll back in my head as he fills me, and I suppress a moan so his driver won't hear us.

"You're so warm, so wet, so made for me, little tornado," Archer mutters.

"I'm all yours, big boy. Every inch of me, yours."

With one of his hands on my hip, the other caresses its way up my body, pausing at my chest to squeeze my breast. He slides under the fabric of my bra and pinches my nipple, commanding a whimper to escape me. "Harder," I beg of him, and thrust down onto his cock, spreading and filling my greedy pussy.

He obeys, his shaft growing harder inside of me. So hard it grinds against me in the best way, pleasure consuming me more and more until I'm nearly ready to explode.

Archer releases my nipple, holding me closer and gripping my ass, his fingers digging in and pulling me into him. Our mouths meet, teeth and tongue and lips and moans we eat up from each other. My clit rubs against him, the perfect amount of friction.

I come hard and fast, cry out, Archer fucking me all the way through it and not letting up, building to another one only seconds after the first had stopped. My pussy pulsates around him, and even though I've already come twice, I want more, of the pleasure, of him, of us, as much as I can get, as much as my body will take.

"You're taking me so well, baby." Archer pants and keeps thrusting his hips into me—harder, deeper, his cock swelling. "I love you, London. Your body, your tight little pussy, your filthy mouth, your brilliant mind."

I slam myself onto him and grind in a circle, baffled by how much of him I can take. Weaving my fingers into his hair, I pull tightly and command his attention. "I love you, Archer. Now shut up and come for me. I want to feel you—"

But he cuts me off, his mouth on mine, his cock giving me exactly what I asked for. He thrusts deeply, exploding in my pussy, and moans into me as he climaxes. We continue making out long after both of our orgasms pass, his cock still buried in me. We must be close to home, but I don't care, I don't want to be separated from him just yet.

Archer's cock twitches, and in between kisses, he says, "You're still pulsating, little tornado. You're practically milking me. It's making me hard again."

"Do something about it."

"Get on your knees and bend over."

I climb off him slow enough it's not a complete shock to my body at his absence and get on the floor, grateful Archer opted for a limo tonight. Once I'm in position, Archer joins me, rubbing his practically hard cock over my empty hole. He swirls it around and I wait impatiently. Teasing me, he dips it in, and out, and around every inch of the sensitive and throbbing area.

"Fucking perfect." He drags my skirt up, exposing me and sitting back to admire the view.

Leaning all the way over and resting my head on my arms, I take him in as he licks his lips and comes closer, meeting my hungry hole with his mouth and tongue. His moans vibrate the already delicate skin and he drives his tongue into me, using his hands to spread my legs. His thumbs trace over my labia and one slips inside of me.

I bite my lip and try to keep my sounds to a minimum, but it's hard when Archer's mouth and hands roam in all the best places. I pulse against him and he licks around my asshole, exploring wherever he wants. Archer grips his cock in his hand, squeezing and slowly moving it up and down, his attention still focused on me. He breaks away, returning with his shaft at my hole, pushing in slowly and then all at once. He buries himself deep and thrusts hard, our bodies bouncing into one another. Without meaning to, my pussy tightens and I back into him, spreading my legs wider as I cry out, my orgasm hitting harder than any of the others before. Archer follows, pumping his alongside mine, filling me once again, his fingers digging into my waist.

My entire body trembles and I find myself unable to move, to do anything other than bask in the pure bliss.

Archer kisses my back and carefully removes himself from my

aching hole. I close my eyes as he's zipping his pants, and a short moment later, he's pulling me up and cradling me in his seated lap. He smooths my hair from my sweat-glistened brow and presses his lips gently on my forehead.

I smile and try to recall a time I've ever felt more cared for, more taken care of, than right now, and realize nothing, and no one, has ever made me feel the way I do with Archer, and if I'm lucky, this is just the beginning of the rest of my life with him.

"I've got you, little tornado. Now, and always."

If you loved reading London & Archer's story, you will fall in love all over again with Scarlet and Leo in Twisted Enemy. Releasing in 2027

Nothing is more dangerous than obsession...

Leo Sin built his empire on fear, power, and absolute control. But one woman shattered it all the night she stole from him and vanished.

And he's hunted her ever since.

Now a new threat to his casino forces Leo to do the unthinkable: recruit the very thief who humiliated him... Scarlet. She's brilliant. Fearless. Impossible to trust.

Forced to work together, their uneasy alliance ignites a dangerous attraction neither of them expected. Revenge drives him. Survival drives her.

But the closer she gets, the more Leo must ask himself one question: Will he destroy the woman who betrayed him... or risk everything to keep his twisted enemy close?

Acknowledgements

This book was so much fun to write. I truly enjoyed Archer and London, and their dynamic may be my favorite to date. I love how opposite they are but have this incredible magnetic pull that cannot be ignored.

What was meant to be an easy breezy 80k words, ended up over 140k, making the deadline to get this one finished chaotic and full of suspense. What was once a self-published novel, is now my very first traditionally published book, and I am overflowing with pride and joy and immense gratitude. *cries happy tears*

The Sin family is wildly dysfunctional, and I cannot wait to dive into the other brother's books and show you more of this dark and dangerous world!

I have many people to thank but I'll try to keep the list short & sweet (unlike this damn book haha!)

Tiny—my reason for existing.

Mom—you can't read this one either. Thanks for not dying.

September—for keeping me alive and sparking my new obsession with tequila, the Sin family thanks you.

Tiffany—for being the best assistant, and even greater friend.

Michelle—for always being my ride or die.

Anianne—for being so excited about London and Archer's story!

Kate—have a cookie.

Rumi—for limiting my commas and fixing my frags.

My agent, Josi—for championing this series and helping it find its home!

The entire team at Keeperton/Arndell. It has been an honor to work on this series with you, and I cannot wait to see what's in store for the Sin brothers! Huge shoutout to Kellie for being a dream to work with!

Everyone over on Patreon: April, Ashley P, Ashley S, Cailean,

Elle, Emily, Harley, Kaylee, Krystal, Mandi, Maureen, Michelle, Payton, Robin, Clayton, Sara, Sherrianne, Teia, and Tyler.

And finally, you, the reader, for believing in me and putting up with my extra thiccc books. I couldn't do any of this without you. I love you endlessly.

About the Author

Luna Pierce is a multiple-time Amazon Top 100 bestselling author of gritty romance novels spanning dark contemporary and paranormal genres. Her work focuses on flawed, complex characters and the powerful connections that form when love collides with trauma, secrets, and redemption. With a heavy emphasis on emotional authenticity, her stories explore the beauty and pain of loving deeply while carrying the weight of the past.

Known for her raw, emotionally immersive style, Luna examines themes of healing, self-acceptance, and resilience. Her characters are shaped by difficult histories and personal loss, forcing them to confront their inner demons as they navigate love and identity. Through high-stakes emotional arcs, her stories challenge what it means to fight for love, especially when it feels undeserved or out of reach.

Luna's romances balance darkness with hope, pairing grit and angst with deeply satisfying emotional payoff. Her work remains rooted in character-driven narratives that resonate long after the final page. She is drawn to exploring devotion, sacrifice, and the courage it takes to choose connection over fear.

Her stories are written for readers who crave intensity, vulnerability, and passion, and who believe love is most powerful when it is tested, earned, and fiercely protected. Luna's work appeals to hopeless romance who are unafraid of emotional depth and the complexity of the human experience.

Based in small-town Ohio, Luna balances her writing career with motherhood. When she isn't working on her next book, she can be found listening to Taylor Swift while consuming far too much coffee, making endless to-do lists, and spending time with her daughter and cats.

Through her work, Luna aims to create unforgettable romance stories that are emotionally honest, boldly imperfect, and deeply human.

Arndell

Connect with Arndell

Love this book? Discover your next romance book obsession and stay up to date with the latest releases, exclusive content, and behind-the-scenes news!

Explore More Books

Visit our homepage: keeperton.com/arndell

Follow Us on Social Media

Instagram: @arndellbooks

Facebook: Arndell

TikTok: @arndellbooks

Stay in the Loop

Join our newsletter: keeperton.com/subscribe

Join the Conversation

Use **#Arndell** or **#ArndellBooks** to share your thoughts and connect with fellow romance readers! Thank you for being part of our book-loving community. We can't wait to share more unforgettable stories with you!